TAKEN
by the
WIND

TAKEN *by the* WIND

Ci Ci Soleil

Copyright © 2022 Beach Reads Books

All rights reserved. Published in the United States by Beach Reads Books

Taken by the Wind is a work of fiction. Any similarity to actual persons, living or dead, events or places, is purely coincidental.

ISBN: 979-8-9850660-2-9

Author: Ci Ci Soleil

Book cover art: Danielle Hennis

Beach Reads Books
PO Box 103
Carrboro, NC 27516
BeachReadsBooks.com

For Linda—may the wind blow all happiness your way

And for Alexander—your creative spirit will take you far

Chapter 1

You never know when it's the last time you're going to see someone. Whether they're heading off to college and starting a new life that just doesn't revolve around you anymore, whether they've just ended your relationship by saying they will never see you again, or whether they fully intend to see you again, they can't wait to see you again because their world is your world, but fate has other plans. It was that "other plans" part that Miranda had a problem with. She was a planner, and nothing interrupted her when she was on a roll. Everything was under control, especially when she was planning for someone else.

"Boy, are you gonna be surprised!" Miranda said with a giggle, a satisfied smile on her face. A sudden splintering sound, followed by a crash, made her spin round. "What the hell?" Her heart raced as a loud thud sounded from outside. She ran to the window to see a large branch had fallen across half the patio; her beautiful giant planter lay in shards among the collateral damage of the once-potted petunias and trailing vines. "Well, shoot!" She clenched her jaw. "That's bad timing." She closed her eyes and took a deep breath. "Okay… time to get a grip. Time to pivot. Change of plans. So, no guests on the patio." She looked up at the wind blowing in the treetops. "Funny, forecast didn't mention storms. Guess I missed it." Never in a million years would Miranda describe herself as someone who "missed things". Planners didn't do that. That's what contingencies were for. Not only was she a planner: she was a fixer. She could fix this. Okay, so maybe not the planter, but certainly the plans.

Miranda made some adjustments to her list and checked the timer. She nodded, feeling an unusual flush of pure satisfaction course through her veins. This was something she was really good at. She could feel the smile spreading across her face and radiating like warm sunshine through her soul. It wasn't very often that she felt really proud of her accomplishments. But no wind was going to ruin her evening. Tonight she had something to prove. With a smile she said, "Yeah, you're gonna be so surprised, uh huh."

"Who're you talking to?" Emma said as she came in, bearing a tray full of empty wine glasses.

"Oh, I'm just talking to myself, I guess. Extraverts do that you know."

"Yeah, right. I'm not sure that calling it 'externally processing' really makes it any different from bat shit crazy," Emma teased. "Thought I heard something go crash, bang, boom?"

Miranda decided to let the dig go by. Kids were like that these days. Dig, dig, dig. "Tree branch took out the patio as a venue for tonight. We'll have to adjust."

"Oh, that heavy old branch covered in vines finally bit it, huh? I always knew better than to stand beneath that monster. Well, where should I put these down? I was about to take them outside." She lifted the tray of glasses.

"You knew that was going to fall? Why didn't you say something?"

"Well, I didn't know *when* it was going to fall." Emma lifted the tray of glasses, her eyebrows raised.

"Yeah, pivot… pivot…" Miranda muttered as she consulted her list.

"You're talking to yourself again."

"Hey, don't knock it. Most days, it's the best company I keep. Now that you're away at college and your father is always traveling or at work, I seem to spend most of my days here by myself. I'm not surprised at all that I talk out loud. To no one." Miranda shrugged. "Anyway, it would be too quiet around here if I didn't." She wasn't going to let any gentle teasing from her daughter get under her skin. Not tonight. Tonight was too important. Tonight she would show him. He would understand just what a perfect wife she was. She could definitely fix this. She could pivot in any way that was required.

Emma raised the tray of glasses in her hands again. "A bit heavy."

"Glasses, right. Um, put them on the sideboard. Extras that don't fit go in the butler's pantry for back up. I'm going to set the wine up on the bar, but we'll need extra glasses given the guest list. With the patio out, everyone will just have to fit inside. Everything gets set up inside the house." She looked out the window again. "Damn. I hope that whole tree doesn't come down on the house when it's full of people. Then he'd be surprised for sure."

Emma went and looked out the window. "Eh… you worry too much. But then again, it is a pretty damn big tree."

"Language, Emma!" her mother reprimanded as the doorbell rang. A look of consternation crossed Miranda's face.

"Don't sweat it, Mom. I'll get it." Emma took her tray and disappeared through the door.

"Thirty minutes until the first guest arrives. That better not be a guest. No, can't be. This is good, Andy, this is good. You're good. Your house is not about to fall down around you. And he'll be home in an hour."

"Andy! I got the banner!"

Miranda shook herself and headed for the front door. She ticked off in her mind, *fresh flowers, check. Chafing dishes, check.* Four of them stood down the center of the dining room table. The water was steaming and they were just waiting for the lovely treats which would be kept perfectly hot in their steel bellies for the party tonight. *Bar, all set. Check.* "Caroline, you're a savior. Have I told you that lately?"

"Not since maybe last month, but hey, you know, you just don't turn, what is this? Forty-three? everyday. Hey, why are you doing this for forty-three anyway? Oh, never mind. I don't think I really want to know. But you must be onto something—even the weather seems to want to make a big ruckus. You wouldn't believe the wind that just kicked up out there."

3

"Tell me about it! A huge branch just axed the patio for the party."

Caroline looked out the window and sized up the devastation out back. "Crazy." She shook her head.

"Pivot… right. I think hanging the banner from the second-floor banister will be perfect. Not so low that anybody will get hit in the head by it as they walk through to the great room, but you know, here." She waved both arms at the large hallway linking the front entranceway to the back of house. She could do this. She could change her plans. She looked around with approval. The house looked fantastic. It would be a little crowded with everyone inside, but it would work. She could make it work. That's what she did. She made things work. She gave a sigh of relief.

"Mom, the balloon guy just pulled up. Want me to handle?"

"Yes, E, that would be great, thanks!" Turning around, she said, "Caroline, I'll help you with the banner."

As Emma went outside, Caroline hung up her light jacket and joined Miranda. "Well, Andy-my-dear, let's get this thing hanging. Time's-a-wastin' and you're going to have a house full of guests soon."

"I really appreciate you coming all the way from Charlotte."

"Lexington's not so far. I'm happy to be here." Caroline shrugged. "But I'm not sure why you needed me. I mean, it's just a birthday party. And if anyone can throw a party, it's you."

Miranda gave her best friend a weak smile as they walked up the stairs. "It's for the courage. I wanted you here for the courage. All his friends will be here tonight. And their wives. Their overly-accomplished wives who I'm sure make him wonder why he ever married dumpy old me."

"Don't be silly. Those bitches are going to come into your larger-than-life house and see your larger-than-life, well, life. The flowers. The food. I mean, Andy, c'mon, everything's perfect. They're all going to be drooling with envy 'cause of how you've overdone everything." Caroline unrolled the large banner along the upstairs hallway. Bright colors screamed out, *Happy Birthday Gregg*. "With that wind outside, it's just too bad they won't get to see your new landscaping."

The two women started suspending the banner. Miranda laughed out loud. "Wouldn't that be something?"

"Wouldn't what be something?"

"The bitch brigade envious of me?" She chuckled. "Nah, they'll just be looking longingly at the food while they all starve themselves and sip on their expensive wine diluted-to-ruin with sparkling water."

"Oh, that sounds disgusting. People actually do that?"

"Yeah. It cuts the calories in half."

"I hope I am never that afraid of calories."

"Obviously *I'm* not afraid of them," Miranda said under her breath.

"Hey, you okay?" Caroline gave Miranda a serious look.

"Oh, I'm fine. I'm just twenty pounds away from perfection. And maybe I have a few other boxes to check." She didn't make eye contact as she said it.

"Come here. Andy, come here." Caroline waved her best friend into her arms and gave her a big hug. She pulled back and, with her hands on Miranda's shoulders and a determined look, she said, "You have nothing to be ashamed of. You are the mistress of this castle. Your cooking will either delight or completely intimidate anyone who crosses your drawbridge. And your husband of nearly twenty years will be totally surprised that on his forty-*third* birthday—not one generally celebrated by mere everyday mortals—everyone in his glittering sphere will be here to toast his health and wish him his heart's desire. Okay? You good?"

Miranda wiped a tear from her cheek and nodded. "What would I do without you, Caroline? I always wish I could be more like those expertly self-disciplined women with their college degrees from fancy private schools that I've never heard of. They stand around at parties with their glasses of low-calorie watered-down wine and they only look at the food… but they never actually eat it."

"And what would be the fun of that? I personally would never want to miss an evening of your cooking. I'm sure it's well worth shaving a couple of years off of my life for!" Caroline gave her friend a wink. "But it's time for you to get dressed. And me, too. I need to throw my bag in the guest room."

The front door opened and Emma walked in with a giant bunch of balloons, followed by a lanky man with straight black hair, longish in a way that was somewhere between needing to be cut or looking very European. At the moment it was quite disheveled, but it only made him more attractive. He was dressed in tight black jeans, black shirt, and a casual black jacket.

"Mama! Look who pulled up just as the balloons were being delivered! And thank God because in that wind I could not have wrestled these in by myself. We lost a few of them."

"Hello, Emile." Miranda thought only Emile could wear that outfit and look elegant rather than like a thin Johnny Cash impersonator.

"Andy, it is lovely to see you again. And you as well… it is Caroline, is it not?" Emile finger-combed and then shook his hair back into place. "Where would you like for us to put the balloons?"

Caroline waved a greeting and then sighed quietly to Andy. "I've got to hand it to him, he's got the best accent ever."

"Belgian. I know. Well, he'll add a touch of class to our affair tonight, huh?" Miranda giggled, once again feeling giddy. She was finding the rollercoaster of emotions an unexpectedly hard part of her day. She was usually so even-keeled. "Thanks for the moral support."

She called down some instructions for the kids to place the huge balloon arrangements inside now that the patio wasn't happening. "And Emma—when you put out the food, please make sure you pick up the labels. Once everything gets placed the tags should all be picked up!"

"I know, Mom, I know. I was raised at the right hand of the party maestro! Emile and I will start putting out the last-minute stuff. C'mon, Emile! There's ice buckets and the charcuterie boards, nut bowls and all kinds of chocolate decadence to lay out in their assigned and marked places."

Caroline laughed as the two young people wrestled with their giant balloon bunches. After spending a couple of minutes untangling the strings, they disappeared towards the kitchen.

"See? It's all under control. You go get dressed. All those bitchy women will be in awe of you tonight!" Caroline smiled and gave Andy a squeeze for reassurance.

"Yeah, you're right. It's all going to be perfect." She walked into her bedroom and pulled out her black dress. "Unless no one comes because of the storm. Unless my party gets taken by the wind. Hmmmm." She looked out the window. The wind was still strong but there was no rain. She pulled on the Spanx that left her breathless but less lumpy, and then her black dress. Making a last-minute change of plan, she ditched her sparkly jewelry and chose instead chunky turquoise earrings and a silk scarf in a lovely Caribbean blue that she'd picked up on one of the rare trips when Gregg had actually taken her along. The blue really stood out. It was so cheering. It gave her hope and courage. She added some mascara to make her eyes pop a bit more. As she looked in the mirror, she said, "Hello baby-face." Decades of teasing about her never-aging face had become something she truly felt grateful for now. At her best moments, she could admit that her face didn't suck, even if below the neck was something she never wanted to look at. Well, neither did Gregg. He seemed to do everything he could to avoid looking at her. She gave another glance out the window and then steeled her confidence. Tonight, he would be so surprised. And his friends would all admire him with his adoring wife and his big fancy house with this ostentatious party to celebrate an otherwise unimportant birthday. That storm brewing outside would add a dramatic flair, a unique accent, to the affair. An evening to remember. And he would be pleased. And he would love her again and everything would be all right. Yes, with enough planning, she could fix this.

Chapter 2

"Mama, when's Daddy going to be here? I mean, he's kind of late, isn't he?" Emma seemed anxious.

"Just keep the wine flowing. He'll be here. He runs late a lot. I mean even more late than when you were growing up. And I'm sure the weather is playing havoc with the traffic lights."

"I'm going to go and take a peek outside again and see if he's pulling up yet. Maybe I'll give him a call."

"Oh, honey, your hair looks so nice and it will be blown to pieces! Don't worry. He'll be here. The point of a surprise party is that he doesn't know to rush home from work." Miranda gave Emma an encouraging nod, although she was feeling a bit deflated herself.

"I'll put on a hat!" Emma gave her mother a smile as she crammed a knit cap over her hair. She grabbed Emile's hand and they slid out the side door of the house.

Caroline came up and stood at Miranda's shoulder. "Andy, you sure know how to throw a party. Have you even taken a moment to be a part of it at all? You should enjoy this, it's got to be the event of the season, even here in Lexington, Kentucky. You know, I've had three of the wives ask me if I knew the caterer. Honey, they think a professional did this. They would hire you! It's a triumph."

"It's an insult."

"What?"

"It's not a compliment, Caroline. They're saying I'm really only worthy of being the hired help."

"Okay, snowflake. I think you're being a bit sensitive here."

"Well, you can think that, but I've lived among them long enough. I'm not significant enough to be in the elite club. My background isn't 'right'. I don't look right. I'm not educated."

"You've got to give that up. You dropped out of college twenty years ago but you're still carrying that old guilt around with you?"

"Oh, you underestimate me. I've got guilt older than that. Don't forget, I'm a product of my mother."

Caroline chortled. "You dropped out for Emma. It was a good reason. And you've been a total over-achiever of a mother. And a wife, I might add. When I see what a devoted wife you are, I think I understand why my own marriage failed. I never did anything like this for Sasutki."

"Hey, marriage isn't easy. Cross cultural marriages are particularly tough. You did everything you could." Miranda sighed. "Gregg would never have married out. He's so…"

"Elitist?" Caroline whispered the answer to Andy's sentence.

"Caroline! How could you say such a thing? No, he's not like that at all. He's just… into his own kind. People he can understand."

"Yeah. People like him. In this case, medical types."

Andy looked up and froze suddenly. "Shh! And in the absolute parade of over-achieving hospital types surrounding us tonight, here comes another. I must have met twenty people I never knew Gregg worked with." Andy plastered a smile on her face as a willowy, young Asian woman was dragged over by Emma. "Evening," she said in her most hostess-like voice.

"Mom, I want you to meet someone. She just arrived. I met her outside." Emma was bubbling with excitement. "She works with dad. She said she wasn't really invited and I told her that was ridiculous—everyone's invited! And she just had to come in out of that wind anyway."

"Hello," the woman said almost shyly and with a noticeable accent. "My

9

name is Chenguang. Thank you for inviting me into your lovely home. This is really spectacular. It's quite the party." The young woman looked around, as if she were trying to drink in the whole scene. She looked a little intimidated. Andy kind of liked her. She recognized another beta when she saw one.

"Hello, I'm Andy. Well, Miranda technically, but mostly people call me Andy."

"Oh, so nice to meet you. People generally call me M.G."

"M.G., this is my oldest friend, Caroline. She's visiting from North Carolina. We were college roommates, way back when."

The willowy woman smiled and nodded at Caroline, who smiled back and said, "So how do you get M.G. from Chen… I'm sorry, can you say your name again?"

The woman's smile was truly lovely. She sounded gracious and almost shy as she spoke. "It's undeniably a hard name. Chenguang. It's the name of a flower, a Morning Glory, and when I explained that to the surgical staff, well, it kind of stuck. So, everyone has called me Morning Glory, or M.G. for short for years now."

"Oh, are you one of the nurses on the surgical team?" Andy asked.

"M.G. is Dad's surgical resident, Mom, isn't that cool?" Emma gushed and turned to her newfound friend. "I'm a pre-med student. I'm gonna be a physician just like my dad."

"I know. Your father talks about you all the time. He's very proud of you. And I'm not his surgical fellow anymore. I just finished my training and was hired by the medical center. Now I suppose I fall into being a colleague. But your father is a fabulous teacher. He's the best teacher I've ever had. It will be quite an honor to be on his team." They talked to the woman for several minutes before she excused herself, seemingly awed and shy in Miranda's house.

"I liked that one. She wasn't bitchy at all." Caroline gave a genuine smile at the back of the woman as she walked away with Emma.

"Well, of course not. She's not one of the wives clinging to their rich husbands. She's got a career. She's a surgeon! She's got nothing to be bitchy about." Miranda laughed. "And I liked her, too."

At that moment, the front door opened and in walked Gregg, windblown and a bit disheveled. He froze and looked around, blinking a few times. Random shouts of "surprise" piped up from different people. As partygoers were alerted to the fact that the man of the hour had arrived, they made their way towards the large, two-story entranceway. Andy wormed her way through the crowd. "Welcome home, honey! Happy birthday!"

Gregg looked at her and around the room, his eyes taking in the banner, the balloons, the crowd. He ran his hand through his hair. Someone brought him a glass of wine.

"Uh, thank you." Gregg nodded to the man, who slapped him on the back a couple of times.

"You sure look surprised!"

Gregg leaned over to Andy, a smile plastered on his face. As the gathered guests were cheering and calling out birthday greetings, he said through his frozen smile, "Honey… what's going on?"

"It's your birthday, silly!" She laughed and gave him a kiss on the cheek. "We didn't do anything for your fortieth, so this is like a make-up birthday party. Consider it your forty-plus-plus-plus." She turned to the crowd and held up her glass. "Everyone, a toast! To Gregg Cochran, my perfect husband. May your birthday bring you your heart's desire!"

"Your heart's desire," the crowd shouted in unison, glasses raised over the sea of smiling faces.

The crowd broke out in a rousing rendition of *Happy Birthday* and then somehow zig-zagged into *He's a Jolly Good Fellow* before they either lined up to wish their friend and colleague well or wandered back to drink and food stations. Gregg made his way to the great room and took up residence by the stone fireplace while his guests filtered by to have a word or to clink a glass with him. Miranda returned to her hostess duties, replenishing the hors d'oeuvres, bringing out more bottles of wine, and picking up abandoned wine glasses.

At ten o'clock, Gregg came up to her as she was making the rounds and seeing if she could get the guests anything else. "Andy, can I talk with you for a moment?"

"Oh, sure." Andy turned to the guests she had been speaking with. "Would you excuse me please?" She gave them a warm smile. This party was a huge hit. Even the bitches were making up to her, inviting her to their county club luncheon next weekend, and one of them had asked her if she'd like to go shopping sometime. Andy felt like a celebrity. The perfect party at the perfect house for the perfect husband. She followed him as he ducked around the giant stand of balloons blossoming from the first step of the staircase and they snuck upstairs for a private conversation in their bedroom. He shut the door behind her as she came in.

She put her arms around him and kissed him. "Surprise! Are you surprised? Are you happy, Gregg? Isn't it a great party?"

"Yes, it's a great party. You did… it's… I'm just at a loss for words."

"All your friends are here. I had your secretary, Madge, get me the list of everyone you work with and are friends with at the hospital. All our neighborhood friends. It's a huge turn out and it's all for you!" She felt radiant with her success.

"Where did you come up with this idea? I'm so, uh, surprised. Um, I just didn't expect it." He looked so awkward, so apparently, he was actually surprised.

She felt victorious. "I wanted to give you your heart's desire for your birthday."

"And you thought this was my heart's desire?" He loosened his tie and took a few steps away from her.

"To be celebrated by everyone who loves you? To be surrounded by your friends… in this house you insisted we buy so everyone would be impressed? Sure. I mean, you were pretty miffed when you made full professor, and no one marked it other than a sentence in the Chair's newsletter. And the award you won, you said that hardly anyone even congratulated you for it. This is my way of wrapping all that into your birthday and all these people are here celebrating you. Gregg Cochran. Surgeon extraordinaire."

"That's not my heart's desire."

Andy walked up to him and put her arms around him, her head resting against his back and her fingers dancing lightly on his chest.

"Well then, what is your heart's desire?" She was a teeny bit afraid that he might want a special little birthday present right here up in the bedroom while they had all those guests downstairs. It was the only kind of sex they had anymore, she suspected because that way he didn't have to touch her. But right now? It wasn't what she thought was proper, but there was nothing she wouldn't give him if it would make him happy. Oh, the things she had done to try to make him happy. She started to undo his belt. "I want to give you your heart's desire."

"I want a divorce."

She froze. Her fingers went numb. Not even cold like ice, just numb, as though they weren't connected to her body. Dully she could feel his hand prying hers from his waistline and putting them down at her sides. His hands let go of hers a little too quickly. He took a small step away. He turned his head, but he didn't turn around and face her. She could see him, but he wasn't looking at her. Just like usual.

"My heart's desire is… is… Andy, I want a divorce."

"A what?" She felt bewildered. Lost. Deaf. Spinning. Nauseated. Dully, the thought drifted across her mind that it was impossible to feel so many sensations at once but no emotion at all.

"I was going to talk to you about it tonight when I got home. But this… this party? Why in the world would you… you know I hate surprises."

"No, honey no. You don't have to like the party… but you don't need to divorce me over it." She heard the words coming out of her mouth and wasn't sure she'd said them. A part of her brain was grasping at straws, but anything that might give her a lifeline at this moment was worth clinging onto. This had to be a joke. He couldn't be serious.

Gregg turned and looked at her. "Andy, I'm so sorry. I'm not joking. I'm not kidding around. I can't… I can't do this anymore." He sighed heavily and ran his hands through his hair. "I can't go on like this."

"You're not happy?"

"Are you? Have we been happy even once in the last decade? I'm ready to be happy. I'm finally ready to be happy. What did you call it? My 'heart's desire'? Yeah, I want that. I want a divorce. I want you to move out."

Andy didn't know how she managed to stay standing. He just looked at her and said, "I'm sorry. I want you to move out," then he left the room and went back down to the party. She was frozen for several minutes, not even noticing the time passing by. At last, laughter from downstairs broke through her shock and she shook herself. She needed to get back to her guests. Balling her fists and steeling herself with a deep breath, she took a step towards the door. It was getting late. It would all be over in less than an hour. She opened the door and went back down the stairs. She watched Gregg work the crowd now. He was a different person. People gathered around him, laughing at his jokes. That was how he'd always been in college—the most popular guy in the room. Why had he fallen in love with her? Maybe he hadn't. Maybe she was just the girl who he'd gotten pregnant.

It wasn't long before Caroline found her. "Wow, that's a change. That wind stopped blowing, thank goodness. Tell you the truth, I was getting a little worried there for a while. And Gregg even seems to have lightened up a lot. I haven't seen him that loose in well, I dunno… must be years. He actually looks like he's having a good time."

"Yeah. I think he got something off his chest. He seems to feel much happier now, doesn't he?"

"What are you drinking?" Caroline looked at the amber liquid in Andy's glass.

"Scotch. I decided that wine wasn't going to do it for me. So, I pulled out Gregg's eighty-five-dollar bottle of scotch. Want some?" She hadn't noticed that the storm had blown itself out until Caroline mentioned it. She was too consumed with calming the storm inside her head.

"Uh, sure? Since when do you drink scotch?" Caroline followed Andy to the butler's pantry where Andy poured her about four fingers' worth. "Andy, is everything all right?"

"Oh sure. It's fine. Yeah, fine. We just need to make it to the end of the party. Can't be much longer now."

It turned out to be much longer. People didn't pack it in until long after midnight. Gregg seemed to have come to life and be suddenly determined to celebrate with a vengeance. Andy and the bottle slipped upstairs without being noticed long before the last of the guests took their leave.

Chapter 3

The doorbell rang. Andy didn't move from the couch. One of the pillows was over her face. The doorbell rang again.

"I hate that doorbell. Go away," she mumbled. Then she heard the key in the lock click and the door open. "Oh shit. It'll be my savior again. Ugh."

"Andy? Andy? Look, I know you're here. Your car's parked out front. Andy?" Caroline peered around through the dark as she walked through the condo. "Andy? Oh my God, there you are. It's eleven o'clock in the morning. Why are you on the couch? And all the drapes are closed. It's so dark."

"What else do I have to do?" Andy rolled over and turned her back to Caroline.

Caroline sat down. She picked up a bottle of scotch from the coffee table. It was mostly empty. "Well, at least you're still drinking the good stuff." She shook her head and put the bottle down.

"Glad you're able to find some redeeming qualities to my alcoholism."

"Andy, I don't think you're an alcoholic." Then she added more quietly, "Not yet anyway." She picked up three empty glasses. "But I do think you're in mourning. You know, there are more effective ways to grieve." She walked into the kitchen and set down the glasses. When she came back she asked, "Who were you drinking with anyway?"

Andy took a few moments before she answered. "Well, there was 'me'. Then there was 'myself.' And I think 'I' was there too, but I don't think I know who she really is anymore. I don't recognize her at all." Andy started to cry again. It was all she could do to keep from shaking, from the tears taking hold of her and turning into sobs. She really didn't want Caroline to know she was still crying, and crying this hard, after all this time. It had been months and months.

Caroline leaned over towards her friend and started to gently rub her back. "Andy, you're gonna make it through this. I promise you, you'll make it through."

"I was happy. I had everything I ever wanted. It's like my whole life has been blown apart."

"Andy, you're strong! You haven't been blown apart."

"I'm not strong. You went through your divorce without giving up a single tear. I gave up my home, my life, my daughter, everything. I'm a doormat."

"First, you are not a doormat. Okay, well, maybe you did give up a lot. And just because you didn't see all my tears, just because you were on the other end of the phone when I went through my angry phase, doesn't mean I didn't spend my time as a puddle. Everyone cries when they go through a divorce."

"He's not crying. He's celebrating. And I abandoned my daughter."

Caroline's voice was very gentle as she spoke. "Emma is a senior in college. It'll be really good for her to have to do her own laundry. To have to figure out how to feed herself." Andy wasn't looking at Caroline, couldn't see the concentrated look on Caroline's face as she chose her words carefully. "I know you were so… supportive of E during college, making meals for her and checking in on her and checking all her papers and all. But this gives her a time to grow up a bit. Some adulting would be good for her."

Andy turned over on the couch, wiped her tears and looked at Caroline.

"You know, it might be good for you, too. Even if things had been perfect between you and Gregg, you would still need to find a new you. A you that isn't E's doting mother, because she's growing up. She'll graduate from college next spring. Even in a perfect world you would still be crossing some of these bridges."

"How can I find a new life at forty-one? Almost forty-two?"

17

"You will. You've made great strides already. You have this lovely condo, and Andy, this is really a gorgeous place. You're starting to establish yourself here in Charlotte. A new city. A new you!"

Andy thought her friend's voice sounded fake, it was so optimistic, but she decided not to call her out on it. Who knew how long anyone would stand by her through this awful funk? She was grateful for Caroline's friendship. It wasn't like she had a Monday friend, a Tuesday friend, a Wednesday friend... her calls of desperation all went straight to Caroline.

"So, tell me, how's therapy going? You went this week, right?"

Andy sat up and rolled her eyes. "Yes," she said sullenly, "I went." She flopped against the back of the couch. "I hate it. I really hate it. Now she's making me journal. I loathe journaling."

"But you wrote that paper about journaling? Wasn't it like a book chapter, or something? You made me read that, about a decade ago. Even by your own admission, you said it was super effective, or something like that."

"I know I did. And it is effective, just for other people. Not for me. For me, it just throws my failures back in my face. Over and over again, I write about how I've lost my whole life. He took my whole life away from me. My house. He wanted the house. He just didn't want me in it." She took a deep breath and looked up at Caroline. "Last night I was journaling about the latest developments. That's why I ended up having all the scotch." She picked up her journal lying on the coffee table and flipped it open to the latest pages. "You remember the woman E introduced us to at the party, the one whose name is a flower? The surgical fellow who gushed on and on about what a wonderful teacher Gregg is?"

"Her? Oh yeah. That young, pretty willowy thing? I kinda liked her."

"You're not helping, Caroline. He's with her now. They'd been having an affair. Apparently for quite a while. It turns out Emma met her in the yard when she went out looking for her father. Morning Glory was there as moral support, waiting for Gregg to come out after he'd told me he was leaving. Neither of them expected the party. Neither of them knew what to do and when Emma found her and dragged her in, well she just… just…"

"Oh. That's weird. Maybe that's why she seemed so shy. She knew she was the *other* woman. And she was meeting *the* woman. The wife. Wow, that's really awkward. And there we were, being so… so nice to her."

"Yeah. There we were. I've been gone less than six months and she's now living there. So, I was journaling about that. Hence my pity party with my two other best friends."

Now it was Caroline's turn to give a heavy sigh. "Well, sorry I couldn't join 'myself' and 'I' while they were drowning their sorrows with 'me'."

"I get that journaling is a standard therapeutic technique. When I share my journaling with my therapist, she seems as traumatized by it all as I am. I don't know if she's trying to be empathetic or whether I'm genuinely triggering her. But I hate the process. I hate the living it. And then writing about it. And then sharing the misery. It's like pen and paper as instruments of torture."

"Yeah, I get that. I'd way rather write about what I wish had happened. Or wish was happening. Yeah, way more than sucky reality. That would be much more fun."

"Tell me about it." Andy looked around the room, feeling rather forlorn. "Well, I suppose I'd better get dressed. I think I've gained five pounds since he left me."

"You have?"

"I don't know. I don't own a scale. I didn't take that. I actually didn't take much with me. I was in shock, you know. I just packed up some suitcases and left. We never even said goodbye. It was more like I died, and my ghost slipped out of the place unnoticed."

"Well, I've come to save you from yourself today. And this weekend. You're going to spend the time with me at our place. Mimi's back from her art show and I know she'd love to see you again."

"Your mother is the coolest little old lady." Andy wondered if she could worm out of the invitation. She just wanted to stay where she was, curled up with her expensive scotch and see if another attempt to drown her sorrows might not be successful.

"And my brother's in town, without his full crew in tow this time. The wife and kids are visiting their other grandma, so the entourage is back in Paris. It's going to be a quiet house."

"Actually, maybe not. I think I'd be more embarrassed to hang out with a superstar. Particularly in my condition." Andy felt mortified to think that she would be in the company of someone like Chase Watkins just when she was feeling her most defeated.

"Nope. Pack your bags, baby. You're comin' with me. We are headed to weekend rehab at the Watkins place!"

* * *

Andy woke up in a new bed on Saturday morning. The sun was streaming in through the guest room windows and the birds were singing. Past the pool and over the large lawn stood the edge of Old Town Park's woodland forest. Andy felt like she was at a retreat center. The huge old house was a historic site, in effect, if not on an official register. Mimi had lovingly restored it over three decades and filled it with art from friends across the country and locally. Andy snuggled down into the blankets and felt a tiny ray of hope. The knock on her door was loud and disruptive by contrast.

"Um? Hello? Who's there?"

"It's Chase."

"Chase? Uh, what do you want?"

"Can I come in?"

She pulled the blanket up higher. "I'm still in bed… um…"

"Okay, no problem." The door swung open. "Hey, Andy, nice to see you again." He entered the room like they were siblings and he'd done this a thousand times. In reality, she might have met him twice when she was in college and he was in middle school. Long before he had made the grade. He sat down on the edge of her bed.

A part of Andy wanted to object, but she had to admit that a part of her was starstruck as well. Here was Chase Watkins, one of the most successful male models in Europe, sitting down on her bed. If only Gregg could see this. She cursed herself for not having any kind of social media account to which she might post a selfie of this moment. She couldn't believe that anyone could look better than their photographs and magazine spreads, but there he was, sitting there and smiling at her.

"Hi, uh, Chase."

"Caroline told me what's up. I think I have an idea for you."

"You do?"

"Yes. You're depressed. I went through a real funk, too. I found a way out. I think it could help you like it helped me. It saved my life."

It was like a strong wind blew through Andy. This wasn't the pussyfooting around her therapist did, waiting for her to venture first into any territory at all, too cautious to suggest or name anything that might be happening. This was calling it out. Laying it bare. She was depressed and her life needed saving. Now that she heard it, she recognized it.

"Andy, your life is worth saving. Will you give it try?"

She could feel herself nodding. She thought her eyes might be wide like saucers, like a kid visiting Santa Claus and staring, too afraid to whisper her most ardent desires in his ear, afraid that like every other adult he would dash her hopes and tell her she was silly, stupid, uneducated. But all Chase said was, "Good. You won't regret this. It won't be easy, I'll be honest with you. But the way out isn't easy. It's a lot of sweat and tears. From what I understand you've got the tears part well covered. Now comes the next step. Get dressed. We'll start off by going for a walk and talking it all out." He patted her foot under the cover, but it wasn't comforting. It was more like a command. Encouraging but firm. He gave her his brilliant smile, one that had made him millions of dollars, and got up. As he left the room, he said, "See you downstairs in ten minutes!" And he was gone.

Chapter 4

Caroline put her reading glasses on top of her head. "Damn, girl. This is funny. This is seriously good. You'll be sending this in, getting this published, right?"

Andy blushed at the praise. "I wouldn't even know how to start getting this published. And you're such a dear friend, to actually read it and give me feedback."

"Don't mention it. It's hilarious. The story of your life. Well, sort of. More like the story of your life on some kind of crazy steroids. How did you come up with all these wild ideas?" Caroline was still laughing. "Did you actually cut up all of Gregg's clothes?"

Andy picked up her iced tea and shook her head. She didn't drink scotch anymore. And never a soda. Not even diet soda. No chemicals. She wouldn't have recognized the woman who sat across from Caroline now from the derelict wreck she'd been a year ago. Chase's intervention had transformed her. For a time there, she thought it would break her, but eventually it had revolutionized her body, her mind, her diet, her habits: herself. She felt like Andy Cochran 2.0. except she wasn't Andy Cochran anymore. She was Miranda Wright. Going back to her maiden name was part of her spiritual journey to reclaim herself. Chase said that names mattered. Owning your name mattered. She still felt timid and shy on the inside, like if anyone actually took the time to get to know her, they wouldn't find any juicy skeletons worth the search… just the fat girl in the closet. They'd only find that girl who'd never graduated from college. The one who wasn't really worth it. The truth of Miranda Wright. But eight months of working out like she was a movie star and eating like she was a super model, with a super model as her coach, bootcamp director, and cheerleader gave her the outside visage of a much more confident and put together person than she actually was. "Fake it 'til you make it," she had told herself many times. Well, health-wise she'd made it. The rest was mostly faking it.

"From you. I got the idea from you."

"What do you mean?" Caroline asked, obviously confused.

"Well, you said it would be more fun to write what I wish had happened. Or what I wish was happening. So, when I found journaling too much to bear, too much truth staring me in the face, I thought about that. And I started to write what I wished I'd done instead." Andy shrugged. "Kind of like cutting up all of Gregg's clothes. I really wish I'd done that rather than drinking down my anger."

"But please, please tell me you really put the seafood shells and leftover shrimp in the curtain rods, to make the house smell hideous before you left?" Caroline was looking at her with absolute awe.

"Nah. I just read about that someplace and I thought I wish I'd done that. I wish I'd infected the house with something nasty, something they would never find but that would ruin their happiness and make the thing that Gregg loves more than anything else be what he deserves—a gorgeous, huge, fancy but nasty house that no one can actually live in."

"You don't have to look guilty, you know," Caroline said. "You didn't actually do it. But I love the idea of the house as his picture of Dorian Gray. So, this is all your fantasy… of revenge?"

Andy blushed and shrugged again slowly. "Well, yeah. I think it's normal for the spurned woman to fantasize stuff like this."

"No. No, it's not normal. The average woman fantasizes things that are much more violent and much less hysterically funny. I'm glad you went for hysterically funny. And yes, I think you should see if you can get it published, like for real. I don't mean self-publish. That would seem, under the

23

circumstances, to be petty. But send it to a few agents. See what happens. It can't hurt."

"Maybe I'll give that a try. It's a pipe dream. I know it won't go anyplace. Anyway, I'm feeling particularly good today because my attorney called, and she's feeling confident that I'll get a massive settlement from Gregg. And boy does he seem pissed about that, as if half of his riches from being a top surgeon aren't rightfully mine. And there's alimony. Plus, he'll have to buy me out of the house. I left, so he gets to keep it, but he can't keep the value of it."

"Knowing Gregg as I do, I bet he's pissed. Serves him right. You deserve all that money. And now I'm glad that you didn't cut up all his clothes or poison the place or the judge might not have been so generous to you. See, I promised you that it would get better. You are strong. And just look at you now!"

Andy smiled on the outside. Inside she still felt like one strong wind might blow her over again. Her newfound dedication to the gym and her personal trainer and her strict healthy eating plan was better than her rebound relationship with a bottle of scotch, but it still felt like an addiction. It still felt like she was running and hiding, making herself too exhausted to feel or think about what the last year had done to the only happiness she had ever known.

"So let me broach another subject with you." Caroline gave Andy a hard look.

"Uh oh? Um, what?" Andy could feel her heart skip a beat. She couldn't imagine what Caroline was thinking behind a look like that.

Caroline took a deep breath. "I think it's time that you started to get out there again."

Now Andy felt her heart skip more than just one beat. All she could do was shake her head.

"Why not? It's been over a year. If any not-quite-middle-aged woman should be confident about herself, it's you, my dear."

"I… I just couldn't. I can't imagine being comfortable even speaking to a guy."

"You speak to Chase all the time."

"Yeah, but he's not like a guy. He's Chase. And he's married. And a superstar. And he's…"

"What?"

"Safe. He's safe. I can relax around him because I know there's no question, of, of well, anything. I can't imagine being around men socially. It would be like being with wolves."

"They aren't all like Gregg."

Andy shuddered. "The things I did to keep him happy. I'm so embarrassed now that I look back on it. The things I did to please him. Or to try. I really thought I could fix it all. Make it work."

"You know some day you're going to venture out there again and meet someone."

Andy shook her head. "I'd be too afraid of my terrible judgement in men. How would I ever know I wasn't picking another Gregg? Or someone even worse?"

Caroline smiled at Andy. "I think you'd know. You'd know when you felt safe. When you found someone you could open up to. And be just you."

Andy was still shaking her head. "That day is not today."

"You know, Andy, that day will come. And when it does, you'll have to take a chance."

Caroline was giving her that really hard, intent look again. Andy squirmed in her seat. "Okay, okay, I promise you that someday, someday I will pluck up my courage and take a chance."

* * *

Andy pulled up in front of the Watkins home. She didn't mean to screech the tires like that when she parked the car. She looked down at her hands and could see them shaking. She felt nervous and excited at the same time. What she really needed was Caroline. Or maybe a killer Pilates class. By now she could control any emotion through enough sweat and sheer exhaustion. But she didn't want to control this emotion. She wanted to feel it. Feeling anything at all was a strange sensation. She'd kept herself numb for so long that even feeling something good was foreign territory. She got out of the car and ran up to the door. Before she reached it, Mimi came out, a concerned look on her face. She brushed her gray hair back from her eyes.

"My goodness, Miranda! You drove up like the devil was after you. Are you all right?"

Andy smiled at Caroline's mother, marveling at how much she looked like Audrey Hepburn would have, if she'd lived to be seventy years old. She held up an envelope. "Is Caroline here? I have something to show her."

"She got home from the dental office about a half hour ago. She's in the den. She's been binge watching some series on Starz, so you might have to whack her on the head to get her attention."

Andy laughed. Caroline could always become obsessed with a good story. Probably why she was such an ardent supporter of Andy's work. "I'll go find her. Come along. I think you'll want to hear this too." Andy gave Mimi a little hug as she went in through the front door. As predicted, she found Caroline glued to the screen. Caroline hit pause on her remote.

"Oh, you know that you're my best friend when I'll stop watching him in that role. Oh my God, what a hunk." Caroline dramatically clutched at her chest.

"I appreciate that you can spare me a few minutes away from your historical fiction!" Andy laughed. "So, Mimi, do you watch the show too? Is it that good?"

"Oh no. It's not quite to my taste. I let Caroline have it all to herself."

Andy looked from mother to daughter, a question on her face.

"Don't let her tease you, Andy. My incredibly liberal artist mother disapproves because it's a love story and on cable, and, well, it can get pretty earthy."

"Explicit." Mimi threw out the comment as she cleared her throat.

"We tried watching one of their series together before we knew how they, uh, handle the love scenes, but that didn't work out very well."

"Because it was porn!" Mimi said, but Andy could tell the old lady wasn't really laughing.

"Yeah. And it was like watching porn with your mother," Caroline whispered with mock disgust. Then she burst out laughing. "Honestly, a really good and well-done story can become otherwise if you're watching it in the wrong company."

"It was probably my fault," Mimi added. "I thought it would be like regular TV, or at the least like an R-rated movie. Now I am no prude…"

At this Caroline made a face behind her mother's back and shook her head vigorously.

"…but it was even worse than what they show on the BBC!"

Caroline's smile was mischievous. "I decided that a little bit of skin and sin wasn't going to make me miss a really good story. But anyway, what's up? Unless you're here to indulge the less noble side of your character with me?"

"I'd love to, although I'm sure that seeing how real authors become truly successful and have their books made into a mini-series would only intimidate me. Thanks anyway. I wanted to show you this!" She held out the letter, happy that her hand was now steady.

"What is it?"

"It's an offer letter. From a publisher. The first one the agent took the manuscript to. They like it. They. Like. My. Story." She glanced over at the paused show on the big screen television. "Even without all the uh, 'skin and sin'. They thought it was funny. They want to publish it!"

"Oh my God! Oh my God! Andy! Oh my God!" Caroline was jumping around. The letter ended up in Mimi's hands.

Mimi carefully opened the sheets of paper and read the letter. "Oh Miranda! This is wonderful! And just look at the advance they want to give you! This is… my goodness. They must really believe this is going to be

27

popular." She turned her attention back to the paper in her hand. "Movie rights. They mention *movie rights?*"

Caroline was still jumping up and down with Andy in her arms. "Movie rights!" she shouted. "Just think—three months ago you were a nobody with a great manuscript. And now you're a woman with an offer letter!"

"This calls for a celebration! I hope you'll stay to dinner, Miranda?" Mimi was all smiles, but she didn't join in the jumping.

"I'd love to. Thank you, Mimi!" Andy gave her a hug.

"I'll go and attend to dinner while you two jump around like a couple of five-year-old's."

Caroline grabbed the letter and started to read it. "You see—it's a whole new you. It's a new start. Your new life. You're an author! *Miranda Wright!* So, tell me, how does it feel? You're a huge success."

Andy could feel the blush pinking her cheeks. She knew she could be totally honest with her best friend. "Exciting. Terrifying. I mean I'm not a success. Remember, I haven't sold one book yet. And I don't know how to be a successful author. Down on the inside I'm still a timid little girl who has only ever had one serious relationship and doesn't know much about the world."

Caroline looked at the letter, shaking her head as she read through it. "Well, that may be so, but there's a big difference now. Look at that advance! Now you're a woman with a hell of a huge settlement from your asshole ex-husband and a book about to be published! What will you do with your newfound riches? Go and see Europe? Buy a big house? My God, buy a racehorse?"

Andy thought about that. She hadn't given any consideration about what to do with her money, not from Gregg and certainly not any that might materialize from the book. When she'd been married to Gregg, it had always been his money. He'd been very clear about that. He'd desperately wanted the impressive house, but with her, he was a total skinflint. Until she'd gotten her settlement from him, she'd been penny pinching like back in college. She hadn't shaken that habit yet.

"You know, I like the condo. It's a nice little home base, but it doesn't really feel like home. I kinda' just knock around over there and look for something to do. I do think I need a home. I know this sounds like a wild hare, but I think I might buy a beach house." Andy amazed herself as she heard the words come out of her mouth. She had never let herself say it before. "I always wanted a place at the beach, but Gregg always said it was a stupid idea. That people wasted money on beach houses, and we could rent anything we wanted for a vacation." She looked out at the evening sun sending its rays through the picture window. "Except we didn't. I always dreamed of a quiet little beach cottage away from everything. And now I actually have the money to do it." She felt a sense of something building within her, expectantly, like a new dawn, full of promise and mystery.

"Oh my God, Andy, that is such a coincidence!"

"What is?" She pulled herself from her reverie and looked at Caroline.

"I always wanted a best friend with a beach house!"

Chapter 5

Miranda didn't know why she'd done it. Maybe it felt like a dare. Her daughter had urged her to "Try it, just try it once. It won't take you very far, don't worry, Mom. You worry too much. You need to try new things."

Maybe it was when Emile offered her the windsurfer and chuckled in that snide little way, as if to say, 'No way can your mom handle this.'

So, she'd done it. In defiance of their knowing looks, their expectation of her utter failure, their poorly suppressed smiles. Without even a thought for putting on the life jacket she said, "Okay. Have it your way. I'll try something totally new." After falling over the first couple of times, she managed to stand up and get a firm grip on the bar. Then the wind came, and what a wind it was. Shit. She really hadn't been ready for that. What do you do when you get out on the open water and realize that you don't have a life jacket? Or when you're holding on for dear life, throwing every ounce of your weight into balancing and pulling against the sail and you realize you're completely on your own. She hadn't been ready for that either.

After about twenty minutes, zooming up the coast, her hair a tangled mess, her heart thumping, but her feet still firmly planted on the board, she spotted half a dozen bright red jet skis by the shore. She had no idea how far she'd gone but it felt like miles. The jet skis lined up like that could mean only one thing: a little rental place. If she could just steer the windsurfer into the shore, she could drop the damn sail when she hit the shallows and rest her aching arms and her complaining back. She swore that she would never, ever windsurf again.

She adjusted her body, balancing her weight a little more to the right and the board turned into shore. She leaned a little harder and it turned a little bit more. "It's like having a baby, Miranda. One big push and you're there!" She leaned hard and pulled against the sail with all her might. She never could have managed this just a year ago. A huge wind gusted out of nowhere and picked up the sail, making the board jump three feet out of the water. Quickly she bent her knees to absorb the shock of the board landing on the waves and tried to grip the surface with her toes. Every part of her ached now, but the shore was rapidly coming closer. As she leaned hard the board made a graceful arc and, as if it were steering itself, took her towards the jet skis. The proprietor was standing by his machines, refilling the fuel tanks, frozen as he stared at the incoming craft. She quickly let go of the sail and bent down to grab the board with both hands. Sure enough, the sail acted like an anchor, a dead weight in the water. She felt grateful that her abject fear had told her to hold on to that board for dear life or she would have been pitched forward in a spectacular wipeout as the board came to a sudden halt. It wasn't her pride that she was worried about. She didn't have much of that remaining after the humiliating and public way Gregg had ended their marriage. No, it wasn't her pride that she was worried about. At her age, she just really didn't want to get injured.

She realized she was trembling all over: a mixture of exhaustion and fear. She stepped off the board into the waist-deep water.

"Wow. That was the most interesting technique I've... um... ever seen. I think that defied all the laws of physics. Where did you learn how to windsurf?"

"At the Salvo Day Use beach."

"Three miles down the coast?"

"Oh, is that how far I came? That was fast." She looked back down the coast. She realized her trembling didn't seem to be abating. If anything, hearing how far she had come seemed to make it worse. She took a deep breath and turned back to the caretaker, trying to sound lighthearted rather than panicked. "What a ride. You have a phone I can use?"

"Uh, yeah," he said, still looking at her.

His look made her feel even more flustered, if that were possible. She was wearing a Caribbean blue two-piece and a pair of sunglasses anchored to her head with a funky, hot pink neoprene eyeglass strap. Emma had practically forced her to buy this suit and it was only the second time she'd worn it. He had on bathing trunks, a beach hat, and shades too, but there was no question about it, he was definitely checking her out. She thought that was marginally inappropriate given that he couldn't be over thirty and she had more than a few years on him.

"This way." He jerked his head towards the shore, hefted both his gas cans, and started the slow slosh towards the large chunks of cement that lined the shore. She dragged the windsurfer behind her, her arms still trembling. As he climbed out of the water she hefted the wet sail and lay it on the barrier so it wouldn't drift off while she put in her mayday call. She followed him on shore. "Here's the phone." He pointed to a handset lying on the counter at the Tiki-style shack that served as a headquarters.

"What is this place?" she asked, surveying the countertop that offered a variety of items for sale, including mugs, unattractive homemade-looking earrings that were labeled 'artisan', and random mass-produced beer huggies that were the opposite of artisan.

The man looked around. "Great question. The property's a mishmash of businesses. We rent jet skis, kayaks, paddle boards, canoes." Miranda followed his gaze and saw that the place also had a stack of beach bikes. The small plot was ringed by camp sites, more like camping slots, each with a parking space, a tiny cement well for a fire, and a split rail fence to separate each space from its neighbor. There were four pull-behind campers and two pop-up tents in the fifteen or so spaces available, and laundry drying on lines strung about. In the middle was an A-frame house on high stilts. "You aren't going to sail it back to Salvo, are you?" the young man asked. "Of course, if you leave from here, I need you to rent a life jacket. It's not worth the risk to go without one."

She stared at him. "I'm not sure I can contemplate a more horrifying thought than that at the moment."

He smiled. "Hey, life jackets are cool. No one thinks less of you for wearing one. In fact, if you want the real scoop, around here they'll think you're definitely un-cool by going without. We really hate making the rescue runs. Search parties are no party. It usually just turns out bad. Look, I'll let you borrow one for free. Just no more dare devil stunts like that."

"No, it's not... what?" Miranda was trying to process what he had just accused her of. "Never mind." She dialed her daughter's number. "Hi Emma, yes it's me. Yes, yes, I'm sure you've been worried. Yes, I'm sure Caroline is out of her mind. No, I didn't know how to turn around. I barely knew how to stand up! You what? Well, you'll need to call 911 back and tell them I've popped up, still alive. Well, I'm up the coast, at, oh, hang on..." She turned to the caretaker, "Where am I?"

"Chicamacomico Watercraft Rentals."

"Chicama... what?" Then she looked up and saw the water tower. "Emma, I'm at the watercraft rental place close to the water tower about three miles to the north of you. Great. See you in a few. And make sure you call 911 first." She hung up the phone. The young man was standing behind the counter with a smile on his face. She looked at him and had to remind herself to close her mouth. He was cute. Suntanned. Fit. Sloppy sun-bleached brownish hair. He took his sunglasses off. Hazel eyes. Damn. Her favorite. And that smile. Wow.

"That's funny. You don't know how to sail." There was no hint of a question in his tone. It was a statement of fact.

"Nope." She blushed, not sure if it was because she didn't know how to sail or because he'd just checked her out again. Since she'd married Gregg, she was sure that no man had looked her over. Not even Gregg. She didn't want to think of how long that had been. She was trying to puzzle out how it made her feel to have this man glance at her that way.

33

"You should know how to sail. You are seriously lucky that you were able to handle that windsurfer."

"No kidding. I went on instinct."

"Then you've got good instincts. You're lucky. I've known people who have suck-ass instincts and it always steered them wrong."

Miranda thought about that. Did she have good instincts? She wasn't sure. She had this uncomfortable feeling that she usually listened to her head rather than her instincts. That hadn't worked out so well. After all, she'd married Gregg. Of course, she'd been pregnant and back then that's what you did. Now, after all that therapy and journaling and fantasizing, she could see that her college-aged gut had told her he was too controlling, too bossy, too driven, but her college-aged head said she should love him. He was super cute. They'd been dating over a year, and that was an eon for college students. He'd 'pinned' her the fall of his senior year, which meant they were serious. They were the perfect couple. He was going to medical school the next year. Of course, she loved him. If you could draw an ace from the deck of college sweethearts, Gregg was it. How could she not have loved him? He was Mr. Perfect on his way to becoming Dr. Perfect.

"You should take a sailing lesson."

"Yeah, uh, what? I should do what?"

"You should take a sailing lesson. I can take you out on the catamaran. That's a good place to start. Once you know the basics of sailing, you're much less likely to get in over your head like that. You here for the week?"

"No, I'm an owner. I'm here for the summer."

"The whole summer? No kidding?" He looked at her intently. "Then you definitely should learn how to sail. You'll be back every summer now. Yeah, you need to know how to sail. I could show you the sound side here, where the little coves are. There're some spectacular birding grounds if you're into that kind of thing. Vacationers aren't but residents usually are. If you're going to be a part of the community, you need to know your island."

Andy felt guilty. This man was trying to be helpful and all she could think of was that she'd just escaped a near death experience. Then it struck her that she wasn't sure if she meant the trip up the coast or the marriage with Gregg. Her house guests were leaving in the morning. Tomorrow she would be alone. Alone in the new beach house. For the first time. Her beach house. It was going to be pretty quiet without them there. Was she ready for quiet? "Sailing lesson? Yeah, sure, okay. When?"

"How about tomorrow?"

Good timing. She could avoid having to face her aloneness. Stave it off for one more day. Surely loneliness was going to come snapping close on the heels of being alone. Then she would think of Gregg with his young new wife. In her house. "Tomorrow sounds good. What time?"

"Arrive at eleven. I'll show you how to get the boat ready. Take you around the islands."

"Okay, great. How much?"

"Tell you what, I'll give you a really good deal if you're willing to bring a picnic lunch."

She looked at him. "You serious?"

He just smiled at her, his tan face contrasting nicely with his white teeth. He still had that old, bedraggled beach hat covering his longish, shaggy hair. He was so cute he probably could have sold her a turnip at this point. She hated turnips. But she loved picnics. Sailing lesson. Seeing the island. Spending an hour or two with this man who was destined to be the world's greatest salesman? Why not? She deserved some fun. She glanced at the prices on the board for rentals. While sailing lessons weren't listed, all the posted prices seemed quite reasonable. "You're on. Anything you can't or won't eat? Anything you particularly love?"

"No allergies. No dislikes. I do like surprises, and I love good food." He went on to tell her about the coves he would show her the next day, what kind of storks and cranes inhabited the marshes, in addition to the several varieties of ducks. She began to feel seriously excited to see the world of Hatteras Island as it was known to the natives. A quick two-beep pulse of a car horn pulled

35

her away.

"That's probably my rescue party. I'm looking forward to tomorrow. Oh, hey, what's your name? And do you need me to do any paperwork for the reservation?"

"I'm Austin."

"Well, hi, I'm Miranda. But people mostly call me Andy."

"People mostly call me Austin."

"Nice to meet you, Austin. Any paperwork?"

"Nope. Here, I'll help your friends get the board out of the water."

Emile helped Austin haul the windsurfer out of the sound, chatting good naturedly. Andy caught a few of Emile's words on the breeze, "…like a pro. She knew how to do that? Who knew? And Emma went into total panic attack mode…." But the rest was drowned out in Caroline and Emma's concern.

"We were so scared! You just zoomed off and you were gone." Emma was shaking slightly.

"Oh my God, girl!" said Caroline. "You always were so much more daring than I was. You know, E, always in college she was Ms. Adventure. You should have seen her then."

Miranda laughed. "Oh hush, Caroline. I don't think I want her to know those old stories! E, you did call 911 to cancel the alarm?"

Emma nodded. "Oh yes, geez. You're such a mom!"

The women laughed and hugged again.

The boys walked by with the surfboard, Emile saying, "Don't you love it when they laugh like that?"

"They are awfully cute; I grant you that. Where're you from?"

"Oh, you noticed my accent?"

"Well, yeah. Kind of hard not to. France?"

"I'm Belgian."

"Oh, like the waffles?"

"Actually, waffles are not from Belgium. I first had them in a place called Waffle House. While the waffles were pretty good, the place… it was kind of dumpy. Made me worried about what Americans think of Belgium. But Emma, she reassured me that a lot of Americans don't think of anyone but themselves."

"Yeah, that would be about right. But hey, we associate Belgium with waffles and chocolate, what's not to like? So, Emma's your girlfriend?"

"Oui! She is lovely."

Austin looked over his shoulder at Andy, a smile on his face. He and Emile finished strapping down the board on the top of the car.

"Thanks!" Emile said as he climbed in the driver's seat and beeped the horn twice. Caroline and Emma climbed in.

"So, Andy," Austin said, "I'll see you tomorrow?"

"Picnic in hand."

Chapter 6

Andy examined the flexible cooler. While it was convenient to carry the picnic in, it wouldn't do squat to keep the food dry sailing on a catamaran. She hoped the inner bag was as waterproof as it was advertised to be. She wondered what the picnic would be like. 'Ms. Adventure' Caroline had called her. "Pregnancy was my last adventure," she said to herself as she added another little jar to the hopper. "You haven't done anything in the least adventurous since then." She looked around the kitchen. "Well, Miranda, you did buy this beach house. And that's adventurous." She smiled and pulled a small jar out of the cupboard and slid it into the pack.

Everyone had pulled out at nine-thirty this morning. It was a seven-hour drive to get to Charlotte, where Emma and Emile would stay with Caroline and Mimi for a couple of days. From there, Emma and Emile would head on to Lexington, Kentucky. Emma was starting medical school in August, and she needed to get settled in her new apartment.

Picnic prepared; Andy checked herself out in the mirror. She was wearing what she called her 'lifeguard bathing suit' with a super light, long-sleeved Caribbean-blue sun shirt over it. It hung open and framed her figure. She loved it. "You look… good, Andy. Huh Yeah, you look good. And I don't know that you've ever said that to yourself before." She liked the suit. It was conservative, offered good coverage, but also showed off her shape. "And it's not like this is a date. Far from it. You're not taking a chance. That day is not today." This was her being a sucker and being up-sold by an entrepreneurial young businessman who was too young for her but could probably sense her loneliness and was totally cool with making a buck off of that. "Okay. Time for a sailing lesson. It's all business, but that doesn't mean it can't be an adventure!"

Parking at Chicamacomico Watercraft Rentals, she picked up the cooler and her towel, took a deep breath and walked towards the Tiki shack. A nondescript mutt ran up to her and started jumping about. She'd never been much of a dog person. It ran off and brought back a chew toy. Despite her lack of interest, she decided to oblige it, bending over and pulling at the toy, while the dog growled happily and tried to shake the chew out of her hands. When it let go, she threw the toy, and the dog skittered off happily. Andy surprised herself that she laughed at the dog, but she was glad it found something else to poke at and left her alone.

"I see that Junior likes you," the shack attendant said, giving a nod to the pooch.

"Is that your dog?"

"Nah, belongs to a friend but it hangs out here sometimes." He shrugged.

"I'm here for a sailing lesson." She looked about for the man she'd seen yesterday, but there was no sign of anyone else at all.

"Sailing lesson?" The attendant was obviously confused. He was the kind of man who had spent his life in the sun on an island at the edge of the world. He had a graying narrow beard and shaggy dark hair that was punctuated by wiry tufts of gray that stuck out, making him look kind of lumpy. He had a small beer belly, which added to that effect. His skin looked permanently tanned and the smile lines around his eyes also seemed to be a permanent feature. "We don't do sailing lessons."

"Oh." She returned his confused look, not sure what to say. "But Austin said yesterday…"

"Oh, *Austin*. That's why he said he was getting the Hobie. Okay, I guess that's why he wanted me to work today. Sure. He'll be here in a second. Why don't you wait at the picnic table?"

"Okay, thanks." She sat down, followed by the mutt and his chew toy. Suddenly she felt nervous. She hadn't felt nervous like this since... well, since before she'd married Gregg. It was as though she'd been waiting for a date and then realized he was going to stand her up—publicly. Memories of past humiliation drifted across her mind. *I'm not that girl. I'm not going back there*, she said firmly to herself. She sat for another ten minutes, wondering whether she should just go back home. Then she saw it. The sails were tall as it came around the edge of the land and turned towards the waterfront. It glided in like a giant swan, almost floating above the water. It was beautiful. Austin anchored the catamaran and came onshore. "Wow."

"Yeah. It's beautiful, isn't it?"

"Gorgeous," she answered, and then reminded herself to look at the boat.

He smiled at her for what felt like a long time. "Head over to the bin over there and get yourself a life jacket. No one goes on the open water without a life jacket."

The tour was everything he'd promised. They went fast over the open water, which was thrilling. They floated their way down side paths to see the waterfowl. There was no way she could keep track of the coves and small waterways, and he explained that the only way to see them was on a catamaran. The sound was just too shallow for bigger boats and motors scared the wildlife. The birds seemed to treat the sailboat as a gentle giant, watching it glide by but not seeming to be overly concerned. She had never seen so many wild birds up so close.

"There are cranes, egrets, and herons, sure, but they're all over the place. They'll land in your backyard. It's like pelicans. I mean you can't move without running into a pelican. Dime a dozen. Now look down here. See that odd-looking bird with the crazy orange beak and the orange eye? That's an oystercatcher—and that's what it eats. Clams, mussels, that kind of thing."

"Damn. That thing looks like it could star in a movie. A Halloween slasher movie... for birds." Andy laughed. "It's almost creepy looking, you know, for a bird."

Austin laughed at her. "You're funny." He looked at the oystercatcher again. "And you're right. It has that creepy clown kind of look." He pulled a face. She laughed at him. Then he turned his head and pointed to a new bird that had just come into view. "Hey, look over there. That's a Tundra Swan. It's only here 'cause it's injured. It should be long gone by now. They rest on their migration path, but something must have happened to it. It's been here for a while."

"Poor thing. It looks lonely."

"Maybe it is." He shrugged. "They mate for life but looks like its mate found better things to do when this one couldn't keep up."

"And here I was thinking that I was anthropomorphizing the bird, but I can totally relate to that. That bird does feel lonely." She suddenly felt like she'd said too much.

"Oh, I'm sure animals have an emotional life. It's just like people to think that we're the center of the universe rather than just one little part of the whole picture."

"Oooh, a falcon just flew over us!"

"That's an American kestrel. And look over there: that fluffy one. That's a black-bellied plover."

"Wow. That's striking with that black belly. That's pretty."

"Yeah, and you're really lucky. They only dress up for breeding season. Unlike humans, who plume out all year round, these birds just do it when they're serious about it. But he must be an immature one that somehow missed the bus north, and now thinks he's been stood up! It's really unusual to find one in plumage here. And this is really late in the breeding season, too. Maybe it was injured and couldn't fly."

"I think that's my new favorite bird! Are they only here in summer?"

"Nah, they hang out all year here, but the mature adults breed way up north. They mostly like to winter here, but you can find them year-round, particularly juveniles. You can certainly hear them. They make that haunting whistle. Listen. They're warning all the other birds about us."

She listened. "Yeah, I hear that day and night. Wow, you're like the sailing and bird encyclopedia. What's your story? How do you know all this?"

"For that, we'll have to stop for lunch."

"For that, I came prepared."

He sailed them to a lovely, uninhabited little beach. Before they could disembark, a large sea turtle swam up next to the boat, pulled its head out of the water and looked at them before swimming away.

"Oh my… is that a… a huge, wild turtle?"

"Yeah, that's a sea turtle. Cool, huh?"

"You said it." They both watched for a moment as the turtle swam away and then they sloshed up to shore. "Amazing."

He smiled at her delight in the wildlife. "So, what did you bring me to pay for your sailing lesson?"

She looked at him with a smile. "Well, you said you love food, so this will be a real test of just how true that statement is." She felt so confident when it came to food. From the top of her cooler, she pulled out a small, round red and white gingham oilcloth. She handed it to him, and he spread it out on the beach. She began to pull out small Tupperware containers "First, I'm sure you're dying of thirst, as am I. Here's a strawberry-mint lemonade." She handed him a clear plastic milk bottle-like container. Dancing in the yellow liquid were several slices of lemon and strawberry and long leaves of mint. "I hope you like it almost sweet."

He nodded at her, looking impressed. He pulled off the top and took a sip. "Damn, girl. That's good."

"Or maybe you're just really thirsty." She smiled at him. He smiled back. "We have two dishes in our main course, one hot, the other cold. Here are Vietnamese wrapped spring rolls. I hope you like shrimp—it's also got tiny stick carrots, lettuce, sprouts and other veggies with that jumbo shrimp inside. And here's a packet of the sweet chili sauce. The hot dish is asparagus puffs, although if they are even still warmish then we're lucky. But they're pretty tasty even at room temp."

"What are they?"

She took out a foiled hot-mitt pouch wrapped around a container. "Oooo, still warm! Score! It's puff pastry with asparagus, obviously. Prosciutto, and a mild gruyere cheese. They're French. You met Caroline briefly yesterday? I learned about these from her sister-in-law, Claudine, who's French and an amazing cook." Again, Andy felt like she was saying too much. Only she could be interested in all these details. "And then there's other stuff," she said a little too quickly, to cover her embarrassment. She pulled out a container that came in three parts. One part held chopped egg whites, the other chopped egg yolks.

"Hard boiled eggs? And crackers?"

"These are deconstructed hard boiled eggs. Oh, don't make that face. Just trust me, it's a thing. The crackers are sea salt bagel rounds. And this," she pulled out a small bottle and opened it with a *pop!* "This is caviar. You put the white, then the yolk, then the caviar on the little bagel rounds. It's divine. Here's a little remoulade sauce. Trust me."

"I trust you. What other amazing surprises do you have in there?"

"Um, here's a few skewers of fresh mozzarella with grape tomatoes. They're good but not stunning. Some fresh cherries. Ah, and the *pièce de résistance*: dessert."

He held up the tiny jar she'd handed him and looked at it. "It's a, a, s'more?"

"Yeah."

"In a tiny mason jar?"

"Yeah, aren't they cute? So, how'd I do, captain?"

"Don't know. I'll have to try it. But I'm looking forward to it."

"No plates. We'll have to make do with what we have. But I have these little wooden sushi mats." She handed him the rolled-up mat and then unrolled one in front of her. "And this." She handed him a tiny wooden spatula, almost like a knife. "You can use that to eat, build your crackers,

43

devour that dessert. Bon appetite!"

"Yeah. OK, I'm officially impressed. Where did you learn to do food like this? Are you a chef?"

"No. I'm a writer, of sorts. I guess. But I had a lot of time to cook over the past few years."

"You're a writer? Like a reporter?"

"No, um, well. Like a book writer. An accidental book writer."

"How do you write a book by accident?" he asked, picking up a skewer of tomato and fresh mozzarella.

"Well, I wrote two books, actually. Oh my God, if I answer this question, this is going to be like telling you my life story."

"I want your life story."

She looked at him. This was definitely taking a chance.

He looked back at her. "You show me yours and I'll show you mine."

She took a sip of lemonade and picked up an asparagus puff. "Wow. My life story. That's a huge trust issue. I mean, shouldn't we do ropes course exercises first?"

"What are ropes course exercises?"

"You haven't done one? Oh, it's a big thing in business back on the mainland, in the cities. My husband did one with his department and I heard all about it. You do all these exercises to learn to trust one another. Catch each other as you're falling. Hold each other up on high wires in the trees. Stuff like that. He hated it."

"So, you're married?"

She took a deep breath. "I was. Oh shit, this is getting to the life story part."

"If you're not comfortable, hey, that's okay. I just like life stories. The great parts. The shit parts. I mean, it's all life."

They were quiet and watched the birds fly overhead.

"I was married."

"Newly divorced?"

"March. Um, yeah, March. Married my college sweetheart. Got pregnant. By accident, I mean. On my twentieth birthday."

"You know the *day?*"

"Well, our, uh, celebration got a little out of hand. So, we got married and Gregg went to medical school. I quit college because of the baby and we lived our early years in abject poverty. God bless his parents during that time. They bought us a tiny condo and we would never have made it without their help. It was supremely embarrassing. His parents always seemed to think it was my fault. They loved their granddaughter and I think they just tolerated me because I was the conduit to her. And then Gregg surprised me a year and half ago when he came home from work and asked me to move out. In the middle of his surprise birthday party."

"Ouch! Awkward."

"No kidding."

"No warning?"

"If there was, I missed it. But to me, no. He just came home and told me he couldn't do it anymore and that he wanted me gone."

"So, what did you do?"

"I moved out."

"I thought the wife always got the house?"

"When I realized that, it was a little bit too late, so apparently that does not happen in my story. In my story, I got a big settlement. Boy, was he pissed at the judge, but I bought the beach house."

"And you're an accidental writer?"

"Well, while we were married, once our daughter went to school, I had a lot of time on my hands. You met Caroline—part of my rescue party?"

Austin nodded.

"Caroline's mom is an artist, I mean the real thing, not a hobby painter like me."

"Oh, you paint."

"Well, I haven't for years now. Caroline's mom taught me to paint. But back then, I got really interested in art. I had all this time on my hands. I mean my daughter was gone at school all day. God knows Gregg never came home. So, I needed something to do. I ended up reading about art therapy. It started off as just a little interest project, but you know, it became like an obsession. I wrote a paper, like I'd written back in school, you know, just to prove to myself that I *could*. That I wasn't an idiot even though I was a dropout. I wrote about how painting could be used to augment therapy—and be a therapy in itself. Then I started to wonder about writing and how writing was therapy."

"And that made you an accidental writer? So, are you a therapist?"

"No." She laughed. "Not me. But I ended up writing another paper on how therapeutic writing was. Then I got the idea that a lot of different art was great therapy, so I did a chapter on dance as therapy, poetry, finger painting, sculpting—now there's not much on that one. In the end I had ten chapters."

"So, you had a book."

"Well, yeah, sort of. Yeah, it was a book."

"And you published it!"

"No, I couldn't. No one would take my work seriously 'cause I didn't have a college degree. They treated me like I was some kinda quack. Shut the door right in my face."

"So, what did you do with it?"

"It's sitting in a drawer. It's like my life's work and it's sitting in a drawer."

"That's a bummer. I bet that could really help people."

"Not from my drawer it won't."

"Why didn't you self-publish?

"I don't know. It felt like just putting it out there into the black hole filled with people's manifestos and passion projects that they couldn't get anyone to really believe in. It would've been too much like I was confirming the total failure of my project in my husband's eyes. To him, a respected academic, self-publishing is the height of embarrassment."

"Woah, that's heavy. So… accidental writer?"

"Oh yeah, back to the life story. You're sure you want to hear this?"

Austin looked at her as he sipped his lemonade. "Anyone who can make strawberry-mint lemonade like this has to have an interesting life story. Now, given the s'mores in a jar, your life story will be stupendous, I'm absolutely convinced."

She laughed. "Oh, you judge me by my food, do you? But will you still respect me after dessert?"

"Somehow, I get the feeling that I won't be able to do anything other than respect you."

She smiled at him and felt much more confident to go on. And somehow, she couldn't believe how good it felt to just talk about it. "Okay. So, I wrote my life's work on how to heal through various kinds of art therapy. And there it sat in a drawer. And one day Gregg tells me he wants a divorce. So, I gave it to him. I always gave him anything he wanted. And I went into a serious depression. I didn't have anyone to give anything to anymore. I don't think I knew who I was. Caroline was my college roommate. She and her brother basically did an intervention with me and made me get my act together. Of course, she'd read my art therapy book. I mean, what are college roomies for if not your best friend in the whole world? They're as supportive as a mom." She laughed at the memory. Austin looked away and out over the water. He looked pained. She was sure she was boring him and decided to get to the point.

"Uh, yeah, so she made me re-read the book and badgered me into writing. I swear, all I did for a year was to write and meet with a personal trainer."

"And what did you write about? Like journaling?"

"It started out as journaling, after all, that's what I'd found out in my research was so helpful to people who were suffering. But no, it turns out I hate journaling. With a passion."

"So, what did you write?"

"I wrote a novel. I mean, I had no idea how to write a novel, and believe you me it underwent many, many edits. But I created a character based on me and one based on Gregg. In the novel I did all the things I wished I'd done in real life."

"Like what?"

"I got revenge. I got even. I found love again, actually with Gregg, isn't that pathetic? In real life, he and Chenguang are deliriously happy. He calls her his morning glory. That's what her name means. She goes by M.G. She was his surgical resident. Then surgical fellow. He was her boss. She was his lover. And now a surgeon he works with. Now lives with. In my house."

"Not bitter, are you?"

"Sure, I'm bitter. Of course, I'm bitter! I got revenge in *fantasy* life, not real life. Of course, I'm bitter. But that's life, isn't it? And the real irony? I submitted this book and it found a home with a publisher almost immediately. It got published."

"So, you're a novelist?"

"Well, Captain Austin, you have the very great pleasure of dining with Ms. Miranda Wright, who, as of a few weeks ago, became a *New York Times* best-selling novelist and will soon have a movie made of her romantic comedy and imagined life story, *Taken by the Wind*. It's a southern thing, like *Gone with the Wind*, only this was my whole life blown apart by that damn wind. So, you, my new friend, are dining with kind of a famous person. But I'm in hiding, so don't tell anyone." She held her finger to her lips and smiled broadly.

"Wow. That is quite a story. If you write like you cook, then you don't need to be in hiding."

"Well, like I said, I had a lot of time to cook for many years. I spent most of my marriage trying to please Gregg, doing anything to please Gregg, while all the time I could never be smart enough or pretty enough or even attempt to be successful enough for him." She played in the sand with her fingers, feeling the confession coming out. "I think he felt that I embarrassed him, me with my dropout, non-degree status. I do plan to go back and finish up. I really do."

"Wait a minute. Why? For him or for you?"

"What do you mean?" she asked. "Of course, it's for me." She knew she sounded defensive.

"Just askin'. I mean, what do you have to learn there? What do you need to learn there? Sounds like you might have this writing thing figured out. So, you want to go back to school 'cause it feels unfinished? Or because you want a different career? Or because you want to prove something to him? Like he made a mistake to dump you, because you're educated, beautiful and successful. You're everything he wants?"

The questions made Andy anxious and now it was her turn to look out over the water. She was going to cry. Damn him, she was going to cry. She'd sworn she would not shed one more tear over that man.

"Yeah. That's a good story." Austin was nodding his head. "And now you're not living the fantasy one anymore. Now you get to live your real story. From here on out, the real thing. That's cool."

She wiped a tear from her cheek, resolutely not looking at him. "So, what's your story?" she managed to choke out with a reasonably calm voice. She didn't want to eat anymore.

Austin picked up the mason jar and his tiny wooden spatula. "Well, I'm an island boy. Born here. Raised here. By my dad. I've had to help in the family business."

"The rental place?"

"Yeah. It's a messy mishmash of everything under the sun. My uncle runs it, and although it's not my dad's first love, he has to help out a lot. But they're into, how can I describe this? 'Subsistence living.' It's an island thing. You see, on the islands, we only make money about four or five months a year. God forbid we have a hurricane during the season, or anytime really. We have to make all our money during the summer season. Winters, well, they're long and quiet. So, if you make sixty grand in the summer, that's all you all have for the whole year. As you can tell from the state of the business, we're lucky if we make that. I've been working the business for years. As long as I can remember actually. I'm going to school to earn a business degree so that I can come back

49

and change things. I want an MBA."

"You want to change the business?" She didn't remark on how shabby things looked. After all, it was part of the charm of the beach and the southern islands, part of the relaxed atmosphere.

"I want it to run like a business! I want the whole island to run more like a business. Everyone's barely surviving. Now Dad, and my uncle in particular, that's fine with them. You get what you need when you need it. Have faith, it will come. If not, you didn't need it."

"That's quite the philosophy. Gregg's philosophy was you make a butt-load of money and buy anything and everything you want that will impress others. The big house. The Jaguar. The Rolex. The new, younger, more successful wife. All while I was expected to pinch pennies."

"Pinching pennies is all I've ever known. I want to figure out how to help all our businesses do better. I want to help the island, the community."

"That's noble."

"It sounds noble, but we have a real problem. Kids who were born here, lived here just like me, they graduate from high school and go off. Some to college, others to jobs. But they see the larger world and they don't come back. Why would they? It's subsistence living. And it's boring. The winters are hard."

"You make it sound like Minnesota. This is North Carolina. The winters aren't hard."

"No, it's not the weather. It's the people. You can't get people to stay the winter. Because there are no people, there's no businesses open. Because there's no businesses open, there's no people. Take my dad, for example."

"What about your dad?"

"He's lonely. He won't admit it, but he's lonely."

"Where's your mom?"

"Complicated. Died. Mother and father actually. A whole car full of people. Killed by a drunk driver when I was five. My seven-year-old cousin was killed too. It's a problem on the island. The tourists, they come and get drunk as skunks and try to drive back to wherever they came from. Occasionally they take one of us out with them. Or like in this case, a whole car full. The boy who killed my family was only twenty-five years old. Driving without a license. No insurance. Totally messed up." Here Austin took a deep breath. "I don't drink."

"I don't blame you."

"I'll never drink. Anyway, it's just been me and Dad ever since."

"Your dad? You just said…"

"Yeah, like I said, it's complicated. My father died in the car accident. My uncle, who also lost his wife and daughter, took me in. Raised me. He's my daddy. He's done everything for me. I loved, and lost, my father. I'll never know him. Or my mom. I was just too young. But I still have a dad. Yeah. I love my dad."

"Wow. You've been through a lot. I'm glad you have your uncle."

"He's my *dad*. And he needs me to take care of him, so I feel really guilty leaving for the mainland to go to school. Man, he went into a real funk for a couple of years after the accident. He doesn't talk about it. He's doing all right now, I guess. Yeah, he does great while things are going great, but he can triggered by stuff. I really worry about him without me here."

"And he's never remarried?"

"How could he do that? There are no women."

"What do you mean, there are no women? It's the Outer Banks! It's covered in women."

"Sure, in summer it is. In summer it's crawling with people. But they don't stay. Mainlanders can't hack it here."

"Can't hack it?"

"Yeah, you won't find this out, because you're a summer owner. But winters—there's no society here. Nothing to do. It's boring and isolating. That's why everyone moves away. I know more than a half a dozen eligible guys who would give their right testicle to have a woman in their lives."

"Well, there's got to be ample women on the mainland?"

51

"It never works between a mainlander and an islander. If you weren't raised here, you can't handle the isolation. Dad's dated women but once they experience life here, winter life here, they leave. There's no hope for it. It's just a summer romance."

"Summer romances can be fun." Andy blushed furiously and looked away, wondering why she had said that.

"But they aren't satisfying. They're like teenage girls. Jesus, they're like college girls. No substance. No depth. And my dad is just not the revolving-door-relationship type of guy."

"And are you?"

"Am I what?"

"The revolving-door-relationship type of guy?"

"I don't know. I haven't had a chance to figure it out yet. If I am, then I can live happily on the island. If not, I'll still live on the island, but I'll be lonely."

"Loneliness is tough."

He looked at her with a sideways smile. "The toughest role you'll ever play."

She laughed and decided to test him. "But Hollywood made you a movie star."

"And pain was the price you paid."

"I can't believe you know that song," she said.

"Music is timeless. It brings people together."

Later that afternoon, as they splashed about in the water, he suddenly said, "Stand here. Just stand still. It's back. Very unusual. Don't talk." They stood almost arms-length from one another, but he had taken her hand and continued to hold onto it. Then he nodded at the water, and she followed his gaze. The turtle was back. It swam around them once, coming so close it almost brushed Andy's leg, and raised its head to give them a look. Then it drifted off, paddling its way to wherever the turtles hung out.

"Oh my God, I have died and gone to heaven. Thank you, Austin. Thank you."

He gave her a long look and a sweet smile. "You're welcome."

As four o'clock neared, the catamaran rounded the edge of the land and approached the watercraft rental lot. Andy was sad to see it all end. They had raced the wind, scooting across the waves. She'd learned what it meant to 'tack' and how it took you backwards against the wind. She had been greeted by a wild turtle. They had basked in the warm waters of the sound and picnicked on the private beach. She must have seen a thousand birds, none of whose names she would remember. She decided that no matter how much this trip cost, it was worth the price of the excursion. But it was ending, and it was time to get back to reality. Austin was a very nice man, but this was business. He had promised her a sailing lesson and a magnificent tour, and that's just what he'd delivered. It wasn't a date. She was just fooling herself. He was too young for her. She was too old for him. This wasn't her chance. But it had been fun, for just a moment there, when they had been holding hands and the turtle swam by them, to think what it would have been like if it had been a real date. It was the most romantic time she had ever spent with anyone and now she had to hand over her credit card and pay for her little vacay to Fantasy Island.

He hooked the Hobie up to the anchors that lined the coast and took down the sails. Then he unhooked her cooler and carried it back to shore. She followed him, sloshing through the thigh-deep water.

"That was an amazing day, Austin."

"My pleasure. That was an amazing picnic."

"I'm so glad you liked it. Um, my, uh, car keys and phone and credit card are in your drawer there."

"What? Oh, yeah, sure."

As he handed them to her, she asked, "So, how much do I owe you for that fantastic five hours of near bliss?" She took a deep breath, readying herself for the price tag that would leave her speechless. If her daughter had gotten herself in this kind of a situation, Andy was sure she would have admonished her for being so naïve.

"Tell you what. That was a really good picnic. If you're willing to throw in a fabulous dinner, we could just call it even."

Andy blinked at him. "Are you serious?"

"Hell yeah. After eating my dad's cooking since I was five? And don't even get me started on my uncle's," he said as he nodded at the house. "That man would barbecue anything."

"Wow. You're hypnotized by my cooking? Well, okay, sure. You're on. Not tonight, surely? Sometime in the next… week?"

"Right, not tonight. In about fifteen minutes the parade of returns will start up with everyone bringing back all the toys they've checked out for the day. And it's Saturday, so we'll have campers checking in until about ten." He sighed deeply and looked around at the lot. Four more cars and pull-behind campers and one pop up tent had been added to the scene. "You know, I've got some stuff going on the next few nights. Thursday works for best me, but after six-thirty. I have to close up shop again that day."

"Thursday it is. I'll write down my address and number for you."

"Text it to me." He picked up his phone and typed in her number. "I won't keep track of a piece of paper."

"Great, so I'll see you between six-thirty and seven?"

"Absolutely. I wouldn't miss it."

"I'll try to impress you."

"Somehow I know you will."

Chapter 7

Miranda pulled down five of her favorite cookbooks, stacking them up on the kitchen table and taking a seat. She felt really excited about making dinner for Austin. They'd had such a lovely time on the water. She hadn't cooked for another man since, well, since Gregg. At least her cooking was one thing he had actually liked about her, pleased that it never failed to impress their friends. It was funny, in a sad kind of way: she had never actually liked to cook. She'd learned how simply to please him. She had done everything to please him. To make it up to him that she had accidentally gotten pregnant and subsequently ruined his life.

But now she was cooking for someone new. A new possibility? A new friend? A new man in her life? A new chance? What was Austin? "I don't even know what I want from this," she muttered as she tossed the books around, trying to decide which to delve into first. While she was eager to display her skills for an appreciative audience, she hadn't actually dated anyone yet. Eighteen months since her separation. Three months since the final decree. She was a free woman with a huge settlement and zero self-confidence, best seller notwithstanding, who had only ever been seriously involved with one man. Now there was this other man. What did she want from him? What was she ready for?

"Shut up, Andy! This is a dinner. It's just a bunch of food on the table. You eat it. And then he goes home."

Her phone rang. A part of her was certain it would be Austin, realizing, like Gregg had so long ago, that she was 'not an asset', and cancelling their date, but it was only Emma.

"Hi E, what's up? Are you having fun at the Watkins place?"

"Hi Mom. Oh, yeah, they're terrific. All of them—and man are there a lot of people here! I'm out walking in the grounds now to get a few minutes of privacy. It's just beautiful here. But you won't believe what just happened…" Emma went on into a long string of complaints about how her rather impromptu girls' trip to Paris that summer had just fallen through. She had heard from her college friends and they were too busy to get together since they had all started jobs. Andy made a coffee and listened. She was well-acquainted with this routine. "And it's my last summer that I'll have free, in like forever!"

"Well, honey, they have jobs. They aren't going on to more school. They probably don't have any vacation time yet. They all just started work." Andy tried to reason with her daughter.

"But this is special! This is our last time to get to do these things. I want to go to Paris with my girlfriends."

"It may be a special opportunity, but I doubt they can simply ask for the time off to go on a vacation."

"Why not, Mom? I mean, what do you know about it? You never worked."

That should have stung more than it did, but Emma was ever full of zingers and Andy had long since learned that her baby girl was a little high strung, a little high maintenance, and a lot like her father. She had spent twenty-two years soothing her little perfectionist. "I would say it was work to run the household, manage the finances, keep you all fed and clothed, help you with your homework. I loved it all, but it was a full-time job to keep you and your father running at top speed. Honey, I was like your pit crew. I fixed everything."

"Speaking of Daddy, he's being really difficult."

"How so?" This was a surprise. While Gregg had barely sheathed his sword of criticism around his wife, he adored his daughter. She could do no wrong. Well, that wasn't quite accurate. As long as she got top grades and never got into trouble, she could do no wrong, and he would buy her anything. There had been a parade of huge stuffed animals. Then the thousand-dollar gift cards for straight A's, which resulted in the need for extra closet space. That girl had more shoes than a small-world dictator. The car when she turned sixteen, but not a convertible because her SAT scores were good but not in the top ten percent. Oh, the whining with that punishment.

"Well, I have a couple of things I need, and he won't help me."

"What do you need?"

"Well, the credit card..."

"How much is it this time?"

"It's just twenty-two hundred dollars and I've only got seven hundred to put towards it. But, Mom, I found the most gorgeous jacket. Lime green. Lambskin. It was so cool. It was at a trunk sale and it was..."

"I don't even want to know. I have your credit card info. I'll go online and pay it off. But E, this is the last time. You can't keep spending on these things, no matter how wonderful and unique they are. Besides, pretty soon you'll be wearing scrubs for the rest of your life. You won't even have the occasion to wear all those clothes." Andy thought with a smile that E certainly hadn't inherited any skin-flint genes from her father.

"Thanks, Mom. You're the best. I love you."

"Oh, honey, I love you too. You're my everything, you know."

"Yeah, I know, Mom."

You're the best. I love you. Andy loved those moments with E. Beneath all the drama there was an undercurrent of mother-daughter closeness that had buoyed Miranda through the unhappy years with Gregg. She always had her wonderful little E.

"And, uh, Mom? There's something else I need your help with. Daddy was so mean on the phone tonight."

"No? He wasn't?" Miranda had worked hard to protect little E from

57

Gregg's tempers and demands. "What happened, honey?"

"Well, it's about the apartment. I know I signed for it for the year, but it just won't do. Emile and I have decided to live together and it's way too small for two people. I think having Emile right there will be so important for me in medical school. He'll help take care of me while I'm studying all the time. And this is the start of our lives together."

Andy stared out the window. Emile as a son-in-law? Starting their lives together? Sure, he was nice. Ish. She wondered why Emma and Emile hadn't mentioned this while they were visiting?

"I don't know how I can live without him."

Andy struggled with what to say. "You two are like two peas in a pod, aren't you? Even your names sound alike."

"Emma and Emile. I know. It's so cute. And the way he says it, with his accent."

Andy thought for a moment and took a different track. "Emma, you're going to be really busy next year. When your father was in medical school, he practically killed himself studying. He was never around. I was a new mother, not even twenty-one yet, all on my own. My mother was in Texas and your other grandparents were good with presents but not with things like changing diapers or getting food on the table. I was like one of those pioneer women. Have the baby and not miss a step with the chores!"

"You were a great mom. You've always been there for me. And I love Emile. I just don't want us to start off our lives together in some cramped, dingy little place where we'll ride on each other's nerves. I want us to have a good start together. I think we need a decent place to live. You're right—it'll be hard enough with me being in school and all."

Andy breathed a deep sigh of acquiescence. "And your father won't help you get another place?"

"No. He's being a real jerk about it. I think he only wants to spend money on M.G. He seems really distracted."

"He is paying for your medical school. And he's newly married."

"Yeah, and she's great. We talk about medicine all the time. She's really supportive, but man, she's strict. I think she might be telling him to push me out of the nest or something. I mean, geez, Mom, I'm still a student. You know, to be honest I think he's still kind of pissed that I didn't get into Yale or Harvard. He went on about that so much. But U.K.'s a great school. He should love it. He teaches there. And I love Lexington. I never want to leave Lexington. I mean, except to go to Paris. Or visit you."

Miranda smiled. So, the wonderful, the fabulous, Dr. Morning Glory was showing a crack of imperfection? Emma never realized the effect it had on her mother to hear about how smart, how stylish, or how young Chenguang was. Emma extolled her virtues rather endlessly, as if she had at last found an 'appropriate' role model for herself in her new stepmother. "So, Daddy's all too wrapped up in his new family to remember us, huh? I'm sorry about that, honey. I think men go through those phases. He'll remember you and find his way back. So, what are you and Emile thinking?"

"Well, we've found this little condo. It's not fancy or anything, but it's nice. And it'll be a really good place for us to get a start. A safe place to call home while we're making it through my med school years."

Andy sighed again. "How much?"

"Under five-hundred thousand."

"Wow, that's a lot, E!"

"Not for Lexington. And this is nice. It has lots of big, open space. Not claustrophobic."

"You know the place your dad and I had while he was in school was the tiniest little thing. His parents helped us to get it so you'd have a good place to grow up. It was a stretch for them to help us. Certainly, my mother was in no kind of situation to help out at all."

"So, you'll help me?"

"I don't know, E. This is a lot of money!"

"Aw, Mom, c'mon. Don't be like Dad. Besides, you have a best-selling novel. With a movie-option. I mean, they're going to make the movie, right?"

59

"It looks like it, but I don't know. I don't have anything to do with that. I just wrote the book."

"And Daddy gave you that huge settlement. I mean he complains about it, like, all the time. Particularly since he says you're rich now with the book."

Andy laughed. "You don't exactly get rich off of one book. Or a movie option. Honey, it's not like I wrote Star Wars."

"Can't you please, please help me?"

"Ummmm."

"What else do you have to spend money on? You have your beach house. And you know, property is a good investment. Tell you what, I won't ask that you give it to me. It can be your investment. And that's a good thing, right? Your property."

Andy thought about that. She had a condo in Charlotte. That was home. If her beach experiment failed then she had a place to run to. But if E settled in Lexington…. If she and Emile settled down, had kids, she'd want to be closer than Charlotte. Or where she was now. The islands were at the end of the earth.

"There's three bedrooms. So, we'll have a guest room for you! You'd always be welcome!"

"Maybe. And I'll talk to your father about it."

Chapter 8

"Damn," Andy muttered as she looked through Julia Child's *Mastering the Art of French Cooking*. She slammed the book closed. "No one eats like this anymore. Why did I say I'd try to impress him? How stupid. Why didn't I offer to order pizza? Oh yeah, because of the turtles." She didn't want to admit to herself just how much she wanted to impress him, but after another two hours of searching the internet for ideas she gave up and called Caroline.

"No worries, Andy. The peas-in-a-pod are being excellent house guests. But, oh my God, you went out on a boat with that sound-side Adonis? For five hours? You're kidding me? That turtle sighting sounds amazing."

"Yeah, um, Caroline, please don't make such a big deal about it. Is Emma around? I don't want her to hear you."

"Okay, but why?"

"Oh c'mon! This man is way younger than me. He can't be too many years past thirty and to be honest, really low on my list is to hear E laugh at me and call me a cougar. I'd prefer to skip being humiliated in front of my own daughter. And I really, really don't want her to tell Gregg. Besides, you and I both know this isn't going to turn out to be anything anyway. Even if he thinks he's attracted to me now, which I'm not saying is true, but if he did, when he finds out that I'm a decade older than he is... well, it's going no place. I'm just going to get my hopes up, and then have them dashed with the reality check that all this man really wants is a personal chef."

"Maybe you could take a chance? Andy, going on a date doesn't mean dating someone. And dating someone doesn't mean it's a forever commitment. It's just a date. Besides, you have a secret weapon: the way to a man's heart is through his stomach. Just ask Claudine. She totally seduced my brother with food."

"That's what I need! I need to talk with Claudine. Is she there?"

"Oh my God, Andy, *everyone* is here. Claudine, Chase, the kids, the tutor, their French chef, their whole entourage. It's a zoo. Believe me, Emma and Emile fit right in."

In the end, Andy got more than just a list of recipes from Caroline's sister-in-law. In exchange for the promise of Claudine shipping her morel mushrooms and very specific instructions, Andy had to promise to come to visit Claudine's book club in the fall. Claudine also told Andy what to wear, how to do her hair, what perfume to use, and what to cook. While it should have seemed overbearing, that heavy French accent made it seem more like she was getting coaching from a celebrity make-over artist. "You are at the beach, no? *Oui?* So, Andee…" When Claudine said her name, it sounded like she was saying 'undie', as underwear. Really sexy French underwear. "…you must steam the seafood. Buy live crabs, two or three kinds, and serve with fresh lemon wedges and bowls of clarified butter. It is very romantic to bash the crabs with the hammers! And corn on the cob. And a big bowl of butternut squash and roasted potatoes. Cut into chunky circles and then stack them up like little cakes."

Claudine was right. It was the perfect meal. Tuesday morning a box arrived of fresh morel mushrooms, along with a pouch of dried ones labelled 'just in case'. A bottle of white wine. French, of course. Bordeaux—a Semillon. Expensive. Fresh, live, growing herbs. A few cans of real French foie gras. An absolutely gorgeous pair of crab crackers, two wooden hammers, complete with a small wooden board to use them on. Comprehensive instructions. "Wow, she is nothing if not thorough!" Then she found a little bottle of perfume. It smelled absolutely gorgeous. Andy pulled out the morel mushrooms and a little note.

"These will keep in their special box in your refrigerator for up to two weeks. Enclosed is my secret recipe for poached eggs in morel mushroom sauce. Serve it for breakfast the first time he stays the night." A hand-drawn smiley face gave Andy a big wink.

"Oh my God, I will never live this down." But she put all the items away carefully and was thankful to have the recipe. Having tried it once, she thought she could probably fall in love with Claudine too.

She found the days weighed heavily on her. She tried to write. Lord knows, she had a contract for her next book and an agent breathing down her neck. She had no idea what to do about it. She was a one-off writer, as far as she knew. A one-hit-wonder of the written word, as it were, but she would never say that to her agent. Agents were a tricky bunch. They loved you if you smelled of success, if you could pump out two or three books a year, if you could give them a steady income and keep bread on their tables as well as your own. There were millions of wannabe writers. That's what she was. A wannabe that had somehow gotten lucky. Apparently, her fantasy of revenge, of getting even with the man who had jilted her, and then of reeling him back in, had struck a chord with millions of women readers. Would she ever be so desperate for love on the outside as she was on the inside? That kind of loneliness could drive you to do really dumb things. Like thinking that you had any hope of a thirty-something MBA student finding you attractive.

Then she remembered what Austin had said when she'd asked him if summer flings could fulfill him. *I don't know. I haven't had a chance to figure it out yet. If I am, then I can live happily on the island. If not, I'll still live on the island, but I'll be lonely.*

She went to her computer and pulled up her playlist. She put on *Candle in the Wind* and listened to the lyrics. *Loneliness is tough. The toughest role you ever played. Hollywood created a superstar, and pain was the price you paid.*

"I'm not going that route. I am not going to let loneliness dictate my life. Or my choices."

She still couldn't write. But she did get three rooms painted.

* * *

Thursday came much more quickly than she expected it would. All of a sudden, there wasn't enough time to get everything done. She'd wanted to get some fresh flowers for the table, but it was either that or clean up after her painting frenzy. She hoped the smell of fresh paint was gone at last. Too late, she realized that no matter how much it needed it, it wasn't very smart to repaint the house right before a dinner party. She looked in the mirror as she got ready for Austin to arrive. "You know what's going to happen to you, don't you?" she said to her reflection. "You're going to develop a teenage girl crush on this man who is a decade younger than you are. He's going to see you as an old lady. You're going do the whole stupid rebound relationship thing, and get your heart broken without the benefit of actually having been in a relationship, because this is all in your head. Stop thinking of this as your chance." Then she heard the doorbell. "Oh damn, he's early."

There he was, wearing khaki shorts and a light pink polo that really complemented his tan. "Hi."

"Hi back. C'mon in. How was your week?"

"Good. Kinda busy. I had to run up to Manteo to do some errands for the business."

"Manteo? I liked Manteo. It's cute. It's like going to the city compared to here."

"Is the quiet of the islands getting to you already? This is high season. You just wouldn't believe it in winter."

"So you've said. I'm looking forward to the quiet, but since I've had constant house guests since I arrived, that sounds like a bit of a mythical concept to me. I plan to head back to Charlotte sometime in the fall. I have a condo there that I've barely moved into. Would you like something to drink?"

"I don't drink."

"So you said, but I imagined that you were referring to alcohol rather than all liquids. After all, you don't meet a hundred percent of your fluid needs by soaking it in from the ocean."

"Sorry." He smiled sheepishly. "Am I being too sensitive?"

"Not at all. I have more of that lemonade or I can make you an icy, fruity kind of island-y thing."

"What is it?"

"I don't know, I'm making it up. If you like it, you'll have to both remember how it came to be and give it a name."

"Like Fido?"

"Yeah, like Fido, Rufus, or Bad Dog. Sounds like you want to live dangerously?"

"Oh yeah. If it's good, we'll call it the 'Sans Life Preserver'."

"Ha, ha. Very funny. Or we could call it 'Taken by the Wind', in the sense that you don't even know you need a life preserver."

"Oh, you always need a life preserver. But I do hear 'Taken by the Wind' is a very successful name to give something. Sure to be a hit. So how do you invent this, this, uh, fruity island-thing?"

"Right this way," she said, but he moved first, right though the living room and into the kitchen, as if he already knew where it was. The step-down from one room to the next didn't seem to surprise him at all.

"Nice kitchen!"

"Yeah, it's the nicest thing about the house. I've replaced most of the appliances, except for the dishwasher, which is so loud it's like having another person around." She sighed. "This is a wonderful place. I loved the house the minute I saw it. It has such a good feel."

"Hayward House does have a great 'real people live here' vibe to it. I've always liked this place. It's far from a mega-mansion summer rental."

"You know this house." It was a realization and not a question.

"Oh sure. It's had several owners in my time. It was kind of a shack when my dad was little. The Haywards originally lived here. Nice couple, he always said. Mr. Hayward fished and played guitar. She taught school way down in Hatteras. They lived here until the end, like fifty years. Then it stood empty for quite a long time. A little over twenty or so years ago a builder bought it and did all these amazing renovations to it. He was a friend of my dad's, so I heard all about it. Came by a few times with him. They worked on it for years. My dad helped him build this kitchen. Yeah, the guy had about eight friends help him on this house."

"Really? Wow, you know way more about my house than I do. Most beach houses have kitschy names so I've been wondering about this being called Hayward House. I bought it from the nicest old couple, who weren't named Hayward, I just adored them. It was so sad—they owned the house for quite a few years, but eventually it just got beyond them. They live central state and as they got older just came less and less. Their kids couldn't wait to dump it."

"Yeah, you bought a bit of a fixer-upper," he said as he looked around. "It seems to be this house's karma. You should have my dad come over and look at it. He could give you a list of what you need to do to get this place back in shape. I think it's gonna take more than paint."

She smiled. He could smell the paint. "Well, I suppose I have to start someplace. What happened to the builder?"

"Went bankrupt. Had to sell. Sold it to your friends."

They weren't really her friends—she barely knew them. She decided to let it go. "Went bankrupt fixing up this house?" She looked around.

"Beach houses are expensive propositions. The sea air, the salt, the humidity, the hurricanes are all really hard on everything here—houses, cars, boats, roads, electricity."

"You know, for someone who absolutely loves the island, you're a terrible salesman!"

He laughed. "True island life is not for the faint of heart. The other thing that happens all too often is you take a place like yours here—right now

Hayward House is back on this secluded, lovely little undeveloped section. But they fixed the road back here in the spring. It's been a mess of potholes and broken pavement for about as long as I can remember. Before you know it, all those lots out there will be snapped up, and then you'll be living in a little neighborhood of mega-mansions. On stilts."

"Really?"

"Oh, yeah, I've seen it so many times. But you won't have neighbors, not real ones. Just summer renters, partying their way through their vacations."

"All that open space out there… they're lots?"

"Lots for sale. Yeah, it's all lots for sale. What's not owned by the government to be kept as a preserve and thank God for that or this wouldn't be the Outer Banks, it would be Miami, but everything else is owned by someone who's just waiting to make a buck on it."

"Sounds like I better enjoy my little slice of paradise while I can."

"I'm afraid that's progress, my dear. Doesn't make me happy either, but what can you do? What can any of us do? We don't own the island. We just live here. So, anyway, how about that 'Bad Dog' drink you promised me."

"Sure." She went to the refrigerator and pulled out a small bowl of sliced strawberries, pitted cherries, and sliced orange, and another full of long sticks of thinly sliced fresh pineapple with a few zests of lime, lemon and orange, which she handed to Austin. Then she grabbed a bottle of mango juice and one of pineapple juice and set it on the counter. She handed Austin two glasses from the cupboard. "Can you fill these with crushed ice, please, while I get the rest of the mixers?"

He watched her line everything up on the counter and pull forward a two-tier stack of decorative bottles with pump tops, sitting on a wrought iron two-tier stand. "What are those?"

"Oh, I love these. These are my syrups. I have to warn you, all but two are sugar free, but these are great. The front row are for coffee." She pointed to the chalkboard labels on which she had written 'Salted Caramel,' 'Chocolate,' 'Belgian Sugar Cookie' and 'Special'. "This one is empty right now," she said

67

as she tapped the one labeled 'Special', "but it will be pumpkin pie flavor. It's my favorite, but I won't let myself have it until after mid-September."

"Why? If it's your favorite?"

"Because you should enjoy things in their season or they lose their meaning. It takes discipline to really enjoy life to its fullest. When everything is easy and there's instant gratification, it's not gratifying at all. Pumpkin pie is a fall flavor. Its season runs from September fifteenth through January fifteenth."

"Damn, Andy. That's being really rigid."

She smiled at him. "Or, that's having standards, which can be a really good thing. The front row is for coffee, the back row has your options."

"Coffee? Is that your coffee maker?" He took several steps over to the silver square appliance that was Andy's pride and joy. "Holy shit. What is this thing?"

"Oh, yeah, uh, that's my coffee maker. I'm happy to have it back, actually. It's a Jura and it does everything—lattes, cappuccinos, espressos, macchiatos, foam, tea, you name it."

"Wow, this thing's a beast. Lot of moving parts here. You just got it back? Did it break?"

"No, it's worked like a dream. No, um, when I left my house, um, I mean my house with Gregg, I didn't take the coffee maker. Then he refused to give it to me. But my house guests brought it last weekend."

"Oh, so he relented?"

"No, Morning Glory said it reminds her of me. She's total tea. No coffee. Seems she's gotten him to kick his coffee habit, too, and was happy to get rid of the thing. She sent it by way of Caroline and Emma."

"Oh, so she's trying to expunge you from the house. She sent it with your friends."

"Uh huh, I guess. Erase me from Gregg's memory." She could feel a stinging sensation in her eye and took a deep breath. She wasn't going to let Gregg or his new wife hurt her. Not now. Not in this moment. *Please, not in this moment.*

"Yeah, well, Andy, I can see where you'd be hard to erase."

She had to catch her breath. It was such a sweet thing to say in that moment where she had been feeling so vulnerable. He might be younger than her, but he seemed totally comfortable with the fact that she'd had a real life before they met. It wasn't this ungainly thing between them. It just was. And it was okay. She tried to think of how she felt and came upon the word *safe*.

"I really love coffee. That's my thing," he said, looking at the machine in fascination.

"You, my friend, may drink all the coffee you want from this marvelous machine. But I don't think it will taste quite right with dinner."

"After dinner?"

"Of course. After dinner you can have anything you like." Andy blushed hard, hearing the words that had just come out of her mouth. *Oh my God, what am I saying? Shut up, Andy.* She could just hear Emma's voice in her head, calling her the worst type of cougar. Happily, Austin was still staring at the coffee maker as she walked back over to the before-dinner mock-tail set up.

She didn't notice Austin's gaze as he closely watched her walk away with a wry smile of his own.

"So, back to the second row." She pulled each bottle from the rack as she announced its flavor. "These are mango, passion fruit, coconut, and cherry. And I know people really don't like coconut, but I do. I also have pomegranate in the pantry."

"I love coconut. It's one of my favorites."

She smiled warmly. "So, you just take your glass here, put in some juice and seltzer and hit it with whatever flavors you want to enhance it with. Then add your choice of fruit. You can be whatever kind of bad dog you'd like to be."

While she popped her appetizers into the toaster oven, he made his drink. "I feel like I'm a kid again. These are like slushies all grown up."

It didn't take long for her little dish to heat up. "In a quick minute, I'll have an amuse bouche for you."

"A what?"

"An amuse bouche. It's an appetizer. It's supposed to tickle your palate, amuse your tongue in the French way, before you eat."

"Amuse my tongue. In the French way?" He smiled at her.

The toaster oven went *bing*, and Andy was saved from having him see her face turn bright red again. Nothing was coming out quite like she meant it. Hopefully the food wouldn't turn from her intended path, as her words were seeming to do.

"Here you go!" She sprinkled tiny slivers of fresh herbs over the plate that now held eight little squares and set it down on the counter. "Amuse yourself." The plate held four round and four square little appetizers.

"What is it? I mean, it smells amazing, but it, it, looks like…"

"It looks like what?"

"It looks like dog food."

"Oh!" She burst out laughing. "You're right! I never thought of that before, but you're right. It does. I can guarantee you that it doesn't taste like dog food. It's foie gras. Also French. This one is a toasted baguette with foie gras while the other is a base of spice bread with a layer of fig aspic, topped with a block of the foie gras. Try it, you'll like it. I got the recipe from a friend of mine from France. Excellent cook."

With some trepidation, Austin picked up one of the appetizers and looked at it. He smelled it. Then he tasted it. His eyes flew open wide. For a moment, Andy thought she'd poisoned him.

"Oh my God," he said with his mouth full of food. "This is… incredible."

She took a bite of hers and sipped her Coconut-Mango-Tango. It was divine. She owed Claudine big time.

"Oh, I almost forgot. I picked up something for you." Fishing around in his pocket, he pulled out a small bag labeled 'NC Aquarium' and handed it to her. She opened the tiny bag and pulled out a necklace. "After your reaction to the turtle, I saw that and thought you'd like it. That it might remind you of your turtle sighting. I have to say, that was a pretty rare and precious thing. They don't just come by and say hi like that every day."

The turtle was shaped in fine silver lines, white crystals dotting its shell. A delicate silver chain hung down and a smaller turtle, made in the same fashion, dangled there, making them look as though they were swimming together. It was so light and delicate. She could see the skin of her palm through the lines of the silverwork. She was going to cry. Damn it! She was going to cry.

Austin seemed awkward. "It wasn't expensive or anything. After all, I'm really just a glorified never-ending college student, aren't I? But I saw it and it struck me and I thought you would like it. Here, can I help you put it on?"

She was grateful for the excuse to turn her face away from him. She used the opportunity to wipe away the tears on her cheek while he did up the clasp on her neck under her short dark brown bob. "Thank you, Austin. That turtle was like, like having a mystical experience. This is so sweet of you." His hands were on her shoulders. "You are such a sweet man." She turned to look at him, in control of herself once again. "We should amuse ourselves while the foie gras is hot."

"Amuse our 'booshes'?"

"Something like that."

"Those were so good, I could eat my whole dinner of just that." He sighed as he took another bite.

"I bet. But you'd die of a heart attack before you could ever leave this house. And then what would I tell your dad? Besides, you're cooking dinner with me tonight."

"What?" he asked in mock astonishment. "That's the rest of my payment? To work?"

"Ha! Yes! From what you told me, your food life has been sorely lacking. We're going to fix that. But the best way is to start teaching you how to cook great food for yourself. So tonight, we're cooking together. C'mon, let's get started. This food won't cook itself." She pulled a huge pot from the gas stove.

"Ooooh. Crabs. I love crabs. You know, I do know how to cook crabs. I did grow up on a beach."

"And we're making this." She pulled over a basket containing sweet potatoes, squash, whole stemmed garlic, corn in the husk.

"What is that?"

"What is what?"

"This one?" he asked, holding up a gourd.

"That's a butternut squash. You don't know that?"

"Yeah... sure, I do. I mean, I've had it before. Frozen. From a box. What's this one?"

"That's an acorn squash. You haven't had that either? Not fresh? Okay, change of menu. We're having crab and squash-fest apparently. You totally have to try these. You really have never had these?"

"Remember, my dad did the cooking when I was growing up. Totally uninspired. He's great at seafood. And at grilling anything. Well, meat-anything. But vegetables to me are corn, peas, and green beans. Frozen boxed stuff. Salad is iceberg lettuce with fresh tomatoes and some blue cheese crumbled on it."

"Have you tried sushi?"

He shook his head.

"My dear, you haven't lived. If you like this, and if you survive the evening, I'll make you sushi next time. Barbecued eel is the best."

He gave her an unsure look.

"You know, maybe I'm too into food. It seems like ages ago now, but when I first wrote my novel and my now-agent said she'd give it a read, I was so nervous that when I sent it in, I attached the wrong document."

"What'd you send?" he asked, as he took another foie gras appetizer.

"Oh, I accidentally sent her a recipe for bouillabaisse. She must have thought I was an idiot."

"But she still read your book."

"Oh yeah. It was a great recipe. I lucked out in that she loves food, too."

"Trust me. You're not too into food. Not at all." He gave her a wink.

The evening flew by with her teaching him how to cut and prepare the vegetables. They ate at the large kitchen table, where they could watch the sunset over the sound through the huge windows on the west side of the house. They ate steamed Dungeness and snow crab clusters, roasted butternut squash and sweet potatoes all stacked up like little tiered cakes, corn on the cob, and acorn squash crescents dusted with brown sugar and cinnamon.

"Oh my god, I've died and gone to heaven." Austin sat back in his chair. Andy was seriously amazed at how much food the man could put away, thinking he must secretly be an athlete of some type. Well, that would be easy to believe.

After dinner, Austin played with the coffee maker. "It's set up for decaf, so it should be relatively safe," she told him. He drank three different cups, making all different kinds of specialty coffees.

"Woah there, dude! Even decaf isn't caffeine free. You'll be up all night."

"I'm not afraid of caffeine. But I am in love with your coffee maker. Look at what I did with the espresso and steamed milk!"

"Wow, well if the whole MBA thing doesn't work out, you've got a career as a barista waiting for you. I mean, given that your creation there looks like a mushroom cloud, you have a career as a post-apocalyptic barista." He laughed and handed it to her for a taste. "It's good. Damn, you make that better than I do, but still, stick with the MBA."

"Oh yeah, MBA. Definitely MBA over barista." He smiled back at her. "Let me help you do the dishes."

They chatted as they cleared up. Andy hit the start button on the dishwasher, and as it ground to life she picked up several things to return to the pantry.

"So, where is your daughter now?" he asked her as she disappeared through the door.

From inside the pantry, Andy called back, "Oh, she's in medical school, in Lexington, Kentucky, with her father."

73

"Oh, middle school," he said over the growling dishwasher, "I remember that." He stacked a pot on the towel for the washed items. As she came back into the room, he added, "Yeah, that's a hard time. It makes getting an MBA feel really possible by comparison."

"Of course, you'll get the MBA! Just don't give up. I gave up. Don't you give up. I'm living with this feeling that I have something to be embarrassed about because of that. Don't make my mistake. Go all the way. Finish the job."

"You had a really important job to finish. You didn't make a mistake. You had your daughter to raise. So, she's living with her dad?"

"Oh no, while she's at school she's living there."

"Oh, like a prep school?" he asked.

She burst out laughing. "Yes, like a prep school. Like the most intense prep school experience ever. Oh, she's just like her father. She's going to love it. She's always been all about the academics. Always the smartest one in class. You know, it wouldn't surprise me to learn that she's a little embarrassed about me too, never having finished."

"You put too much stock in a degree. My dad never finished his degree and he's done just fine."

Andy looked at Austin curiously. "Didn't you say he was into, what did you call it, subsistence living?"

"Yeah, absolutely. It's not like he's not smart. He's damn smart. And he's happy. He doesn't have anything to prove to anyone. I mean, he's a real character, but I just think you won't find your happiness until you decide that you don't have anything to prove to anyone either."

She took another sip of the fabulous decaf latte he had made her. "Well, there is one person I definitely have to prove something to, and that's my agent. I'm here to find solitude and write my next great bestseller. I have no idea what I'm doing or how I'm going to do it. Oh my God, going back to school would be easier than this, even at my age."

"Hey, you're never too old."

"To go back to school?"

"For anything. Don't limit yourself."

When Andy went to bed that night, she thought back on the evening she had shared with Austin. He had looked at his watch and noted the time, and that he had to open the shop in the morning. He thanked her for dinner and she walked him to the door. There was not even a question of a goodnight kiss. They parted as old friends or family members might after a nice, but rather routine dinner. She stood at the door and watched him walk down the front porch steps. She felt so incredibly safe with him and sighed deeply. As he reached the bottom step, he stopped and turned around.

"Andy?"

"Yes?"

"Would you like to go sailing again on Saturday? Weather's supposed to be nice. My uncle said he'd take the afternoon shift if I close up."

"Dream come true. I'd love it."

"Eleven again?"

"Perfect. Picnic again?"

"Perfect. And please don't feel like you have to go to a huge amount of effort. Something casual and easy would be just fine."

"But how else will I pay for my sailing lesson?" she asked with a laugh.

"Just time spent will pay the bill."

She climbed into bed feeling like she hadn't felt in a long time. Pretty. No, that wasn't it. If he'd kissed her or made any move on her at all she might feel pretty. But it wasn't that. Interesting. She felt interesting. Respected. And liked. She couldn't ever remember Gregg making her feel interesting, respected, or liked. It wasn't about what she looked like or what she represented. It was about who she was. She found Austin an interesting mix; probably more suited to being a psychologist than a businessman. He had this deep wisdom interspersed with the inexperience borne of a secluded upbringing. Imagine not recognizing a fresh acorn squash? Never having had sushi or foie gras? Of course, some people just liked what they liked. They sought out or created the comfortable ruts they kept themselves in and then forever steered straight. Certainly, she had done that, hadn't she? Absolutely, but her road had come to an end. She'd had to plow a new way. And here she was, about to go sailing with a much younger man on what could potentially be considered a date… maybe. Just maybe.

"Oh, shut up, Andy! You need to stop thinking of this imaginary rebound relationship and get to thinking about your editorial deadline." She rolled over and tried to fall asleep, but she tossed and turned, her mind spinning too quickly to settle down until the wee hours of the morning.

Chapter 9

Austin readied the catamaran, looking forward to the day's sail. He was glad to have a day off from the rental business. Usually his summers were seven days a week with maybe a day off each month. He had never complained because that was the life and he was, after all, trying to pay his way through school. At least he was getting paid for it now. How many years had he worked just to help the family make ends meet? However, he could feel the strain now of never taking a break. After all, he wasn't exactly a kid anymore. He deserved a day off. Saturdays were the slowest days at the business, with all the rental houses swapping over, and a good day to take a day for himself. His uncle and his dad could manage without him.

"C'mon wind!" he said as the sails filled and he navigated the Hobie towards the sliver of the shoreline that belonged to Chicamacomico Watercraft Rentals. The boat responded to the pull of the sails and picked up speed, taking him faster toward his goal. He could see her waiting there already, the surprise of his summer. The way she had come in on that windsurfer out of nowhere. Crazy, insane, dangerous—to be that far out on the sound without a life vest. The way she made the pivot in the wind defied all the laws of physics—she must have had an errant gust cross-cutting over the water to bring her to shore like that. She had pulled that contraption up and stopped it on a dime. Crazy. Totally crazy.

There was something about her that had really caught his attention, particularly when she turned out to have been kidnapped by the wind. With how buff she was, he wouldn't have been surprised if she'd been a stupid daredevil, risking her life to show off for her friends. But she wasn't. She was scared, that was obvious. She'd been shaking when she got out of the water, but she'd also held it together with impressive aplomb. Jenna, his last girlfriend, used to get hysterical when things didn't go according to plan. He had taken her to a rock concert on campus once, but she had gotten scared in the crowds. They had to leave. After a few months he decided it didn't matter how pretty she was, he couldn't stand the helpless damsel-in-distress routine. She didn't want a boyfriend: she wanted a bodyguard. And an audience for all her damn drama. *Well, count me out for that shit,* he thought. No, this woman had really held it together. He could tell she was a few years older than he was. Maybe that was the problem with the people he'd been dating. With a kid in middle school, he estimated Andy could be up to ten years older than him. That wasn't that much. And their day's sailing had been unexpectedly interesting. She had been funny and insightful. She had an amazing life story. And she was so open. Damn, she'd written that novel. Not that he'd ever read it, it just wasn't his type of thing. But she was interesting. And the exact opposite of Jenna. Or Meredith. Or Whitney. Or any of the girls he had dated while wintering in Wilmington.

His dad had been passingly curious about the sailing when Austin had asked him if he could take the Cat out.

"It's for a lesson, Dad."

"A lesson? What are you charging?"

"Not a customer. Don't know. Maybe lunch?"

"Ohhh," his dad had said with a small smile. "A girlfriend!"

"An, uh, lady-friend."

His dad smiled. "A class act then. Absolutely, take the Cat. Have a good time." If his dad wanted to know more about Austin's plans, he didn't ask. Actually, his dad did a great job of respecting Austin's privacy. Now his Aunt Mad, not so much. She always wanted to know what was going on in Austin's life, what he was feeling, if he needed to talk. She tried to be the mother he had lost and struggled to remember. He could appreciate that it was well meant, but it was misplaced. He didn't care if his dad found out about Andy, but he sure didn't want Aunt Mad to start nosing around. There would be no end to that.

Austin pulled the Cat up and dropped the sheets, stepped off the platform and hooked it up to the anchors beneath the surface of the water that he had laid out just that morning, just like he did every morning.

"You look happy," Andy said, as he sloshed up to the shore.

"It's a beautiful day. We've got a totally fun catamaran to play with for hours. One of your fabulous picnics awaits us. I enjoy your company. What's not to be happy about?"

She blushed. He found he really liked the way she blushed. Here she was, this totally accomplished, successful, mature woman and yet she was unpretentious enough to blush at a simple compliment.

"I'm enjoying spending time with you, too."

Man, she was direct. That was so refreshing. It didn't hurt that she was nice to look at. She had one of those ageless faces. *I bet she'll still look this good when she's in her forties,* he thought. *But that's a long way off.* "All aboard! I have a new cove to show you. Maybe we'll see some new birds." He noticed she was wearing her turtle necklace. "And maybe some turtles, too."

Andy reached for her necklace. "I'm hoping it's a good luck charm. That and my life jacket."

"I'm sure it is," he said with a laugh. That was a nice little necklace. He was almost embarrassed that he'd bought it for twelve dollars at the aquarium gift shop. He and his dad always got season passes, along with his Aunt Mad and her family. When he had been in Manteo he passed the turn-off for the aquarium and spur-of-the-moment decided to go in and look, just to see what they had. He had found it in the children's section, but it seemed to fit the bill, nonetheless. It looked great on her. She was back in that Caribbean-blue two-piece she had been wearing when they met. It really set off her brown bobbed hair and light brown eyes. He didn't know where their relationship was going, but it didn't really matter. She was going back to the mainland and he was going to back to school to make progress on his degree. Just two more years and he would have this thing done. That was, as long as there weren't any more interruptions. Whatever it was between them was a summer thing. That's all it could be. But that didn't mean it couldn't be nice.

He sailed them fast across the sound for the first hour. They couldn't really talk that way, since he had to shout instructions to her, but he knew a very secluded little cove up closer to Pea Island. He hoped no one was there today. Shortly after noon he steered the catamaran slowly up the narrow waterway towards an empty little beach.

"Oh, this is sweet! How do you know about this?"

"Sailing. I've tried to discover everything there is to know about these islands. We can pull up here. Make sure you put on bug spray."

As he anchored the boat and let down the sails so it wouldn't move in the wind, Andy set up their picnic on the beach. She laid out the gingham cloth and started pulling lidded cups out of the cooler.

"My, my, my, what have we here? Looks like something amazing."

"Well, you did say something more relaxed."

"Yeah, I was hoping you wouldn't take me too seriously and hit Subway or something." He winked at her.

"No worries about that! No, but I did go for a healthy angle this time. These are salads."

"In cups."

"Yes, everything is in cups. Super easy to pack in. Keeps sand out of it. And all the cups are recyclable, biodegradable corn-based plastic."

He held the cup up in front of him. There was a fork sticking up in the slot for the straw. "Andy, there must be ten different things in here."

"Thirteen actually. It's called Baker's Dozen Salad. And these, I love these. These are fruit cups." She pulled out smaller cups that contained a mixture of fresh berries. "That's yogurt and some granola down at the bottom."

"Okay. You know this is girl food, right?" He thought it probably wouldn't hurt him to eat healthy stuff for once. He reached into the picnic basket. "Wow, what's this?" He pulled the top off a small Tupperware, the whole bottom of which was an ice block, and peered inside.

"Oh, that! That's my take on a charcuterie board."

"It looks like boy food."

"Yes, 'boy food'. That's prosciutto wrapped around asparagus. Thin slices of hard salami. Some Chèvre cheese. The really hard cheese is Parmigiano-Reggiano and it's really good. Here, this container has the olives and here's a tiny little jar of honey. These are the figs in here; put them on the board, please. That container has some almonds. And we're done."

"Wait... what's this?" He pulled out little mason jars. "Dessert?"

"Bingo. That's strawberry shortcake."

"I'm eating like a king with you."

"Oh, don't let me hypnotize you with my cooking! That wouldn't be a fair fight at all. I'm sorry, but you wouldn't stand a chance."

"Oh, wouldn't I?"

"No. Cute as you are, you would be easy pickins."

He leaned closer. "So, I'm cute?"

She smiled. "Incredibly."

He leaned into her just a little bit more and their lips brushed. It was the whisper of a kiss. "I think you're pretty incredible too," he said as he leaned back.

As they ate, they chatted. "So, do you miss your daughter? Do you mind me asking? I mean, it's just you live so far away from her."

"I don't mind you asking. It's sweet of you to care about her. Yes, of course I miss her. But E is where she wants to be. And school's very demanding. Just because I don't see her, doesn't mean we aren't close. We talk a few times a week and she emails me sometimes. She's not a big emailer in general. She loves to text me, which she has been known to do several times a day. There's nothing I can really do for her while she's at school, but you know, if she needs me, I can be there in a day. And from Charlotte I can be there in half a day.

It's not like I'm on the other side of the world. I would be there in a heartbeat if she needed me."

"It's just that children need their mothers. They never stop needing their mothers."

"And I will never stop being there for her. I will always be her mother. So, does it bother you that I'm so far away from her, given your, well, given that you grew up mostly with your father?"

"With my dad. Not my father." He thought about her question. Why was he so concerned for this daughter of hers he'd never met? Maybe he needed to know that she was a good mother and hadn't run out on her daughter, abandoning her so she could lead the glamorous life of a famous author? Maybe he just wanted some reassurance that she was someone his mother would approve of, were she still around. "I wish my mother hadn't died, of course, or my father, but it was a really long time ago. A lot of the memories are fuzzy. My dad is a great dad. And a great mom. He had to do it all. He's my best friend. A great guy. A real character, but a great guy."

"He sounds like he has a lot of qualities important for being both a great dad and a great guy. My daughter is very close with her dad as well. To a great extent, they're two peas in a pod. Just alike."

"And how does she get along with her dad's new wife?"

"Oh," Andy said and rolled her eyes. "It's disgusting actually. They love each other. I mean they *really* enjoy one another. No wicked stepmother syndrome here. Morning Glory, sorry I'm being nasty, Chenguang, or Chen as she goes by professionally, is a surgeon, which is just what E wants to be. So, I sit by and watch my daughter idolize her new mother."

"She's not her new mother. You can never replace your mother. If E had a crisis, if some boy broke her heart, it would be you she'd be calling, not Chen."

"As long as it wasn't a school-related crisis, probably true. But still, I *feel* replaced. It's hard to not feel replaced. You know, that's just a space you don't want to share. And it leaves you a little empty feeling inside. I guess that's one of the reasons I'm here. I can't fill myself up with other people's needs any longer—nobody needs me. I have to fill my own space. On a wild hare I bought the beach house because I could, suddenly, surprisingly, I was able to do that. I thought it would give me the solitude to force myself to write and it would give me the space to build my own life around me."

Austin didn't know what to say. This was so totally beyond his experience that he was having trouble relating to it. His life certainly revolved around himself. And the business. And keeping him and his dad and his uncle's family in the black all year. But when he was away for the winter in Wilmington, when classes were in session, he was all about Austin. And he relished that time. Well, maybe he got it after all.

"I'm sorry, I'm rambling." She looked embarrassed.

"No, it's all right. I was just thinking. I've never been a parent, so it's a bit hard to relate. But my dad had to be both my parents. And honestly, I had to grow up pretty fast after the accident. Like I said, Dad was great, but he certainly never lost himself in me or in my world. He made sure I was fed, well, he and my aunts did anyway. And I always had clothes to wear. And he'd make sure I'd done my homework, not check it, mind you, but just got it done. It was a two-word conversation. But he always had interests. His Hobie and sailing. Birds. Books. Music. The business, of course."

"Didn't he come to your games and sports events?"

"Yeah, but I didn't do a lot of those. I wasn't interested in competitive sports that much."

"Really? You look like an athlete."

"Running the rental place is pretty constant movement, constant lifting and schlepping around fairly heavy things. I don't need to join a gym. I work in Mother Nature's gym every day."

"I always checked on E's homework. Always went over every question and re-explained everything to her from school. Gregg was adamant that she get straight A's. Go to an ivy league school."

"Wow, that's a lot of pressure to put on a kid. I guess she's well on her way at the school she's at."

"Yeah, she's doing great. Far outstripping her tutor." Andy giggled. "Me," she said pointing to herself. "I think I would have made a great teacher. I was studying arts in college before I had to drop out, but raising E showed me that I would really have enjoyed teaching. We had the playroom set up as a little classroom. And we did the best birthday parties, full of costumes and events. I would make these stupendous cakes for her. Of course, she's way too old for any of that now. Oh, they grow up so fast. It all passes by so fast."

"Wow. You were an awesome mom. Would you do it again?"

A warm smile broke across her face. "Thank you. As I look back on it, it really was the best part of my life. The most important job I will ever have and yes, I would live it all over again in a second if I had the chance. I'd probably do some things differently, but I would totally do it again."

"My mother would have loved you."

"Austin, I think that is the nicest thing you could possibly have said to me."

Austin agreed. There was no higher compliment he could ever have given to anyone.

Chapter 10

Austin stretched and scratched, rolled onto his back and, putting his hands behind his head, looked up at the ceiling. "Wow." After laying there for several minutes, thinking, he rolled out of bed and headed to the bathroom for a shower.

As he towel-dried, he went to the mirror over the sink and wiped off a circle so he could see his face to shave.

"That was awesome. Damn. That was awesome."

He flinched as he nicked his chin. Dabbing at the blood he said to his reflection, "If you ever actually sleep with her... she is gonna be one kinda hellcat in bed." He stuck a little wad of toilet paper on the nick. "Damn." He washed off his razor. "Austin, you are one lucky bastard."

He finished shaving and went to pull on his swim trunks. Since he spent half his time in the water, that was his uniform for the summer: swim trunks and a killer tan. He looked in the mirror, deciding that he still looked good. He hadn't thought about how he looked for... well, he couldn't remember when he last given it a second thought, but suddenly he was acutely aware of how he looked, of what he wore, of how he smelled. It was an odd feeling to think about this thing that had never held any meaning to him before. But before he'd dated girls without any life experience. That wasn't Andy. She had a ton of life experience. And it showed. Boy, did it show. Certainly, he was physically up to the challenge, but he wondered if he was mentally? Could his relative lack of experience keep up with her? Or would she quickly get bored with him?

He usually asked a lot of questions when he didn't quite know what to say, not just with her, but with anyone. He found that if you asked questions in the right way, people would tell you what they really wanted to know. Then you could just repeat it back to them and they would call you 'wise beyond your years'. An 'old soul'. He gave a wry smile as he grabbed a T-shirt out of his drawer and pulled it on.

Coming out to the kitchen, he grabbed the bag of ground coffee out of the freezer and started to brew a pot. He always made enough for both himself and his dad, who would rise in about an hour. If they saw one another in the morning that was lucky. Austin was usually off and on his way to the business by the time his dad got out of bed. Austin had taken over the books for Watercraft Rentals and in the morning, before the customers came, was his most productive time. He knew his dad was going to be working on repairing the broken jet skis today. They had a dozen of them, but only eight or nine were working at any given time.

He poured a bowl of cereal and a cup of coffee. "Man, that was a cool coffee maker." He would never own anything like it. He'd come home and looked up the model. It had cost nearly six thousand dollars—and her husband had given it to her as a Christmas present.

He shook his head. He'd given her a twelve-dollar necklace and she'd gotten tears in her eyes. He didn't quite know what to think.

He'd given her the barest kiss yesterday before their picnic. It was incredibly sexy the way their lips had only just met. He knew it from the moment he heard himself say his mother would really like Andy that he was going to kiss her again. They never even made it to the strawberry shortcake. That second kiss led to a totally wild make-out session. The only reason they'd restrained themselves was because a motorboat started to putt-putt its way up their little waterway, causing them to roll apart from one another and sit up, acting like nothing was happening. The boat passed them by without turning into their cove. Then they'd laughed and packed up the lunch and sailed back so he could close up shop. Yes, he definitely wanted to see her again.

He made sure there were a good two cups of coffee in the pot on the 'warm' setting and then left for the little A-frame where his Uncle Ben and Aunt Mad lived. He knew his aunt would bring him another cup soon after he arrived.

By ten in the morning he had laid out all the anchors in the sound, hauled out the six jet skis reserved for today, pulled up the beat-up old sunfish some dad wanted to rent so his twelve-year-old could have his first experience sailing, and laid out the four kayaks that should be picked up at eleven. He'd been to the gas station and filled up four large gas cans, hauled them back to Watercraft Rentals, and schlepped them out through the water to refill the jet skis. He tried to keep busy. Usually that was no problem at the rental shop, but today he found it to be a bit of a challenge. He would do a task and then head to the Tiki Shack to check his phone, see nothing, and then head back out in the water to do the next task.

He made it to noon before he tried to call Andy, but he only got her voicemail. He'd never left her a voicemail and suddenly felt awkward, not knowing quite what to say and not wanting to sound totally stupid, so he just hung up. At three p.m., just when his uncle was taking over and he was heading back to help his dad with the jet ski repair work, he got a text.

Hey, I saw you called. Three times. What's up? Emergency?

No. Just wanted to say how nice yesterday was.

Want to come over to dinner this week?

Sure. When?

How about Wednesday? I should have a surprise for Wednesday.

Surprise? What?

It's a surprise…

Wednesday is great. See you about seven?

7 is magical.

Austin found the time went by much more slowly than he thought it would. On Wednesday, while he was between customers and waiting for the day to pass, his phone buzzed. He felt this strange little jolt as he picked it up, and then an odd sense of disappointment to see that it read 'Taisei Abe'.

He swiped to accept the call. "Konichiwa, Ah-Bey-Say-Day."

"Greetings, Austin Powers." The voice came through in a fake British accent. "How's it hangin'?" Taisei always got tired of people calling him Taisei Abe, as in the famous president of centuries past, so he always clarified that it was pronounced 'Ah-Bey, as in Ah-Bey-Say-Day'. While that in itself didn't make much sense, it did work. He was rather acutely aware of being half-Japanese and half-American. When anyone was rude about his heritage or called him a 'halfie' or 'part Chink', he would only talk to them in Japanese, completely bewildering them, not to mention annoying the heck out of them. Austin always knew when Taisei was on the phone with his mother, as they held long conversations in Japanese. It certainly was one way to keep their calls private. Sometimes it made Austin wish he could speak another language, too, so that he could have more privacy when he was on the phone.

"Dude, life's good. Life is good."

Austin smiled. It was always great to hear Taisei's voice. They had been roommates the past year and had signed a lease on a great place for the upcoming one. Close to campus, but not too close. Fully furnished, so no pain-in-the-ass move-in day. No scrounging of nasty used furniture. It would be fun to live with Taisei, but not too fun. Taisei had enjoyed way too much fun in the past and had almost flunked out of his program. He was a guy with a lot of anger and daddy issues and tried to drink them out of his system. Austin supposed that was what you should expect when your dad was a raging alcoholic/workaholic who lived overseas and was on his third marriage. Eventually Taisei had told Austin about the divorce that had unraveled his life before he was ten. It sounded ugly. Full of drama.

Austin was a positive influence on him. A calming influence. Bringing him out to the islands for visits during long weekends when classes took a break was really good for Taisei. Settled him down. "All's hangin' well, my

Yūjin. How's the luck holding out?"

"Ah, my friend. I am calling with bad news. My luck continues to sucketh."

Austin could feel his stomach clench. What had he done now? "You didn't, uh, wreck your car again, did you?"

"Did not wreck the car. Did not crash my bank account. I'm being a good boy. My Uncle Moneybags is here and practically sitting on me. Still my lottery tickets are a waste of money."

"Dude, that trick only works when you give them away. You can't make the luck work on yourself. You have to give the scratch cards away for them to be lucky."

"I never should have told you that story. No, this time your luck's bad too. You know our great apartment? At the luxury complex?"

"Yeeeahhhh…"

"It burnt down."

"Holy fuck!" Austin quickly looked around to make sure no customers were within hearing distance.

"Yeah. There was a wiring issue or something. Mom keeps correcting me, saying we were totally *lucky* this happened in summer when we weren't living there. So, I guess the good luck part is that we weren't burnt to a crisp come fall."

"Damn."

"Yeah."

"We need a new place to live." Austin sighed. He really didn't want to leave the beach right now.

"Yeah. You nailed that one, Powers."

"Let me talk to my dad and my uncle to see if I can get a few days off. I'll head to Wilmington and check it out. Surely there will be something decent left."

"Hey, you're making money for school. That's one thing I don't have to do. Let me take care of it."

89

"Uh, that's not very fair on you."

"Mom says she'll come with me and help. We can make the drive from Charlotte tomorrow."

Austin instantly felt himself relax. This wasn't the kind of decision he would trust to Taisei alone, who tended to overlook some of the practical aspects which Austin found important, but Mrs. Abe seemed like a rock. She was one of those helicopter moms. "OK, great then. I'm glad your mom can make the time. Please tell her I said thanks."

"What, and make her love you all the more? She already sees you as my savior. She'd do anything for you."

"She's awfully nice about a boy she's never actually met face-to-face before. Hey, Taisei?"

"Yeah,"

"Don't be bummed, man. It's going to work out. It'll be fine."

"Yeah, you're right. It'll be fine. Looking forward to the fall. I'll let you know what we find."

"Cool. Thanks for taking this on. I owe you one."

"I owe you many. Sayōnara, Austin Powers."

"Hasta la vista, baby."

Austin shook his head and sighed heavily. *What a total pain in the ass.* "Well, that kinda sucked. I'm looking forward to this day getting better." Then his phone went *bing*. A text message.

Can you give me a call when convenient? Change of plans.

He was about to ring her back when two cars pulled in. The kayak people. Eight in the party, six kayaks. They were early. Luckily, he had the kayaks already out in the water and clipped to the anchors. He would have to get them fitted in life vests, get them seated in their boats, probably provide some rudimentary instruction with the paddles, and see them off before he could call her back. That would be twenty minutes at the very least. Probably thirty.

Half an hour later, when Austin waded back up to shore, his uncle sauntered out of the house, cup of coffee in hand.

"Nice timing. How come you didn't come out to help?" Mild annoyance tinged Austin's voice.

"You looked like you had it under control. Besides, that was funny! That old man just couldn't stay upright in the kayak at all."

"Yeah, he fell out few times, but I think he's got the hang of it now."

"No, he doesn't," Ben said. "He just fell over again." He took another sip of his coffee. "I'll bet his wife is pissed. Boy, are they gonna be wet."

"I did recommend they stick to the shallows. And they're all in bathing suits." Austin shook his head.

"Those are the kind of people who should have their own sitcom. That's funny."

"Glad you're here. We've got five reservations coming in…" Austin checked his watch, "ten minutes. Hey, I've got to make a call. Hold down the shack, will you?"

"It's what I do every day."

"Yeah, right," Austin said, but it was under his breath and his Uncle Ben didn't hear him. 'Change in plans' she had written. Maybe she wanted to go out to dinner. Maybe she might ask him to stay the night. *You're dreamin', Austin.*

"Hey, Austin." Her voice sounded nice over the phone.

"Hey, Andy, sorry it took me so long to get back with you. Loads of customers this morning."

"Well, the sun is shining. You've got to make hay while the sun shines."

Austin smiled. That's what his dad said. "So right. What's up?"

"You won't believe this. I mean it's really good news but it's bad news. I'm afraid I can't make dinner tonight. I have to leave town."

He could feel disappointment well up in him. "Something happen?"

"Something wonderful. Yeah, my agent just called me and she's locked in a series of promotional events for my book. It's a book tour. Wow, I can't believe I'm actually saying those words. A. Book. Tour. I'm pinching myself."

He made his voice sound light. "Hey, that's great news! Congratulations. And you leave today?"

"Yeah. Bummer. I have to fly out of Charlotte tomorrow. So, I need to head to my condo there and pack my real clothes. They're sending me to New York. Austin—I'm going to be on the Today Show next Wednesday!"

"Television? Wow, that's huge." *Her real clothes. Back to her real life. That's right. She's a summer resident. She's a mainlander.*

"I won't be back for two or three weeks. Looks like two right now but my agent told me to be prepared for three, just in case. She called it a 'best case scenario'—on the road for three weeks. Obviously, easy for her to say since she's not making the trip."

"So, what will you do?"

"Well, first D.C then New York. She said I need to have a professional make-over. I'm 'too frumpy and not television ready'. Honestly, I don't know whether to be totally offended or totally excited."

"Wow. You're pretty perfect just the way you are."

"Oh, you're sweet. Then it'll be book signings, a couple of radio shows and a writer's conference. I'm going to be on a panel discussion. Can you imagine that? Me, on a panel?"

Austin felt an uncomfortable little feeling in his chest. *I should have slept with her the other day when I had the chance. Now she'll move on to her real life.* She had asked him if he wanted to come over for dinner after their sail, but he'd declined, wanting to take it a bit slower despite the attraction between them. He didn't like rushing into relationships, even though the most they could possibly have was this summer. By the third week of August they would each be heading for the mainland. And now half the time they had left had just instantly evaporated. He had a weird feeling. Then he realized that he felt lonely. He wasn't going to see her tonight. He wasn't going to see her for three weeks.

"Austin? Austin are you there?"

"What? Oh, yeah, sorry, Andy. What were you saying?"

"I was just saying that while it's really exciting, it's unexpected and a bit inconvenient. I have, let me correct that, I *had* furniture being delivered this week. It was supposed to come today, but when I checked it online it's gotten stuck in transit and won't be here until Thursday or Friday. But I'll have to cancel the delivery and it will go back into storage and God knows when I'll get it. So, while this is good news, it's also bad timing."

"I can take delivery for you," Austin said as he moved another twenty feet away from where he'd been standing. His uncle had manufactured a reason to come and stand by his nephew, all the better to overhear his conversation.

"You could? How?"

"Well, I could watch the house and arrange to be there when the delivery comes. I could sign for it."

"You would house sit for me? Really?"

He hadn't been thinking of house sitting actually. He'd been offering to track the stuff online and then show up in time to open the door for the delivery.

"This is about having non-ending access to that coffee maker, isn't it?"

He laughed. The more he thought about it, it might be nice to have a place of his own for a little while. Living with his dad was fine, but he never got the chance to be alone in his own place. The island was way too expensive; when he was on the island he stayed at home, period. When he was in Wilmington last spring, he'd had three other roommates and that was complete chaos compared even to island life in season. This fall it would be just him and Taisei, unless they couldn't find anything and had to cram into some overcrowded off-campus house. "Yeah, the whole thing is about that coffee maker. I'd be happy to house sit for you while you're traveling, Andy. Happy to do it." His uncle moved closer.

"Oh, house sitting. That's nice," he said. "Take some good books. And your own sheets!"

Austin rolled his eyes and walked another twenty feet away.

93

"Oh my God, Austin, how did I get lucky enough to ever run into you?"

"I don't know. You must have been taken by the wind."

She laughed. "You *are* the best. I'm leaving here in the next two hours. How about I drop by work and give you a set of keys?"

"Sounds great. Right now, I'd better get back to it. We just had five cars pull in."

"All right. I'll see you before lunch time. Want me to bring you lunch?"

"You would do that?"

"I've got food in my fridge. Tons of it. I went shopping yesterday for our dinner tonight. I'd be happy to bring you lunch."

"That sounds great. I'm starving."

"Perfect. See you around noon."

She was there by twelve-fifteen, lunch in hand. He met her at her car. His uncle was watching him closely. He could see a couple of suitcases in the back of her small SUV.

"I hope you like these. It's what I had for lunch, so it's kind of like we'll be eating together, only apart. I'll stay in touch while I'm away, let you know how things are going."

"I'm counting on it. And I want to see you on TV."

"I'll get E to DVR it for me, not that I'm excited to see myself on the small screen. I'm so nervous, I've no idea what to say."

"Just be yourself and they'll love you."

She smiled at him so warmly, he leaned through the window of the car and kissed her. As she drove off, he held his lunch cooler and was glad she hadn't gotten out of the car. Both his dad and his uncle were at the shack now. Austin was sure his uncle had called his dad to alert him that something was up with his boy.

As Austin sauntered back over to the Tiki shack, his uncle called to him from over by the huge bin of life preservers. "So, where did you order lunch from that it comes delivered with a kiss?"

"N.O.Y.B., Ben, N.O.Y.B.," Austin answered, but his tone was friendly. He sat down and unzipped the cooler pack, curious. He pulled out a giant hoagie-type bun filled with grilled vegetables. He could smell the grilled onions and portabella mushrooms. One half was filled with that Chèvre cheese she liked so much. The other side looked like it was smothered in provolone. He took that half. He pulled out a very large water bottle filled with the strawberry-mint lemonade that was almost, but not quite, sweet.

"Man, what's that?" his dad asked him.

"It's a sandwich."

"Wow. Hey, you gonna eat all of that?"

"This half has goat cheese. You want it?"

"Do I like to sail?" His dad reached over and took the other half just as Uncle Ben walked up.

"Hey, you guys ordered lunch without me? No sandwich for me? And no kiss?" Then he looked at what they were eating. "Oh, well good then. That looks disgusting, damn vegetarian food."

"Did your girlfriend, excuse me," his dad quickly corrected himself, "your *lady friend*, make this?"

Austin nodded, his mouth full. He reached for the lemonade bottle but missed it just before his dad snatched it away. He took a long drink from it, set it down and nodded.

"What do you think?" Austin asked.

"I don't know who she is, but I think you should marry her."

"Oh, you've been hypnotized by her cooking! You're such a pushover."

His uncle took the lemonade and took a long sip from it. He nodded. "It's not bad. It's not beer, I'll grant you that, but it's not bad. Yeah, I give you my blessing. Marry her."

* * *

Later that night Austin pulled up at Hayward House. He'd had to close up shop and then go home and pack. That took all of five minutes. His dad had made dinner, but after three bites Austin just couldn't eat the tuna casserole with crushed potato chips sprinkled on top. He might have liked that when he was ten, but now he found it hard to choke down. He decided to find something at Andy's. His dad had only nodded when Austin told him he was going to house sit for a couple of weeks. He didn't ask him where or for who. Island people commonly did that for one another, helping out with pets and the like. Sometimes an owner would ask an islander to stay in a house when it wasn't rented, worried that it would be a target for thieves if left unoccupied. Hardly. That kind of crime just wasn't an issue on the island. But what a treat—fancy rooms, pool tables, private pools, huge Jacuzzi bathtubs awaited the fortunate islander who got that kind of a lucky draw. Islander homes were someplace between shabby chic and just plain shabby, but they were the kind of comfortable that could restore your very soul. Andy's place was someplace in between an 'owner home' and an 'islander home'. Austin couldn't wait.

He unlocked the door, remembering his uncle's advice about sheets. Austin snorted. Everything at Andy's was crisp and new and nice. Really nice. Compared to his dad's house, he was going to be living in the lap of luxury. And sleeping in her bed. He was going to be sleeping in her bed. Without her. He pushed the door open and went in.

He left his suitcase in the living room and went into the kitchen. Andy had left a note clipped to the side of the fridge telling him where everything was. He opened the door: there were four bottles of lemonade. And dinner made for him, with a note that more were in the freezer, were he so inclined. She had made him dinners. He looked in the freezer and there they were, five little freezer containers of meals. She had a ton of food in her fridge, and fresh fruit everywhere. He felt like he was at camp. A really grown-up camp. He saw a small oblong cardboard box in the fridge and pulled it out. It was filled with the strangest mushrooms he had ever seen. At least, he was pretty sure that's what they were, but he wondered whether they were poisonous. They were like the ones he'd seen in kitschy drawings with gnomes. Since gnomes didn't exist, he had also assumed that those ugly, oddly capped, white stemmed anomalies were similarly imaginary. But here they were, in a box in Andy's fridge. He wasn't going to eat those. He put them back in the box and returned it to the shelf.

He was starving. Her sandwich at lunch had been tasty, but he decided that vegetarian food wasn't exactly 'stick to your ribs' kind of stuff. He pulled out the plated dinner. She had left a little card taped to it with reheating instructions. It was a roast chicken thigh, a big one, with some kind of breadcrumb crust on the top and weird little purple fingerling potatoes and white baby carrots and pearl onions on the side. It was sitting on a bed of polenta. At least that's what the little card attached to it said. "I'm so glad my dad isn't seeing this. Damn, the man would run me over and marry her himself!"

At first, it was really, really weird to sleep in her bed. Particularly to sleep in her bed and think about her. He loved soaking in the tub. Apparently, before she moved into the house she had re-done the master bathroom and added one of those huge Jacuzzi tubs like the rental beach mansions had. Austin drank the lemonade as he enjoyed the bubbles. The room still needed to be painted. There were paint samples on the wall. He thought the dark reddish one would look the best, but he was sure she was going to go for that bland light green color. She had written 'toasted cranberry' by the red stripe and 'sage green' by the bland one. The third was a stark white color. He would bet anything that she would never go for the stark white.

He found the hardest thing about being in Andy's house was his growing desire to know her better. He wanted to explore the Hayward House, after all he hadn't been here since he was a kid and his own father had helped to remodel the place way back when, but he didn't want to violate her privacy. He resolutely refused to look through her desk, except when he needed to find a pen.

Her wall of books was interesting. She had a lot of books he thought he should probably read. His dad would like these—he loved books. She had a lot of books on art. Austin found he liked those much more than he would have expected. Then he found her music collection. She had nothing contemporary. "Gregg, you bastard. You must have kept all the good stuff." She had a ton of classic rock, bands he had heard of but wasn't really acquainted with. The Moody Blues. He'd never heard of them. The Alan Parson's Project? Fleetwood Mac? What the hell was that? Rush, now them he'd heard of. The Rolling Stones. Eagles. Michael Jackson. Yeah, those had some potential. Then he found some oldies that he'd at least heard play on the oldies radio station that his dad liked, some Ricky Martin, some early Pink, at least she was still making music. Maroon 5, didn't they brake up? "Wow, a Beatles CD. Well, okay, everyone still had a Beatles album. Who the hell were Styx? And Kansas? Maybe he'd find one from Texas or Connecticut? He sifted around. Maybe it was a state thing? But there wasn't much to listen to other than her classic rock and early seventies throw-backs, so that's what he played in the evenings as he heated up the dinners she'd left for him. And he found the music was all right. Yeah, it was all right.

He tracked the furniture shipment on his phone. It was delayed from Thursday to Friday and then to Monday afternoon. On Saturday night he got a text from Taisei.

New nest secured.

Awesome, Dude. What's the damage?

9 big 1s

Apartment?

Condo units. Small but nice. Mama Abe thinks we'll stay out of trouble there.

On a bus line?

Mama Abe made sure of it. I'll text you pic.

The pictures came through. It was an older, rehabbed condo with what looked like original but refinished wooden floors. "Nice, granite countertops. Nice new fridge," Austin said as he went through the photos. Rooms looked decent-sized. Kitchen was open to the living room. It had one of those fake fireplaces. "That should be fun."

Looks spacious, he thumbed into his phone back to Taisei. And then he added: And empty.

Yeah. Furnished not happening. This was the best we could find.

Then another text came: *Also, no pool.*

"Shit," Austin said aloud. "Unfurnished."

His phone binged yet again. *Want me to rent furniture?*

Nah. Let's scrounge Austin typed back. He knew that four-fifty-a-month plus utilities would put a strain on his budget. The last place had been running a terrific deal, which had made it affordable for him. He didn't want to keep piling on bills he didn't need. This condo was going to cost him a hundred dollars a month more. He didn't want to ask his dad to help him make up the difference. His dad had his own problems.

Scrounge it is. U ready 4 the storm?

Just a tropical depression, Austin wrote back. Lots o' rain. Shop closed, prob Mon/Tues. Over in 2 days max. Looking 4ward 2 the R&R.

Stay dry. C Ya Powers.

The tropical depression was moving in slowly from the ocean. With looming dark clouds and absolutely no customers, they closed the shop by three on Sunday, planning to come back Tuesday if they were lucky, and for sure by Wednesday. While the clouds threatened, the rain held off until Monday evening. That turned out to be convenient, since the delivery guys actually showed up at four o'clock, three hours after their guaranteed time. Austin had been hanging out all afternoon. Despite the fact that he didn't have any place to go, he was feeling antsy just sitting at Hayward House and waiting with nothing to do. He was relieved when the truck finally pulled up in the drive.

"We got an order for a Miranda Wright. You Mr. Wright?"

"Nope. I'm here to take delivery of the furniture while Ms. Wright's out."

"You the caretaker?"

"Yeah, sure, I'm the caretaker."

"Like the pool boy, huh?" The man had a rather unpleasant look on his face as he said it.

"No. I'm not the pool boy," Austin said, slightly annoyed. "Right now, I'm living here."

"Right." The man chuckled rather nastily. "Sign here." The man looked around him at the beach house. Then he looked Austin over again. "Some people got all the luck. Oh, I bet she's a yoga teacher and you collect butterflies. C'mon Danny, let's get this shit moved in."

* * *

The men proceeded to haul in a new dining room set, a canopy bed, a leather couch, two leather chairs, an ottoman, the coolest coffee table Austin had ever seen, and four lamps. Austin was kept busy trying to move the furniture that was already there out of the way so that the new stuff could fit in the rooms. It was crazy, like being in an overloaded furniture store.

"So, what about this old stuff?" he asked the head moving guy.

"What about it?"

"Ms. Wright left me instructions that you were supposed to take away the old furniture."

The man consulted his clipboard. "Not on here."

"But you can't leave it. This is a crazy... what a mess."

"Not my mess. Not on my list, not my mess. Enjoy your new furniture."

Austin spent the evening setting up the new canopy bed and moving the queen mattress and box spring onto it. "Oh, she's gonna be pissed," he muttered. They had talked nearly every day and every day she had asked about the delivery and reminded him that all the old stuff was supposed to be picked up.

The next morning he texted her.

Your furniture came.

Oh wonderful! How does it look?

It looks crowded.

????

They didn't take the old stuff.

His phone rang. He swiped to talk to her.

"What do you mean they didn't take the old stuff? That was part of the deal. They guaranteed me… what? Oh, yes just one minute." She was obviously speaking to someone else. "Look, Austin, I'm so sorry, I've got to run. It's makeover time for tomorrow's TV thing. I'll have to handle that problem when I get back."

"Uh, Andy? Do you want me to take care of it?"

"Oh, would you?"

"Yeah, sure. I mean, do you care what happens to it?"

"As long as it's out of my house, I don't care. It was supposed to be donated."

"I'll take care of it. I know just where to donate it to."

After she hung up, he texted Taisei.

Furniture found. We have sofa, love seat, a dining room table (2 big), coffee table, 2 lamps

Taisei wrote back: *Shipwreck? U pick it up on the beach?*

Something like that

It poured and poured all day Tuesday. Austin did his best to break down what furniture he could and stack the rest out of the way so he could move around.

On Wednesday morning he took his perfect mushroom-cloud latte along with egg and cheese wrapped in an English muffin and sat on Andy's new L-shaped, deep-red contemporary leather couch in front of the TV. He put his feet up on the world's coolest coffee table. "Couch, I love you." He had slept on it for hours the previous afternoon. He'd been reading one of her art books and listening to The Moody Blues in the background as the endless drone of the rain beat on the house, and he'd zonked out. He thought about the furniture he'd always had. It was early Ikea picked up at a garage sale. This, this was grown up furniture.

He turned on the TV to catch the Today show. He had to watch it for more than half an hour before they got to her interview. "How can Kat stand this crap?" he asked no one in particular. His aunt watched the show every morning like it was a religion. No wonder she was bonkers. Then there was Andy. "Wow, you look even better on TV." Her hair had been dyed darker. Her clothes made her look like a professional woman. She looked different in make-up. Even her nails were done. It was quite a make-over. It made him uncomfortable, but he wasn't sure why. She looked great, after all. Maybe she just didn't look like herself. She looked older. Or maybe just less carefree.

The host was interviewing her about her book, asking her about being a first-time novelist and talking about the movie that was currently being planned. Andy was explaining about the story line of the book.

Austin listened for a while as his eyes glazed over. "Wow, I might love you but there is no way I am going to read that stupid book of yours." He came up short. *Love?* That was heavy.

His phone buzzed. It was his dad. He picked up the remote and hit the mute button, silencing her mid-word as the interviewer was asking her about her life before becoming a best-selling author. "Hey, Dad."

"Hey, I didn't know that house sitting meant you would totally disappear. Where'd you go? When are you coming home? I thought we'd spend the storm together."

Austin felt a twinge of guilt. "Don't know. Two to three weeks."

"How about coming over for dinner? And, Junior…"

"Dad, Junior is the dog's name."

"Yes, Junior, but this time I do mean the dog. I'm heading out to Beaufort for a couple of days. I need you to take the dog while I'm gone."

"You going to see your lady-friend?"

"Yeah."

"You don't sound too excited there, Dad."

"Eh. We'll see."

"She's a mainlander, Dad."

His dad gave a heavy sigh. Poor Dad. He really needed a girlfriend. A permanent girlfriend. A new wife, if Austin were being honest with himself.

"I know. But I keep trying. I'm not too hopeful, but I've got to go. So, can you take Junior?"

"Oh sure."

"It's okay with the house owners?"

"I'm sure it will be," he said, not at all sure it would be.

"Great. So how about coming over for dinner?"

"Uh, yeah. How about we go out?"

"My cooking is really that bad? I suppose you're still eating your girlfriend's, oh, excuse me, your lady-friend's cooking, aren't you?"

"Oh yeah, every night," Austin said happily.

"Lucky dog."

"It's Junior who's the lucky dog."

"Yeah, I suppose so."

"How'd the roof do in the storm?"

"What? It's fine. I know how to fix a roof. I'm your dad, remember? I'm not Uncle Ben. I had to fix his roof, too."

"Oh, you didn't? In the rain? You should have called me!"

"It was easy. Your Aunt Mad was grateful. No worries."

"Hey, Dad, is there any space in the storage unit?"

"Yeah, sure. It's more than half empty since I sold that fishing boat. You have something you want to put there?"

"Someone gave me some furniture when they got new stuff. Need it for the apartment this fall, but I only get it if I can help them get rid of it now."

"Need help moving it?"

"If you can cover for me for a couple of hours at the Shack tomorrow, I'll ask Sam if he'll help me move it."

"To get out of moving furniture, I'd be more than happy to take your shift at the shack. Hell, I'll even cover lunch for you and Sam."

"Thanks, Dad. So, I'll come up and we'll hit, what? Top Dog?"

"Sounds good. And you can take Junior back with you?"

"Sure, no problem."

Chapter 11

Being on the road was exhausting. Miranda Wright, author of the New York Times Bestseller, *Taken by the Wind*, was suddenly in high demand. She was interviewed. She sat on a panel for a discussion at a conference she'd never heard of before. She spoke to groups. She was on TV. She answered a million-and-one questions as she signed copies of her book. She thought people would ask her about her characters. She thought they might ask her about her process of writing, not that she wanted to admit that for her writing was really like vomiting words onto a page when you were so wracked with emotions that you couldn't sort them out. But trapping them in ink, separating them from you, meant that you could hold them at bay, examine them, and have some hope of escaping and eventually, moving on. She was sure that real writers had a more formal, structured process than that. But no, these people asked her different questions. What they asked her about was *her*. Her personal life. Her views.

Are you still in love with your ex-husband?

Do you still dream of revenge? I got great ideas from your book. I can't wait to try them out.

Did he really grovel at your feet like that? After all that crap he did, that must have felt wonderful.

Are you happy now? You have everything you wanted. Have you punished him enough?

She found the people and their questions intrusive. Their fantasies about her life and character made her uncomfortable. She tried to handle it all with grace, explaining that the book was fiction. She wrote *fiction*, but that wasn't what the people wanted to hear. They wanted drama and dirty laundry. It made her want to retreat back to her beach house hideaway. She missed Austin.

Was this what it was like to be a celebrity? What if people started following her around, watching her every move, who she was with and what she was doing? Did she want the world to know about the intimate details of her life? That was easy to answer: no! That romp with Austin at the secluded little cove had been amazing. And private. Would anyone care that she was having a hot little affair with a younger man? The ten-or-so years between them wouldn't raise too many eyebrows. Not really. Those kinds of things happened. Then she reminded herself, it actually wasn't a hot little affair. Not yet. They had been interrupted. She felt her heart flutter and fanned herself with a nearby flier, her own face smiling back at her. She felt a little sweaty just remembering that day. Yes, it surely would be a hot little affair when she got back to the beach. She felt nervous and shy, but also like for the first time she might be ready to take that chance Caroline kept talking about.

Chapter 12

Austin was counting the days before Andy got back. She'd been on the West Coast for more than a week and it had been hard to talk on the phone given the time difference. She never seemed to be free until close to ten, which was one in the morning to him.

The first day he had Junior at the house he realized that he might have made a mistake. Junior was all over the new furniture, muddy paws and all. He claimed a favorite pillow on the couch and would curl up on it. Austin found some old blankets and covered up the couch and chairs. He found a towel that looked old, at least compared to all her other ones, and kept that by the door so he could wipe off the dog's feet. "You know, Junior, this is more grown up than I ever actually wanted to feel," he told the pooch as he cleaned off his paws when they came in from a walk.

After a few days of sun where he worked at the shack, they had another three days of rain. Junior had been excellent company, but once his father returned from his very disappointing weekend with his lady friend from Beaufort, he wanted the dog back. Bored again, Austin looked around for something to do. He decided to paint the bathroom. That took a day, but it poured again the next, so he painted the upstairs room that served as her office and library. He sure hoped she liked sage green.

Then he got a real surprise. He came home one day from the rental shack and found a huge box from Bowflex on the porch. He eagerly scanned the weather for the next day of rain, so he could put the thing together.

107

After twenty days Andy came home. She had landed in Charlotte, stayed for two days to catch up on life there, and then had made the drive back to the Outer Banks. She was waiting for him when he showed up back at her house.

"Hello, Austin," she said with a smile. "I have to say, I was so impressed at the transformation of the place. You are nothing if not efficient."

"Well, it rained a lot while you were gone. Bad for business but great for here. I had to do something."

"I love the sage green."

"I knew you would."

"And the flowers."

"I knew you would." His father had suggested that he occasionally buy flowers for his lady friend. Austin figured the lack of flowers must have figured into his dad's disappointing weekend, but it sounded like good advice, so he'd put fresh flowers in a vase on the table the day before she came home.

"I'm so happy with the furniture!"

"Yeah, it's gorgeous." He noticed that she had rearranged the entire living room and had hauled the bench to the other side of the table in the kitchen. "I hope you're not just saying that about the sage green."

"No, no, really, I love it. And the work-out room you set up."

"Thanks. Putting the Bowflex together was a bitch, I have to say. Don't send it back. I'm sure it will never go back in that box."

"Then I double appreciate it. I've really been missing my personal trainer. I need to do something, so I thought that would fit the bill. It was kind of an impulse buy. One of those one-step Amazon purchases. I really have to delete that app."

"I like your impulses."

Hours later they had made dinner, snuggled together to watch a movie that they never paid any attention to, and started making out on the couch. She was wearing a little tank top over these brightly colored short shorts. She had absolutely amazing legs. With her shirt pulled up and him kissing her stomach, he found these interesting, faint stripes on her lower belly.

"What are these?"

"Those? Stretch marks. Almost everyone gets them with pregnancy."

"They look like tiger stripes." He looked up at her, a wicked grin on his face. "They suit you. I knew you were going to be a little hellcat, just from the way you kissed me at the beach." He kissed her stomach again. "Guess I was right."

She laughed and gave him a little roar. "No hiding the marks on my never-will-be-quite-flat tummy."

"A woman looking like a woman is what makes her interesting. And I think you're very interesting," he said as he started to explore.

He found that he loved everything about her. He thought their evening might end in the bedroom, the bedroom where he had been sleeping for the last three weeks and wishing she were there. "This is amazing. You're amazing," he whispered in her ear as he nibbled her neck.

She gave a little giggle and squirmed in his arms. "I missed you when I was away."

"What was it like? Being a celebrity?"

She laughed but then became more serious. "People asked crazy questions. So personal. I didn't think anyone would care about a book author. But it was like I was some type of famous person. Hey, what if you being with me means that your picture will be plastered all over the place? Because mine sure was. What if your life becomes subject to people's curiosity? Maybe their ridicule?"

"You mean, my having a love affair with you would make me famous?" Raising one eyebrow, he said, "Imagine me, Austin Mitchell, boy from small town Outer Banks, becoming famous!" Then he laughed. "I could probably live with being famous. That is, if you were part of the picture." He kissed her again, slowly, on the mouth. "I think you're beautiful." He pulled the spaghetti strap of her tank top down over her shoulder and kissed her collarbone. "I think your shoulders are beautiful." His mouth followed down her arm. "And I think your arm is beautiful." He ran his tongue in a line up her arm, making

109

the loop over her shoulder and then down her chest. He could feel the soft roundness of her breast against his cheek. He loved how she trembled in his arms. He tried to pull her shirt off over her head, but it got stuck and made the moment very awkward.

"Do you love this shirt?"

"Um, no. It's just a shirt."

He put his two hands on it and ripped it up the seam.

Later on, they found themselves in the Jacuzzi tub. She raised one leg out of the tub and towards the ceiling, stretching, and then drew it back down to the water.

"That was amazing, Andy." He wondered how he could tell her. If he should tell her. Did adults who had regular sex lives talk about it with each other, like they talked about work, world events, or the weather? He wasn't sure. It had been amazing. But it was almost too amazing.

"Yes, you were wonderful, Austin."

"Was I?"

"Yes, of course, silly." She massaged his chest with her foot. "Don't tell me you're worried. You don't have anything to worry about."

"No, no, I'm not worried. It's just that… just that…" He had no idea how to say this.

She sat up and looked at him. "It wasn't wonderful?"

"Come here, come here." He turned her around and had her lean back against his chest. "Relax." He could feel that she wasn't relaxing. "Relax." It was clear that despite her efforts she was not succeeding.

"What did I do wrong?" she said in a small voice.

"You did nothing wrong. You just need to relax. You are amazing, Andy. Truly amazing. I just always thought that making love should be a two-way street."

She froze in his arms. "I don't know what you mean."

"I just mean that I'm here too and I'd like to please you as much as you please me."

"You did please me."

"Really? Really, Andy?" There was a heavy silence. He thought about how to approach it. "This might be a really indelicate question, but tell me, what was it like between you and Gregg?"

"Me and Gregg?"

"Yeah. Did he ever, did he ever do for you what, uh, you did for me?"

Andy was quiet. Austin decided that he would let her take her own time. Until then, he would just hold her.

"No. He didn't. He didn't seem to really like me that much."

"But you were married."

"Yes, but he rarely seemed to want to touch me. And certainly not to look at me." She was quiet again for a long while. Austin held her a little more tightly with one arm and stroked her leg with his free hand. She looked down at his arm stroking her. "He never wanted to see me naked. I think he was really bothered by the fact that I was a little pudgy. He used to pick at me for what I ate and how heavy I was."

"Well, that's nasty. I think you're fabulous."

"Thank you but remember that I practically lived in the gym for a year. Even I'm not quite used to how I look. But when I was married to Gregg I was about twenty pounds heavier. One of the reasons I ordered that Bowflex is that I have no gym to go to. I mean it's not a lap pool, which I really miss. And my personal trainer. I just can't face going back to that…"

"That what?"

"That, that sense of utter rejection."

He bent down and kissed her neck. "I'll never reject you. You're amazing. I've always heard that when two people love each other and they're together for a long time, they don't even see the other person's body."

"Well, Gregg seemed to do all he could to avoid seeing mine."

"I'm not sure that's what I meant," Austin said softly. "I'm sorry, Andy.

He should have wanted to please you."

"He never wanted to please me. Well, maybe in the very early years, but he was so tired all the time. We really lived parallel lives. And as for our love making, somehow it became about getting him off so he could go to sleep, get up the next day and do it all over again."

"So, you basically performed for him?"

"Performed on him would be more accurate. He was always pretty happy to have me, uh, relieve him."

"Would you mind if I asked you why you did all that for him?" She didn't say anything right away. Then he realized that she was crying quiet, soft tears. "You don't have to answer…"

She took a deep breath. "Be… be… because I didn't want him to leave me. I thought if I gave him what he wanted, that he would love me. Eventually."

"Oh." Austin didn't know what to say. What could you say to something like that? "You were unbelievably amazing."

"I've had a lot of practice." She sniffed and wiped away a tear with her hand. "And he left me anyways."

"I want us to be different. Can we be a two-way street here? I mean, you wouldn't let me do the same for you."

"I haven't had a lot of practice at that."

He readjusted his position and kissed her neck softly. Now he could feel her leaning into him and actually relaxing. "Then let me practice, okay? Let me try to keep you wanting me as much as I want you."

She exhaled deeply. "Yeah, I'll try to let you practice."

He kissed her hair and her neck, then she turned around to face him.

"Austin, I know I'm a bit older than you. I've been married. I have a daughter. I come with baggage. While you've had some experience, you don't have baggage. This is wonderful, but I'm not sure it's going to work."

He reached out and touched her face. "Does it have to work? What does this need to be?"

She looked confused. "I guess I don't know. I got pregnant the first time I had sex. It's always been forever for me, so that's a really tough question."

"I move back to the mainland in three weeks. Then you move back to the mainland, too. This is a summer gig for you. We don't have to force this to be anything but wonderful. There are no requirements. No expectations. I won't be disappointed. I hope I don't disappoint you."

She stroked his face. "So, we have three weeks together?"

"Looks like it. What does this need to be for you? I want to make you happy. Should this be happening?"

"Absolutely yes," she answered quickly. "I haven't felt like this in… well, I don't know that I've ever felt like this. And you do make me happy. I don't want this to be nothing. But it can't be forever, either. This whole Demi Moore, Ashton Kutcher thing just won't work."

"Who's Demi Moore?"

She laughed. "Precisely. I'll see if I can just let this be a summer fling and then let you go in the fall."

"The reality is that our lives are headed different places. But that doesn't mean we can't love each other now. And who knows what will be in the future? We shouldn't force it out of being anything either."

"Oh, Austin. I got very lucky when the wind blew me to you, for however long it lasts."

He stayed the night with her. They climbed into bed very late and he held her. Just listened to her breathing. Just watched her in the moonlight until sleep took him as well.

* * *

Austin was back at work, wading out into the sound, laying out the anchors that would hold down the rental equipment for the day. The weather looked gorgeous for the next week. That meant he wouldn't see Andy as much as he would like to. He was living back at home and his dad wanted to do all kinds of things together before he left for the classes that would to start back up in just a few weeks.

Over breakfast that morning he had asked Andy more questions about her baggage. Gregg must have been quite a trip to be married to. From what Andy described, he nitpicked all her decisions and joked about her in front of their friends and family members. It sounded like a constant stream of subtle put-downs, one after another. He wouldn't let her make financial decisions because she didn't make any of the money. He had been controlling, bossy, manipulative, and cheap. Their life primarily consisted of Andy doing everything she could to please him, keeping his house immaculate, wowing him with amazing food. From what Austin could deduce, sex could best be described as performance art. It had been a one-way street for so long that Andy wasn't even sure how to make that tango a dance for two.

Whatever happened between them he wanted it to have a positive effect on Andy, not to drag her back to where her unhappy marriage had left her. Above all, he certainly didn't want to do any damage. He looked out over the water. He was beginning to understand some of the complexity that his dad's generation felt. All their breakups, heartaches, relationship bumps, and recoupling in different configurations had always mystified him. But in the past few days, he felt like he had made a step toward being a grownup. Not for the great sex, but for seeing the complexity and suffering and resilience of the human heart.

Chapter 13

"Answer, c'mon, answer..." Austin said into the phone. Then he heard her voice. "Hey, Andy, last minute I know, but I wonder if you're free tonight? I just found out that Duckbill Blues, it's a little bar up in Duck, is playing bluegrass tonight. It should be great—want to go?"

"Sure, I'd love to. When?"

"We need to leave soon if we're gonna get a table. We can eat there. Do you eat bar food? I mean, like really-not-very-good bar food?"

"I think I'll survive it. You're calling from Chicamacomico? How about I drive up and get you and we'll just head up to Duck in my car?"

"Sounds great. See you in about twenty? I'll be at the produce stand across the street, so you don't have to make the left turn. Great! I hope you like it."

"Austin, I'll like anything we do together."

Austin marveled at how easy she was to be with. How warm and open and affectionate she was, without being clingy. Of course, he wouldn't have minded a little bit of clingy. He felt like he couldn't get enough of her, and now the days were flying by. He would be leaving soon and wouldn't be back to the islands until the Thanksgiving holiday. Surely, there must be a way they could get together during the fall. Maybe she could come to Wilmington? Since their time together was so precious they seemed to spend it together very simply, making dinner, watching movies, having awesome sex, but not going out, not diluting their time with other people. It would be fun to go out and catch some music. Austin thought he could share Andy with the world for just

115

one evening. Besides, he'd just heard that Grandpa was going to swing by and join the band. No one wanted to miss Grandpa. He was a legend on the island.

He switched out of his swim trunks into some white shorts and a pullover top. Andy had bought him these and he knew it would please her if he wore them when they were out. She loved to buy him things, a habit he didn't want her to develop. She made sure he had everything he needed at her house, from clothes to deodorant to what he liked to drink. She was the most nurturing girlfriend he had ever known. She actually anticipated his needs, before he'd even thought of them himself. He would just be thinking he was getting thirsty and one of her amazing iced teas would plop down in front of him. They would be snuggling on the couch, watching a movie, and just before his neck would begin to feel sore she would reach for a pillow for him. She was so in tune with him. She would see things when out shopping and pick up items she thought he would like. He always respected the fact that she had great taste. She was introducing him to whole new worlds. Of course, money was nothing to her. He couldn't even imagine living that way, not having cash as a concern. Someday, when he finished this damn degree, he would apply these business skills to the islands and then they would make real money too. Well, maybe not real money but they would be doing more than subsistence living. There had to be a better future for people on the island than that. He could feel what that would be like when he was with Andy. It was like having a real life.

She pulled up right on time and they headed up Highway Twelve to Duck, on the north side of the Outer Banks. He pulled a thumb drive out of his pocket and held it up. "Look what I have—new music to load into your car."

"You can load music from that thing into this?"

"Andy, seriously, you don't even know how this car works. I'm kinda surprised you don't have a self-driving car. Yes, look at this." He pressed the radio/media button on the console. Then he punched the touch screen to bring up JB. "See this? It says 'JB' and it means your jukebox. You can load it up with whatever you want. I'm loading it up with all your favorites. I made this while I house sat for you. It's got ABBA, the Doobie Brothers, Moody Blues, Electric Light Orchestra, Billy Joel, Elton John, and I know this will be totally jarring, but some Stones and Rush in there too—a great mix that you'll love."

"Oh my gosh, you're going to make me love driving! How do you get the music from the drive into my car?"

"Okay, Andy, see this little button. With the squiggly kind of lines on it, look: it pops off. This is your car's USB port."

"My car has a USB hookup? Really? That's so cool. I didn't know that!"

"Honey, do you know how to change a tire?"

"Honey, that's why I have Triple A." She smiled at him. He loved her smile.

"I'll load this up and then you'll be a driving machine… in your ultimate driving machine. Oh wait, this is a Lexus."

"It's still an ultimate driving machine. And I'm not the-self-driving-car-kind-of-girl anymore. It was too much like driving with my mother correcting me all the time. Tried that, but decided that I'm an old fashioned, independent type." As they made the trip up the coast, they talked about his departure. "Is there anything you need for resuming your mainland life?"

"Andy, you've got to stop buying me stuff."

"I like buying you stuff. Besides, I have no one else to buy for."

"You have E," he reminded her.

"E has everything she needs."

"Hey, I get it." He put his hand on her shoulder. "Part of who you are is taking care of everybody and everything. But I just want us to be. Let's not fall into old patterns. Let's create our own. While we can. Besides, remember where I've donated all your old furniture to."

"I'm so glad! It would have broken my heart for all that stuff to have just been thrown away."

They arrived at Duckbill Blues in time to get the very last small table for two. They were a bit to the side and against the wall but still had a view of the tiny stage crammed into the corner. The waitress took their drink orders as the band arrived and began to set up.

Andy leaned over to Austin. "So, this band is called Grandpa?"

"Oh no. This band is called The Dare County Line. Grandpa just shows up sometimes to play with them, and it's not to be missed. He doesn't always come out. He's not exactly a spring chicken."

The waitress brought their drinks and took their dinner order. Andy watched the band set up. "You know, every one of those guys looks familiar to me. I think I've seen them at the grocery store, the gas station, and I'm not sure where."

"Oh sure. That makes sense. While you're on the island, you'll learn who's here for the duration and who's just a tourist. It doesn't take long to see who's an islander. They live here, so of course you see them all over the place, over and over again. In the sea of temporary faces, the permanent ones will jump out at you."

The band took the mic and, sure enough, introduced themselves as The Dare County Line. They announced that they expected Grandpa to show up that night. The considerable number of locals in the crowd cheered loudly. The tourists looked around, a bit confused, but then politely joined in. The band played four songs in their first set.

"Clearly you love this music," Andy said as she leaned into Austin. He put his arm over her shoulder.

"Oh yeah, this is fun. I like a lot of music, but I grew up with this. My whole family is into music. I've always heard this, so I have a lot of good memories built around these old tunes. Just wait until you hear Grandpa. You'll feel like you've been transported back in time."

As if on cue, an old man shuffled in the front door. Dressed in tight-fitted jeans and a white button down, he made his way over towards the stage. He was wearing the rather ugly, but comfortable-looking shoes common to men of his generation. The band finished the song and the baseball-capped banjo player went to the mic. "Well folks, we know why you all really came out tonight. And he's here, the man of the hour. Grandpa, come on up and take the stage." The locals in the crowd went wild again.

Grandpa took the stage. He actually needed some help getting up there. He shuffled over to the mic. "Aw, thankee all for that warm welcome. You all know why he calls me the man of the hour, don't you? It's because I'm only good for about an hour." The crowd laughed. "But since you've been so kind, I'll oblige you all with a few tunes."

Austin leaned over to whisper into Andy's ear and caught the scent of her perfume. He loved the way she smelled. "If you've liked this so far, then be prepared to love this now. Grandpa is one of a passing generation. There just aren't many men left like him."

Grandpa started swaying with the music as the band struck up their next tune. He sang old time bluegrass, his voice slightly nasal but pitch perfect. As he sang the years seemed to fall from him. The band did five songs with him, the audience clapping along and some people getting up to dance in the tiny area in front of the stage. At the end of his set, Grandpa once again thanked the audience, who stood and cheered and clapped loudly. "Aww, you are awfully sweet to a little old man. Watch out now fella's, 'cause I'm comin' after your ladies!"

"Now watch him," Austin said as they took their seats again. "He'll work the crowd just like he said. He'll come over and say hi, so I'll introduce you."

Indeed, Grandpa made his way through the crowd and either received or bestowed kisses to all the ladies, young and old alike. "It's like they're lining up to smooch him!" Andy laughed.

"Oh, he'll want to kiss you, too. Just be ready." He winked at her. "Grandpa's great. I hope I'm just like him when I'm his age."

"At this point I think he'd better kiss me! I'm not sure I'd be okay with being the only girl in the room to not get a kiss from that cool old man."

Austin laughed. "Don't let him hear you calling him an old man. Only he's allowed to say that about himself! He's young at heart. Be careful, or he'll try to steal you from me." He lifted her hand and kissed it. They watched Grandpa make his way through the crowd. Everyone was shaking his hand, clapping him on the shoulder, giving him a kiss or accepting one.

"He knows everyone," Andy said.

"Well, just about. Probably not the tourists, but he loves to play the celebrity. All the permanent folks, sure he knows them. He was born here. Other than to fight in the war, I don't think he ever left."

"He seems amazing. Do you play?"

"A little bit of guitar. My dad taught me. I took violin for a few years. He taught me that too. But while I have the love of music, I'm afraid I don't have the gift like all the other men in my family. Oh, here he comes." Austin stood up again and as Grandpa shuffled over to their table, Andy joined him.

"Well, well, well, if it isn't Austin!" the old man said with a laugh.

"Hi Grandpa. You did a great set. I'd like to introduce you to my girlfriend, Andy. She's new to the island."

Grandpa gave Andy a once over and then nodded approvingly. "Mind if I kiss your pretty young lady?"

Andy laughed and leaned in, presenting her cheek to him. "I'd be hurt if you didn't! It's nice to meet you, sir. You're quite the local celebrity."

"Nah, they're just happy I didn't die up there on stage before I finished. I'm sure they were cheering with relief that I didn't ruin all their vacations."

"Do you join the band often?"

"Every once in a while. You know," he added conspiratorially, "I just do it for the kisses!" He winked at her. "It's nice to meet you, young lady with the boy's name. Oh, there's a lady there I haven't kissed. I don't want to get in trouble with her. I'd better go and spread some love. Austin, you be good."

"Or be good at it. Yes, sir. I know."

They stayed late at the bar listening to the music and then Austin drove her car as they made their way back down the island to Andy's house, where they stayed the night.

*   *   *

Three days before he was to depart they had their big fight. He hadn't been prepared for that. They were having dinner of some type of seared salmon with vermicelli noodles. It was one of her typically complicated dishes that tasted fresh and light. English peas and kernels of corn mingled with Asian flavors. It was delicious. They'd had a fun day, then been tangled up in each other in the late afternoon, and then made dinner together. They'd cooked together so much that he was pretty sure he'd be able to do it on his own this fall and make some pretty impressive stuff.

Then she let the bomb drop. "Austin, I think you need to start dating when you go back to school."

He paused, wondering where this conversation could possibly be going. It had certainly come out of left field. "I am dating someone. I'm dating someone I think is very special. You."

"Thank you." She paused and took a sip of her fruit tea. She sat back in her chair and looked at him. "I think you're very special too, but it's best if you have a social life when you go back to the mainland. I want you to know how much I care about you. How very much. But even I recognize that this has no future."

He set down his fork and sat back in his chair. "Why do you say that? Who knows what'll happen in the future?"

"We talked about this weeks ago. After my trip, I came back to you and, you know, we talked about this. In the jacuzzi."

"That was weeks ago." His head was spinning. "Why do we have to make any decisions now? This is just starting. This is just getting good." This felt like a relationship between real adults and not like the silly drama he'd always experienced with insecure girls his own age. He shuddered at the thought of going back to the social scene in Wilmington. He didn't know what he wanted from his relationship with Andy in the future. That would be what it would be. But he didn't want it to end now. "We can find a way to overcome the distance."

"We've talked about this. We have to be real, Austin. This is a summer fling."

"We talked about letting this be what it is. And it's great. We talked about not forcing it to be anything it wasn't. You're forcing it out of existence."

Andy looked away for few moments, as if she were trying to compose her thoughts. "You're going to need more from a relationship than I can give you. Eventually. Eventually you're going to realize all I can't give you. And you'll want all those things. I can't keep you from having a full life, Austin. I think you're wonderful. And I care too much about you to do anything at all that would harm you. I want to make everything perfect for you—but I can't. And I'm not perfect for you. I'm too old for you."

"So, you're a few years older than I am. A lot of people have age differences. Even those TV people you mentioned. What were their names? They made it work."

"Ashton Kutcher and Demi Moore? They got divorced."

Austin blinked a couple of times as the fireworks went off in his head. "No. I know what this is about. This is not about you and me. This is about you and Gregg."

"What?"

"Yeah, it is, isn't it? This is you rehearsing for the end of our relationship. You were surprised by Gregg and the divorce. You don't want to be surprised again. So, you're getting yourself ready now. Well look, I have news for you— I'm not Gregg. Maybe to me this isn't a summer fling? Maybe it was when it started. But maybe it isn't now."

She looked stunned. Tears welled up in her eyes. "Maybe you're right. Gregg did surprise me. And it's true: I wasn't ready. But this—what can this be but a summer fling? You're headed back to school to finish your business degree. This is a summer house. I'm not an islander. I'm a mainlander. I'm headed back to Charlotte by mid-September. I'm not coming to Wilmington. I'll still live, what, three-and-a-half, four hours from you? We can't keep this going."

"I think you should stay on the island. I think you should write. You should make this your home. You belong here. It's so obvious. And I'm coming back. It won't be that long."

"Oh, Austin, I can't stay here. I'm not an islander. I'm a mainlander. I live in Charlotte."

Austin tossed down his napkin. He didn't want the dinner any longer. He shrugged his shoulders. "It never works between a mainlander and an islander."

After another hour of going in circles they gave up and he went home to spend the night. He was very out of sorts when he walked in. His dad was reading a book, obviously waiting up for Austin. Maybe waiting up to see if he came home.

"How was dinner with your girlfriend?"

"It was dinner."

"So, um, you leave in three days to head back. Will you be riding with her? Or would you like your old dad to take you? I'd like to take you back to school."

"Dad, I have my own car. I'm driving myself." Then Austin realized that this was his dad's way of being nosy. Austin looked at his dad and saw a strange look in his eye. Suddenly he felt guilty about all the time he hadn't spent with him this summer. Since he'd met Andy, it had been all about her. All about them. He knew his dad missed him in the winters. Now Austin got it: his dad had missed him all summer too. "She's not coming with me, Dad. She's a mainlander. I think it's over."

His dad closed his book and set it down beside his chair. "I'm sorry, son. It's hard… with a mainlander."

"Yeah, like you say, it never works."

"Well, it didn't for me. I had hoped you wouldn't get your heart broken, though."

Austin winced. "Yeah. It's ironic. I always said it would be… whatever it would be between us. But now that I'm not getting what I want, I regret letting go of the reins." He sat down next to his dad. "So, when I go up, I'm taking that U-Haul of furniture for the apartment. There's no way you want to tag along and help me move in, is there?"

His dad smiled. "I'd be happy to. I'll call Mike and ask him to help if you want. Then I can drive back with Mike."

"You guys will have to stay overnight. Drive's too long to go there and back in a day." Austin felt even guiltier that now his dad and Mike would lose two days of work. He was going to spend every minute he could with his dad, and he would do a much better job of staying in touch with him once all his classes started up.

His dad grinned at him. "Maybe we'll try to see what all those mainlanders think is so great over there."

"They just don't know what they're talking about, Dad. They don't know anything."

Chapter 14

They had left one another at the end of summer with hurt feelings, Andy unable to find a sufficiently kind and compassionate way to end this fantasy and Austin unable to find a graceful way to let her go. She had been surprised, not to mention touched, by how fiercely he fought her to keep their relationship going. She knew he would realize that this was for the best. Eventually, so would she. "You never know when's the last time you'll ever see someone," she said over her coffee cup as she looked at the sun on the sound. "My God, I would love to see you again."

She was tough with herself and the four times she picked up her phone to call Austin, she made herself put it back down. Then she surprised herself with letting the days slip by without packing up her house. The fifteenth came and went. Charlotte remained a far-away place. She tried to write, had only a little success. She did another short book tour and was interviewed at another writer's conference. Luckily, she was away when Austin's school was on fall break, so she didn't have to face the temptation to see him, should he even decide to come home. When she came back to the beach house it finally dawned upon her that she wasn't ready to give up the memory of him, and this house held the memory of him. She felt happy here. The happiest she could remember being in at least a decade. Lonely too, but happy. Then she got an email. It was titled 'I need help'. It was from Austin. She opened it immediately.

"I have a problem. I need your help. I failed my paper. I asked my dad for help, but he told me that he always failed those papers too. He suggested I get a tutor. You're the best writer I know. Will you please help me? I need to learn to write. And fast, while I still have time to save my grade."

She looked at his email. He was asking her to do something she was great at. She wanted to help him, if only to make up for the pain she had caused him at the end of August, but she was afraid of starting their relationship back up and probably even more so of sending him mixed signals. It was a Pandora's box that she was afraid to open and yet struggled to walk away from. "I guess that's why they call it temptation," she sighed as she re-read his note.

The next email came. "If I fail my course, I won't graduate. I need your help. Please?"

Chewing on her lip she could feel herself sliding back from all her discipline. "Damn. Why am I such a sucker for being needed?" She wrote back, *Of course.* She sighed. "I owe it to you, sweet, wonderful Austin, to give you any help you ask for."

The days turned into weeks with her tutoring him. "Oh, this is much better, Austin. Much, much, much," she commented as she read on. After she finished, she composed a note to him with some suggestions for strengthening the clarity of his analysis in a couple of places and pointed out a few grammatical errors.

"Thanks for your comments on my writing," he emailed her. "I have to say, you are really a great teacher. I never got this kind of tutoring before and I surely didn't learn all this stuff in college!"

They proceeded to have slow-motion conversations, each typing in a careful comment to the other and then doing something else while they waited for the response.

"Well, maybe you weren't paying too much attention way back then. But it's a whole new ballgame now. You're not like some young unschooled undergraduate."

"No, I'm not," he answered. "Now I have a best-selling, famous, fabulous author as my tutor! I've learned so much with these last three papers. Hey, how's the book coming?"

"Ugh," she typed. "Don't ask. I have major writer's block. I did great after that little book tour this summer, whipped out all those pages when I got back. I did a few after my trip to that conference. I think that inspired me, but now I sit around here bored and stare at my computer screen. I can't think of what happens next."

"You need to do a book club."

"I suppose I could reach out to my agent, but I dread being sent out on another three-week odyssey of travel," she typed and then clicked on send.

"Just do one on the island."

She read his words and thought about that. Then she typed, "Where? How? I hardly know anyone, and I certainly don't have connections here. I have no island-friends."

"I think I can help. Would you mind if I gave your email to someone I know? She's really into books. I'd bet she'd be excited to find out that she's got a real author on the island."

"Well…" she typed.

"She's really nice. You'll like her."

The very next day, Andy found an email from a Katerina Guion in her inbox, inquiring whether she might be willing to come to their book club. They could hold it at a little bookstore down in Buxton called The Book Shelf.

"Wow, Austin, you are nothing if not efficient."

One evening, two weeks later, she followed the instructions Mrs. Guion had sent her and drove the twenty miles south. She arrived at a cute little building with a large sign out front saying, 'The Book Shelf.' A little bit nervous, she parked her car and went in. There were more than a dozen people waiting for her—an astonishing crowd for a beach town in post-season. She hadn't seen fourteen people together on the island since Labor Day. Four couples and a half a dozen more men. She thought that was a bit of an odd turnout, given the genre of her work. Usually, the audiences were strictly women. Wine bottles were open, plates of cheese and crackers were about.

Someone had brought a bowl of hush puppies. Maybe it was the snacks that had lured them out? Maybe it was the promise of seeing other human beings for a change? Certainly, that's what had brought her.

A thin, middle-aged woman with long, steadily graying dark brown hair came up to her. "Hi?" she said tentatively. "Are you Ms. Wright?" She reached out to shake Andy's hand.

"Yes, I am. Are you Katerina?" Andy didn't quite know what to do about this woman. She was shaking her hand with a surprising amount of vigor and looking at her with big, wide eyes.

"Yes, yes, please call me Kat. I saw you on the Today Show! I thought you were marvelous. I actually read your book right when it came out. I've read it three times. Did you know that that ring she owns, the one that's blue, did you know it's red later on in the book? Was that intentional? I always wanted to ask that. Wow, is it nice to meet you. I saw you on the Today Show. It's such an honor to have you here, Ms. Wright."

The woman was still pumping Andy's arm up and down, talking a mile-a-minute and repeating things she'd already said. Andy wondered if this was what it was like to have her very own fan girl? "Kat? Yes, Kat, it's so nice to meet you." Andy retrieved her arm, surprised at how sore it felt. "You're so kind to reach out with your invitation. Please call me Andy."

"Wow! New York Times Best Selling Novelist Miranda Wright and I are on a first name basis! Oh, we are just so excited to have you… Miranda! C'mon in. Meet everybody. My sister-in-law can't wait to meet you. She's read your book twice, she missed you on TV though. She didn't pick up on the ring thing," she whispered conspiratorially.

"Oh, well, thank you. I'd love to meet her."

Kat signaled over a larger woman with big blonde curls. She was also middle-aged and wore heavy eye make-up. "Miranda," Kat said it, like she was savoring it, or perhaps lording first name status over her sister-in-law, "this is Madeline."

"Madeline, it's so nice to meet you."

"Please call me Mad, Ms. Wright," she said in one of the strongest southern accents Andy had heard yet.

"Mad, it's so nice to meet you. Please call me Andy."

"I can't believe Kat brought you in! Miranda Wright! I thought she was pulling my leg when she told me. Can I call you Miranda too?" Mad shook her hand in a firm and friendly way, without the workout Kat had given her. "I'll hope you'll sign my book tonight, Miranda! Hey, Frankie, come over here, bring my book, honey."

Okay, Andy told herself. *With these people, apparently I'm Miranda.* That was okay. She only went by Andy with close friends anyway and she had gone by Miranda Wright on the whole book tour. That's how the world knew her as an author. She supposed that as much as she would like to have friends, she wasn't here to make friends: she was here as a professional visit. She was an author. They were book lovers. She needed to be the somewhat famous Miranda Wright. At least for the night.

A portly blonde man, a little older than Mad, came over, book in hand.

"Frankie?" Miranda smiled at him. "Mad, is this your husband?"

"Frankie? Oh, heck no, he's my brother. My husband's Ben, he's that guy over there in the blue shirt. But there's hardly any of us on the island who aren't related to one another. Second, third, fourth cousins, you know. Or once married to one another and now married to someone else. But there's so few of us. We all get along."

Miranda had a hard time looking away from Mad as she made that statement but managed to glance over to where the woman was pointing and saw a man standing by the sales counter on the other side of the smallish space. He was standing a little apart from the others and wearing a Caribbean-blue pullover shirt. He was blonde and in his mid-forties. He had kind of a square-ish face and a really nice smile. He was holding a glass of white wine and looking directly at her. She thought Mad was a lucky woman. Ben exuded an air of gentleness. Reluctantly she turned back to Mad and her brother, Frankie.

129

"Well, Frankie, it's nice to meet you."

Frankie picked up her hand and kissed it. Miranda was sure she looked absolutely as awkward as she felt. She forced herself to relax and smile, but took her hand back as soon as she could.

"Now, Frankie's not married, so if you ever want to look around the island, he's your man!" Madeline shoved the book into Miranda's hand and led her over to a table. "Can you sign my book before we start?"

Miranda found her most gracious smile. "Of course." There was no worry that anyone would be disappointed tonight about not getting their book signed: with her there, a total of fifteen people were in the room. On her tour she'd had to sign dozens upon dozens of books at a time, writing her name until her hand cramped and continued to ache late into the evening.

"Can you sign it, 'To my new friend, Madeline. Love, Miranda Wright'?"

"Of course." She ended up writing the same affectionate inscription in Kat's book as well. A woman named Maggie was pleasant but not fawning about the book signing, so Andy gave her usual inscription, 'May the wind take you to fabulous places, Miranda Wright.' Cynthia, the last woman there, seemed far more interested in the wine than in having her book signed.

In the end, all of the women and six of the men asked for books to be signed as well. The last in line was that attractive gentleman in the blue shirt she had noticed earlier. *Ben* she reminded herself. *Madeline's husband.* As he approached the little table and chair they had set up for her, she noticed he was carrying a dozen books. His shirt had the logo of 'The Book Shelf' stitched onto it.

"Oh my!" she said as she surveyed the stack.

"Hi. I own The Book Shelf and I wondered if you'd sign some of the books we have for sale."

"Oh, this is your shop? It's really lovely. So quaint and beachy." Indeed, it was a comfortable kind of place. Bookshelves along all the walls, a few freestanding shelves dotting the open space. They looked as though they had been lovingly made by someone who enjoyed doing woodwork and had rather a lot of time. There were all kinds of chairs: squashy comfy ones, love seats, a wingback chair that reminded Andy of one her grandmother had once owned, and one of those old antique courting chairs where two people sat on opposite sides and were separated by the back but still faced each other. There were two pod-chairs that looked like bird nests suspended from chains hung from curving floor stands made of metal. Someone had gathered most of the chairs and loveseats into a sort of a circle and a few folding chairs had been brought out to complete the set so there was seating for everyone. The sales counter had been turned into a serving table, and held the bottles of wine, glasses, and most of the snacks. "I guess you love books?"

"I do love books. I love bringing good stories to the people who live here."

"It was very kind of you to open your shop this evening and host. I was so pleased and surprised to get Kat's invitation."

"Oh, we're pleased to have you here." He set the books down on the table.

"Have we met?" Andy asked him.

"Oh no. I would totally remember it if we'd met."

"Okay, I'm sorry, you just seem familiar somehow. I'm sure that seems so odd. I'm new on the island and I've been meeting all kinds of people. I must be getting people confused."

"You have a gift then, if you're meeting people in October. It's pretty quiet around here. Even all the restaurants are shutting down for the winter."

"I'm sorry," she said again, distracted by his blue eyes and his smile. Why did he keep smiling like that? "I actually met a lot of people in the summer when I moved here. Lately it has been very quiet. I'm happy to sign these for you. Thank you for asking."

"My pleasure."

"Pleasure's all mine." She signed the books, happy that all she had to write in them was 'Miranda Wright'.

She mingled with the collected guests. They seemed more interested in socializing and drinking the wine than talking about the book. She felt a bit shy to be doing a book club anyway, so she was kind of grateful that they didn't get down to business right away. There were no book club discussion questions in the back of her book. It was a romantic comedy, falling into the classification of 'upmarket women's fiction'. It was fluff. She knew that. She didn't feel apologetic for what she had written, but she also didn't think anyone could pass it off for being more than what it was.

"So, I saw you met Frank?" said Cynthia. "He's a nice man. Lost his wife a few years ago. It was sad."

"Oh. That's horrible." Miranda wondered if it had been another drunk driver.

"Yeah. For some reason, women don't seem to like to stay on the island. I can't imagine why. She just took off one day. Paul's wife left him too. She got a really good job on the mainland and just never came back." She pointed to the balding, short man in the black button-down shirt. Miranda wished he had done up two more buttons.

"Oh, so Paul and Frankie are both… um, single?"

"Yeah, Paul, Frankie, Lawson, they're all single. Their wives all left. Couldn't hack it. Gone for years. Burke and Darnell's wives died. Tragic. Really sad. One of breast cancer and the other in an awful car accident. Oh, don't bring that up. I probably shouldn't have. Neither of them like to talk about it. Adam never married. He's a fishy kind of guy," she said with a wink. It was a swarm of names that Miranda couldn't possibly hope to keep straight. She felt rather speechless and hoped she didn't have to face Cynthia again, with her gossip that seemed designed to be more for shock and awe than for acquainting you with the community.

After Cynthia moved on, Adam sidled up to her. He was flat-out gorgeous. Their conversation started out well. He asked her a few questions about her hobbies, however in short order it seemed as though his questions were actually leading to something. "So, you're into fishing, right? Exciting stuff!" He proceeded to tell her about pulling in and tagging sharks in the surf. He seemed to be very caught up in a rather heroic story of how he wrangled the monsters of the sea. He assured her that he carefully photographed each of his conquests, releasing them to the ocean and their pictures to Instagram. He pulled out his phone and showed her at least a dozen pictures, most of which featured him and only one time did she see something that could have been a shark. She found it oddly creepy and hard to get a word in edgewise.

Darnell turned out to be quite a character. He told her all about his motorcycle, offering to take her for a ride anytime, assuring her it was the only true way to see the islands. He was an imposing kind of guy with that bald head, the single hoop earring, and all those tattoos snaking up his arms. She could see the edges of them peeking up his neck out of his shirt and wondered just how much of the man was left unaltered? And he seemed a little on the old side to be quite so covered in ink, like he was trying to pull off cool. He had a way of speaking that was a bit loud and very direct. She had to fight off her desire to shrink away from him. Then she remembered Cynthia saying "tragic" and mentioning Darnell. She had a horrible thought... *The car accident. What if this is Austin's dad? He lost his wife. Austin lost his parents and was now being raised by his uncle—the man he identified as his dad.* It certainly looked like subsistence living described him. *Austin described him as being a real character. Wow, father not like son.* But then she wanted to shrink away from him for another reason—even the thought of being flirted with by Austin's guardian made her distinctly uncomfortable. *No surely,* she thought, *he wouldn't have sent his dad to this event.*

Lawson slid into the rotation, bringing her another glass of red wine. Not just an accountant, but a CPA, he assured her. He traveled up to Manteo every day for work. He seemed to be very excited about tax codes and told her in some detail about how the new bill proposed by Congress was going to affect small business owners. She wasn't sure of even half of what he said to her, but that might have been because of the parsley stuck between his teeth.

All in all, by the time Kat dinged her knife against her wine glass, calling for the start of the book club, Miranda felt she had been in the strangest speed dating event of her life.

"Hi, everybody, and I want to welcome you to The Book Shelf!" Kat said,

133

as though they hadn't just spent the last hour socializing. "We're so excited to have Miranda Wright join us for our book club this evening. As you know, Miranda's book was on the New York Times Bestseller List! And she was on the Today Show over the summer. I saw her." She turned to Miranda. "You did wonderfully, by the way. I can't wait to hear all about what it was like to be on TV!" Then she turned back to the group. "Before we start discussing the book, does anyone have any questions for her? Oh, uh, give her your name when you ask your question."

"Hi, I'm Paul," the man with the unbuttoned shirt said. He sounded so nervous. Miranda would have expected anyone showing that much chest hair to be far more confident. "Your character in the book is single but then gets remarried. Is that autobiographical?"

She froze. More personal questions. "Um, you know, while authors draw inspiration from life, few books are truly autobiographical. For example, my character has a son who is younger, and in my life I have a daughter, so both my character and I are parents, but my daughter's older. She's just starting medical school."

"Yeah, but did you remarry your husband?"

"Um. No. I'm not married. But I do have a boy, um, er, a man-friend." She felt weird to say she had a boyfriend when she wasn't sure what Austin actually was, particularly now that they hadn't successfully let go of one another. And even though he was a decade or so younger than her, she didn't want to advertise that fact to anyone. The word 'boy' made her feel nervous.

Paul looked over at Darnell, who shrugged. "I don't have any questions."

The women dove in to save the day, talking about the funny things they liked from the book. Some agreed with her protagonist winning back her ex, while others disagreed. One thing they were unified on: they all loved the revenge plot against the wayward husband. The men retreated into silence, killing off the bottles of wine. At last a man in a faded blue t-shirt with wiry tufts of gray hair and a salt and pepper beard said, "Why did we have to read that stupid book anyway? It's a chick story. All about… relationships. Man, it was like, like having to eat weird Asian vegetables."

Mad kicked him in the ankle.

"Now, now Ben," interrupted the man in the Caribbean-blue polo. "That's not quite fair."

"Sure it is. Last book we read was a real book. A real good book. This one is a damn romance novel!"

Maggie yawned. "Oh, shut up, Ben. We read all kinds of books. Last time we read one you recommended. Now that we have an author actually living on the island, this one was a good one to choose." She turned to their guest: "I thought your book was okay. Had me laughing out loud in parts." She then turned back to the man in the faded t-shirt, and said, her voice ripe with sarcasm, "And our last book was one of those military sci-fi wonders." She snorted.

He rushed in to agree with her, not appearing to pick up on her tone, "Yes, it was a wonder! Good way to put it, Maggie!" He seemed happy to have someone support him. He turned to Kat, "And you made us read a damn love story. A stinkin' romance book." Then he turned to Miranda. "With a name like Miranda Wright, you think you'd write crime novels."

Miranda would have been more taken aback but she had already sensed that the men here represented a captive audience. And there was that joke about her name. It never took long for that to come up. "I'm so sorry you didn't like it."

Mad jumped to Miranda's defense "Yes, I'm still wondering *why* we read that sci-fi crap. It was hardly literature. Now this story," she shook her signed book, "this was fabulous! This was on the bestseller list. It's movie material!"

"David Drake is the best damn author. Action. Sci-fi. Military might. Now *those* are good stories. It's not… *re-la-tion-ships.*"

Then the Caribbean blue polo-man, who had been mostly quiet up to now, spoke up. "Actually, Ben, all books are about relationships. Even the one you had us read. I agree with you that David Drake tells a good tale. But you know, Ben, if you think about it, his characters are driven by relationships too.

135

Who they loved, who they lost, who betrayed them, where their loyalties lie. It's all about relationships and how well they understand themselves. In that way, I don't see Miranda's book as being all that different. Here, her protagonist is driven by a lack of self-awareness and a desperate need for affirmation and love. You can see how her demons lead her to concoct that crazy scheme to get back at this man, who is so obviously worthless. But you know, in the end, water seeks its own level and it's just two rather shallow desperadoes ending up together since they are a lonely two-of-a-kind. It's like the road less taken, only this is a sadly hilarious story of what happens when you never, even once, think of taking the high road."

Miranda felt like she'd been stabbed in the heart. Was that what her book was about? For her, it had been better than therapy. All of a sudden, she felt revealed and vulnerable in a way that was strange and frightening to her. Did every one of those people who had waited hours in line to have her sign their book see her as a shallow desperado unworthy of the love of a decent person? Haunted by demons? Had she just been a freak show? She could feel her cheeks getting hotter with every passing moment.

"Oh, is that what it was about? I thought it was just a lighthearted beach comedy!" Cynthia said as she finished her fourth glass of wine. "Fluff!"

"Actually, it's quite a treatise, quite a statement on the human condition, all wrapped up in the guise of humor. It's brilliant," the man in The Book Shelf shirt said.

Miranda stared at him. He had called the other man, that Sci-Fi fan, Ben. If he wasn't Ben, then who was he?

By nine-thirty Miranda made her escape. She drove home thinking that was one of the most bizarre evenings she had ever experienced. She was absolutely mortified that people might think her book was the autobiographical depiction of a loveless and unworthy desperado, or, on the contrary, classify her as a brilliant analyst of the human psyche, ruthlessly dissecting and passing judgement on woman's baser qualities. She really just wanted to get back to being Miranda, author of a fun, lighthearted beach novel.

Chapter 15

Burke was up in Nags Head doing some errands. Kat was holding down the bookshop. There was so little traffic in November that it would be easy for her to manage, single-handed though she was. After the book club, Kat had gone on and on about how fun it was to sit around with all the books and have wine and the snacks. She now wanted Burke to hold a whole series of special events, even though the attendees would just be their friends. She also insisted that Burke needed to add a café to the bookstore. That way, people could sit around and read and decide about their book purchases while they drank a coffee.

He had objected. "But then they'll just read the book while they drink their latte and they won't buy the book." He had to admit it though, he was mulling over her idea.

"Nah, Burke. The people who are going to read your books without paying for them will do that anyway. They already do that. They already treat you like a library. Now at least they'll be paying for coffee and muffins while they freeload off your literature."

So, he had gone with her suggestion. Quickly he learned that just buying a Keurig for the shop wasn't going to cut it, but he couldn't invest in a whole Starbucks-like set up; that was way beyond the capacity of his little bookstore. Surprisingly, it was his son away at college who had advised him via email on fancy coffeemakers. Burke selected a Jura model that came highly recommended. His son even researched and found a reconditioned one that Burke could pick up for just shy of a thousand. While Burke bemoaned the fact that he would never, ever make that investment back, he was surprised at how quickly word spread that The Book Shelf was now The Book Shelf Café. It did bring in traffic. And they did buy coffee—lattes, cappuccinos, espressos, macchiatos. He didn't even know what some of those were, but happily all he had to do was press a button. People were as amazed by the machine as they were by their fancy new coffees, but they happily handed over their five-fifty for a cup. Then he had mugs made with The Book Shelf Café logo on them. Surprisingly, people bought those too. Then he ordered some t-shirts.

It all was a great innovation, but it added to his long and growing to-do list. It also had the surprising outcome of making him want to try everyone else's coffee wherever he went, sizing up the competition and checking out what real coffee shops offered and how they did their pricing structure. Today he was at a funky little Nag's Head coffee shack called New Morning View. He had just ordered a skinny cappuccino with two pumps of caramel syrup, half-caff. He felt silly ordering it, but Kat insisted he try the different variations of everything, so he knew the lingo the summer customers would use and understand what they meant when they ordered. The clerk handed him his beverage with a bright smile, saying, "You have a great day now!"

"Thank you." He nodded and picked up his coffee. As he turned around, he saw the author from the book club walk in. "Well, well, imagine running into you here! Miranda, right?"

"Yes, Miranda Wright. That's me."

"Oh, I'm sorry. I meant 'Miranda, correct?' I got your first name right? Uh, correctly? Uh, I mean correct." Burke stumbled over his words and felt rather foolish, thinking he wasn't making much of a good impression.

"Oh! Yes, so sorry. I should have, uh, caught on."

He thought that at least she was making light of the situation.

"It's not like that mistake doesn't happen all the time. You're right, I'm Miranda Wright. It's kind of an inconvenient last name at times."

"Miranda Wright. I think it sounds nice."

"You're sweet. You own The Book Shelf—that darling little bookstore in

Buxton?"

"Absolutely, that's me."

"You know, I don't think I ever caught your name. I only found out that you aren't Ben."

He laughed. "Nope. I'm not Ben. Far from it. I'm Burke Mitchell."

"I've met other Mitchells."

"You've met quite a few—at the book club. There's only about four families on the islands. We're almost all Mitchells, Guions, Midgetts, or Tanners. About every third person you run into will be a Mitchell. Hey, are you, uh, getting coffee? I'd be happy to treat you to a cup, as a thank you for being so willing to come to the book club."

"Oh, that's so nice of you."

He noticed that she looked unsure. "It would be my pleasure. After all, I really appreciate you supporting my little business. It's hard to keep everything going, particularly in winter, so while you doing a tiny book club like ours is a small thing to you, it's a pretty big deal to us here on the island."

"No, it was my pleasure." She smiled at him and looked more relaxed. "Sure, why not. That's what I came in for: a cup of coffee." She ordered a skinny cappuccino with two pumps of sugar-free caramel. Half-caff. He couldn't help but smile.

They took a little table together. As they sipped their coffee, she said, "I'm so glad I was invited to the book club. It was very kind of you all to read my book. Really, I should be buying you a coffee."

"It was a pleasure. But I'll take a raincheck on that coffee. Now don't be surprised if I call in your I-O-U." He was happy at the warm smile she returned. She looked like she actually blushed a little bit. She looked cute when she blushed.

"Thanks. You know, I feel a little shy confessing this but yours was actually my first book club... ever. You know, it's not the kind of book that Oprah typically chooses or that book clubs usually focus on."

"You mean it's, uh, lighter material?"

"Well, that's a nice way to put it. Yes, it's 'light', your generous comments about the depth of its analysis of the human psyche notwithstanding. I, myself, have referred to it as *fluff*."

"Oh, so Cynthia wasn't the first?"

"No, I actually did beat her to the punch. I'm so glad for the experience, though, because I'm doing another meeting with a book club over in Charlotte, the weekend before Thanksgiving, so at least I have some idea what I'm getting into."

"Oh, that'll be a big city book club."

"You mean it'll be different?"

"You look a little concerned there. Why?"

She took a deep breath. "I guess I just wonder what's gonna happen. I suppose I shouldn't be too thin-skinned about it. All books get criticism of one kind or another."

"Oh, I expect it will be quite different. Good ole Ben won't be there, so if they don't like what you wrote and would rather be reading shoot 'em up novels set in space, then they will still probably fawn all over you and tell you how great you are anyway."

She laughed out loud and the few other people in the tiny coffee shop looked over at them. "They certainly don't do that here, which is perfect. I haven't actually drunk the whole celebrity Kool-Aid, so I'm not attuned to the fawning attention."

Burke chuckled. "I don't know about Kat and Mad; I think you have a couple of fan girls in them."

"Oh my God, they were so sweet." There was real warmth in her voice.

"Hey, it was a serious highlight for them. That was a big night with a famous mainland author coming to visit. Why are you here over the winter anyway?"

"Oh, ostensibly I'm here to write. I bought a place, a summer place, but I'm staying on, hoping the seclusion will spur me to write the next great novel. Or at least my agent is hoping that."

"What place?"

"Hayward House."

"Oh, I know that house. I love that house! I helped renovate that place decades ago." Burke could remember well working with Pete, the owner, a slew of weekends on the place with about a half dozen other friends. Those were happier days.

"Yeah, I heard the guy two owners ago had quite a few friends pitch in to make the place a home. Thank you for all your contributions. I probably owe you coffee *and* lunch for that!"

"I'll take you up on that. You know, I'd love to see it sometime. I'm really curious how the whole thing turned out and what the next owners did with it."

"Oh, not much. It was a private summer house to them. I actually had quite a few repairs to do when I got a hold of it. I'm still working on some, but I love the house. Makes me lose all interest in heading back to my condo."

"And where's your mainland house?"

"Charlotte. Well, I have a condo now in Lexington, Kentucky, but that's more of an investment place. My daughter's living there."

"Charlotte's a long ways away."

"Yeah, about seven hours. I'm not looking forward to the trip."

"So, then you'll be coming back for Thanksgiving? You should join us rather than be alone in that big house of yours. We have a whole bunch of us getting together for the holiday. My young son will be coming home from college. It'll be fun."

"Oh, wow. That sounds… great. I'm so… touched that you would even think to include me."

"Oh, we islanders might be very outspoken, some a little harsh even, but we're very welcoming just the same."

"I'll be staying at the condo and visiting dear friends for the holiday. My old college roomie. Her sister-in-law is from France. Believe me, I try to never miss Claudine's cooking. Then Thanksgiving weekend I'll fly for a quick trip out to Lexington and visit my daughter. So, thank you for your kind invitation, but I'm afraid I'm not going to be around."

"Well, I'm sorry you can't join us. That would have been nice. But that sounds great. Really." He could tell his voice didn't sound like he thought it was great. She was looking at him curiously. "You know, we have another tradition where everyone will get together—and I know they'd enjoy seeing you again. It's the winter solstice bonfire on the beach. It's really special. Probably not quite French food, but we ring in the longest night of the year in our own special way. If you'll be around then, you should join us. You'll have met mostly everyone who comes already, at least to our fire. But it's pretty; you can see bonfires burning and twinkling all up and down the beach."

"That sounds magical!"

"It *is* magical." Burke felt his pulse quicken a bit as he caught an image in his mind of spending the solstice with her, next to a bonfire, late into the night. He could feel himself smiling.

"Gosh, I would love to. Actually, I'm going skiing with my daughter and her boyfriend and I think my, um… my…" She struggled to find the words, as though she couldn't figure out exactly how to put it.

"Your sister? Your mother? Your astrologer? Your boyfriend?" He made the suggestions in rapid succession.

"My astrologer? What? Silly. My, uh, friend, man-friend."

"Your *man*-friend."

"Yeah. Umm, it's complicated." She looked oddly uncomfortable, like she wanted to change the topic. "We're all going skiing."

"Oh, where?" he said, not actually that interested. The nice images in his mind had changed from warm romantic bonfire to cold mid-winter rain.

"I think Aspen. I like Aspen. Yeah, probably Aspen. My daughter adores Aspen."

"I've never been. I'm not a skier." He shrugged as he felt the distance between them grow. "Well, if it's so special to your daughter, it must make for a good trip."

"We used to go there as a family. It's a cute little town and the slopes are great. You take a gondola for about fifteen minutes and at the top of the mountain is this great lodge at eleven thousand feet where they have live music and a café. Not much oxygen, but beautiful scenery. It's really incredible. A ring of mountaintops all around."

"Nice trip." He nodded and sipped his coffee. "So, you were married? Are you widowed or divorced?"

"Divorced. Newly. Just official last winter. I'm still getting used to it all. And the book was not autobiographical."

He really admired her sense of humor. "But you have a man-friend already." He gave her a wry smile.

"I'm getting used to that, too." She smiled back. "E, that's my daughter, loves Aspen and my ex is taking her and her boyfriend to the Caribbean for the week after Christmas, so I'll take the kids to Aspen before the holiday."

"Ooooh, I don't hear any competition there, do I?" He laughed gently.

"What?"

He was caught off guard by her surprise. "The Colorado trip. Uh, I'm sorry. It just sounded like you might be trying to compete with your ex. He's doing the Caribbean thing and you're trying to stay in the game with the ski trip to Aspen."

Miranda stared at Burke but then broke into a wide and confident smile. "I'm not competing... truth be told, it's just that I'm trying to connect with my daughter, woman to woman, you know."

"Oh, well, that's wonderful then. Your daughter is a very lucky girl. Um, mind if I ask? How does it work connecting with your daughter with all the men folk along?"

"What do you mean?"

"Well, it's just that when I want to connect with my son, man to man, we do something that is, you know, just the two of us."

She laughed lightly, but there was a tightness about it. "Emma always insists that Emile comes along. They're like two peas in a pod. Inseparable.

She insisted that he go on the Caribbean trip with her, and once her father acquiesced, well, of course he has to come to Aspen."

Burke nodded, his mind spinning with the complexity of women's relationships.

"You look pensive. Penny for your thoughts?"

"You sure?"

She nodded.

"Okay. Here goes. It is possible that she is, I don't know, playing you off each other? I'm a single father, so no one for my boy to go to other than me. It just sounds like she might be, uh, I don't know, confused?"

Miranda shook her head.

"No? Or maybe just a little bit self-absorbed?" It was the only explanation that made sense to him and he couldn't believe it wasn't obvious to her. As he looked at her face he registered her shock. She probably hadn't yet realized just what she was being drawn into. He decided to back off, having inadvertently looked into his imaginary crystal ball and gone too far. "Really? Oh, okay. Good to know. I guess you love to ski? Probably great at it." He looked at her very intently. Her brown eyes were really pretty.

"Actually, I like to cross-country ski. I'm a terrible down-hiller. I can't turn left."

"Oh. Can't turn left? I don't ski, so I don't really know what you mean."

"It's my knee. I think it's my knee. I can bend and turn right but then eventually you have to bend and turn left or else…"

"Or else what?"

"Or else you go off into the trees, which I've done a lot. Or—and this is much worse—you get turned back straight, which is about all I can do, and then you go screaming down the mountain."

"Screaming down the mountain?" With his hands he indicated going very fast. "Or screaming as you go down the mountain?" He raised and flailed his hands on the second 'screaming'.

She chuckled. "In my case, both. Screaming in every definition of the word. The wipeouts are spectacular. Truly spectacular. Let me just say I have a real thing for not injuring myself at this point in my life."

"Why did you agree to go on those trips?"

Miranda shrugged. "E and her dad love to ski. I wanted to make them happy. They would always hit the slopes and I would go to the cross-country track and buzz around there for a while. Then I'd go shopping and we'd all meet up back at the condo at some point."

"Forgive me for saying this, but that doesn't sound like a family vacation."

"Sure it was. They had a great time together on the slopes." Miranda's face fell.

He stared at her for a moment and then took a sip of his coffee. Making sure that his voice was very gentle, he asked, "So, Miranda, you go skiing, why? You can't ski. It sounds like it terrifies you. And yet this is your idea of a Christmas vacation with your adult children? Are you sure this is what *you* want to do?"

She opened her mouth and then she closed it. Then she took a sip of her coffee. She took a deep breath and looked him straight in the eye and smiled. "I'm taking them skiing. It'll be a great holiday."

It was like a door had just slammed between them. The warmth that had been building was doused, much like his little daydream of the bonfire being rained out. With that remarkably composed smile, she had just told him to butt out of her life and he supposed he deserved it. He hadn't meant to analyze her situation like that, even though he was pretty sure he was right. In fact, he was absolutely sure he was right.

He lifted his cup and realized that it was empty. Yup, empty.

"I want to thank you for the coffee and the conversation, Burke. Maybe I'll see you around."

She gave him a half-smile, walked over to the trash can and threw away her cup. He remained seated, watching her as she walked away, sorting through this sad feeling that was growing in him. When she got to the door, she stopped and turned around and looked at him. He smiled at her and waved. She looked confused, but gave him a small smile and a little wave. Then she turned and disappeared through the door.

Chapter 16

Wheel in hand and unable to concentrate on her audiobook, she turned the sound off. She had long passed Raleigh and saw Williamston coming up on the navigation system as she drove down highway sixty-four. "At what age do mothers and their daughters actually become friends?" She wondered what had to happen to bring about that magical turning point? How could you coax that relationship into being? She'd certainly tried, but it didn't seem to be working very well. She wasn't sure about several things. One, what else she could do for her daughter? Two, how she could help her daughter to be happy? And three, how could she finally win the same love and affection the girl lavished on her father? Somewhere deep inside she felt that number one might magically unveil number two, which would grant her number three.

Over the holiday, she'd visited with Caroline, making a grand appearance at the book club the weekend before Thanksgiving, just like she'd promised Claudine. Those poor women—they'd been expecting someone interesting. Someone special. Someone worthy of writing a best seller. Someone they could tell their families about round the holiday table, relishing in the glow of a brush with fame. What they actually got was someone very much like themselves who had just found that therapy sucked, and fantasy was a much more pleasant place to hang out. And in the end, in fact, pretty damn rewarding. Reality though, could still bite.

Caroline and her extended family welcomed Andy like they always had and it was a lovely holiday. Then she'd taken a quick flight over to Lexington to visit with Emma for Saturday night and Sunday. She endured a dinner with Emma and Emile, then got Emma all to herself on the last day of her visit. Andy had been hungry for Emma. She'd missed her and missed taking care of her. Four years ago, when Emma had gone away to college, Andy had still seen her nearly every weekend. While Emma lived in the dorm, Andy would stop by and take her to lunch. After she moved into an apartment, Andy would swing by on Saturday or Sunday and load up Emma's fridge with meals for the week. While Emma could get top grades, she really couldn't cook at all. That was okay. Miranda relished pulling together creative meals that would delight her daughter and also give her the opportunity to enjoy a nice dinner in with a friend, should she choose to invite someone over. Miranda always tried to support Emma in making friends. School was really competitive. It was hard for top students, particularly when that student was a girl, to find real friends. While Andy was there, she would pick up Emma's laundry. It gave an empty-nester something to do during the week, and Emma had so many clothes that sending off a week's supply with her mother wasn't likely to result in a wardrobe emergency. While they were together, it was like old times. Miranda would read her papers, fix her grammar errors, restructure her arguments. There were some rules of the English language and essay composition that she was sure her daughter would never learn. Well, Gregg had never excelled at those tedious details either. It was like his bedside manner—it just wasn't his thing. Emma was so like her father!

She missed Emma needing her. She had missed her daughter's entire last year of college, and now Emma was in medical school and Miranda didn't live across town. She lived two states away. Her little girl was all grown up. Having Sunday alone together, well, that was just precious. She wanted to make it special. So, she took Emma out for a nice lunch. She thought it would be pleasant to engage in girl talk and there was some girl talk she thought they needed to have. She tried to tell her about Austin, which was difficult since she was still figuring out just what she wanted with him. But Emma needed to know, particularly since Miranda and Austin had just decided to spend the next holiday together, on the ski trip with E and Emile. Miranda tried to bring it up. Three times she tried, but somehow the conversation always ended up back at Emma and Emile, or worse yet, on Gregg and Morning Glory. Miranda couldn't seem to recover her confidence after that one. She found she was afraid of confessing to her daughter that she was dating. Or was it *who* she was dating?

"Confessing?" Her voice rang through the silent car. "Confessing? I should be bragging! He's a hot, younger guy." She tried to sound smug, but even in the privacy of her Lexus she could hear the lack of bravado in her voice. "Yeah, that would have been confessing," she said with a heavy sigh. Confessing that she'd moved on. Finally. Getting her own life together at last. Long after Gregg had moved on with his. But it wasn't like Emma to greet this news with cheers and enthusiasm. E seemed to filter everything through "What would Daddy do?" Well, Andy had already had a lifetime of that. That wasn't where she was at. Wasn't where she was willing to go. Indeed, when Miranda managed to squeak out a timid, "E, I'm dating someone", Emma just rolled her eyes with a dismissive, "'Bout time" and then moved the conversation on to something more interesting to her.

After her failed attempt at girl bonding over breakfast, she took Emma for something that always worked: retail therapy. While Miranda had to be judicious about what she bought, given that she was flying back to Charlotte before her long drive back to the beach house, she was happy to do some real shopping while she was in a real city. For Emma, they hit Costco to pick up household stuff and Whole Foods for the kinds of things that graduate students just couldn't afford. She now had lots of treats to get her through the rest of her classes and exams. Some excellent organic chocolates. A wheel of brie and a big wedge of Gouda and a block of the best aged parmesan Miranda had tried in quite a while. A freezer full of ready-made meals. Nothing as good as what she would have made Emma, but in a pinch, they would do. Andy was happy to get some decent blonde-roast, whole-bean decaf coffee for herself, something that was in not existence on the Outer Banks. Then they hit their favorite clothing stores. Emma was even willing to make a quick stop into J. Jill and Chicos after they had explored some of her own personal favorites. Miranda bought two new shirts and a pair of pants, while Emma ended up with two huge shopping bags full of shoes and outfits. In the end, Miranda also slipped her daughter a Starbucks gift card that she'd put a cool hundred dollars on. All in all, it was a good day. A real mother-daughter bonding day.

Reluctantly she drove Emma back to the airy new condo Miranda now owned. It was painful to let her go, but she had to turn in the rental car before her flight back to Charlotte. Emma picked up her bags from the back seat.

"Thanks, Mom. This was fun." Then she looked at her phone. "Oh my God! Look at the time! I can't believe I wasted the whole day. I have to go study. Have a good trip home. Love you. If you find that cute shirt in the mango color, please ship it to me. Bye!" Emma blew her mom a kiss, which was muffed by the big shopping bag in her arm.

So now Andy was driving back to her own life. A life where she wasn't a mother anymore. Where she was a writer. Where she lived in a big, empty beach house. Where her weekend with her daughter had just made her feel even more lonely than she had been feeling before the trip began.

Chapter 17

Austin heard his cell phone ring. Now he just had to find the stupid thing. The semester was over. He didn't have to be back in Wilmington for a whole month. He knocked a stack of sweaters off his bed onto the floor and there it was. He looked at the screen. It was his dad.

"Yo, Daddy-O."

"Hey Junior! Grandpa and I are looking forward to having you home. When do you arrive?"

"On the twenty-third. Remember, I told you. I'm going up to New Hampshire for a few days."

"Oh, yeah. Must have conveniently slipped my mind."

"Dad, you're like forty-five years old. Don't tell me you're turning into Grandpa already. He's seventy-five and can't remember shit."

"Language, Junior."

"Sorry, sir. But yeah, I'll be home for Christmas and staying past the first week of the New Year. I'll be there for the New Year's Eve bonfires. Your boy's comin' home, don't worry!"

"I guess it's just that Grandpa and I really enjoyed seeing you over the Thanksgiving holiday. Having three generations together was a great thing. Who knows how many more opportunities we'll have to do that?"

"Oh my God, Dad. Grandpa isn't dying anytime soon. Dude's one tough old bird!"

"What? I don't think your grandfather's *dying*! I meant that you'll fall in love with that girlfriend of yours. I'm afraid you'll move away, become a mainlander and I'll never see you again! Except in summer when you and the wife and kids want to vacation at the beach and need a free place to stay."

Austin was quiet for a few moments, caught off guard by the joke. He and Andy had ended it when he came back to school. But then she'd helped him with his paper. He'd pulled an A in the class, much to his professor's surprise. It was great to feel so confident in his own writing ability now. Better yet, their emails about schoolwork had gradually turned into long emails which then turned into phone calls. The day after Thanksgiving she'd asked him if he might like to go skiing with her and a couple of friends; he couldn't remember their names, but he'd meet them soon enough.

"Dad, I like her a lot but I'm never leaving the island."

"Oh, you say that now. But maybe you'll head up north-east and decide you love it there. Want to live there with her."

"She doesn't live there, Dad. We're just going cross-country skiing with some friends."

"What's up with skiing? It seems like everybody loves skiing all of a sudden. I've never known anyone to go off skiing and now it seems like I'm surrounded by people who are crazy about skiing."

"I didn't say I was crazy about skiing."

"Of course, you're not! You've never been."

"I know, Dad, that's kinda why I want to go. Check it out. See what it's like."

"It's expensive. Money doesn't grow on trees."

Austin thought he understood what this was about now. "My friends have a place, Dad. They told me the rent is free and rental skis are cheap. Plus, they have a bunch of old skis around and if any fit me, I won't even have to rent any at all. It's not like down-hilling it. Who knows when I'll have the chance again?"

"And you'll get to be with your girlfriend the whole time."

"Well, yeah. That's kind of the point."

"So, when do I get to meet her?"

Austin wondered what that would be like.

"Why are you so quiet? What's wrong?"

"Nothing's wrong. I was just thinking about you meeting her. I think you'd like her, but I'm not sure where this is going. She's a little bit older than I am."

"Well, that doesn't surprise me. You always were a little old man in a young man's body. You've been that way since…" His dad's voice trailed off.

"Yeah, I know. I miss them, too. All of them. All the time."

"The accident kind of took away your childhood."

Austin wondered if his dad was going to cry. He sounded a bit shaky. "Hey, you gave me a great childhood. You've always been my best friend."

"Yeah, we've been best buddies." He didn't say anything for a while. "But now you've got a new buddy."

Austin could tell his dad was trying to lighten the mood. "Don't be jealous. I'll introduce you when the time is right. I have to figure out what this is, where it's going, if anyplace. It's a little confusing."

"Well, I'd like to meet her sometime."

"I don't know, Dad, you might try to steal her from me," Austin joked.

"Then she's pretty special if I'd like her that much!" His dad laughed. "You know, on that topic, I'd like to ask you a little question. I have kind of… a little situation."

Austin felt his heart skip a beat with sudden concern at the word 'situation'. He wondered about his dad's health.

"I, uh, met somebody."

"Met somebody? That's great, Dad! Where? How?"

"Social event. She's really, really, interesting. Ran into her a couple of times, just out and about. I want to ask her out."

"Wait, is she an islander or a mainlander?"

"She's uh, an islander. Yeah, she's an islander. Lives here year-round."

"New islander?"

"She's been here a while. I just never met her before."

"That's great, Dad. So, ask her out. What's the problem?"

"I did ask her out. She's not exactly available."

"What? She's married?"

"No, no, no. She's not married, but she's got a boyfriend. Some type of boyfriend."

"You haven't met him?"

"No, he's a mainlander."

"Ooooooh. He's a mainlande*r*. He's not around."

"Nope."

"But you are."

"Yup."

"And you like her, huh?"

"Really like her. Really, really, really like her. I feel this incredible connection with her. I just *get* her."

"So, ask her out."

"She'll say no. And I don't know what to do. I really want to get to know her better. So… I thought I'd ask…"

Austin sighed. He suddenly realized that a man becomes an adult in stages. First there's the time in your late teens when you sneak out of the house and meet your girl on the beach. You hang out by the campfire and lose your virginity. And you think you're an adult. Then comes the time you move out of the house. For Austin, that time came when he first went to college. For the first time no one was there, looking out for him. It was a little strange, but it was more independence than he'd yet known. He felt like an adult. And now, here was his dad asking him for dating advice. He had suddenly crossed into a new stage of being an adult. This was uncharted territory.

"Okay, Dad, I'll tell you what you do. She's off limits. You need to respect that. But you can become her best friend. Then, when it falls to pieces with the mainlander, you'll be there, in the wings, very well positioned to knock that dude off his pedestal. Now you might go through this awkward broken heart phase, but just wade through all that. It'll pass. And then she'll be ripe for the picking and all yours."

"All mine…"

"Yeah, but don't move in on her until either she's free or she moves on you first. Even then, move slow. If you really like her, like you say, you need to reel her in."

"You make her sound like a big fish. "

"Yeah, except you'll enjoy it a lot more than landing a marlin. The rewards are much better."

"She's not a big fish, Austin. She's a really nice woman. An interesting woman. I don't think she's just some summer fling."

Those words stung Austin a bit. A summer fling wasn't synonymous with 'doesn't have any meaning'. It didn't mean it was a relationship you necessarily threw away. Or didn't cherish. "No, of course not. I hear ya, Dad. Does she have kids?" Austin wondered what it would be like to bring that kind of complexity into his relationship with his dad. It had always been just the two of them and he really couldn't remember it any other way. Sure, he'd met some of the women his dad had dated, but it had always been clear to Austin that none of those relationships held any hope of becoming anything or of jeopardizing what the two of them had. He had never thought a woman would come between them. Then he had a very uncomfortable thought. Andy had a kid. What if it did turn out to be something real between him and her? What if they brought her middle schooler into this relationship? And then his dad? Then her ex would have to fit in somewhere, wouldn't he? It made his head spin to think about it all. He was sure he was nowhere near ready to be that much of an adult.

"Yeah, but grown and flown. No worries there."

"What?" His mind was still back in that nightmare of family entanglements.

"Her kid. Grown and flown. Older than you."

"Okay, then." Austin felt a sense of relief. "You said she's special."

"Yeah."

"Well then, that's why you want to become her best friend first. Does she like books?"

"She loves them. I mean, like she's devoted her life to books."

"Okay then, there's your first entrée. Does she like birds?"

"I dunno."

"Take her birding. Every islander needs to know about the birds. I guarantee you, it will be a hit. I've had good experiences with that. I highly recommend it."

"Good idea. We could pick a nice day. Go out on the boat. Real islanders love the birds."

"Great idea, Dad."

"I'll let you know how it goes."

"No details, Dad. No details. I don't think I'm ready for that."

"Alright, I'll spare you. Have a good time on your ski trip, son. I'll see you soon. We miss you."

Chapter 18

Miranda put down her book. "Geez. This is not an advice book. It's magical realism. People actually do this?" She looked at the back cover, as a woman's face smiled back at her through the artificial glow of soft filter enhancement. "There is no way that woman is old enough to have a grown daughter, gray strands notwithstanding." She made a mental note to remember that if her face were ever to be pictured on the back of a book, she needed to request that particular trick. She flipped it over. *How to Be Best Friends with your Daughter*. That's what she wanted, wasn't it? For Emma to say, "Hi Mom! How are you?" and to mean it. To care. To care what her mother thought, like she cared what her father thought. She looked at the author's picture again.

"Well, you got this book published and lord knows, that's not an easy process. You must know what you're talking about. Ph.D. in what?"

She went back to the chapter she'd been reading, her brows raising with each successive paragraph. A few minutes later, her eyes widening, she kept reading but held the book away from her, as though it might bite. The phone rang.

"Hi, it's Miranda."

"Hi, Andy, it's Caroline." She sounded surprised. "So, you're not screening your calls? The guys from the book party finally getting the message?"

"Oh no, nothing so wonderful as that. They call. Frequently. I answered the phone purely by accident—or by prescience. I must have known it was you."

"Uhhhh, I'll take 'by accident' for three-hundred. I mean, you really suck at telling the future."

"No shit, or I'd never have married Gregg."

"But then you wouldn't have Emma!"

Andy looked down at the book on the counter. "I ordered this, um, book. To help me with my relationship with her. It's about how to be your daughter's best friend."

"So, nice lunches. Shopping therapy. Getting your hair and nails done together. Girl talk. Taking trips together. And what else?"

"Multiple checks there. And I'm taking her on a holiday trip right before Christmas. Wait a minute!" Andy quickly flipped back four chapters. "Caroline, everything you just said is on a checklist in chapter three. You don't even have a daughter."

"Naw, but I've seen a lot of sappy movies. *Postcards from the Edge*… you know, that Carrie Fisher story. Oh, wait a minute, that's probably not the role model you want."

Andy flipped further in the book. "Oh, this book is total trash. Towards the end it has advice for how to handle the bumps in your relationship when one or the both of you face jail time, and how to avoid the blame game." Andy threw the book down. It slid across the counter and tipped over the edge, falling to the floor. "Maybe I'm not destined to be her best friend."

"Maybe that's not what mothers do," Caroline said. "My mom surely didn't. It was more like… well, nagging, if I'm being honest. She expected a lot of me and I wanted to live up to her expectations. Not sure I did, in fact, on second thought I'm absolutely sure I didn't, but she loves me anyway."

Did I have high expectations for Emma? That was kind of Gregg's role. My role was to take care of my daughter. I loved Emma. I just wanted to make things okay for her. I just wanted to make her happy. Isn't that the road to having a great relationship with her? She mused on that as she gazed out the window.

Chapter 19

To break her boredom, Andy found herself up in Nag's Head on a December afternoon. As she was walking down the sidewalk from The Kitchen Store to her next destination, her phone rang. "Miranda Wright."

"Hi Andy. So funny, you answering as Miranda Wright."

"Oh, hi, Caroline! Yeah, I'm sorta becoming my alter ego here, living at the beach. No matter how I introduce myself, everyone calls me Miranda. Or Ms. Wright."

"Oh well, it's how they know you, from the book and all. Just go with it. And remind yourself that you're not always in trouble when you hear that name. What're you doing?"

"Me? Out shopping. I'm at that Outlet Mall we went to when you were here. I'm walking down to the Nautica store and looking forward to getting out of the cold!" She thought it might be nice to get a shirt or two for Austin for Christmas. She was taking him skiing, she had told him as a Christmas present. Really, the present was to herself: days away with Austin and not having to be solely hostage to Emma and Emile and their endless mirth at her lack of prowess at the downhill slopes. At least she had changed their plans and they were going up to Jackson, New Hampshire. Cross-country skiing. Something she could do. Something she enjoyed. She had a new life now. She wasn't going to sit it out on the sidelines any longer. E had whined fiercely—she wanted to go to Aspen. Aspen was cool. Everybody who was anybody would be in Aspen.

She walked into the Nautica store and started browsing the men's shirts, still chatting to Caroline. She wandered over to the gloves and hats and found a set in deepest cranberry that she thought would look lovely on Austin. She put them in her basket. Then she turned around and accidentally bumped into another customer.

"Oh, excuse me. I'm so sorry…" she started and then she froze. Suddenly she was facing Burke.

"Hi." He smiled at her, complete surprise on his face, but a warm expression, nonetheless.

"Oh, hi. Oh, sorry, Caroline. I didn't mean you. I meant someone else. I just bumped into a friend here." She held up her index finger to Burke, gesturing to give her a minute. He waited patiently. "Sure, I promise when I'm in Charlotte over the holidays that we'll get together. I'll come and stay for a few days. Yeah, it'll be fun. See you soon. Love you, too." She hung up her phone and slipped it back into her purse. He was still standing there, just looking at her and smiling. "Well, hi again. Funny, running into you. I hope you had a good Thanksgiving."

"It was great. The whole family was home. It was really nice. And you had your big city book club? How did it go?"

"It was fun. I remember you promised that they would be nice to me."

"And were they?"

"Oh, yes, they were wonderful. Honestly, I think it was more about wine and local gossip than anything, but several said they got a good laugh from the book. That's all it ever was for anyway. Not great literature."

"Ah, you sell yourself a bit short, Miranda. But yes, your book is very funny. I've enjoyed it each time I read it."

She was stunned. "You've read it… more than once?"

"Oh sure. I've read it three times."

"Burke, I'm glad to hear that but, but really, it's not *that* interesting."

"Oh, I really like your writing. You have a nice turn of phrase. And each time I read it I found hints in the storyline that I'd missed before. You know, they were always there, but until I knew how the story turned out I didn't catch them. I actually thought I might give it another read to see if I could find more. It's very clever how you did that."

"I don't know what to say."

"Kat, you remember her? She set up the book club meeting? She loves to do that with books. She's convinced that authors hide little easter eggs in their books, if you only know where to look. She pointed some out to me after I'd read it once and that got me started. She really is a big fan of yours. Hey, do you think you'd ever come back and do another meeting with our little group?"

"Um..." She hesitated. "Will Ben be there?" She smiled.

He smiled back. "I'm quite confident that you can hold your own against a raging fan of military sci-fi."

"Well, maybe I could at that. If Mad is there to defend me I'm sure I'd have nothing to fear. Yeah, it would be fun. I'd be happy to. I have a lot of time on my hands so that would probably be good for me."

"That's great! I'll pass the word to Kat. Hey, you know something else you might enjoy, if you have time on your hands, is seeing the island."

"Burke, I live here. I see the island every day. Particularly when I make this huge drive up to here or Manteo. I've seen a lot of sand."

"I'm not talking about sand."

"Water? You mean, like go sailing? In the winter?" She glanced outside through the huge glass windows. "In winter?"

"Actually, I mean go kayaking."

"Kayaking... Burke, that would be freezing."

"Oh, no. You'll be warm in a wet suit. One thing I've got is a ton of wet suits. Talk about peaceful and quiet—and so beautiful. It's great exercise and you won't believe what you'll see." It was obvious that she was hesitating. "We can pack hot cocoa..."

"I don't know, Burke. I'm going to have to think about it." A part of her really wanted to kayak around the island. That sounded so adventurous. And fun. Her life at the beach in winter consisted of a lot of cabin fever and staring at her computer screen. She had to drive up to Nag's Head just to go to the gym or swim laps. She missed the summer when she got a workout by having fun. She noticed the gloves in her basket and suddenly felt strange even thinking about going kayaking with this bookstore owner, given her upcoming vacation with Austin. She could feel her face growing warmer.

"Is this about your man-friend? You know, we could just invite him to come. The kayak only seats two but we could get another boat. And we'll have others joining too. It's not like it'll be just us."

"It's sweet of you to ask. And, to be honest, yes, I was thinking about my man-friend."

"Ask him if he can join us." Burke shrugged nonchalantly as he said it. "Look, Miranda, there aren't that many people here on the island, not in winter. We all need to be friends. We need to hang together. I would advise you to make friends and not worry about someone being jealous that you have people to do stuff with. It can be pretty lonely here if you don't have friends."

"I see your point. You know, you're probably right. I think he would say I should get out and meet people. In fact, he's pushed me to do that."

"Good man."

"Yes, he is a good man. Sure, I'd love to kayak around and see the island with you and your friends. When?"

"How about tomorrow? Mad and Ben and I are already planning on going. I promise I won't let him talk about any book at all. The nice thing about kayaking is you can easily paddle out of earshot. Weather is supposed to be in the high sixties, sunny. Couldn't get a better day. It's supposed to get stormy later on in the week."

"That won't impinge on your schedule?"

"Nah. I'm going anyway, with or without you. I love to kayak. You can ride with Mad if you want, but fair warning: you'll have to do a lot of the paddling."

She laughed. "All right then. Where should I meet you? Where do we put in?"

"There's this little watercraft rentals place up by the water tower…"

"I know exactly the place!"

"Great! It's one of the few rental places with the right bit of shoreline. See you there at ten-thirty?"

"Sounds fantastic."

"I'll have some wetsuits. I know the owners of the place. We can change there."

"Of course, you know the owners! Mad told me everyone knows everyone. Is related to everyone, in one way or another." She chuckled at the memory.

"I suppose that's true. We're pretty inbred here. Well then, I'll see you tomorrow." He smiled at her again and then turned and left the store.

"Okay, I'm going kayaking," she said under her breath. She felt kind of excited to be doing anything at all. And he was right. She needed friends. Austin had told her she needed friends. Several times he had encouraged her to get out and meet people and to start doing things. It would be fun to tell him about seeing more of the island.

* * *

She got to the watercraft rentals at ten-fifteen. No one was there. She sat in her car and re-read a printout of her current manuscript, but it didn't help. She just couldn't get into the story she was creating. She didn't feel any empathy for these characters. She had no idea what to do with them. She chewed on her pencil and got lost in thought.

Suddenly there was a *tap, tap, tap* on the window. Burke was there. She hadn't even noticed him pull in.

"Oh, hi!" she said, surprised at the clear excitement in her voice.

"Hi. Is it just us this morning, or did you get in touch with your man-friend? Is he coming?"

"Oh him? No. He's on the mainland. He can't easily get here. He's really busy right now."

"Okay, then. Just you and me. Mad broke a crown last night and Ben's taken her to the dentist this morning. Have you kayaked before?"

"No, never."

"Right. Then we'll take the two-person kayak. I've got one of those too. And let's get you in a wetsuit. Ben said we could just grab what we needed."

"Oh, is this Ben's place?"

"Yeah, Ben and Mad mostly run this. They were cool about us taking out the boat. I have the keys to the storage shed—the wetsuits are in there."

She followed him over past the Tiki Shack, feeling haunted by the ghost of Austin the whole time, reminding herself that if he were here, he'd be encouraging her to go. Burke led her into the little shed and showed her the row of wetsuits hanging up. He looked at her up and down and then eyed the suits. "I think this one should fit. You'll be amazed at how warm it will keep you. Water's cold. We'll try to not get wet, of course, but just in case. And it's a great day today."

He left her in the shed and she pulled the wet suit on over the snug athletic wear she had worn. When she came out, he was in his wet suit. He was in good shape for a man in his forties. Not beach buff like Austin, but he had nothing to be ashamed about. "Ben and Mad have a lot of wetsuits. Do they use these? Do they come out much?"

"Oh yes, they love to double kayak. Since they aren't here we're taking their kayak, 'cause it's the nicest one."

She almost laughed out loud at the image of Ben and Madeline squeezing into the wetsuits. They would look a lot like penguins. She would have liked it if Mad had come, at least. Ben, she wasn't so sure about.

Burke sloshed out into the water of the sound. The kayak was sitting on a slab of concrete that made a runway of sorts into the water. He started pulling at the edge of the kayak. She followed him. Before it was barely in the water he told her to hop in and he would get them started. "Here, hold onto these. We'll need them," he said as he handed her some paddles. "Why don't you sit up front? If you're not used to paddling, it can feel like hard work to sit in the back."

She had tried to be diligent at maintaining her workout but realized that she was slipping a bit. Even sitting in the front of the boat her arms felt like limp noodles long before she expected them to. When it came to the paddling, Burke did the heavy lifting. While he took her in and out of some beautiful and secluded coves, she was glad he didn't take her anyplace she'd already explored on the catamaran.

They talked about weather and politics. She was grateful that their leanings were in the same direction—it was hard to imagine how tedious this excursion would have been had he been as passionate about his beliefs as she was hers, except in the opposite direction. He told her a lot about the history of the islands. It was interesting. They stopped on a quiet little patch of water and he pulled out a thermos and poured steaming hot cocoa into the cap that served as the cup. He handed it to her. "Sorry, we have only one cup."

"Oh, that's okay. It was a good idea to bring this." She took the proffered cup and sipped it. "Hey, this is good stuff."

"Yeah, it's got Baileys in it. It's really good stuff."

She smiled and took another sip, then passed the cup back to him.

"So, how's the writing coming? When can I put your next book in my shop?"

"Ugh. I'm not sure I want to talk about it. I can't seem to get in the groove. I can't seem to find a good story that I want to write about. I think I hate my characters." There. She'd said it. Somehow, it felt good to confess.

"Have you tried writing about what you know? That's what writers do, isn't it? That's what gives them an authentic voice."

"What do I know about? I know about raising a daughter, by myself, while my husband worked a million-and-one-hours and we never saw him. Then she started lessons and clubs and teams, and she was gone, too. Write about that? About being abandoned by the both of them? Left alone in the empty shell of a totally privileged life? Who wants to read about that? It would just be whining."

"Hey, just because you weren't starving doesn't mean you weren't suffering. It sounds lonely. I understand lonely. I live here. You were living on your own island. Mine is full of birds and yours was invisible to the naked eye, but no less real."

"Damn, just listen to you. You should write the book, Burke. I don't like to think back on it too much. It was… solitary. But I can't write about that. I can just hear my agent snort and say, 'Now, Miranda. I just think that people don't want to read about a lonely, privileged woman. Let's go back to the drawing board. Maybe you could write a novel about human trafficking? Or maybe a future dystopian horror story?'"

Burke laughed. "Is that what people want to read these days?"

"It would seem so. I mean, I get it: I have very first world concerns. But there's no lure for me in being emotionally traumatized by diving into an imaginary world full of kidnapping, murder, rape and torture. I can get all my emotional trauma needs met just by checking the news every day. I got traumatized just by seeing all those nasty bumper stickers last summer."

"I can guarantee you those weren't island people. Those were visitors. We know better than to take sides. We can't help it if someone who's a real jerk comes to the island, but islanders keep their beliefs to themselves."

"No one stands up for what they believe in?"

"Sure. But we believe in the island. And it does no good to piss people off and lose business. We have four or five months to make eighty percent of our yearly income. Jerks come, and jerks go. Their karma will catch up with them, but hopefully *not* while they're on our island."

"Karma, huh?" She turned around in the kayak and looked at him. "You believe in karma? What did I do to deserve such an unhappy marriage?"

"Do you want my honest opinion?"

"Sure? Yeah? Okay? I'll give it a try. Give me your honest opinion."

"Well, from putting together two and two, my guess is that you got unexpectedly pregnant, and you and Gregg did the right thing. After all, he was Mr. Wright. So, you became Mrs. Wright, whether that's who you were or not. When you become someone you aren't, it really messes with your karma."

"Wright is my maiden name. His name is Cochran. I went back to my maiden name when we separated."

"Oh, well then, you're on the right track now, aren't you? You're yourself again."

"But I did the right thing! Having E was totally the right thing."

"I didn't say it wasn't. I'm not judging. I just said that you weren't living your own karma anymore. You asked what you did to deserve such loneliness. You were living for other people and you forgot to live for yourself at the same time."

"That's not true! That is so not true! Where do you get these psychic powers from anyway?"

He laughed at her. "So, how is it different with your man-friend than it was from your husband, if you don't mind me asking?"

She was glad she was facing forward in the kayak since she could feel the blush turning her face bright red. It was the sex. She was sure it was the first fucking awesome sex she'd ever had in her life, but she was not about to say that to Burke. "He listens to me. We help each other. We like to cook together. He respects me."

"But he lives on the mainland."

"Yes, yes, he does."

"Then how come you aren't lonely?"

Now that was a good question. She thought about it. She was lonely, but she also wasn't. She lived in that beach house with far more space than she needed. She was alone a lot of the time. She was suffering with writer's block, and yet she wasn't lonely. It wasn't the desperate isolation of being married to Gregg. "Because I have friends."

"Thank you. I'll count myself among that group."

"Because I have meaningful work. Because I have my art."

"Those are all good things."

"And because... he's healing me. I don't have to please him to prove myself. For the first time, I'm respecting myself."

"Then he's someone you should hang on to. So, you'll have to leave the island."

"Leave the island?" She was surprised to hear alarm in her voice.

"Yeah. It never works between an islander and mainlander. He's on the mainland."

"For now. But that's not the real issue."

"Oh, what is?"

"Uh, well, uh, we have this age difference."

"Older men are nice. They know who they are. They know what they want."

"Yes, I suppose that's true," she said, but she was thinking, *Younger men have their assets, too.* They paddled along for a while "Never mind, I don't want to talk about it."

"Sure, no problem. Can I ask what made it so lonely with your ex?"

"With Gregg? I never saw Gregg. He must have worked fourteen hours every day. Probably more than that. He loved it. He absolutely loved being at the hospital. We got him on Sunday, when he would work out and sleep."

"So, no quality time?"

"I tried. He would come home about seven-thirty or eight or later and want dinner. Of course, our daughter couldn't wait that long—she went to bed at about that time. But she wouldn't eat if I wasn't eating with her, and that's a big part of socializing a child. And I *wanted* to spend time with her, particularly as she had less and less time for me. But Gregg would want us to eat together. So, I would make these lovely dinners for him and I would have a salad, but that would make him mad. He kept expecting me to have some kind of eating disorder and watched me like a hawk. He wanted to see me eat."

"That's weird."

"There's a reason. We had friends: he was another doc at the hospital, she was bulimic. We didn't know until she had a cardiac event. She died. It was incredibly sad. That brought out confessions from more than a few friends of the extremes some of the other moms were going through to keep their figures. So, he was always watching to make sure I had a normal relationship with food and didn't pass anything on to our daughter." She paused, her paddle dragging through the water.

Then Burke whispered quietly, "Hey, look over there. It's a black-bellied plover! They're really shy."

She turned her attention to where he pointed. He handed her the binoculars. "But it's gray and white? Where's the black belly? I thought they were supposed to be this striking contrast?"

"Oh, the pictures you see always show them in their breeding plumage, which is incredibly pretty. But they breed in Upper Canada. They're almost always mottled when they're here."

"No, I saw one. Last summer. I saw one for real, in its black and white coat. It looked just like that, only with a pitch-black face and belly." She handed the binoculars back to him.

"I suppose you must have seen a juvenile in early summer. Well, you are fortunate. Occasionally, very occasionally, a juvenile will miss the migration north. Mature too late to make the trip, or maybe sustain an injury and be unable to fly off with the crowd. These guys only dress up for breeding season."

"Tell me, is everyone here obsessed with birds?"

"Nope. Just most of us. There's not much to do eight months out of the year. If you go around the island, you see a lot of birds. Eventually you want to know what you're seeing. It's just natural."

"I guess so. I mean, I do like them much more than I thought I would. Once you know something about them, they're kind of interesting."

"I'm curious. Back to your story. So, what did you do?"

"About what?"

"About the two dinners."

"Oh! That. Sorry, I'd totally moved on to birds. Yeah, so I made these lovely dinners for the two of us and I'd eat with Gregg."

"But you'd already eaten."

"Yeah, so I'd make dinner twice. I'd eat dinner twice. And I'd starve myself all day because I knew I was going to eat so much food in the evening."

"How'd that work?"

"Didn't. I couldn't hack it, and it made me stressed and hangry all day. I fell into drinking wine with dinner."

"That sounds good."

"Yeah, but a two dinner, two glasses of wine habit every night leads to a fat girl."

"Doesn't look like it to me," he said.

"Well, I've lost about twenty pounds since Gregg and I split. Funny, when I was dying of loneliness inside my marriage, food was a good friend. But when I was really alone, I could hardly eat."

"Humph. It's good to be a little rounded out. Women should be women and not all boney thin. A man likes to have something to hold onto."

"Well, I fit that bill," she said, but it was mostly under her breath. "What was so weird was that Gregg had all these impossible standards that I could never meet. Never hope to live up to. I wasn't thin. I wasn't pretty. I wasn't successful. Until I left. Then, finally, for the first time since I was twenty, I focused on myself. I lost the weight. The book became successful. Once he was out of the picture, I suddenly met a couple of the standards I'd felt so completely overwhelmed by."

"You're selling yourself short. You totally have three out of three there."

She could feel herself blush again.

"I have to say, I find it rather nice when you can compliment a woman and she blushes. There is something so modest about that. So unpretentious."

"You're very sweet," she replied. It was a little stunning the things he was comfortable saying. He just put it out there. It was he who was unpretentious. But it was a little bit like he could read her. She didn't know how she felt about that.

"And how are you now?"

She thought about that for a moment. She thought about Austin. It would never work. There was no hope for anything long term. Surely, he would want to have children someday—if he was moving through his thirties, probably soon. No matter how wonderful she thought he was, she couldn't stand in his way of having a full life. Yet, she felt more whole than she could remember feeling for years. "I'm healing."

"Island's a good place to heal."

"You mentioned once you had a son. Tell me about your son."

"Junior? He's a good kid. Named for me."

"That's probably why you call him 'Junior'."

"It was my brother's idea, he insisted, and well, anyway…" Burke looked uncharacteristically awkward. "Junior is really old for his age. He's off at college. He'll never come back. He hates the island."

"Hates the island? I can't imagine anyone hating Hatteras Island." She could agree that it was quiet, but it was so beautiful. So peaceful. "Is the isolation too much for him? I've heard that a lot of kids move away when they grow up."

"No, I think he's fine with the isolation. He thinks it's dumpy. Thinks we need to come into the twenty-first century. Loves change. Wants to change everything around here. He'll never come back now that he's experienced the wider world. But the island will never change. It shouldn't change. It should be one of those places that you can always come back to and it's always the same. Always here for you." He was quiet for a minute. "Yeah, the mainland has ruined him."

"Maybe he'll find an island girl and settle down? Come back?"

"Nah. He's got a girl. She's a mainlander. I don't think he'd look at an island girl. It never works between an islander and a mainlander. Once the islanders take up with a mainlander, if it gets serious, they leave."

"You've dated mainlanders. Why didn't you ever leave?"

"I'm an islander."

A sudden movement caught her eye. "Oh my gosh, look at that. Isn't that one of those wigeons? But its head's the wrong color. Why is that?" She handed him the binoculars.

Burke took a good look and then handed them back to her. "You're one lucky lady. And you're right, that's a wigeon, but no ordinary one. It's a Eurasian Wigeon. Birders will be on the lookout for years just hoping to see one of those."

Miranda looked through the binoculars again. "Well. I have to say, that's really satisfying."

"Well, I have to say, Miranda, you're an islander."

Chapter 20

Andy pulled on a pair of jeans. She felt fresh from her shower. They had arrived at the inn early in the afternoon. Since the weather looked to turn a bit sour the next day, she had taken Austin out right away to experience skiing for the very first time. He looked so handsome, with snow in his hair, that look of wonder on his face at the stark winter whiteness all around them. He quickly picked up how to cross-country ski and she enjoyed his natural athleticism. They had come in from a wonderful snowy excursion and had jumped into a hot bath to warm up. That had led to a romantic interlude and the need for the shower. They didn't have much time. They had dinner reservations and she really didn't want to be late. She towel-dried her hair and ran a comb through it. She was amazed to think that this was what a relationship was *supposed* to be like. Looking back, she shuddered at the realization of how emotionally abusive Gregg had been to her. How much shame he had instilled in her. At this moment, she felt great.

"We have about twenty minutes," Austin said, coming into the bathroom shirtless.

"Oh my God. You look gorgeous."

He winked and wrapped his arms around her. "The better to seduce you, my dear," he said, kissing her on the neck.

"If only we had the time. But we're meeting E and her friend." Feeling sexy and cared for and empowered was still a pretty novel feeling. She smiled and playfully whacked him on the butt. "I have to get ready." She turned on the hairdryer and he walked into the bedroom in search of a shirt while she dried her hair. She threw some make-up on her face, glad she didn't need to wear much. She looked in the mirror and was grateful for her baby face, her caramel-colored skin. She'd been teased so often when she was younger, but now she really appreciated that she sometimes was mistaken for thirty. Sometimes people even asked if she and her daughter were sisters. Not that that question made her daughter too happy. "Thirty," she said to her reflection. "I'd love to have some of that time back that I wasted on Gregg." She turned her head and saw Austin pulling on that long-sleeved shirt she'd gotten for him. It looked amazing on him. Just the right amount of cling.

She turned back to the mirror and finished her make-up. Austin came into the room. "Seven minutes. Hey, I have a question for you. We're meeting your daughter for dinner? Why didn't she come up to New Hampshire with us?"

"Oh, she's so independent. She would never do that. She would say I embarrass her."

"I have to say I think that's incredible. I'm not sure it's legal, actually. She can find her own way?"

"Of course! She's the most capable person I've ever met. Puts me to shame, to tell you the truth. She's an amazing kid. We should go downstairs. Emile and Emma will be waiting for us."

"Emile?"

"Yes, they go everywhere together."

"Oh, she's with your *friends*! The windsurfer people. Oh! Well, that makes more sense. Is Emma your sister?" he asked, but Andy didn't hear him. She was rooting around trying to find her room key.

"Here it is! Okay, let's head down. And we're late. Because of you."

He pulled her into his arms and kissed her again. "Oh yes, but the pleasure was all mine."

"Actually, I thought we did a very good job of sharing it this time." She giggled.

He kissed her again. "Okay, let's go. I'll follow your lead." They walked through the hotel hand-in-hand. Andy felt like a young woman again. She couldn't believe she'd found Austin. She'd missed him during the fall, much more than she wanted to admit. The beach in winter was a challenge for her to bear. This trip was wonderful. Being with him was wonderful. That nagging idea that he would someday want to have children, children she couldn't hope to give him, she shoved to the far recesses of her mind.

As they walked into the restaurant, the maître d' asked them, "Do you have a reservation?"

"Yes. Cochran. For four. Oh, there they are!" Andy led Austin over to the table, still holding his hand. The young couple at the table stood up. "Hi, Emma," Andy said as she kissed the other woman on the cheek. "Hello, Emile. So nice to see you again."

Emile kissed Andy on both cheeks. "Ah, Miranda, you look radiant." His accent made the compliment sound even nicer.

"Thank you. Emma, Emile, I'd like for you to meet Austin."

Everyone shook hands and greeted one another. Austin turned to Emile. "I think I remember your accent. You're the not-French guy from the rescue party last summer? We put up your windsurfer together."

"Oh, oui! I remember you. Oui, I am Belgian. Not French."

"Yes, I remember. We talked about waffles."

Emma said, "You do know that Belgian Waffles are an American invention? They aren't Belgian at all."

"Uh, yeah. Emile told me. Last summer. Anyway, I hope you haven't been waiting for us long? Do we need another seat at the table? Won't we have one more joining us?"

"Oh, no, we're good. No one else," Emma said.

"And we haven't been waiting long at all. We've been traveling all day, so we're glad to sit down and relax for a while," Emile said. "It has been a day of planes, trains and automobiles. I worried that we would not all make it to dinner tonight." He shook his head sadly.

"It's been an afternoon of snowy fields and skis for us." Andy smiled back at him. "Really fun."

"Yes, cross-country skiing, how quaint! I never thought to do this, but it's just so, well, New England-y. Like in an old movie," Emma said, looking around her. "I guess it's the thing to do in winter here since they don't have any real slopes. Hey, the menu looks… interesting. I guess these things are New England specials?"

"I haven't looked at the menu yet." Andy picked up hers. "What looks good?"

"It'll be hard for anyone to live up to your cooking, Andy," Austin said as he turned his attention to the menu.

"So, you liked the skiing, Austin?" Emma asked.

"Oh, yes, very much. I've never been skiing before. This is great. It's a real workout."

"We usually go to Aspen or sometimes even Vail, so this is quite a change. I've never been to New Hampshire. But it's nice to do something that everyone can do and enjoy." She sounded very smug as she said it.

Austin shot a look at Andy, but if she noticed, she pretended not to see him. "Who wouldn't enjoy cross-country skiing?" he asked Emma. "We skied a big loop from this hotel around to two, no three, little, what were they called, Andy?"

"Bed and Breakfasts."

"Yeah, B&B's. They were great. We took off our skis and stuck them in the snow. Wow, so much snow, it's crazy here. The skis could actually stand-up in the snow. All on their own." Austin was all enthusiasm.

"Of course, they stand up in the snow." Emma laughed as she said it.

"Austin is from the Outer Banks. They don't really get snow," Andy explained.

"We went inside to check out the little inns. They were serving up hot cocoa and cookies."

"Yes, they were so welcoming!" Andy said, giving Austin's hand a

177

squeeze.

Emma and Emile exchanged a look. "Must be a marketing ploy," Emile said. "To try to get you to stay there next time."

"Cocoa and cookies? Like for little kids?" Emma looked skeptical.

"Then it worked for me. I'd love to stay at one of those places sometime," Austin said as he picked up his glass of water and took a sip. "Although I have to say, this hotel is lovely."

"Well, it's not quite the St. Regis." Emma gave a disappointed little sigh as she sipped her water. "In Aspen we have a condo and all the equipment." She turned to Emile. "We'll have to rent cross-country gear, you know."

They were interrupted by the waitress coming over to tell them the specials.

"Hi folks! Welcome. Are you staying with us? Good! You'll love the skiing here. The trails are great. Tonight, we have two entrée specials: maple glazed shrimp and butternut squash for twenty-eight-ninety-five and a chicken roasted in cider with herbed bread stuffing and gravy, also for twenty-eight-ninety-five. Our dessert special tonight is pecan turtle bread pudding and that's six-ninety-five. Can I get you all something to drink?"

"Water's fine for me," Austin replied.

"Oh, let's get a bottle of wine," Emma said enthusiastically.

"Wine list is right there next to you." The waitress pointed.

"Austin, do you like red or white?"

Austin looked frozen for just a moment. "Water is fine with me."

"Oh, we'll get a bottle and share it. Do you prefer reds?"

Before Andy could get in a word, Austin said, "I don't drink." He turned his attention to the menu to study it. "Don't worry about me."

"Oh, you don't drink. How, uh, healthy of you."

"More for everyone else," Emile said, as he shrugged at his girlfriend.

"Surely *you* want a glass of wine?" Emma looked at Andy, arching her brows. "Maybe two?"

Andy rarely drank anymore but tonight was a celebration. And after the workout of skiing a bit of wine sounded delightful. "Sure, I'll take a glass," Andy answered. "I'd prefer a white."

"We'll take this one," Emma pointed out her selection to the waitress.

"Oh! That's a nice one! You've got good taste." The waitress left them to put in their order.

"It's easy to have good taste when she's paying." Emma giggled, pointing to Andy, and then Emile joined her. Austin just stared at them. Then he looked at Andy.

"Yes, yes. Very funny, you two. Merry Christmas."

"Lamb chops for me," Emile announced. "Double E, what are you getting? Let me guess, the salmon."

"You know me so well. Of course!"

"Double E?" Austin asked.

"Yeah, my name is Emma Evangeline, or E-E. But for as long as I can remember people have called me just E."

"E. Your name is E? You're *E*?"

"Well, it's Emma Evangeline." She sounded a little exasperated. "My nickname is E. Emile calls me 'double E', because of course, he's 'E' too. We're so alike. It's so cute." She squeezed Emile's hand.

Austin stared at Andy and back again at Emma. "E."

"Yes, that's right. E. It's pretty simple." Emma sounded snide.

"I'm not sure anything is simple…" Austin's voice trailed off.

"Hmmm. I think I'll get the risotto with the scallops. That sounds good. What looks good to you, Austin?" Andy asked.

"What?" Austin quickly looked back at his menu "Uh, still trying to decide." He looked at Andy.

She nodded and looked back at the menu. "You know, you might really like either the chicken under a brick or maybe the lamb chops, like Emile is getting."

"Thanks for the recommendation. I always trust your judgement when it comes to food. Do you guys know she's like a personal chef? I mean, Andy should have her own TV show."

Andy blushed at his praise.

"Yeah, personal chef was about her career until she suddenly started writing books," Emma said with a little snort, taking a sip of her water.

"Now Emma Evangeline. Be nice," Andy said.

"I'm nice, Mom, I'm nice."

"You are her daughter?" Austin asked Emma. "You're E?"

"Yes." Andy was mystified at this whole conversation. "This is Emma. I told you we were meeting Emma for dinner."

"Yes, your friends Emma and Emile, from the beach last summer. You said your daughter would meet us here."

"This is my daughter," Andy said.

"But your daughter is in middle school."

"Excuse me?" Emma said. "I'm in medical school."

Austin was about to say something when the waitress came back to the table with the wine. "Know what you'd all like?" They each gave their order, with Austin opting for the lamb chops, sounding very awkward and unsure of himself.

"Before I serve the wine, I know this is funny, but I have to see some ID from you all."

"Ah, she is worried that I am an illegal alien!" Emile said in mock humor, his accent particularly strong.

Emma laughed as she pulled her wallet out of her purse. "Never fails. I always get carded."

"I'm afraid I must give you my passport. I am Belgian," Emile said with a smile.

"Everyone, ma'am," the waitress directed the comment to Andy, who hadn't moved.

"Me? You want to card me? You're kidding." The waitress nodded. "Well, hell yes! This never happens to me anymore." Andy fished out her driver's license.

"Oh, just enjoy it!" Emma teased.

"I'm enjoying it. Don't I look like I'm enjoying it?" Andy laughed as she handed over her card.

"Everyone, sir," the waitress said to Austin.

"Oh, I'm not drinking."

"Doesn't matter. Everyone at the table has to show ID. That way it's all in the open who can and who can't drink. We had a little problem last month with of-age people ordering for the table and sharing with under-age people. We almost lost our liquor license. So, we have pretty stringent rules now. I'm sorry." She shrugged. "If I don't card you, I could lose my job."

"My God, Austin, just show her your driver's license." Emma nudged him with a brittle laugh, a clear edge to her voice.

He handed the waitress his license. "I don't drink," he said simply.

She read his license. "But in two months you can! It won't be long. Then you can enjoy a glass with your mom here and big sister!" She smiled at him, handing him his license back. The rest of the table was dead silent. He put his license away. Andy was frozen in her seat.

No one moved or said anything as the waitress uncorked the bottle of wine, poured three glasses, and set the bottle on the table. She took away the empty wine glass that had been sitting in front of Austin. Then she left to put in their orders.

"What did she say? You turn twenty-one in... when? Two months?" Emma turned to her mother and said much more loudly than she could possibly have intended, "Mom, you're dating someone younger than me?"

Conversation stilled to silence across the room. Everyone in the restaurant turned to look at them.

Andy looked at all the strangers looking at her and then back at Emma. "No, no." She looked at Austin. "He's only about a decade younger than I am."

"About? In whose world of math does that exist?" Emma turned on Austin. "What are you doing with my mother? What are you up to?"

"Emma! Stop that."

"No, I'm serious. This, this boy... Mom, what are you doing with this boy?"

Andy felt her heart beating in her ears. She was trying to take it all in. The recrimination in Emma's face and voice. The amusement on Emile's. The confusion on Austin's. She couldn't even imagine what her face looked like, but she was sure it was beet red. She reached for the bottle of wine and added a bit more to her glass. Her hand was trembling.

Emma turned on Austin again. "So. You're twenty."

"Yes."

"And you are, um, let me see, a pool boy?"

"No. I'm a college student."

"You told my mother you were getting your M.B.A.," she said, her voice full of accusation.

"No. I never said that. I said my goal is to get an M.B.A. I run an equipment rental shop on the outer banks in the summer. It's a family business. I'm studying business at school."

"Mother, how in the world could you have failed to pick up on the fact that your boyfriend here is practically jailbait?"

Andy could hardly breathe. She looked from Emma to Austin and struggled to process what was happening.

"Oh, Dad is not going to believe this." Emma shook her head.

"What does he have to do with anything?" Austin shot the question at Emma.

"This is all about him. Can't you see that? This is all about how much she hates M.G."

"Who's M.G.?"

"Morning Glory. His new wife. This is all about trying to make Dad jealous and get back at him. You know, Mom, she's going to have a baby. You need to let this go." She rolled her eyes. "But this, this is just pathetic." She sneered, looking from Andy to Austin and back again. "What? Are you trying to live out that silly book you wrote?"

"I think I've had enough," Austin said as he pushed his chair back. "Emma, your mother is a grown woman. She is creative, intelligent, capable, and kind. Knowing her has been one of the high points of my life, young as I may be. What has been between us isn't about Gregg, or you or anyone but Andy and me. And you and I may have been born about the same time, but girl, I have to say that you are just about the most disrespectful daughter I've ever met. Your mother is a grown woman. She can make her own decisions. It's not your place to insult her."

"Mom, can you believe how he's talking to me?"

"What I can't believe, Emma," Austin continued, "is how you put your mother down. She's your *mother*. Dig after dig. Within five minutes of me meeting you, you were already digging at her. Did you learn that from your father? You don't think she got enough insults from him?" He pushed his chair back further and stood up.

"You snide little... Mom, clearly this boy is after your money!" Emma stood up, too.

"Stop it! Stop it! Both of you!" Andy shouted. Again, the whole restaurant went quiet. The waitress showed up a few feet behind them with a large tray, bearing their appetizers and a basket of bread. She was frozen, not knowing what to do. "Austin," Andy said in a small voice, "maybe you shouldn't stay."

"Believe me, Andy, I wouldn't stay for five more minutes of this. And I certainly won't stand around to hear your own daughter continually put you down like that. It's completely disrespectful." Austin turned to face Emma again. "Maybe it's because I lost my mother and didn't have the blessing of having her around while I grew up, but I would never in a million years have treated my mother the way I've seen you treat yours tonight. It's pathetic, Emma. You are not better than your mother, so stop judging her. I don't think you even know her." He turned to Andy. "I'm going back to the room. I'd like for you to come too. I think we have some things to talk about. In private." He shot a look over at Emma. "But I understand if you want to stay here and finish this with your daughter."

Andy looked at Emma. She was red-faced and angry. Emile was smirking. No, she didn't want to stay with them. She wasn't sure she wanted to be with Austin either. "We'll talk later, Emma."

"Mom, you've got to be kidding! You can't be leaving with this, this pool boy."

Austin turned to the waitress. "Please have our meals sent up to room four-twenty-one."

Andy took Austin's outstretched hand and followed him out of the restaurant. She could feel her head spinning, her heart slamming in her chest. They were headed back to their room but she really just wanted to crawl under a rock.

Chapter 21

She sat down on the bed. He sat down next to her. They didn't say anything for a while. They just sat, staring straight ahead.

"So, you're twenty?"

"Yeah. Uh. Do you mind if I ask how old you are?"

She felt sick. "I'm forty-three, Austin. Forty-three. How old did you think I was?"

"A bit over thirty."

"Oh. That's how old I thought you were."

"So, she's not in middle school. I thought you had a daughter in middle school. You know, about thirteen. You got pregnant at twenty. And your daughter was thirteen."

"No, not middle school. Medical school." Andy sighed loudly and then fell back onto the bed and lay still, looking at the ceiling. "How did we end up here?"

"You really don't look like you're forty-three."

"Uh, thanks? No, that's a definite thanks."

"You don't act like you're forty-three."

"I don't know. I've never been forty-three before. How are you supposed to act? I haven't been single in more than two decades. I've never lived at the beach. I've never been successful on my own. How am I supposed to act? I don't understand how we got here. I don't understand what I did so wrong."

Austin lay down on his back next to her and also stared at the ceiling.

After a while he said, "Maybe you didn't do anything wrong. Maybe this just happened because we really like each other. People like each other all the time and aren't the same age." He turned to look at her. Andy was still staring at the ceiling.

She turned her head to look at him. "But I am old enough to be your mother." She looked back up at the ceiling. "Oh my God."

"True."

"Austin, I'm so sorry. I never meant to mislead you. I really thought you were older. You act older. You seem older."

"I've been told that."

They both stared at the ceiling. It felt like neutral territory. A grayish, in-between space to seek safety.

"We skirted the issue of age. Think about it. It could have come up a dozen times, but we just seemed to evade the topic. Maybe we knew? Maybe deep down we knew." She sounded a little horrified.

"Maybe so. We never brought our friends or family into this. I never introduced you to my dad, my aunts or uncles or cousins. There just never seemed to be time. And, to be honest, I didn't want to share you."

"I know. Summer went by so fast. I met you, had to go on that book tour. Then you were leaving almost as soon as I got back."

"Yeah. You felt like mine. Like my secret." He turned to look at her again. "I have to say, like my wonderful secret. I'm not sorry for what happened between us."

She turned to look at him. "I'm not sorry either, Austin. I love you. You've been wonderful for me. I'm not sure how to say this… but I don't think I can go forward with us."

He sighed heavily. "Nah." He turned to look at the ceiling. "Me neither."

"Oh my God, if my mother ever finds out."

"Yeah, or my dad…"

Suddenly she started to giggle, which turned into a laugh. Austin looked at her, a bit shocked, then he started laughing too. They both laughed so hard they were rolling on the bed. It took them a while to catch their breaths. Andy spoke first. "Here we are like two kids, afraid at being caught by our parents. Oh, I'm so embarrassed. That was my daughter. Did you see the look on her face?"

"I'm not embarrassed."

"Only because your father isn't here. Tell me, if your dad had been sitting there during that scene that you wouldn't have just died on the spot."

Austin was silent for a bit. "Yeah, I suppose you're right. That would have been a game changer for me. I wouldn't even want to imagine what he would say."

"I'm going to have to talk to E tomorrow. I'm not looking forward to that. Not at all. Ugh, and M.G. is pregnant. Oh, that's so weird, and to find that out from Emma. In a fight."

"Andy, why do you let her treat you like that?"

"Well, she was pretty upset tonight."

"She was totally disrespectful even before. She made put-down after put-down. She used the news about the baby like a weapon. You told me once that she took after her father. I felt like I saw a bit of what it must have been like to be married to Gregg."

Andy stared at the ceiling again. "Emma loves me." Hurt and pain were evident in her voice.

"I'm sure she does, but it's complicated how a kid feels about their parent. She's independent, not a little girl anymore. She made that clear. She judges you, too."

"Austin, she's my daughter, and she'll change. She'll grow up. I know she's a little… high maintenance."

"Self-absorbed?"

"She's my daughter and I can't cut her out of my life." There was a clear warning in Andy's voice.

"Okay, hey, I'm getting outta line here. It's not for me to jump into your relationship with her. It just strikes me that it doesn't have to be that way,

187

Andy. It doesn't have to be that way. I would never treat my mother that way. I would never treat you that way."

"If I were your mother."

"If you were my mother."

"I could be your mother. I'm old enough to be your mother."

"But you're not my mother."

Andy thought for a while. "Do you think that's what this is for you? Somehow, you with me, it's some search for the mother you lost? Only all mixed up in coming-of-age hormones? Oh my God, are we caught up in some real-life oedipal fantasy?"

Now Austin was very quiet.

There was a knock on the door.

"Room service."

Andy got up to let them in. "You can set it down here, please." She signed the bill, which she noticed was for all four meals. Emma had directed the waitress to bill Andy even after they left the table. "Well, our dinner is here."

"I don't think I can eat."

"Oh, I probably can't either. I notice there's no wine."

"I don't drink."

Andy burst out laughing. "Of course not. Man, but I could use that glass of wine now. Are you okay, Austin?" She came over and sat down next to him.

"I'm just thinking about what you said. About searching for my mother."

"Yeah, well... it's like a made-for-TV movie. A really bad made-for-TV movie."

"Nah. More like direct to DVD. Or straight to stream."

Andy and Austin moved their flights up by two days, returning to Wilmington on the twenty-first. In the wee hours of the morning they had to drive to Portland, Maine and catch a flight through Charlotte to Wilmington. Austin said he felt badly that she had to land in her hometown, then fly to

Wilmington, and then make the drive right back to where she had just been.

"Or I could buy a new car," she had answered with a bit of a forced smile. "I did leave my car at the Wilmington airport." They parted much more awkwardly than Andy would have liked. Not a hug and most certainly not a kiss. Kind words though. Sad looks. She felt like the whole experience had aged her.

He drove to the Outer Banks from there and she drove back to Charlotte. She needed to process the whole event. She needed Caroline.

Christmas was going to be quiet for Caroline's family. This year Chase, Claudine and the kids would be visiting her family in France. Caroline's younger brother would also be with the other side of the family. It was just Caroline and her mother, Mimi, this year and they were thrilled that Andy could join them. It gave Andy and Caroline lots of time together, as they helped plan the menu, shop and cook, but Andy had avoided the topic of her failed ski trip. A couple days before Christmas, they were out doing some last-minute shopping.

Caroline threw a duster in her basket. "Great! That will be the last of my shopping. So, that hot little sandwich from the beach turned out to be a college student, huh?"

"Yeah, can you believe it? I could have died of embarrassment. And to have found out in front of Emma!"

"Yeah, I want to hear more about that, but first, Andy, I have to say, really, way to go, girl! I could never pull that off. I'm sure that anyone we knew from school would be just dying of jealousy now. Hell, I'm dying of jealousy! Isn't that like every woman's fantasy as they hit forty-something, to be just as attractive as they were in their twenties? You never age. Like I said, you go, girl You go!!"

"Oh, hardly!" But Andy felt a smile creep across her face. She hadn't thought of it way. "Leave it to you, Caroline, to be so supportive. I tell you, I certainly haven't felt triumphant. I feel totally confused. Embarrassed. Yes, those feelings. A bit lost. And I miss him. But not triumphant."

"You miss him?"

"Yes, of course. You know, our time together totaled less than five weeks, spread out over six months, but he is the sweetest, dearest man. And I miss him."

"And the hot sex?"

"Caroline!"

"Are you going to call him?"

"No. No. I can't get over the age thing. Now that I look back on everything, I just crucify myself when I can see all the little things that should have tipped me off. Dozens of conversations that if I'd just asked different questions, I would have spared myself this whole ordeal."

"Now that's Emma talking. Spared yourself? Why? You've been happier in these last six months than you've been in a decade. Why would you want to spare yourself that? And it's not like he's a teenager."

"Uh, he's one year away from being a teenager."

"Okay, it's not like he's under-age."

"Uh, he's less than three years away from being jailbait," Andy said as she returned a blouse to the rack. She couldn't seem to find much interest in shopping. She didn't have anyone to buy anything for anyway. E's gift had been the ski trip. Andy was sure that Emma and Emile had continued to have a very good, and very expensive, time on Mommy's charge card, particularly after Mommy left early. To Austin she had given some little things, clothes mostly. And the trip of course. "Oh shit."

"What's the matter?"

"I just realized. I bought Austin Christmas presents."

"And you need to return them?"

"No, I gave them to him. But it's what I bought him. Clothes. All summer he wore swim trunks, shorts, t-shirts. You know, beach wear. I hadn't seen him since then. And I bought him some winter things for the trip."

"Like what?"

"Shirts, pullovers, a sweater, hat and ski gloves, long underwear..."

"Oh my God! You didn't."

"Yes, I did. It seemed so logical at the time. And he didn't know what to pack for a ski trip. He'd never been skiing. But it was… oh I can't even believe it."

"You totally bought him mom stuff."

Andy glanced over at Caroline, a look of horror on her face. "Yes, I did. Maybe I knew? Maybe deep down I knew?"

"Well, don't tell Emma about that."

"Never. Emma was actually horrible. Really horrible. She said the meanest things."

"Oh really?" Caroline didn't sound surprised.

"Yes, she and I had a real blow-out the next day." Miranda halfheartedly slid hangers down the rack. "It was absolutely awful. You remember that book I bought?"

"The one about how to get arrested with your daughter and call it girl-bonding?"

"Yeah, that one. I'm not recommending that one. That advice sucked."

"What a shocker. You know, maybe it's not about being best friends. Or maybe being her best friend doesn't mean being buddies. Maybe it means being there when she needs you. Or putting limits on her. Or being the one person who is really honest with her. Maybe it means loving her even when she's an asshole like her father." Caroline quickly backpedaled, "I mean, goes through a quick phase of that. Yeah, just a quick phase." Caroline didn't make eye contact and turned to face another rack.

Miranda turned away to hide the tear that was starting down her cheek. She felt angry with Emma for all the things she had said but with Caroline, too, for putting a name to what Miranda had witnessed. Deep down a part of her had to admit that Emma had spoken with the voice of Gregg during the last fifteen years of their marriage. He would accuse her of being stupid, of not thinking things through. Of being so damn helpless. Of having no judgement. Maybe that was why she was such a planner? To try to prove it to him that he was wrong. Through innuendo he would ridicule her to their friends. The scorn in his tone had always been searing. And she had heard it again, in Emma's voice. Even the look on her daughter's face was a reflection of her father's. Emma had almost delighted in being, well, cruel. Like there was some kind of victory or triumph in shaming her mother. Miranda came around the rack. She took a deep breath and decided to tell Caroline that nagging fear growing in her since the fight. "She accused Austin of trying to seduce me for my money. Wanted to know if he'd asked me to pay his tuition."

"And did he?"

"Never. I actually wanted to do something for him when he went back to school…"

"That's the mom thing again."

"In hindsight, yeah. I think you're right. Oh, the humiliation with this one never ends, does it?"

"And what did Austin do when you tried to, what? Buy him new school clothes?"

"No, not school clothes. Okay, well some. But I did want to give him money for books. He wouldn't take it. Wouldn't even hear of it, even though I know he missed a lot of work spending time with me. Lost out on making money for school. My offer actually kind of offended him."

"What other mom things did you do?"

"Well, I helped him with his papers. He emailed in the first weeks of school and he'd failed a paper. He asked if, since I was a writer, if I could help him with some pointers."

"And you did." Again, there was no question in Caroline's voice. "You never could say no, Andy. Anyone who needed help. You always were a sucker for being needed."

"Well, he was a terrible writer. It was like when Emma was in junior high. So, I helped him. I'm good at college papers. I used to visit Emma nearly every weekend when she went to college. I'd always look over her work before I went back home." Miranda recoiled. "Caroline, don't look at me like that. I didn't write his papers for him. But I did teach him how to write. In a lot of ways he was a better student than Emma. And by the end of the semester he really improved. There weren't any more corrections for me to make. Which was, um, kind of unlike Emma."

"So, he's bright?"

"Yeah, he's a smart cookie."

"Speaking of cookies, did you send any care packages? My college kid is always pushing me for those."

Andy flushed bright red.

"So… you did. How many?"

"Just one. But I didn't make it myself. I just ordered one of those boxes with fruits and cheese and goodies in it. He said he and his roommate really enjoyed it."

"So, Andy, you were lover, teacher, friend, playmate and mother to this man. I have to hand it to you, that was one complicated relationship. What was he to you?"

"Other than everything? I don't know. I'm going to have to mull that one over. Ugh. I might need therapy again."

"And where do things stand with E?"

"Not good. I think we're not speaking. At least neither of us has reached out in the last few days. She's leaving soon to go with her father and M.G. to the Caribbean. I just die inside every time I think of her telling Gregg about it."

"Oh, let him stew in his own sauce! Let her tell him and may it drive him crazy. The more condescending he is, the more you'll know it bothers him. Serves him right, the jerk."

"What do you mean?"

"I mean I think it's great that Gregg knows you've had a fling with a hot man who is twenty years younger than you are. From what you've said, Austin comported himself in a very mature way, in very difficult circumstances. He did better than Emma did. What can she say about him that isn't to be respected? And Andy..."

"Yes?"

"It's like in your book. It's like how your character got part of her revenge on her wayward husband. The super-hot younger guy. Just do me one favor?"

"What?"

"Don't, under any circumstances, take Gregg back again."

Andy enjoyed celebrating the holidays with Caroline and Mimi as much as she could possibly enjoy anything right now. Mostly she was grateful that they'd taken her in. She and Caroline got together several times over the week and, along with Mimi, stayed up watching old movies on New Year's Eve. She could tell that Caroline was really waiting for her college-age son, Ty, to come home from his evening out with friends. He was a great kid, but like many young men of his age, he couldn't be trusted to always act responsibly. It weighed heavily on Caroline. She must have texted him ten times.

"Did he text back?" Andy asked when Caroline's phone went *ping*. "Yes, finally. I told him he's spending the summer with his father if he didn't let me know that he was still alive and not in jail. That seemed to get a response in a hurry."

"Whatever works," Mimi said. "Miranda, honey, I'm going to freshen up my cup of tea. Would you care for another cup?"

"Oh, sure, Mimi. Thank you."

Mimi put all the cups on a tray and took them from the room.

Miranda watched Mimi leave. "I remember how hard it was to stop calling her Mrs. Watkins and start calling her Mimi."

"She's never made the switch to Andy. I think she might have this thing about girls going by boy names."

"Miranda, Andy, it doesn't matter to me. I have a whole group of people at the beach that I introduced myself to as Andy and they insist on calling me Miranda. It's okay. Whatever."

"It's probably the author thing," Caroline said. "When are you going back?"

"I don't want to go back."

"You mean, not 'til summer, or you mean not ever?"

"I don't know. I feel like never going back. It will be so painful, so humiliating to walk around that big empty house and remember." Andy sunk back into the cushions of the couch.

Mimi came back into the room with fresh cups of tea and some additional snacks. "Did I miss anything?"

"Just that Miranda might give up the beach place."

"Oh, that would be a shame. It sounded so lovely. And you've put so much work into it."

"And I was hoping to join you there for part of the summer every year for the rest of my life." Caroline sighed, giving Andy a wink.

"Oh, Caroline, honey, there are plenty of beach houses. You can always find someplace else to visit, but to have established a home there and then to let a man drive you from it." Mimi shook her head. "Miranda, you've done that once, at great personal cost. Do you really want to do it again?"

Andy froze. She tried to say something, but spluttering sounds came out of her mouth.

"Now, Miranda, I don't mean to upset you, my dear. You've seemed pretty upset already. It's just that at some point you have to live your own life and not let these men deter you or steer you along the way. Even when they keep coming by. Even when they bring their new girlfriends or wives into the picture. Your life is yours. And your home is yours."

Caroline looked from her mother to Andy. "She *is* the voice of experience. Kept this house when Dad left. Clung onto it even though it probably was way too much to manage. And Dad did keep bringing by that string of substitute moms." Andy could see Caroline shudder. "Although I have to say, I'm glad he settled down with Nika."

"Yes, she's lovely. She's a good fit." Mimi smiled knowingly.

195

"Mimi, how did you make peace with that?"

"Let me ask you a question, Miranda. Do you want Gregg still? I mean, are you really still in love with him?"

She thought about that. "No. What I had with Austin showed me just how awful my relationship was with Gregg. No, Gregg's hurt me too much for me to have any love left."

"That makes sense. I got to that point, too. I just didn't want George anymore. He wasn't my concern any longer, and that thought became very freeing. Once I deeply realized that I didn't want him, I stopped making choices in reaction to him. I was free to make my own choices."

Andy turned to Caroline. "You told your mom the whole story, didn't you?"

"Let me just say in my daughter's defense that you two talk much louder than you think you do, and I'm not nearly as deaf as you think I am!" Mimi laughed. "I probably know more than you want me to though, yes."

"So, what would you do, if you were me?"

"Miranda, I would not give up your home for a man. I wouldn't have done it the first time, but it did give you the chance to establish a beautiful new home that's all your own. Now you're letting another man, or the positive memories of him, drive you away from a place that you love. That place is yours. I hope you have many men to, well, have a good time with there, and that none of them can take your home away from you."

"Andy," Caroline said, "I think Mom's right. Gregg forced you from your home."

"And now Morning Glory is living there." Andy sighed.

"Living with the ghost of you, I might add," Mimi said. "Don't forget that that house is filled with your essence after all those years of you being there. This young man was in your house for a matter of weeks."

"I think it's so tough because he was my first love post failed-marriage."

"He was your rebound relationship! And do you love him still?" Mimi's voice was so gentle. "Tell me, was he unfair to you? Or unfaithful? Was he cruel? Or mean-spirited?"

"No! He was wonderful. In fact, if he'd only been twenty years older, or me twenty years younger, who knows, things might have been different. But I can't get over the age difference. I'm seething with shame over it, actually."

"Well, every silver lining does have its cloud. Take it from an old lady, Miranda: be grateful for the love that life brings you. So, you can't go forward with him. I understand that. We all understand that. But if you are worthy of the love of such an exceptional young man, doesn't that say that you're worthy of love in general? So, it won't work out with him. There'll be others. It sounds like he wouldn't want you to suffer because of him. He's not trying to drive you out of your home."

"You think I should go back?"

"I think you should live your life with pride. And if you were able to have a twenty-year-old boyfriend for a while, well, good for you! You're a beautiful woman, inside and out. Of course, he loved you. My advice is, roll with it."

"Mimi, I wish I'd known you when we were all twenty-five. Somehow, I think none of us would be quite the same women."

"Like they say, youth is wasted on the young. It took me a lot of years and a lot of heartache to become myself. I wouldn't want you to wait until you're nearly seventy to come into a sense of yourself. It took me way too long. Just live your life with pride and joy, Miranda. Pride and joy. You have nothing to apologize for."

"Hey, what about that kayak guy who's into birding?" Caroline asked, "What about him?"

"I think they're all into birding."

"Yeah, that sounds pretty awesome," Caroline said with a yawn, clearly unimpressed.

"Actually, the birds were kinda cool."

"And Mr. Kayak's name was?"

"Burke."

"Burke. That's nice. So, what about him?"

"Caroline, I'm still reeling here from a broken heart and you're suggesting I chase down some other guy already? Give me some time, girl! I only stopped crying about five minutes ago!"

"Moving on soon will be good for you. You tend to dwell too much on stuff, and that's *not* good for you. Well, unless you're writing a best-selling novel, it's not good for you. And if you are, it's probably *very* good for you."

Miranda couldn't help but laugh.

"What's his deal? Not married? Any kids?"

"He's been married. She's not part of the picture. He doesn't seem to want to talk about it. It seems that all the single guys there have these tragic relationship stories—wives who've left them, or worse, died. I've never brought it up with any of them. Figured if they want to talk about it, they will. He's got a son though."

"Oh? Young kid? Grown up? What's his name?"

"Named for Daddy. Burke, Jr. He's in college someplace. Doesn't want to come back to the island. Burke senior seems to be pretty put out by that, so I haven't talked much about that either. I didn't want to go down the road of major bummer. My own major bummer is enough for me."

"Well, I'll come back with you for a bit and cheer you up!" Caroline's phone went *ping*. She read her text. "Or maybe not. Ty is on his way home." She let out an exasperated breath. "He dented the car. I might have more parenting to do. I swear this kid is going to kill me. Unless I kill him first."

"Do we need to go and pick him up?" Mimi asked.

"I'm ringing him now. I told him if he puts one more foot out of line, we're shaving off all that long hair."

Miranda looked wide-eyed at Mimi as Caroline left the room to talk to Ty.

"Ty's hair is down to his shoulders. Drives Caroline crazy. Their deal is that he gets to keep his hair if he can stay on the straight and narrow. She says, 'with great hair comes great responsibility', but if he's been drinking and drives home, she'll shave his head."

198

"And if he lets her pick him up?"

"She'd probably let him keep his hair for showing such restraint. But denting that car... He's a handful, that's for sure."

"It's a good thing he has two good parents."

"Well, his father isn't much of a parent, I must say."

"I mean you and Caroline. He clearly has two good parents."

Chapter 22

Burke pulled up his email and started sifting through the messages, marking intrusive ads as junk and blocking those senders. He followed up on some that were related to book orders. Then he saw it. She had written him back. He froze for a split second. She had already answered him once, explaining that she wasn't coming back to the beach again, maybe until summer. Maybe not even then.

"Happy New Year, Miranda. You must have had a wonderful time in Aspen," he had written her back, "to forget about the spectacular beauty of the ocean so quickly! I didn't realize you had done all the winter-proofing to your beach house before you left. I'm impressed that you got through that list so quickly—it can be quite a lot to do to protect your investment for the long months and the possibility of bad weather. When you do come back next summer, if you'd be so kind as to come by The Book Shelf Café, I would appreciate it if you could sign some more books. I've sold so many of them already—and I'd like to do a special event once the season opens and we're busy with tourists. If you let me know your schedule, we can arrange for some book signings, if that would be of interest to you. Of course, I would be more than happy to bring copies by your house near Pea Island, when it's convenient for you, and you could sign them there, if that would save you the hike to Buxton."

He was afraid he was pushing it and being dreadfully obvious. Clearly, she was caught between being an islander and a mainlander. If only he could nudge her towards 'islander'. But now her response was sitting there in his in box. He was afraid to click it. Afraid it would be a terse response. He took a deep breath, moved the mouse over the message and clicked.

> Hi Burke,
>
> I hope you had a happy holiday. I appreciate your note about winter-proofing the house. Being a new beach homeowner, I'm learning how much I have to learn. I didn't do anything special to the house at all, but I'd be most grateful if you could point me to a winter-proofing list or book that I should consult so that I know what to do. So, it looks like I will have to come back to the island after all. And of course, I will come by The Book Shelf Café and be happy to sign whatever books you'd like me to. Thank you for your kind support of my work. Please order the appropriate book for me and I'll pick it up when I come by. Please let me know when would be convenient for you after January 10th.
>
> Sincerely,
> Miranda Wright

Her note was all business, but that was okay. That was a start. He hit reply and composed a note that was 'business-friendly', someplace in between where he thought they were and where he wanted them to be. He invited her to swing by on the fifteenth, if that worked for her. She wrote back to confirm that the fifteenth would fit into her schedule.

He went to the shelf and looked. She had signed a dozen copies back in October. He had ten left. Traffic was light during the winter. He wondered whether he should even be open for the two days a week he ran the shop outside of tourist season. He was only here on weekends now, and then only for a few hours. Islanders respected the winter schedules and they always checked first and hit the stores when they were open. The last restaurant way down here on Hatteras Island always closed in November—the remaining islanders traditionally packing in for the final weekend 'goodbye dinner'. As a community, they were tight knit, and they stuck together, supporting one another. He opened a webpage and logged in. He ordered thirty more copies of the book from her publisher. Then he took eight of the books on the shelf and took them up to the attic, with other stock in longer-term storage. There was little chance he would sell more than the two copies that re-mained out before April.

On the fifteenth, he and the dog drove down to the shop. He had three guides for her to choose from that detailed how to winter-proof a beach house, but he hoped she wouldn't need them. He hoped she would stay.

She pulled up in front of The Book Shelf Café just a few minutes after eleven. He met her at the door, with the dog beside him, wagging its tail.

"Welcome back, Miranda!" The dog gave a little woof and sniffed at her leg. "I hope you don't mind dogs?" Then he bent down to scratch the pooch's ears, saying "Who's my good boy? Huh? Who's my good boy?" The dog wagged his tail and licked his master's hand. Burke turned to Miranda. "How were your holidays?"

She hardly seemed to notice the dog. "Oh, quiet. Over, that's the important thing. Back to real life now."

"Yes, it's good to be busy. Holidays have a lot of build-up, gets people excited, but they can turn out to be just regular old days after all, which are a real let-down if you were expecting something different. I saw that all the time in the younger generation once they became teenagers. It seemed nothing could impress them."

Miranda laughed.

"What's so funny?"

"Oh, it's just what you said. I guess I was expecting a great holiday this year and it turned out to be rather ho-hum and boring after all. So, yes, it was a let-down."

"Well, let me perk you up a bit. Your fan base continues to grow. I have thirty more books here for you to sign." He led her over to table.

"Wow, that's a big stack."

"Take your time. Let me make you a cup of coffee. You like decaf, right?"

"Yes, I do. How do you know that?"

"Well, you ordered a decaf when we had a cup at the New Morning View, remember? Up in Nag's Head?"

"Oh, that's right. I'd forgotten all about that."

Strike one, Burke thought. "Well, I haven't," he said cheerily. "How was Aspen? You missed our great solstice bonfire while on your ski trip."

"Oh, it was probably my last trip skiing. It wasn't so great. Maybe you were right, and skiing isn't my thing. I don't really want to talk about it."

Strike two. "Well, let's get you signing. It's what famous authors do, right?"

He noticed that she gave him a weak smile but walked over to the stack of books. "This is going to take a while."

"You're my only priority right now, so please feel free to take as long as you like."

"I have to say, beach hospitality is just the nicest. Thank you."

"Here, let me take your coat. I'll hang it up for you." As he hung up her coat, he looked outside. The clouds were low and heavy. The forecast was for heavy rain. That could easily flood highway twelve in the low spots. "Looks like we might get some real wet out there."

Miranda went to sit down. He made her a cup of coffee, happy that he'd bought the skinny syrup that she liked. He tried to make a cool design with the foamed milk on the top of her cup, but it came out looking like a blob. It would still taste good though. He might not be confident in his art, but he was absolutely sure of his science when it came to coffee.

She signed for a while and he tried to avoid hovering over her. The dog jumped up in one of the chairs, curled up, and fell asleep. Burke moved away the books she had finished with and moved others to be within reach. He wished he'd ordered fifty copies. After signing fifteen copies she rubbed her hands. "I think I'm out of practice."

"Oh, it's probably my fault, asking you to write an inscription in addition to your autograph. I'm sorry about that. It promotes sales."

"Well, my publisher would love you," she said. "I'm sure they'd want to put you in charge of me down here at the beach. They think I need a minder so that I keep writing and do more promotion." Thunder pealed loudly outside, and rain started to drum hard on the roof.

"I could do that. How's your coffee?"

"You know, it's great. You make a really great cup of coffee. I'm sorry, I should have said something earlier. I noticed it right away. I was just distracted by how sore my hand is."

"Here, let me. This weather can be rough on sore joints, too." He took her hand and started to gently rub it. Gradually he massaged the muscles and worked deeper. He rubbed around the wrist and a few inches up the forearm. "If your hand is sore, it could actually stem from these muscles here. May I?" He pointed to her forearm muscles below her elbow.

"Wow, you do a good hand massage, too." She nodded, and he took that as her assent.

"Hey, coffee, hand massages, great literature—we've got it all here. I might have to change the name of the place again!" He smiled as he worked on her lower arm. He could tell she was fit, in fact she was pretty muscular for a woman of her age. He had a hard time believing that she had a daughter in medical school. She didn't look old enough for that. He was curious. "So, tell me about your daughter. You said she's…"

"A jerk," Miranda said and then she blushed furiously. "Oh my God, I can't believe I said that. She's lovely. She just wasn't over the holidays. Wow, it must be bothering me more than I realized if I let that slip."

"It's the hand massage. You're letting down your defenses. Feeling more comfortable. Opening up. Feeling relaxed."

"Are you trying to hypnotize me?"

"Just calling it like I see it. Here, give me your other hand or you'll feel uneven. One hand will be all tingly and refreshed and the other will feel neglected. That wouldn't do." He set down her right hand and picked up her left. He started to work her fingers. The pounding of the rain made for a hypnotic background. "So, tell me what's going on?"

"Well...."

"Or don't. You can just relax. I don't mean to pry. My own son came home from college quiet and withdrawn. Not like him at all. He can be a tough nut to crack. Very private. He was totally out of sorts."

"My daughter was totally out of sorts too. She's in medical school. Knows better than everyone else. She's a handful."

"Oh, that's a fun stage to go through. I hear it's like that with girls. Boys are so much easier. They just don't tell you what's going on."

"But then it's all left to your imagination!"

"Yes, for those of us with great imaginations I'm sure that's a scary proposition, but for those of us who are ordinary people it makes for a lot less drama."

Andy burst out laughing. "Burke, you're kind of funny."

"Nah, I'm just hypnotizing you with a hand massage."

"That really does feel a lot better. Thanks."

They continued to talk as she signed a book here and a book there. The time crept by, passing noon. "Hey, are you getting hungry? There aren't any restaurants open until April, but I always keep some things to nosh on while I'm at the shop. And looking at that rain, neither of us are going to want to go outside for a while." He pulled out some cheese, dried fruit, sliced sausages, and seeded crackers with a jar of olive tapenade, then some roasted mixed nuts and for dessert some cocoa dusted almonds.

"Nosh? You call this nosh? This is a feast! Oh my god, I love these cocoa almonds. Watch out, I'll eat the lion's share if you don't keep an eye on me."

"Oh, I'm watching. You might have to arm wrestle me for them. Hey, look at this! Look what I found! I have one leftover bottle of red from your last appearance at The Book Shelf, in October. Whaddya know? I should give this to you as a gift for supporting my little store." He presented the bottle to her with a flourish.

"That was a lovely wine, as I recall, but I couldn't take your last bottle of it. It wouldn't be right." She shook her head.

"Then let's tap it! Let's be bad. Let's be literary and sit around in the cutest little bookstore on the Outer Banks and while no one is looking let's sneak a glass with our feast. Besides, it's an excellent pairing with the storm."

She looked outside the windows at the rain, then looked at her car. It was already sitting in a rather large puddle and the rain was intermittently coming down in sheets. "Oh sure, why not?" She sighed. "We're trapped here for a while anyway. Twelve will be a mess after this storm. I have to say, Burke, you are fun."

"Thank you. I'm not sure that's how I'm routinely described, but for today, I'll take it." He felt immensely relieved that their morning was turning into a nice time together. They opened the bottle of wine and one hour turned into five. They drank nearly the whole thing, and then had to wait it out while the effects of the alcohol wore off, but they blamed their delay on waiting for the water to drain off highway twelve so they could each make it back home. They spent their time talking about their favorite books and occasionally slipping the pooch small slices of sausage. Burke pulled his most loved works off the shelf and read parts to her, then she hunted up the ones she liked and shared with him. They made fun of literary critics and wrote their own hilarious, pompous reviews of best sellers, laughing hysterically. Burke thought he had never loved a rainy winter day more than this one.

As five o'clock rolled into view, she said, "Oh my God, this has been fun. I didn't expect to have such a fun day again for quite a while. Thank you, Burke. I've been here forever. The roads have got to be clear by now. The rain stopped over an hour ago. I really should be headed home. Well, to the beach house anyway."

"That isn't home?"

"I don't know. I guess I miss the mainland. Maybe it's just that it's so quiet here. I really don't know anyone, so it's really, really, well… *quiet*. I thought that would help me write, but I'm finding that I need people more than I thought I did."

"Oh! That's all? You're just missing society! You need to become part of the island community. There's lots going on. You just need to get hooked in. I can help you with that, if you'd like."

"Sure. I think that would be nice."

"Not a problem." He smiled at her.

Miranda left at five-thirty with a polite handshake, a smile for Burke and shock at her sudden realization that she hadn't ever finished signing the books.

"You can do that next time," he assured her, holding onto her hand and smiling warmly.

"Next time."

He watched her pull out. He cleaned up the considerable mess they'd made, leftover food, empty glasses, empty coffee cups and stacks of books all over the place. The dog sat up in his chair and watched attentively.

"Hmmm," Burke said to the dog as he straightened up. "Now I just have to invent some society around here to make good on my offer."

Chapter 23

Burke turned off the engine and rested his forehead against the steering wheel. He wasn't sure whether he was ready to face this, but he needed Kat's help. The dog came over and sniffed at him. Burke sat up and took a deep breath. Then he headed into the house, the dog following closely.

He walked right in without knocking. Junior took off running through the house.

"Honey, is that you?"

"No, it's the other honey."

"Oh, hi Burke. You're early. I'm in the kitchen. Come help with dinner."

"Sure. Love to," he said as he joined her.

"Oh, hello, Junior!" she said to the dog. Then she turned to Burke. "I've got a pitcher of iced tea right there, if you're of a mind." She gestured to the pitcher and then turned her attention back to the squash she was roughly chopping on the cutting board. A big pot of sauce was bubbling on the stove and another pot of water was working itself up to a boil.

"Thanks, Kat. Don't mind if I do." Burke poured himself a glass. They chatted about work and the kids for a bit. She added some sliced sausages to the sauce pot and stirred.

"So, you're dancing around something, Burke? What's going on?"

"No, I'm not."

She sighed. "You're not standing still. You're nervous as a cat. You've raised that glass to your mouth about a half dozen times and yet you haven't taken a sip."

"How do you know that? You've been cooking this whole time?"

"Taste it."

Burke tasted it, puckering up his face.

"Precisely. It's unsweet. You only drink sweet tea. Had you even sipped it you would have made a dive for my sugar syrup. After the salt, it's your favorite thing in the kitchen."

"You know me too well." He shook his head.

"I am your sister."

Burke retrieved the squirt bottle of sweetener out of cupboard and gave it a good squeeze, watching the thick syrup diffuse through his glass of tea.

"Now, what is it that you want to say?"

"Nothing. Really."

"You know, Ben and Mad will be here in about fifteen minutes. Mike will be home any second. If you don't want to have to say it front of them, you'd better spit it out now." She turned back to the pot she was stirring and added the chopped zucchini.

He took a deep breath. It was better to get it over with. "Um, Kat, I want you to do me a favor."

She turned to him, raising one eyebrow as she continued to stir the pot.

"I want you to schedule a dance party."

She stopped stirring and stared at him.

"A shag beach-dance party. We can all go out to Manteo. There's this little restaurant. I know the owner. We can bring in music and he'll have a dance night. He'll move the tables and clear the floor."

"Burke, have you even danced in at least fifteen years?" She raised both eyebrows at his shrug. "Just who do you want at your dance party?"

"No. It has to be *your* dance party."

"My dance party? I don't dance."

"Mike does. He was always great at it. He would love to take you dancing."

"At my own dance party. So, you're providing the venue. And the music?"

Burke nodded. "Yeah, but you can't tell anybody that. It's got to be all you."

"Uh huh. And the guest list."

"Oh, the usual suspects. You and Mike, Mad and Ben could come. Maybe Maggie and Jim, and me and I thought you could call up that author lady who came to the book club."

"Oh, I get what this is. You want me to set up an event so you can ask that Miranda woman out on a date!"

"No, I can't ask her out on a date. I want *you* to ask her out."

"What? Burke, what are you? In high school? You're a grown man. If you like the woman, just ask her out on a date."

"I can't." He hemmed around for a few moments. "She's got a man-friend. And I'm her friend-friend. I can't cross that line. She has to cross that line first."

"Are you telling me that you want to go out with this woman so badly that you would drag all your friends, all your coupled friends I notice, out dancing, just so she'll have no one to dance with but you?"

"Yeah, that's a great idea, Kat. I like that idea." He added wistfully, "No one else but me."

"So, she has a man-friend. You're telling me that she's got a significant other, and you want to, uh, elbow your way in there?"

"I want to shag my way in there."

"Did you just hear what you said? Oh, by that mischievous smile, I think you did. Seriously, you would make a move on another man's woman? Burke, that's not like you."

"Oh, I'm way better for her than her man-friend."

"You know him?"

"Nah, not a clue who he is. But he's some old geezer and I'm way better for her. She just has to spend time with me and she'll see that. Kat, we were made for each other. And she's not happy with him. Not as happy as she would be with me. So, will you do it?"

At that moment, Ben and Mad arrived. "We're here," Mad called out. "We brought the bread. And a bottle of wine!"

Burke leaned over the counter towards his sister. "Please, Kat."

"My own brother, asking me to be his wingman. I'll think about it."

Soon, Friday night spaghetti dinner was on. Ben talked about the new equipment he was thinking of ordering for the rental shop. Mad talked about whether a custom doughnut cafe would fly over in Rodanthe. Burke talked about maybe having another book event at the shop.

"But it's winter. No one's here. You'll get at best ten people. Just the book club folks."

"Well, that's okay. We're a good group." He gently kicked Kat under the table. "Kat had a good idea. Kat, tell them your good idea."

She looked daggers at him. A pleading look quickly flew across Burke's face. She sighed and said in a tone of forced lightness, "Well, I hadn't really thought it through yet, but I was thinking that it might be fun to get a group together and all go shag dancing. I hear there's this club…"

"Restaurant," Burke jumped in. "You told me it was a restaurant. In Manteo."

"Oh, yeah, that's right. A restaurant. And the owner, I hear, is really crazy about beach shag dancing?" She said it almost uncertainly, glancing at Burke. "If people want to come and dance, he'll open up part of his restaurant space as a dance floor."

"And he's got music?" Ben asked. "Nobody can get a band this time of year."

"It's taped. Kat tells me it's taped," Burke interrupted.

"I think it's a great idea!" Madeline was bubbling with excitement. "Can I help you plan it?"

"I'd be happy to even turn the planning over to you, Mad." Kat couldn't suppress her smile. "Happy to."

"How many people do we need?" Madeline asked.

"Four or five couples, I'd guess. So that's you and Ben, me and Mike."

"Oh, how about Maggie and Jim?" Mad reached for her purse and pulled out a little pad of paper and a pen.

"Okay, I'm game, hon. But who will your baby brother dance with? We've got to dig up somebody for him," Mike said.

Burke looked hard at his sister.

"Well," she said, "there is that new lady who came to our book club? That author?"

"Oh my God, you are such a fan of hers. You were practically drooling on her at the book club." Mike looked at his wife. "Babe, it was like you'd never met someone who'd been on TV before."

"Well, I've never met someone who's been on the Today Show!"

"Do you think someone like her would want to come and hang out with a bunch of beach crackers like us?"

"Oh, Ben, don't you say that. It ain't politically correct," Mad chided her husband.

"I think she liked hanging out with us at the book club." Burke ventured into the discussion rather timidly. "I didn't get the sense that she was stuck up at all. I thought she seemed pretty down to earth."

"That book was horrible," Ben said. "Chick stuff."

"Well, we're talkin' 'bout dancin', darlin', not readin'. Dancin'. And you're goin' 'cause you're dancin' with me!"

"Yes, ma'am," Ben replied, but he was all smiles.

"So, Kat, can you reach out to the author? You actually set up the book club with her," Burke said.

Kat took a deep sigh. "Yes, I'll shoot her an email."

"Great!" Mad smiled at her. "I'll do the rest!"

Chapter 24

Burke pulled his blue VW Microbus up into the drive of Hayward House. He sure hoped he could depend on Madeline. He usually could. He ran his fingers through his slightly shaggy blonde hair to get it to lie down and look a bit more presentable. He wondered if he should've gotten a haircut.

He felt a sense of nervous excitement as he walked up to the front door and rang the doorbell. He could hear decades old music coming from inside and noticed that she had several windows open, allowing the breeze to blow in through the screens. Well, it was an unusually warm day in early February.

"C'mon in, Mad! I'm almost ready. The door's open!"

He looked around, feeling a bit guilty, as though he were about to sneak into her house. "Okay, you invited me in," he said aloud, but he said it quietly. He opened the door and stepped inside the tiled foyer. It was lovely to see this old house again. He hadn't stepped inside in the better part of a decade. Maybe two. He stroked the woodwork around the dual closets in the foyer. He had built these. The room ran straight across to another matching door on the other side that led to the back part of the property. The doors were new, mostly glass to let in more light. Someone had re-tiled the floors, too. They were white—they had been blue. He walked the few steps into the middle of the foyer and turned right, went up the one step and walked into the living room. He stopped, struck by the décor. There was nothing 'beachy' about this house. The furniture looked like it belonged in some high-rise apartment in the big city. It was leather, contemporary, and ultra-cool. He walked over to the coffee table: it was a giant chunk of a tree, finished and beautiful. It made his woodworker's heart ache with envy. He turned around and surveyed the house. He couldn't believe it had changed this much since Pete had lived here. "Pete would love this," he whispered.

Music was playing, the singer saying something about it being *lovely to see you again, my friend.* It was catchy. He thought he might have heard it somewhere before, but a long time ago. He liked the lyrics, thought they suited the occasion.

"Hey, Mad—I need your opinion," she called out. "Should I wear the deep purple or the Caribbean blue? I can't make up my mind. What do you think?" Miranda walked out of a room from the back of the house holding up two blouses. She was looking at the clothes while she walked in, studying them. She was wearing a pair of black Capri pants and black bra. He thought she was the cutest thing he'd seen in a long time.

"Um…"

"Oh my God!" she shrieked and held the blouses on hangers against her. "Burke, what are you doing here?"

"Mad asked me to pick you up. Didn't she tell you? Said she had some errands to run before the dance party and she would be so late as to be rude. So, she asked me to fill in." He hoped he sounded innocent. He was sure he didn't look innocent with that smile on his face.

Miranda blinked a couple of times and looked around her, then backed up towards the room she had come from. "Must've slipped her mind…" her voice trailed off.

"But, I'm happy to give my opinion. Caribbean blue. Definitely." Burke turned around in an attempt to give her some privacy, or at least to appear that way. "Well, that would be Madeline for you. She means well though. Please don't be mad at her."

"Oh, I'm not mad at *her.*" Miranda's voice came from a bit farther away.

"Well, please don't be mad at me either."

She came back in the room. "I'm not mad at you."

He turned around and smiled. She had chosen the blue. He really liked how she looked in that color.

"I'm just awfully embarrassed. I, uh, completely didn't expect you."

"I'm sorry. You did give me shout to come in." He noticed the song had ended and an Elton John song came into play. *Goodbye Yellow Brick Road.* "You really like old music." He wondered if it was from the era of her man-friend and made her think of him.

"I do. I like a lot of old stuff, actually. I'll be ready in just a moment. Thanks for being willing to drive."

"Hey, it's no problem. Would you mind if I got a glass of water?" he asked, suddenly feeling that his mouth was rather dry.

"Oh, sure, the kitchen's this way."

He followed her, marveling at all the changes to the house. He could still see walls he had worked on, hardwood floor he had laid, trim he had nailed in, but not much. They got to the kitchen, and he looked all around at the changes. At least the beautiful deep blue tiled floor was still there—and that was about it. He and Pete and Joe had worked for hours on that, striving for perfection. "Beautiful kitchen."

"Thanks. It's been a bit of a work in progress. I just got the dishwasher replaced, so that's the last of the appliances."

"You've got a Jura?"

"Oh, you recognize the coffee maker? You're kidding?"

"No, I have one too. At the shop. I love these."

"Oh, want a cup of coffee?"

"Hell, yeah. Here, let me make it for you."

She got out the beans and he made them each a latte. He poured the steamed milk into the brewed espresso, carefully maneuvering the metal cup over the ceramic one of hot coffee. He picked up the mugs and handed one to her.

"Whoa! I don't know if I can drink that. Burke, that's art."

He shrugged. "It's about the only design I make with latte art. I'm working on the flower, so I always do the little heart next to the flower since I get to practice both of them. But go ahead and drink it. I can always make you another."

"It's so Zen. It's like you've made me a sand mandala… out of milk foam." She sipped it.

He noticed she was smiling.

"You know, I can never get this to work." She indicated the design on the top of her drink.

"Do you do espresso? Or do you do the drip setting, and then mix it with the steamed milk?"

"Drip. It's a little easier on my stomach than drinking espresso all the time. Damn, I feel old saying that."

"Well, age aside, that's your problem. You see espresso is an emulsion, that's a rich crema that latte art is made with. Instant or drip coffee is an extraction. If you pour steamed milk into drip or instant, you just won't get the definition you need for designs or patterns."

She stared at him. "You really know your coffee."

"I had to learn. And it's quiet in the winters, so sometimes I entertain myself by practicing."

"When you're not reading all those books?"

He liked the way she teased him. "Well, I am waiting for my favorite author to come out with her next gripping novel!"

"If only! Let's go dancing. Maybe I'll get inspired. Or maybe I'll just be able to forget my anxiety about my adoring fans wanting me to do something I'm not sure I can."

"Oh, sure you can. But, yes, let's go shag dancing. I'm sure you'll be inspired."

They finished their coffees and went out to the car. "This is your car?"

"Uh, yeah."

"And you ask me if *I* like old stuff? That VW Vanagon is ancient! And it's so cute."

"Thanks. It's actually a Microbus. She's my baby, that's for sure."

"And I deduce that you love Caribbean blue?"

"Uh huh. Very beachy."

* * *

They had a nice drive into Manteo. It took them nearly three-quarters of an hour, which gave them a lot of time to talk. After they had been on the road just a few minutes, Miranda said to Burke, "You know, I've been really intrigued with something you said once. I'd like to ask you a bit more about it."

"Oh sure."

"It was your comments on karma when we were kayaking. I've come back to the discussion in my own mind quite a few times."

"Okay, what's on your mind?"

"I just want to know more about how you see it. It seemed that you hold a pretty different idea than most people I know. Most people talk about karma as some mystic, unknowable force where crap from some long-forgotten past life runs you over and squashes you like a bug. But you didn't seem to subscribe to that particular theory."

"No, actually, I don't. I don't know whether I believe in past lives. I can't say I know what happens to us, either before or after this. I know what I want to be true, but I'm not sure I can even say I have faith in my case. I think faith is a gift. It's not my gift. Some people have it, that rock solid faith that they *believe*, they *know*. But in my case, if I have faith then I would classify it as a fond wish. Maybe a dear hope. But I live with the uncertainty of not really knowing. So, that's a long answer to say no, I don't subscribe to that version of karma."

"I haven't thought much about faith. I'm not sure you think about faith until you're tested. Maybe you're driven to it. Maybe it isn't a gift. Maybe it's

217

a destination."

He decided to take a bit of a risk. "I guess you might have been thinking about your relationship with your ex, since that's where the karma topic first raised its head?"

"Yeah, actually I was."

"My guess is that you and your ex treated one another very differently? That at least towards the end, there wasn't that level of mutual respect that maybe there had been earlier in the relationship. And I would guess that it was a long road of very small steps that led to that end, but that if you looked at it with the benefit of hindsight, you might be able to see that breadcrumb trail still."

She was quiet for a moment or two, and then said, "Yeah."

"I'm not saying that either of you deserved the destination you ended up at. All I'm saying is that it was probably predictable that you would end up there and that if you knew way back when what you know now, that maybe you would've stopped that train on the tracks and asked each other if what you had was what you really wanted. Did you ever do that?"

"I tried to get him to go to couples' counseling. He insisted that we didn't need it. I think I understand what you're saying. With the benefit of hindsight, I can see the seeds of our end planted right in the beginning. It's kind of like that old 'you reap what you sow' saying."

"And I hope the proverbial train we're on is headed in a very different direction."

"Huh." She made a sound, but it was very noncommittal.

"And, to be honest, I think there's a little bit of karma that just sucks. Shit just happens. Unexplainable stuff. Dying of cancer because you have horrible genes. You can't control that. You can't much influence that. It's circumstances of your birth. It's a type of collective karma that you sort of inherit just because you're here. And other people's bad choices can majorly impact your life. We have to navigate our lives around the ten percent, which can really suck, but at least the ninety percent of the navigating is actually us."

"You lost your wife."

Now he was quiet for a moment. "Yes. I did." He was surprised at how perceptive she was. Not that he wanted to talk about it. It was too dark a place to visit for him, but he realized that he was going to have to say something. Hopefully something to evade actually talking about it.

"I'm so sorry."

"Me too. It was the most painful experience I can ever imagine going through, the whole, losing... It was some years ago now. I know I'll never really get over it, but I have gone on. And I always had my boy to live for. Life is for the living. And on that oh-so-happy note, here we are at the restaurant. Looks like we're right on time. There's Madeline's car. And Mike's. Do you still feel like dancing or are you totally bummed by our serious discussion?"

Miranda looked at him and gave him a small smile. "I think dancing is the perfect thing to do after such a serious discussion."

He smiled her. "Good friends can have serious discussions. And have a good time."

"I'm enjoying being your friend."

He felt his heart lighten. Now *that* train was definitely on the right track.

Chapter 25

Miranda tried to catch her breath. She had been dancing for nearly an hour straight. She had to admit, Burke was pretty energetic for a man in his mid-forties. He'd spent the first few dances showing her the steps and leading her through the motions. She found she really had to concentrate to follow and decided that it must be much easier to do this when you were leading. Then Burke traded partners and she found herself dancing with Ben while Burke danced with Madeline. After a couple of songs, she and Mike danced, while Burke danced with Kat. It was like having friends. Fun friends. She and Gregg had never had fun friends. She'd had Junior League friends, charity friends, PTA friends, but she'd never had fun friends. She found she liked watching Burke dance almost as much as dancing with him. She felt like she could practically see him as a young man, dancing with his wife, before he lost her. *Breast cancer,* she thought. *That's what that Cynthia lady said, wasn't it? No wonder he doesn't want to talk about it. No wonder she told me to not talk about it. Horrible genes you can't control.* Maggie and Jim arrived and joined their little party and Burke was dancing with Miranda again. She was particularly happy that neither Frankie nor Darnell showed up.

"This is such a hit!" Madeline shouted out to Burke as she and Ben danced by.

"Yeah, thanks for organizing it."

It didn't take long for others eating in the restaurant side to wander over and join in. Miguel had emptied the bar area of chairs, leaving only a few small, high-top tables dotting the floor by the wall. He had dimmed the lights and put up some little red, green, and white lights to illuminate the space with their subtle glow.

"So, do you like shagging?" Burke asked Miranda as he pulled her in close for a spin.

"Oh, *be-have*, Burke." She laughed. "I do. This is a lot more fun than I thought it would be. These moves, they're much slower, but they remind me of disco dancing."

"Oh, don't say that. We never, never say the 'D' word at the beach."

As midnight arrived, they left Miguel's, tired but excited. "Oh, we have to do this again!" Kat said as they made their way to their cars.

"Definitely," Ben said, as he swooped up his wife and kissed her. "Honey, I haven't had that much fun in years!"

"I asked Mr. Rodriguez-Vargas if he'd be willing to do it again, and he said we're on for next Saturday night. Did you see him dancing with his wife?" Maggie asked, a big smile on her face. She and Jim were holding hands.

"I think they were having even more fun than we were," Miranda said.

"Do I hear we're all coming back next weekend?" Burke asked. As everyone agreed, Miranda and Burke walked over to his blue, beachy VW, waving to the other couples. "Hey," he said a bit tentatively, "I didn't mean to commit you there, without asking you."

"Oh, no, I didn't feel like you did." Miranda thought he was the most considerate guy she'd ever met. Probably the kind of guy who went to every treatment with his wife. The kind of guy who stayed with her until the very end. Guys like that were pretty special. She wanted to know more but decided to respect his privacy. He had clearly been uncomfortable. He would tell her when he was ready. Until then, she would just wait and listen, and probably fill the silence with too much information about her personal life. She didn't want to do that, either. T.M.I. was an all-too-common trap she fell into. She sighed.

"That's a heavy sigh. Are you just tired or are you stressing about your book?"

Given that Burke's main source of exercise seemed to be turning pages of his precious paperbacks, she was unwilling to admit that he had more energy than she did. "I'm going to opt for door number two. Unfortunately, the deadline is too often on my mind. It keeps popping up uninvited." It was a little bit of a white lie. It did pop up all the time, it just hadn't been popping up at this particular moment.

"Are you making any headway at all?"

"Ugh. Not really. I keep going round and round. It's so frustrating. When I wrote the last one, it just flowed out of me. I couldn't write fast enough. Now I stare at that blank screen."

"Maybe you need readers."

"I'm not old enough for readers yet… thank you very much!"

"No, no. I don't mean eyeglasses. I mean maybe you need people to write for. People who are eager to read your story and give you feedback."

"People to write for?" she asked, but then added more thoughtfully, "Yeah, people to write for."

"Uh huh. They can help with continuity checking, you know, so blue rings don't turn red." He gave her a wink, and Miranda blushed. "You said you came back from your book tour pretty inspired by the fans. Maybe deep down you really like writing for people. For people who enjoy your work."

"You know, you're right. I did have my friend Caroline read everything, pretty much as I wrote it for that book. She would almost hound me for what happened next." She laughed. "We would go out to dinner and talk about these imaginary characters like they were real people. Once we had a waitress ask if those crazy people were local and whether she should be on the lookout for them in case they showed up." They both laughed.

"It sounds like your characters feel very real to you. You shared them with other people as you got to know them. It's like you've turned the characters over and examined them, getting a better idea of what makes them tick."

"Exactly! It's exactly like that! Burke, do you write?"

"No, I don't write. But I can feel it when a writer's done that, when they've really gotten to know their characters. But me, I just love books. Heck, I love books so much that I own a bookstore. I mean, I've got my fingers in a couple of other businesses, too. So many of us on the island are related to one another and we've invested in one another's businesses to help get them off the ground. It's almost incestual the way our affairs are all tangled up in one another's. Darnell and Adam and I all own stakes in the rental place. Darnell's got a toe in my bookshop, and so does Paul now that I think about it. And, of course, Mike and Ben helped me get it open and running. Kat works there. I've got a major investment in Mike's repair shop, and I've worked there too, from time to time." He sighed. "And if Mad opens that damn doughnut shop, I know she'll need a ton of help and she'll come knocking on my door."

"And will you become a doughnut shop part-owner?"

"Of course. It's Mad asking. We're all family here."

"Wow. That sounds so nice. I lived in Lexington for the last fifteen years. Well, until I divorced, then I moved back to my hometown of Charlotte. I have a condo there now. But Lexington, while it is the most beautiful place I can even imagine existing, didn't have a feeling of community. It was big, fancy houses where you never actually saw anyone. No little book club get-togethers with neighbors, no clusters of friends going out and shag dancing. That was really fun, by the way. Thanks for including me."

She liked how he smiled back at her as he said, "The beach is great. The beach in winter is even better. The island is all ours."

"I guess when you have friends and family here, it makes all the difference. Then you get to see people. The fall was so quiet, so lonely. I didn't think I was going to make it. I thought I'd retreat back to Charlotte. Become a mainlander."

"Well, I can help you there," he said warmly. "I'll make sure Kat and Mad keep you on the invitation list. You're always welcome to join us, and they usually have something brewing, from Friday night spaghetti dinners to apparently our new outings shag dancing on Saturdays."

"That's sweet of you."

"Another idea: why don't you ask them to be readers for you? They loved your book, so I'm sure they'd be willing. They'd probably find it interesting to see how a book project develops. So would I, for that matter, but I don't know if you want a guy's opinion or not?"

"Huh." She mulled it over. "That's an interesting idea. Mad and Kat as readers."

"More like cheerleaders, probably, but still, worth considering."

"Absolutely worth considering. Thanks, Burke. Thanks, that's a great idea. And I feel like I owe you for all your kindness—particularly if you can help convince Mad and Kat to read for me. Maybe we can do dinner some night?"

"Well," he sounded hesitant, "it depends. If you're buyin' then there's slim pickins on the islands until tourist season opens up. And it's a trip, quite a trip, to head inland just for dinner."

"I'm cooking."

"Sold. When."

"How about Wednesday?"

"Again, sold."

"What do you like?"

"Well, I do like surprises and I love good food. No allergies. No real dislikes. Except weird stuff."

Miranda had an odd sense of *déjà vu* but found that her mind quickly went to crafting the menu, which was a welcome distraction. It was always so comforting to be on the solid ground of her best skill rather than wallowing in her challenges.

"So, do you think you'll reach out to Kat and Mad? I'm sure they'd be thrilled." Burke interrupted her thoughts of *amuse bouches* and where she could get good bread. She was realizing that four days away was a short time to actually get special ingredients in winter this far out on the outer banks.

"What? Oh yeah, sure. Sure. Of course."

* * *

Burke arrived right on time on Wednesday night. Miranda was relieved that he didn't show up with flowers. She was getting comfortable with being his friend, but she certainly wasn't ready for any kind of romantic relationship. "If I'm being honest with myself," she had told Caroline on the phone just two days before, "I'm still in a bit of shock. Still recovering from finding out the truth about me and Austin."

"Truth about you and Austin? And just what is that?" Caroline's voice sounded like a bark through the phone line. "That you got along famously? That you cared deeply for him? That you had totally righteous sex?"

"Oh stop, you're only making it worse. Don't remind me. I'm old enough to be his mother."

"But you aren't his mother. You aren't related to him in any way. You're a totally hot woman who just happens to be a little bit older than he is, and good for you! Now stop berating yourself and be proud of yourself. Feel lucky. How is dancing man? Is that developing into anything?"

"I don't know. He's really nice. We're friends. I think that's where I want to leave it. If I venture out there again and get my heart torn out, I just don't know how I'd recover."

"Hey, if you don't want him, send him my way! He sounds like a dream. Anyone without an AARP card I'll at least take a look at."

"You'd have to move to the beach. He doesn't go for mainlanders."

"That would be a problem then, wouldn't it? Oh well, *c'est la vie*, as Claudine would say. So when will you see your friend next?"

"Dinner Wednesday."

And he was at the door. She'd spent hours on this dinner. *Why? That was a lot of work to go through for just a friend.* With a sudden drop in her stomach she realized it could be very misleading. Very misleading indeed. She suddenly felt a little panicky and didn't know what to do. She opened the door and tried not to look nervous.

"Evening." He smiled at her.

"Hi! Come on in."

"I brought some wine to go with dinner." He handed her the bottle.

"Oh, thank you. Well, let's open this." She smiled but thought, *Oh shit, I sound nervous.* With a sense of dread, she realized that sounding nervous would probably give him the wrong impression as well.

"Wow, it smells fabulous in here," he said as he followed her through the house to the kitchen. He certainly seemed relaxed. Or was he just faking it? She studied him for a moment, and then realized that could give the wrong impression, too.

She was glad she hadn't set out good dishes or done anything stupid like candles. But she'd chosen a stupid menu, nonetheless. "Will you be good enough to pull down some wine glasses?" She pointed to a high cabinet.

He obliged. "Can I ask what we're having? I'm trying to place what I'm smelling, and I can't quite figure it out."

"What do you smell?" He'd caught her attention now. This was one of her favorite games.

"Wine. Cloves… and some other spice that I can't place. Not pepper. Maybe I smell pepper? And something else, something I haven't smelled in a long time."

"Oh, you're pretty good! I love playing at this. A huge amount of taste is smell. And you *are* smelling wine and black pepper and you got the cloves right. The other smell is star anise. I was just grinding some more of it up."

"Star anise. Wow. That's different. What are we eating?"

"You open the wine and pour some out and I'll bring out our first treat."

He did as she instructed. "I brought a Gamay. These varieties have been around since the fifteenth century, so I thought it might go with just about anything."

"Perfect! You really put all that reading to such good use, I must say, Burke. You are full of surprises. That will go beautifully with our dinner."

"Which is still a surprise? I notice you're not telling me anything."

"Well, while you're in suspense, would you mind grinding this some more?" She brought over a little malachite mortar and pestle. She noticed that he really could flash quite a roguish smile when he wanted to. "I need this to be quite fine and I haven't gotten it there yet. That way I can attend to our first course."

"Ooooh, l like the sound of first course."

She took her wine glass to the side counter and worked on stacking up her tiny appetizers. She popped them into the toaster oven and set the timer for three minutes. They talked about the weather for a bit, remarking on how much nicer it had been in December when they'd been kayaking. After being unexpectedly warm last weekend, February was now the doldrums out there.

"Maybe we can have dessert over by the fire, later on? That would be very cheery on a cold and gray evening like this."

"Sure, if you'd like." *Shut up, Miranda!* she told herself. *Why couldn't I think of some excuse? That's far too misleading.* The toaster oven gave a merry *ping*, pulling her away from her self-recrimination and she pulled out her starters. "Since you're so curious, here's the first little treat. These are *amuse bouches*."

"Oh, I love it when restaurants serve you those. Now, you don't usually get those at the beach."

"You know about these?"

"Yeah, of course I do, I mean, I'm a pretty good cook too. They tickle your taste buds. It's a French thing. And oh no, you didn't. That's foie gras. I love foie gras. Wow, hot foie gras! That will be amazing. Where'd you get it?"

"Oh, I have a friend from France. I think she felt sorry for me that my

227

holidays didn't turn out to be much fun and she sent me this big care package. She's like that. Really direct and actually somewhat bossy but the most generous person you're going to meet. She sent me a few kinds of foie gras and some specialty foods that she likes. I hope to someday make the dish for her that I'm serving tonight. It's one of my favorites, and it's just not something you do every day."

"Oh, it's a special occasion kind of dish?"

She looked at him thinking, *why did I say that?* "Uh, I hope you like it. I quite selfishly decided this was an opportunity for me to make something I've been craving lately, and it's not something you can make for one." She thought that sounded totally self-centered, but it could only be worse to tell him how many hours this dish took to make. Or how many miles she'd driven to get the ingredients. Or to admit that it *was* for very special occasions. She asked herself again why she'd chosen it. "Um, after we munch on these, I need to work on the leeks."

"Oh my. I'm in heaven. I could eat just this and be happy." His eyes were closed.

"Yeah, they're pretty good, aren't they?" She picked up one of the tiny stacks of the pâté and popped it into her mouth. "These are seared foie gras on toasted brioche with caramelized sweet orange. This one is a truffle foie gras and this one has fig. The fig one is really divine."

"Beyond divine. Addictive. And I get this because I took you dancing?"

"No, because you're going to read for me and give me feedback. That's what I'm paying you for, right?" She winked at him and hoped that he bought it. She hadn't been going to ask him actually but realized that in trying to dodge giving the wrong impression, she had just committed herself to including him in her tiny circle of readers.

"I thought you were going to ask Mad and Kat? Did you not ask them? I did mention something about it to them." He looked a bit concerned.

"Oh, I did. Don't worry! And I've delivered the drafts of a few chapters to them already. They're coming over for lunch tomorrow and we're going to talk books. Promise me you won't tell them, but I'm serving them the leftovers from our dinner."

Burke walked over to the pot and looked in. There was the wine broth and soy sauce, a ton of spices and some slices of fruit but nothing else. "Well, you've certainly got me curious. And very excited to taste this dish after trying the appetizer. Can I pour you more wine?"

"Sure. That would be nice. We're having a poached tenderloin sprinkled with the fresh star anise, served warm on this winter evening. It's currently resting. We're going to have sautéed baby leeks and grilled artichoke hearts. Tomorrow I'm serving the tenderloin cold over salad when the girls come over."

"Wow." He stared at her for a few moments. "I might want to come back again tomorrow!" He picked up another appetizer and closed his eyes as he ate it. "I'm glad you're going to let me read your work, see how a book comes together."

"I, um, thought about what you said about a guy's point of view." *And maybe it will help?* she told herself. *Sure, why not? What could go wrong?*

He was looking at her funny. She wondered what he was going to say. She hoped she hadn't offended him.

"Are they getting the foie gras too?"

"I dunno." Miranda hoped she didn't sound too surprised by his question. "Do you think they would like it, or would they think it was… dog food?"

"Dog food? Who would think it was dog food?"

"Oh, I mean by the way it looks. You know, it's a rather unappetizing brown, which is partly why I always dress it up. But if they'd never had it before then I could see where someone might be, uh, wary of it."

"Huh, let me think. Are Mad and Kat that unsophisticated? I mean, it would take someone pretty green to not know foie gras."

Miranda could feel herself blushing. "Well, I wouldn't ever want to make them feel uncomfortable…"

"Of course not. Tell you what, I'll think about it, and maybe if we eat it all then you won't have to make the decision tomorrow!" He gave her a wink.

"Oh! You're jealous!" She laughed.

"Of course! This looks like a real treat."

"It will be, if I get the leeks done. I'd better get going on that, so everything is ready at the same time. Want to help chop?"

"Sure. Oh wait. I left something in the car. I'll be right back."

By the time she had pulled out and washed the baby leeks, he was back, carrying a tissue paper-wrapped package. "This is for you. And particularly appropriate to this moment."

"For me?" She set it down on the counter and started to tear the wrapping. It was a little bit heavy. The paper tore away easily, revealing a beautiful piece of flat finished wood. "It's a cutting board!"

"Well, technically, it's a cheese board. Made from driftwood. Too soft for a cutting board. I collect driftwood in the winters and when I find something suitable, I make the boards. They're pretty rare to find them in that size. They're usually only large enough for a skinny little cheese board, but they're so pretty and they're from both land and sea, it makes them kind of cool. I hope you like it."

"Like it? I love it! Oh my God, Burke. This is so gorgeous, just gorgeous! Thank you. This is so thoughtful of you."

"Kind of a very late housewarming present. Welcome to the island."

"OK, you can have all the foie gras."

"Bingo! Just what I was going for."

They had a lovely dinner on everyday dishes and with no candles. She tried to keep their conversation light and on things they both cared about, like writing. She ended up printing out everything she had worked on for her new book and he promised to read it and be ready to talk about it by the weekend. They got so caught up in conversation that they never got around to dessert by the fireplace. In fact, her little chocolate pots de crème lay half eaten and forgotten long before he left, close to midnight. As she shut the door behind him, she yawned and thought that she had done a good job of keeping it friendly but not 'couple-y'. She walked back into the kitchen to put up the wine they hadn't finished. "Man, you're a nice guy, Burke, a really nice guy." The kitchen was spotless. He had insisted that they wash up after the dinner, run the dishwasher, and later when it was done, put the dishes up. He was so helpful and thoughtful. Of course, all that cleaning up together had felt very couple-y, now that she thought about it. It felt like they had skipped the whole dating part and were in a totally comfortable, settled relationship. "Oh, I'm just not going to think about this now." She yawned again and headed off to bed.

The next day dawned cold and gray again. At ten-to-noon Madeline pulled up to Miranda's house for their lunch date and Kat arrived at a quarter after. Miranda enjoyed her time with them and was glad that they were just as fun off the dance floor as they were on it. She never once mentioned Burke or that he had been over the night before. She really didn't want to admit to them that lunch was just a fancy leftover dinner. As Miranda went to get the dessert, her phone rang.

"Do you need to get that, honey?" Madeline asked.

"Nah, I'll let the answering machine get it. Besides, we're about to enjoy our dessert! You guys want coffees?" She sounded as cheery as she felt as she picked up their plates and took them over to the kitchen sink. She heard her voice on the answering machine saying that she couldn't make it to the phone and to please leave a message. She pushed the button on her coffee maker and put a mug beneath. Then there was Darnell's voice, telling her that he'd like to teach her to shag dance and there was this little place up in Manteo if she was free this weekend. He really was about the last person she thought she would want to dance with. She brought the desserts and coffees to the table.

"So, I hear Darnell knows about the dancing at Miguel's." Kat smiled at her. "What are you gonna tell him?"

"I don't know," Miranda said as she set down the little pots de crème in front of her guests. "Maybe the same thing I tell Paul, who left a message at ten this morning. And Lawson sent me an email with the same invite."

231

Kat and Mad looked at each other and then began to laugh. "Sorry, Miranda." Kat explained, "It's just that there hasn't been an unattached woman on the island in winter in I don't know how long."

"They sure do come sniffin' around like a pack of old hound dogs, don't they now?" Madeline thought this was particularly hilarious.

"Whoever said I'm not attached?" Miranda tried to sound innocent and not betray her guilt at yet another little white lie.

"Oh, that's right! You have a, a what did you call him? A man-friend? That's so cute. I'll bet the guys heard that you were dancing the night away with Burke and don't want to give him the chance to get in too close." Kat nodded her head sagely. "I'm surprised Frankie didn't call, too."

"Oh, he was going to," Mad said, "but when he found out I was coming over for lunch he wanted to me ask if you'd dance with him next weekend. He wasn't brave enough to call you himself, he just wants to tag along with us and work his way in. He'll be happy enough if he's just in the mix. You know."

"How would they have heard about the dancing? I mean, it was just the four of us couples for most of the time."

"Nah, everybody knows everybody here. I bet they all knew by Sunday night. But if your guy is still in the picture that's good to know. Burke will probably be pretty disappointed too. My brother seemed to like dancing with you." Then Kat added, "I'd have to say, he liked dancing with you a lot!"

"I liked dancing with him too, Kat. And Mike and Ben. I mean it was really fun. We're good friends. Wait a minute—did you just say he's your brother?"

"Oh sure, didn't you know? Everyone is related out here on the islands."

Mad interrupted, "So when is your guy coming to the beach? When do we get to meet him?"

"Oh him? He's, uh, really busy. He doesn't live close at all. We're sort of on a break for a bit." Miranda knew she was flailing, not wanting to admit that she was truly single and not wanting to talk about her heartbreak of just six weeks ago. And Burke was Kat's *brother?* She thought it best if they believed she wasn't available.

"You sound like you're kind of in an in-between phase? Not quite taken, not quite single?" Madeline asked, looking intently at Miranda. After all, Frankie was *her* brother.

"A little more to the taken side than the single side. Open to be friends but not open for dating."

"Oh, good to know!" Mad dug into her dessert. "This little chocolate thing is great. And that appetizer you served us, that was good too, but boy, it sure looked like dog food."

"I have bad news for you," Kat said. "They're never going to stop circling until they see you kiss one of them. Or your man-friend. They'll bide their time. But they're like fisherman: they'll wait with their lines in the water for as long as it takes."

Somehow Miranda navigated them away from dating and onto the book. Kat turned out to be a wickedly good continuity checker.

"What happens to Gabe next in this story?" Mad pointed to the stack of papers in front of her.

"I'm trying to figure that out."

"Well, you could have him miss the train and then run into the sister of the dead girl. Wouldn't that be something? You know, it's just like a book I read by Nora Roberts once. It's a great story line. Of course, in that book the dead girl's ghost comes back and then some really weird shit happened."

"Oh, really? Well, uh, you know you don't usually follow the same plot line as another author." Miranda wasn't sure how much help Mad was going to be. In the end, Mad offered several ideas, all of which were tied to another book Mad had read or a movie she'd seen.

The girls stayed for three hours, which was fun, if not much of a contribution to Miranda's productivity. She did get insights into what parts of the story pulled the reader along and where the storyline dragged. Kat found every inconsistency and even brought an itemized list of Miranda's mistakes. They left with excited requests for the next section, and Miranda promised them new chapters as soon as she could get them written.

"I can swing by tomorrow and pick up whatever you've got!" Mad said with a big smile as she was heading out the door.

"Well, it might take me a bit longer than that."

* * *

Saturday night rolled around again, and this time Miranda did catch a ride up to Manteo with Mad and Ben. As promised, Frankie was tagging along as well. Burke arrived at the restaurant by himself, as did Paul, Darnell, Lawson, and Adam. The usual couples joined them but apparently word had spread quickly—the place was easily twice as busy as it had been the weekend before. As they pulled up into the parking lot, Frankie said, "Well! Look at that!"

"Oh my goodness!" was all Mad could say. Ben burst out laughing.

Mr. Rodriguez-Vargas had *really* liked the last dance party. He'd hung a huge sign at the top of the building which read SATURDAY NIGHT SHAG in a glaring neon orange. The parking lot was filling up quickly. Miranda noticed there were a couple of police cars outside as well.

The four of them went into the restaurant. The bar was much more decorated than it had been the previous weekend. The owner had proudly hung multiple Mexican flags, even more colored lights in red, green and white, and various south-of-the-border themed drapes. It was an interesting contrast to the American beach music playing. Burke was there, talking at a table with Mr. Rodriguez-Vargas and the three policemen. He seemed to be in earnest discussion.

"What do you think's going on?" Miranda whispered.

"I bet it's that sign," said Ben. "Burke looks like he's smoothing things over. Oh yeah, he's had them order some appetizers now. Look at him go. He can smooth talk anyone when he wants to. He'll have things fixed in a jiffy."

Miranda had hoped to dance with Burke again. Now that she was here, she realized that she expected to dance with Burke, thinking the evening would be much the same as it had been the week before. However, Burke remained with the officers for quite a while. She noticed lots of smiling, lots of patting on the back, and occasional laughter. Time passed before he made it out to the dance floor.

Miranda danced with Frankie first, but while he loved to dance, he had no sense of rhythm at all. In fact, he seemed to dance to a beat in his own head, regardless of what was happening with the music, which meant that in order for them to move, she needed to lead.

"Oh!" he exclaimed. "You're really good at this." He happily followed her lead and she decided that she actually liked this role much better than following, even though she had to be very firm and muscle Frankie around, a guy who weighed twice as much as she did. It made her realize, by contrast, how different the dancing had been the last weekend when she had really worked hard to respond to the slightest touch from Burke. Frankie seemed to have a wonderful time and complimented her profusely.

Then Darnell cut in and she thought she would sprain an elbow; he moved her around with such force. She was still haunted by the idea that he might be related to Austin. After all, Darnell's last name was Mitchell, too, so it was an easy conclusion to draw. Austin had described his dad as a wonderful guy, but also as a real character. An absolutely awful cook. A man who had been permanently scarred by the loss of his wife and child. For the first time she was up close enough to read those tattoos on his forearms, showing from under his rolled-up sleeves. One said Elaine. Another said Sadie. "Oh, I see you have names tattooed on your arm. Special people, huh?"

"Oh yeah. I got Duke on my shoulder. And his picture."

"Duke?"

"He was my German Shepherd. Best dog ever."

Then she saw the lipstick kiss-tattoo peeking out of the top of his collar on the backside of his neck. *Yup,* she thought as Darnell whipped her around,

Character. He fits the bill.

"You should relax!" he shouted at her. "You're stiff as a brick!" Then he laughed so loud she felt embarrassed, but she tried to hide it behind a smile of her own. The whole experience made her feel lucky that she'd somehow escaped meeting any of Austin's relatives. That would have been beyond awkward. She escaped from Darnell's clutches after two dances by running to the ladies' room. When she came back she danced one dance with Paul, then Burke finally cut in, but Lawson cut in on him. After a few more rounds of this, she decided to get a margarita and joined Kat and Mike at a side table, where Burke joined them.

"I see you're getting quite the workout tonight! That's a lot of dancing you're doing out there." Burke smiled.

"Yes, I'm being kept on my toes, for sure." She rubbed her elbow. "It's good to get a little break and grab a drink to cool down. Hey, what was up with the cops earlier?"

"Oh, that was just a little misunderstanding. They seemed to be a bit distracted by Miguel's sign and were wondering exactly what it meant. After they hung out a while, they saw it was just the dancing. I convinced them to bring their wives next weekend. It seems that one of them had this crazy idea that not everything was on the up-and-up, if you get my drift."

"You're kidding? Someone watch too many movies?"

"Yeah, something like that. But hey, this is a lot of action for a small town."

Adam came up to the table as she was finishing her drink and asked her to dance. With a glance at Burke, she nodded and followed Adam to the floor. While they danced he told her all about his shark tagging over the summer. She couldn't quite hear him over the music, but she smiled and nodded a few times and he seemed good with that. At the end of three dances, Burke asked for a turn.

"Are you having a good time?" he asked her.

"Honestly, I'm feeling a little overwhelmed."

"Would you like me to take you home?"

"You know, I would. Would you mind? I hate to ruin your evening. No, I shouldn't leave. It would seem so ungrateful to Mad and she's put so much work into organizing this."

"Maybe after a few more dances then?"

"Okay. After a couple more." A half an hour later they were zooming back down highway twelve and Miranda felt like she could breathe again. "I'm sorry. It was so fun last weekend, but it felt like a close group of friends. This weekend felt a bit like a fraternity party."

"Oh, it's not supposed to feel that way at all."

"I tell you, I'll feel really embarrassed if Adam ever asks me about anything he said tonight. I couldn't hear him, but I know he was talking about a bunch of tagging expeditions." She thought that no matter how handsome he was, it just didn't make up for his singular conversation.

"Tagging expeditions?" Burke laughed out loud. "He's caught one four-foot shark in the surf. A few babies smaller than that. I don't know whether I'd call any of those an expedition or not." He had a huge smile on his face. "And let's not forget, he was on land the whole time."

"Oh! So, he was telling me fish tales. I get it."

"If he ever asks, which he won't, just talk about a great big shark he tagged. He loves that story. His one Instagram. You'd think he caught a mermaid the way he tells it. Just mention it and he'll take it from there."

"How did you end up so normal, Burke?"

"You only say that because you don't know me well enough yet. I think we're all somewhat eccentric to live out here. I think we have to be. You don't give me credit—I have my bad days. And I can be just as interesting as the rest of them!"

"Oh, I didn't say you weren't interesting."

"Really now? I suppose that's good." They drove in silence for a while. "Do you think you're going to stop going after tonight?"

"No, I'll still go if the girls are going, but I'm driving next weekend. It's my turn to drive."

"Well, I'll hitch a ride with you if that's okay."

"Sure."

As he pulled into the little road that led to Hayward House, he asked, "Do you still want to get together tomorrow to work on your book? I read all the material you gave me."

"Oh yeah, sure. I'll make brunch. That sounds fine. How about ten?"

"Sounds great."

Three weeks later she had danced away each Saturday night, enjoyed several lunches with the girls, and made three successive Sunday brunches for Burke, in reciprocity for their time and ideas. While she appreciated the writing input she got from the girls, she gradually began to refer to them as 'Mad-Kat' in a nod to their highly entertaining, but mostly unusable, plot ideas. While Mad-Kat turned out to be supportive and fun friends, Burke turned out to be an excellent critic.

One thing she had to get used to was his dog, which he always brought with him. She really was not a dog person. Never had been. His dog looked just like every other mutt she'd seen at the beach. She didn't like to admit it to anyone, but her opinion of dogs was that they all jumped on you. They all left hair all over the place. And they all barked far too much. When Burke came for brunch the dog ran inside the moment she opened the front door. The thing had been so calm when she'd first seen him at The Book Store Café back in January, but now he sniffed all over the house and then jumped up on her couch, knocking over a pillow and curling up on it, as though this had always been his home.

"Oh, you brought the dog," she said, her voice deadpan as the pooch disappeared past her, running into the house.

"Yes, Junior, come back! Oh well, he can't get far." Burke smiled at her. Then, as he noticed the look she was giving him he added, "Do you want me to take him home?"

"No, of course not. He can stay. He's welcome. After all the time you're so generously giving me, I can hardly turn away your dog." The dog sat up and barked once, then took off again on a tear through the house. "Does he always do this?"

"He pretty much goes with me everyplace and yeah, I guess he kinda' does. I always thought he was checking out Kat's or Maggie's or my dad's house, to see if anything's changed, or if he could find one of the cats, but we go to the same friends all the time. I can't remember the last time he saw a totally new house."

They both looked at the dog sniffing through the house as he made the rounds and disappeared into a back room.

"Junior, come here boy!" Burke called. If the dog noticed Burke's call, it gave no sign.

"I see, you have a spoiled dog. Doesn't come when called."

"He will if you have food. His name's Junior."

"I thought your son's name was Junior?"

Burke laughed. "Yeah, that's a funny joke. My boy would do something and blame it on the dog when he was just a puppy. And he got away with it for a good while before I caught on. Then somehow, they both started going by Junior. His name actually *is* Burke, but he goes by his middle name which is…" but Burke was interrupted by the dog running back up to him, its claws skittering on the floor, a hot pink lacy piece of clothing in its mouth, tail wagging wildly.

"Oh my God! What's it doing?" Miranda heard the shriek in her voice and was clearly feeling exasperated. She took a few deep breaths to keep her cool.

"Uh, let me get that back. Junior, here!" he said, but the dog playfully growled and leapt around, as if this were a game. While Burke started to chase the pooch around Miranda's living room, she gave an annoyed sigh and went into the kitchen. Burke made a leap after the dog but missed catching him. He did, however, catch an edge of the lace. He pulled. So did the dog.

A sharp whistle got the dog's attention and then Miranda called out in a bright voice, "*Doggy-vac, doggy-vac, doggy-vac!*" from the kitchen. Junior stood alert, looking toward the kitchen and without a second glance at Burke, took off running. Burke followed.

Miranda was standing in the kitchen with a leftover soup bone in her hand. The dog was at her feet, mesmerized. "Drop that," she said sharply. The dog dropped the slobbery, wadded up mess of hot pink lace. "Lovely. Here you go. Stay out of my hamper." She gave the dog the bone. He didn't move from where he was, he just lay down on the floor and started working on his treat. Miranda picked up the pink cloth. Burke stood there looking at her, holding the other half of the torn fabric. She raised an eyebrow and took it from him, opening the lower cabinet door and throwing both pieces in the garbage.

"Um. I'm sorry he did that. I'll replace it, what he destroyed. Anything he broke."

"You're offering to buy me new underwear?"

"That was your underwear? That… lacy, small thing? Um, I'm so sorry he did that."

"Uh huh. Right." Miranda gave him a stern look, but had to suppress a smile. He was blushing. Burke looked so caught off guard, embarrassed by the situation. She had to admit, he was kind of cute standing there and not knowing what to do. "I'll get brunch set up. We're eating in the living room." She began to take a tray with plates and flatware out.

Burke crouched down and scratched the dog's ears. "Who's my good boy?"

"I heard that. That's not something you should praise him for."

"Again, I'll offer to take him home?"

"He can stay. As long as he stays out of my clothes hamper." They set up for their brunch on the coffee table. She noticed that Burke kept stroking it and studying the rings. "I take it you like the coffee table?"

"I love it. I've rarely ever seen anything so gorgeous. I really like wood."

Eventually the dog joined them, having devoured his pork rib. Burke had finished all he wanted of the quiche by now, and as he read, he absentmindedly scratched the dog's ears, and said "Who's my good boy?" every once in a while, running all the words together.

Miranda studied them. Then she said suddenly, "Junior." Burke looked over at her. The dog didn't. Then she said, "Who'sMyGoodBoy?" and the dog jumped up on the couch, ran over Burke and came right to her. She scratched his ears and he tried to lick her face as she held him off. His tail was wagging so hard his back end was wriggling.

"How can you not find him completely adorable?" Burke asked.

"Hmmm. I think a part of your undisciplined dog problem is that 'Junior' is not his name. It might be your son's but it's not his."

"What?"

"Well, obviously, his name is 'Who'sMyGoodBoy'."

The dog wagged even harder and barked twice excitedly.

"Yup," she said. "That's what you say to him all the time. That's what he thinks his name is."

Burke laughed. "Who'sMyGoodBoy?" he said, and the dog turned around and came over to him, wagging expectantly. "Well, I guess that's better than him thinking his name is 'Bad Dog'."

Who'sMyGoodBoy whined and hung his head.

Over the next two weeks of Burke's editing visits, he continued to bring Who'sMyGoodBoy with him. The dog seemed to love Miranda, particularly her leg, which he would hump if she didn't push him away with her foot. The pooch always wanted to sit with her and be touching her. He followed her around constantly and would stare lovingly at her as she cooked. She was surprised at how quickly having a dog grew on her, but she did make sure to shut her dirty clothes hamper up in her closet.

Sunday rolled around again, and she had come up with yet another unusual brunch idea for her meeting with Burke. She loved to surprise him with food he'd never tried before. She found she loved having someone to cook for. Cooking for herself was just not something she could get very excited

241

about. And he turned out to be a bit of a closet foodie.

"This is weird, eggs on a pizza, but I have to admit, it's surprisingly good," he said as he took his third slice of breakfast pizza. She noticed he cut off a bite with this fork and slipped it under the table.

"I don't think you'll win him over. He knows who actually made it."

"I know," Burke said, pretending to be glum. "I've lost the loyalty of my dog because of you. It's you he loves. That surely must say something about my cooking."

She laughed at him. "I'm glad you like the breakfast pizza anyway, and you aren't feeding it all to the dog. You know, it's good that you like *something* when you come over."

"Hey, the writing isn't that bad. You're taking this too personally."

"Nah, I'm only taking it mostly personally. I see what you mean. And you're right—I don't really like my characters, so I can't find their motivation. I feel like I'm spinning my wheels."

"Well, your characters are certainly feeling that. They're really flat. I'm sorry I'm not giving you great encouragement here. I'm just not finding a compelling story in it."

Miranda sunk back into her seat on the couch. "I'm trying to force it. I think maybe I'm not that kind of writer."

"Maybe I'm off base? Maybe it's me. How's it going with Mad-Kat? Are they giving you good feedback?"

"Well…"

"So, not good feedback."

"Well, um, I think I know the kinds of books that Mad likes in particular."

"Oh, and what would that be?"

"Well, she reads a lot of pretty thrilling stuff. I think she has a real thing for vampires. I think she's disappointed that I don't seem to be able to work the undead into my story."

Burke's sudden laugh made him spill his coffee. "Oh, shit. Sorry." He reached for a paper towel to clean up the mess, but Who'sMyGoodBoy was already on it.

"One thing I've learned from Mad has been really helpful."

"What's that?"

"Well, whatever storyline she suggests, I know to avoid because it's been done and she's read it. Even if she can't remember the book or reading that story, that's the genesis of her idea—she's read it someplace. Or it was a movie."

"Well, maybe Kat will be of more help? I mean with the creative side." He picked up the most recent list of errors she had tabulated for Miranda to fix.

"She would have been an excellent eighth grade grammar teacher, to be sure," Miranda said. "But on the creative side, um, well…"

"Oh no. My sister isn't a vampire girl, too, is she? I'm getting afraid for what's coming down the pike for the book club…"

"No, no, not vampires. She seems to want a hero-type character. With a British accent. And he needs to have scads of money. Very handsome. Make that incredibly handsome."

"Oh. You know, somehow that doesn't come as a huge surprise."

"And he should be passionate about the main character, even against his better judgement. And she should be a stark, raving beauty of noble character but who's not rich. Just a hard-working girl, trying to make it in a hard world."

"Ah, the damsel in distress plot line. And the handsome hero."

"Yeah, but a damsel with real spunk. Now I can see where nobody wants to read a story about a dumpy, middle-aged divorcee who's insecure and, frankly, doesn't have such great judgement and makes some decisions that are, well, rather questionable."

"Hey, unless it's hilarious, and then it becomes a best seller."

"Huh? Oh, yeah, funny! Yeah, I guess so." She smiled at him.

"So, Mad wants you to write a vampire-based bodice-ripper romance novel. Sounds like her. And Kat wants a more down-to-earth Harlequin?"

Miranda nodded. "They're very helpful cheerleaders, but not terribly

243

helpful critics. With all this encouragement, I'm finding that I'm writing, actually plunking words out on the page in response to their demands for more, so that's incredibly useful in that it's making me be productive. But I don't know if they're *good* words."

"They're not critical enough, and I'm too much."

She blushed furiously.

"I don't have to be…" he added rather quickly.

She laughed and waved him off. "Sorry, it's just that it feels so personal, you know? It's so unfinished. Writing is like the raw me. To Mad-Kat, it's a story and light entertainment, that is, of course, missing an undead British billionaire, but to me, at least when I'm writing something that I think has any merit at all, it's a lot of how I think about the world and what I think about people and my own faults and errors spilled across the pages."

"That's what makes it so different from most of what's out there. In your book, it's you in those pages. I think your readers connect with the person who's behind the story. Your voice as a narrator comes from a vulnerable place. I don't think you're alone in feeling that way."

"Oh my God, Burke. There you go again! You see, that's what frightens me about you being a reader, particularly while it's in process. You already say the most insightful, stunning things to me. I don't want to be the flawed, neurotic, vulnerable, yet comedic relief in your eyes. I'd much rather be the beautiful, noble, spunky, hard-working heroine! You reading my raw stuff—I don't know. You'll see the real me hiding behind the curtain, while I'm trying to show the rest of world the true fictional character of Miranda Wright."

He looked at her for a while. "I'm your friend. Who else can you be your true self with but your good friends? And you know what else good friends are for?"

She looked at him and shrugged.

"Allowing you to be your fictional self once in a while, too."

Chapter 26

Miranda was elated. She'd had so much fun. She couldn't remember when she'd danced the nights away like this. Probably not since she was in college. Certainly not since she'd gotten pregnant. They say a baby changes everything. Well, that had been unquestionably true in her case. But she wasn't mothering anymore. She'd always be a mother, it was just that Emma didn't really need her now. She wasn't in grade school. Or high school. Even in college, she'd leaned on her mama to take care of the basics of life, right up until her mama fell apart. Miranda had enjoyed the extension of motherhood—an extension of the only purpose in life that she had ever known. Now she was free to create her own life. As painful as that had been at first, those torturous initial steps had eventually led her here—to a place where she felt as though she was flourishing. She had a sense of who she was at last. And a sense of peace. She smiled as she thought of the previous night. Her feet had ached when she came home, she'd danced so much. She was more than a little sweaty but felt like no workout had ever been as fun as moving about the floor, weaving in and out as she did the Carolina Shag. She looked out her window at the sun glinting off the sound. If she was honest, it was rather nice to be done with the mothering phase. Now there was time for… herself. She took a sip of her coffee and delighted in the moment. It was a moment that she could never have even imagined experiencing just twelve short months ago.

Her phone went ping! as it announced a new text.

To her surprise, it was E.

Mom do u have a minute?

She hadn't heard from her daughter since Christmas. For the first few days, Miranda had checked her phone every hour or so, sure E would send her a message. Then she would check it daily, hoping for some sign that things hadn't changed irrevocably. By the end of the second week, she'd finally trained herself to stop checking, accepting the reality that Emma didn't want to talk to a mother who was such an embarrassment. Now two months had passed. She'd never gone two months without hearing from E. Miranda read the text again.

Mom do u have a minute?

That was unlike Emma. E usually asked for things. Her 'ask' generally sounded more like a command. Clearly, E needed something.

Sure, she texted back.

Her phone rang almost immediately.

"Hi, Mom."

"Hi, E. What's up?"

"Mom, I'm glad I caught you in. I, uh, wanted to talk."

"Honey, something's wrong. I can hear it in your voice. What's happened?"

The line was quiet for a moment or two. That pause gave Miranda more concern than Emma's words.

"I'm having a really bad weekend. In fact, I'm really miserable. First, yesterday, I woke up with a headache. Then I had to go to the store and the people there were so incompetent. It was a total waste of time. Time is my most precious thing and they were just idiots. I'm trying to study for a big histology exam and my anatomy lab partners are trying to force everyone on the team to get together this afternoon for an extra session in the lab. We already spend four days a week in there with a dead body. They named her Old Lady Leary after some old song. Isn't that gross? It's Sunday for Christ's sake. Can't we let poor dead Mrs. Leary rest for a friggin' day? And last night

I was telling Emile about my awful day and Mom, we had a terrible fight. He was just horrible to me, Mom. Just awful!"

Miranda sat back in her chair and looked again at the sound. A few clouds had kicked up and she couldn't see the sun glinting off the waves anymore. Go figure. Not a word about the radio silence of the past months. She took in a deep breath. She'd been down this road with her daughter countless times. "Honey, I'm sorry you had such a frustrating day."

Before she could say anything else, Emma started up again with why everything and everyone around her was wrong. Miranda listened for about ten minutes, during which time she made another hot macchiato and unloaded the dishwasher. Every once in a while she would make little "uh huh" sounds or say "oh." Then Caroline's voice played in her head:

Maybe being her best friend doesn't mean being buddies. Maybe it means being there when she needs you. Or putting limits on her. Or being the one person who is really honest with her. Maybe it means loving her even when she's an asshole like her father.

Miranda took in a deep breath. "Hey, you know something, E? It strikes me that you've just told me how the people at the store were wrong. That your lab partners were wrong."

"Yeah."

"That Emile was wrong when he was so unsympathetic with all the work you have to do and was unsupportive because he wasn't willing to help you out."

"That's right! He was such a jerk. He said, and get this, 'I'm not your mother. Stop asking me to get you something to eat or pick up around here. I'm not your servant'. Can you believe that?"

Miranda thought she could and surprised herself that a little smile came to her face. "Go figure. So, all these things in your life are wrong. You know, E, there is one common denominator there."

"What's that?"

"You." There. She'd said it. That was about as honest as she could possibly be. "It's you. If everything in your life is wrong, then the one constant, the one central figure is you. I think maybe you need to take a few steps back and look at yourself and see what you're doing to contribute to it."

"I can't believe I called you. Now you're just turning around and blaming me."

"Emma, I'm not there. I'm not blaming you for anything. In fact, I'm having a great day here, so I have nothing to blame you for. I'm just pointing out what's right in front of you, that maybe you're too close to… to be able to see it. Life doesn't just happen to you, Emma. You own your day. You own your reaction to it. Honey, you have to decide what to do but as long as you blame everything and everyone else for what upsets you, well, I don't think you'll find either an answer there or any kind of resolution."

Emma was quiet for a while.

"I don't think Emile is coming back."

"He left? So, this wasn't just a disagreement."

"No. I think it was a breakup. He said he'd had it. He was tired of the expectation that he'd wait on me. Mom, I don't ask him to wait on me."

"Really?"

"I don't expect anyone to wait on me!"

"You expect me to wait on you, Emma. You have for years. And maybe my mistake has been to go along with that expectation."

Emma was quiet again. Then with a bitter tone in her voice she said, "I'm sorry you feel that way."

"I'm sorry you expect it of me. I'm even sorrier if you expected it of Emile. That's not his role as boyfriend."

"But I'm in medical school. It's so intense! I have no time. I have to study!"

"I understand that. It's a serious commitment. But it's your commitment, not his. Not mine. Yours. You own this. Only you. And I know you can do it if that's what you want."

Emma was quiet again.

Miranda waited.

"I own this."

"Yeah. And you live with however it turns out. Honey, I'm seven hundred miles away."

Emma gave a little sniff. "I feel so alone."

"Have you called your father?"

Emma's answer sounded a little tentative. "I don't think I could. I only thought of you... Mom."

"I love you, Emma. I want you to be happy. But you have to choose to be happy. It's something that comes from inside you."

"I'm not sure I know how."

"I didn't either when I was your age. But you know what, E?"

"What Mom?"

"I'm learning how. And I'm happy."

"You're happy?"

"Yeah. Really happy."

"Really happy?"

"Yeah, Emma. Sometimes it just takes time. It takes work. And it takes being really honest with yourself. You'll be happy, too. You just have to do those things. But you can't be happy if you can't be honest with yourself, because if you can't be honest with yourself, you can't be honest with anyone else."

"Okay, uh, I'd better get back to studying. Um, thanks, Mom. Thanks."

"I love you, Emma. Call anytime."

"Love you too, Mom."

Miranda hit the end button and looked at her phone, feeling a mix of surprise and curiosity. "I wonder if she heard what I said?" She took another sip of her coffee and then put her empty cup in the now empty dishwasher. In her usual way of talking out loud to no one in particular she said, "Damn, I think she might actually *have* heard me."

She looked back out her window at the sound where the sun was once again glinting off the calm waters. She sure wished she believed in signs. But if faith was a gift, it wasn't her gift. No, for her it could only be a destination.

Chapter 27

One thing Miranda loved about North Carolina was the weather. You could have absolutely gorgeous days, warm ones, even in the last days of winter. It was mid-March. The sun was shining. It was beautiful outside. It would probably be in the low seventies. It had been much colder and grayer during the last week, when she had spent her time in Charlotte attending to some business, checking on her condo there, and visiting Caroline. She was surprised how much she'd missed the island in her short time away. She hadn't seen anyone of her 'extended beach family', as she called them, for about ten days now. She had missed two weekends of shag dancing, which was now so popular that it could be hard to find space on the dance floor. Miguel said he was going to offer it on Saturdays and Wednesdays during the season, and he was looking into live band options too.

She made a cup of coffee, setting it to espresso and trying to make fun shapes with the steamed milk. It came out as a blob. She thought back to how Austin had perfected those apocalyptic mushroom clouds in the coffee. She reached up to her cheek and wiped away an involuntary tear, a little surprised that the emotion was still with her. "Now those are tears I don't resent. If anyone deserves tears shed for them, it's you, Austin." They'd had no contact since that fateful holiday trip. She found that she could miss him at odd moments. When she was alone, coffee could bring up the sense memory of him. She had tried to switch to tea, but she just wasn't a tea drinker. That was M.G.'s territory. As she took a sip, she realized that coffee now also brought up associations with Burke. She mulled that over a bit.

Austin had come into her life most unexpectedly. And most unexpectedly he had turned out to only barely be a man. Looking back and examining their relationship she was amazed at how it had developed and how much it had meant to her. She was grateful for it.

She thought about Burke. He was really nice and they had fun together. He loved books. She loved books. He was trying so hard to play it cool, but it was clear he was interested in way more than being friends. Too interested for her to feel comfortable, but Austin had been that way, too, hadn't he? Hadn't he been just as eager to be with her? It was hard to tell. She had been so eager herself back then. Nervous, sure, but ready to take that chance. She had been ripe for the picking, ready to fall. What if she had met Burke first, instead of Austin? Would she have fallen so quickly into his arms? Was she just that vulnerable because of the divorce? Willingly blinding herself to what should have been obvious? But Austin had been blinded, too. He had thought she was younger. Much younger. They'd both seen what they wanted to see. Damn, how wrong could you get?

Burke seemed like he really had it together, but he was undeniably circling like a shark, just like the other desperate single men who worked so hard to chase her down. It was obvious in the way he danced with her. And that hand massage back in January—while that was nice, it was clearly all he could do to keep his hands that much to himself. He appeared relaxed, but he wasn't relaxed, even when he came over for brunch on Sundays to give her advice on her manuscript. Austin, by contrast, was always himself. No excuses. No pretense. No realization that he could be any other way. He wasn't old enough yet to learn to play a game. He wasn't experienced enough to learn to hide his imperfections from the overly critical eyes of others who were looking for any excuse to protect their already damaged hearts from suffering further harm. Austin had never been rejected. Burke had clearly earned his scars, but that came with age. No one was spared. She had her scars too. She hadn't told Burke that she and her man-friend were over. It was a layer of protection from the unwanted advances of those sharks in the water.

She sipped her coffee, looked outside at the beautiful, calm water, and thought about what she was going to do that day. She should write. Every day she should write. She really wanted to go outside and enjoy the beautiful weather.

The phone rang.

"Deliverance! That will be Mad or Kat wanting to go out and do something!" She picked up the phone. "Hello."

"Hi, Miranda. You sound happy. It's Burke. I wondered if you might like to go up to Manteo and see a new art exhibit. There are a couple of new galleries there that just opened up. Local artists and others from across the state."

She didn't say anything for a moment. She hadn't expected him. She'd expected one of the girls. She felt like she should be glad it was Burke and not Darnell on the line. He had called twice. Paul had left her three messages just in the last week.

"Art gallery?" She liked Burke, and because of that she didn't want to lead him on. But to see the art galleries, now that sounded really interesting.

"Yeah, how about I pick you up in an hour? I want to give you enough fair warning so that you'll, uh, have your shirt on when I get there. And maybe your laundry hamper locked in the closet."

She could hear the mirth in his voice and it made her smile. "Surely we're not taking the dog?"

"No, I'm just kidding about that part."

"Okay, you're on. An hour. And I promise to be fully clothed and ready to go."

"Oh, that's too bad."

He arrived right on time. As promised, she was ready to go when he knocked on the door. She went with a bright blue pullover sweater, black jeans, and cowboy boots. "Why don't I drive today? You always drive, and that's hardly fair to you."

253

"Sure, I'm happy to follow your lead. I can give you directions when we get to Manteo."

Arriving in Manteo, they parked in the historic downtown section and then walked to the first gallery, talking easily. Upon entering, Miranda was immediately struck by the variety of work. This was not your typical kitschy beach gallery with multiple versions of the same paintings of waves or seashells. This was real artwork. Like you'd put in a real home. They perused the paintings, each commenting on the styles they liked the best.

"I have to say, I like the giant cow. Look at those crazy horns," Burke said.

"Yeah, it's cool. Kinda looks like it's got polka dots on it, with that sun dappling, but it's cool. Would you want that hanging in your house?"

"Oh, I don't know if it's *that* cool." He smiled at her. "I just like it."

"Yeah, liking it and living with it are very different things. I like all this selection because hardly any of it's beach stuff. It's not paintings for tourists—it's art. It's actual art. It's really wonderful. I'm so glad you brought me. It's so inspiring!"

"How does it inspire you?"

"To paint," she said distractedly as she looked at a large painting of sunflowers. "Just look at this one. These gorgeous sunflowers, so loosely painted. It's like you're standing at the edge of the little patch of these wildly growing flowers and you can see the field off to the side and the hills off to the background. These colors are so vibrant—look at the difference between this, which is an oil, and the cow. Your cow is done in acrylics. This is from an Asheville artist. Man, I love Asheville. How great that they've brought in a bunch of art from all across the state!"

"You paint?"

"What? Oh, yeah. I've painted for years. Just set up my studio at home when I got back after the holidays."

"You paint." It wasn't a question. He followed her as she walked over to another painting. "Will I see your things in here someday?"

She laughed. "Oh, don't infer something I'm not saying. I love painting. I'm developing my own style. But I'm not that good. I'm at the point where you can show your mother and your friends, and they'll be supportive, but not at the point where you'd show it to anyone you don't know who would give you their real opinion. And I'm certainly not ready for Ben's reviews!" She winked at him. "No, for me it's just very therapeutic. At Christmas Mimi, that's Caroline's mom, she's pretty well known…. Hey, I wonder if she has anything in this gallery?" Miranda looked at the paintings with renewed interest.

"What about her?"

"Oh, sorry. I got distracted. Mimi Watkins is her name. She taught me to paint back in college when I would come home with Caroline. Over the years she's given me great pointers and coaching tips. I guess you could say she's my painting mentor. At Christmas she was very direct. She pulled me aside and gave me my marching orders to get my studio set up and get back to painting. So, that's one of the first things I did when I came back to the beach. It's upstairs in the little room with the small screened in porch off of it."

"You have a studio at home?

"Uh huh,"

"What do you mean therapeutic?"

"Look at this one. This is really stunning. Look at the use of light. Oh my God…"

"What do you mean by therapeutic?" he repeated.

"Oh, art is really helpful in dealing with emotions and major life events. It can help you process feelings and move through difficult experiences. It's a wonderful tool. I wrote a chapter on it way back when."

"Why do you need it to be therapeutic? Wait a minute, this is about your man-friend, isn't it?"

She blushed furiously.

"He's gone, isn't he?"

She just looked at him.

"He's been gone… since the holidays?"

"Uh, yeah. 'Bout then."

The silence hung between them. Miranda was very glad they were alone in the shop. Burke put a hand on her shoulder. "Are you okay?"

She couldn't believe the sincerity in his voice. Had this been Paul, she was sure he would have done a little victory dance, but Burke was really thinking of her.

"Thanks. It's been hard, I won't lie. I loved him, but it wasn't meant to be, should never have been. It was a mistake. Just a crazy mistake."

"Hey," he gave her shoulder a gentle squeeze. "You said you loved him. I remember you saying he was helping you heal from the end of your marriage. Just because it didn't work out with him doesn't mean it was wrong. Maybe there's hope in the future?"

"Not with him. No, we had this crazy age difference that we hadn't realized. There's no way it ever should have happened in the first place. So, I've been painting to work my way through it." She was amazed at how much better she felt just to hear the words.

"And has that helped?"

"Yeah, I think it has. Having friends has been nice too, so thanks, Burke, for including me. It's been nice to not feel so alone."

Burke looked at Miranda for a long time. "You don't have to be alone," he said at last. She didn't know what to say, couldn't quite form words. Suddenly he seemed not totally at ease. Looking around the gallery he asked, "So, what's your style? In all this art, where would your paintings fit in?"

She took a deep breath, feeling like a moment had passed. She couldn't tell whether she was sorry or glad she'd missed it. An older couple entered the gallery, the jaunty bell on the door giving its alerting ring to the manager. The wife was dressed head-to-toe in some hideous shade of yellow. Her husband had the expression of a man who'd been dragged around shopping all day.

Miranda lowered her voice and pointed to the sunflowers. "My work looks a tiny bit like that one with the loose and open style, but this," she led him over to a very large painting. "Now, this I love. I wish I could do this. This forest picture with the stream is just incredible. It's painting with a palette knife—no brushes. Look at how the artist has built up the paint. It costs a small fortune in materials to do this, but it's completely amazing." She leaned in close to the painting, fascinated, pointing out features. "Look here, all this build up, and it must be ten colors. It's a bit like a bas relief with the paint so thick. Look here, the artist is using positive and negative space. In some branches the paint is all built up, which makes them really pop out at you, but to create the depth effect the palette knife has been used to scrape away the paint here." As she pointed to the effect on the painting, she stood back up, not realizing that Burke was standing over her, leaning in and following what she was saying. She turned around and found she was practically folding herself into him, inches from his face.

"That's fascinating," he said, but he wasn't looking at the painting at all.

She looked up into his eyes, blinking, not sure what she should do and not sure if she wanted to do anything at all. Then he reached his hand up and ran his fingers across her cheek and back through her hair. With his hand cupping her head he leaned in and gave her a light kiss on the lips. She surprised herself by kissing him back.

As he pulled back he looked surprised. Then a slow smile spread over his face. Very softly he said, "I'd like to be your man-friend, Miranda."

She watched him as he leaned in again. She felt his hand pull her head towards him. Then he kissed her. He really kissed her. She wasn't sure how much time passed before they leaned back away from one another. "Wow," she whispered. "You are quite the kisser, Burke."

The woman in yellow rapped her husband in the arm and with a strong New York accent shouted to him as though he were quite deaf, "Now look, Louis, he just bought her that painting. You weren't fast enough."

"Well, you never kiss *me* that way," the old man replied.

"Hey, if you'd bought me that painting I *would* kiss you that way!"

Miranda and Burke glanced at the couple and giggled softly. "Can I be your man-friend?" he asked.

"Burke, I'm not sure I'm ready for a relationship." She wanted to be honest with him. Totally honest. He deserved that. "I don't want to get hurt again."

"It's okay. We'll take it slow. Very, very slow. And don't forget, I was your friend first. This isn't like some wild wind whipping in and throwing you off course. I've always been here. C'mon. Let me buy you dinner. Let's get out of here so that man can buy his wife this nine-thousand-dollar painting."

Chapter 28

Burke was on cloud nine. He'd done it. His son had actually given him good advice. Burke had been there, been her friend, and the other guy had cleared out. Of course he had: he was a mainlander. Burke had been nearly four-months-patient. Always trying to keep it fun and light and then she'd told him the other guy was gone, had been gone. She said something about art as therapeutic and it struck him why she hadn't quite been her totally put-together self when she came back from the holidays. Obviously, she had been really hurt. He could hear his son's voice in his head saying, 'What would her best friend do?' *Hug her. Kiss her* was what had immediately come to mind. His heart had been pounding in his ears and he could barely register what she was saying. Something about the guy being nearly retired, a crazy age difference. He kept thinking, *You shouldn't be with some old geezer. You should be with me,* but he didn't know what to do next. To be honest, he'd felt like doing a little victory dance, but no, that would have been in seriously bad taste. In fact, that would be something Paul would do.

As he was trying to figure out his next move, he told her she didn't have to be alone. It was an invitation. A clear invitation. She didn't take the bait. She swam on by. *Damn.* His disappointment felt crushing in that moment as opportunity yet again slipped through his fingers. He didn't know what to say, so he asked about her art. She rambled on about piles of expensive paint on a canvas. He stood over her, smelling her perfume, ostensibly looking at whatever the heck she was pointing to, but all he could think of was how to create a second chance, to bring the moment by again. He swore he wouldn't miss it the next time. There might not be another one. Then, as he leaned over her, she stood up and turned around, her lips just bare inches from his. He didn't remember what he said. Hopefully it wasn't anything stupid, but he'd touched her cheek and then he kissed her, softly, sweetly. She didn't react badly. In fact, she kissed him back. Then he said it. The thing he felt he had been saying with every one of his actions for months and months and months: *I'd like to be your man-friend, Miranda.* Before she could say no, he'd kissed her again. Really kissed her. And it happened. He was her man-friend now.

When they went dancing at Saturday night shag, he didn't have to share her with anyone. Darnell looked like he might try once, but Burke had kissed her on the floor right there in front of everyone at the end of a song. She had kissed him back, her eyes shining and happy. They went back to her house and made out on the couch. He hadn't done that since he was a teenager, all that rolling around with all your clothes on. Napping together on weekend afternoons, wrapped up in each other's arms. It was late March and all too soon the tourist season would open and he would be so busy he would hardly be able to see her. They had to do everything together now, while things were quiet.

He tapped in her number. She picked it up before the third ring.

"Hi, Burke."

"Hi, Miranda. I was wondering if you might like to go out tonight and listen to some music?"

"Wow, again? We just danced last night. Is this more dancing?"

"No, this is sit back in a chair, drink a beer and enjoy some great bluegrass. It's a place up in Duck called Duckbill Blues."

"Oh! I know that place!"

"You do? Great. Well, that was easy. I thought I might have to sell you on the bluegrass. They're opening for a pre-season warm-up show. Rumor is that Grandpa's gonna play."

"Absolutely sign me up! I wouldn't want to miss it. That man is legend. Can we go early so we get good seats?"

He couldn't believe his luck with this woman. Now if she only liked Jackie Chan movies, he would marry her, he was sure of it.

He picked her up early and they walked around Duck for a while, hand-in-hand. Well before the show they went to Duckbill Blues to secure good seats but found that Mad and Kat were already there holding a table for them.

"Oh, here come the lovebirds!" Mad gushed happily. Mike returned from the bar, carrying a couple of beers.

"Oh, I see I'd better get more. What's your fancy, Miranda?"

"Anything dark and chewy," she answered with a smile.

"Good woman."

"Hey Mad, where's Ben?" Miranda asked.

"Oh, he's helping bring in the equipment for the show," Mad said happily as she picked up her bottle of Rolling Rock. "I'm just so tickled about the two of you."

Burke had his arm around Miranda's shoulders and he leaned over and kissed her hair. She blushed and leaned into him, giving Mad a smile.

Mike returned with more beers and they all sat down to drink and catch up on one another's news. The band got up and tuned their instruments. Miranda turned to Mad and said, "Why, that's Ben up there! He's in the band?"

"Oh yeah, honey! Wasn't that clear? He's the banjo player. Music runs in his whole family! Oh, here's our dinners. Thanks, Kyle." She winked at the waiter who'd brought a massive plate of hot wings and another piled high with nachos.

"Wow! I never eat like this." Miranda looked at the plates dubiously. "And I'm just getting back into drinking alcohol again."

Kat laughed. "That's probably why you look like you do."

Miranda picked up a wing and sipped her beer. "Oh, I've really lost my edge since last summer. I'm trying hard to fight my way back to where I was.

You know, I had a flume put in. I found I just wasn't going up to the gym and I missed swimming so much."

"What's a flume?" Kat asked.

"It's a lap pool the size of a mini-van. The water moves so you can swim in place and it's just like doing laps in a pool. In an endless lap lane. Of the world's longest pool. You basically swim until you drown."

"I'm not sure that sounds like fun." Kat shook her head. "Sounds like a riptide in a can, but whatever floats your boat."

The band tuned up and introduced themselves as 'The Dare County Line.' They played three great bluegrass songs and in the middle of the fourth, Grandpa shuffled into the bar. Characteristically, he was dressed in his snug fitting jeans, white button-down shirt, and ugly, comfortable shoes. The applause grew for him even before the song was over. He gave a wave to the crowd as he stopped and smiled, clearly happy for their adulation. He shuffled over to the stage and at the end of the song, Ben put down his banjo and helped the old man up to the microphone. He sat in with them for half a dozen songs this time.

"Oh, that's about all I'm good for. Someone needs to get me an iced tea," Grandpa said when he finished his last song. "I'm gettin' too old for this and you all look younger every year." Ben once again helped him navigate the step down from the stage and Grandpa made his way around the room to hug and kiss everyone there as the other band boys took a break. Eventually he made his way around to their table. Everyone stood as he approached them. He walked right up to Miranda. "Well, hello missy with the boy's name."

"Oh, Grandpa!" Mad chided him. "This is Miranda."

"If you say so. Hello Madeline. You're looking beautiful as ever." He gave her a kiss. "Howdy Kat, my darlin'. Say, when are you going to invite me over for spaghetti night?"

"You know my door is always open to you, Grandpa." She laughed back at him and gave him a kiss on the cheek.

Burke took a small step forward. "Grandpa, I'd like for you to meet

Miranda."

"Hi, Grandpa." Miranda was all smiles. "It's nice to see you again."

"Nice to see you too." He turned to Burke. "Mind if I give your pretty little lady a kiss?"

"I think I'd be terribly hurt if you didn't," Miranda said with a warm smile on her face.

"You two have met?" Burke asked, looking from one to the other.

"Oh, she's seen me sing before."

"Yes, just once. But I'm a big fan of Grandpa's."

"I'd say you're a big fan of my whole family." He winked at her. "Heh, heh, heh. So interesting." He shook his head, still chuckling.

Madeline jumped in. "Grandpa, Miranda is a famous author. And she's a painter. I'd say she's about the most interesting thing to hit this island in a long, long time."

Grandpa surveyed the group. "If you say so, Mad. If you say so." He turned to Burke, "Now there, son, I think you're outta your league." He nodded to Miranda as he spoke.

"Absolutely, sir. She's one of a kind."

"Then you're a lucky man."

Burke smiled. "Yes, yes, I am," and gave Miranda's hand a squeeze.

"Well, I'm gonna go and see if I can be a lucky man. Gonna go and stir up some trouble! I see there's a set of groupies over there who will be mighty sore at me if I don't pay my respects." He nodded to a table of four older ladies, who were all waving and winking at him. "See you all later. Be good!"

As one, the group responded, "Or be good at it." Everyone laughed. Burke noticed that Miranda had joined them, not missing a beat. He felt elated that Miranda fit in so well. This couldn't be more perfect. Well, if she just liked Jackie Chan movies, that would clinch it.

* * *

Burke felt there was one thing left undone. Something he had to address, and he had to do it alone. Very early on Wednesday morning he'd gotten up. He needed to see Joette. He needed to set things right with her. He picked up a dozen roses on his way. If a thing was worth doing, it was worth doing right.

Getting out of his car, he walked across the dewy grass, feeling his nervousness grow. He didn't know what he was going to say, didn't know how he was going to phrase it, he just knew this couldn't go on any longer until he had done what needed to be done. He walked past the trees and down the little lane to where she was. Instantly he felt guilty.

"Look at these weeds," he said. "I'm sorry, Joette. I know these are my responsibility. I brought you some flowers." He stood the roses up in a stone vase and arranged them so they looked nice. He knew they wouldn't stay that way for long. He picked up his water bottle and poured some into the vase. "I'm sorry I'm neglecting you." He started pulling the weeds. "I needed to come and talk to you. I want you to know that you're the love of my life. You'll always be the one." He took a deep breath into the silence. He looked up at the sky and blinked away a tear. No, it was right to cry. Some things hurt so much that they deserved tears. He stroked the stone. It was so cold. "I've missed you every day of these last fifteen years. At first, I didn't know how to go on. Remember how I used to come and talk to you all the time then?" He fussed with the flowers a bit, moving them so they weren't crowding their fellows. "And I've dated over the years. I've told you that. We both know that was never a big deal. It's always been you."

Burke took a deep breath. He knew he had to say it. He knew it wasn't for Joette. It was for him. She would never answer him. "I wanted you to know that I've met someone. Someone special. Someone I think you would like. And I want to be with her. I think for the rest of my life. You asked me to take Austin, to make him family, to raise him as my own. I think you knew you were all going to leave me. I've never been able to find another mother for Austin. No one could ever replace you. But I wanted you to know, and you too, Pumpkin, my darling Juliet, about her, and know that I would never choose anyone who would tarnish all my memories and love for you both. I would never choose someone you wouldn't approve of. But, Joette, I need to say this to you: I don't want to be alone anymore. The boy's at college now. College. Can you believe that? The winters are so long these days. He wanted to come home a lot his first two years, but now that he's a junior he hasn't come home at all, except for holidays. Of course, you know that. We came to see you both on Christmas day." Burke pulled a handkerchief out of his pocket and blew his nose. This was so much harder than he'd thought it was going to be.

"She's wonderful. She's smart and talented. She's your age, Joette. Or the age you would have been. She has a daughter, too. We've been friends since the fall, but things have taken a different turn now and I think she's it." He pulled a few more little weeds, looking around for something to busy his hands. "I hope you can forgive me for needing to move on. But after all these years, I think I feel safe enough to go on. I think, finally, I've found someone I can go on with. She's really perfect. I hope you can forgive me. Please, please forgive me." He dabbed his eyes with his handkerchief. It took him a while before the tears ended. "Please forgive me." His voice was barely a whisper.

As he crouched by their graves, silent and still for a long while, a bird came and landed on top of Joette's headstone. He kept very still, and the bird chirped at him, whistling out a quick tune, and then it flew away. Burke felt an instant wave of relief and sobbed into his handkerchief. "Thank you, honey. Thank you. I won't let you down. I promise."

Chapter 29

Burke read the manuscript, while Miranda typed on her laptop, capturing her thoughts from their discussion over breakfast. The dog was lying on her feet.

For the first two months of the year she had struggled with one dead end story after another. Then she went back to Charlotte for a short week to take care of some business and to visit Caroline, who was feeling lonely with her son away at college. She welcomed Miranda's company and introduced her to Jane, who happened to be visiting. "Jane's baby sister married my little brother, so that makes us either sisters-in-law or some other convoluted kind of relatives, but it's always felt like we were family," Caroline said.

"So, you're Miranda Wright?" Jane asked with a sincere smile. "I've read your book. Really made one of my long flights actually enjoyable." They instantly hit it off. Jane was a huge fan and happily offered Miranda her own story if it would help break her writer's block. "Years ago now, while I was in school and doing study abroad in France I fell in love with Nick, a Brit studying green architecture. Oh my god, I thought he was the most gorgeous thing I'd ever seen. We finally got together. It was that old romantic tale—we didn't have two Euros to rub together, but we loved just to be with each other. He proposed on Christmas day with the most beautiful ring, his grandmother's wedding diamond."

"I have to say, this is sounding pretty perfect."

"Yeah, I thought so too. But then his stuffy, snobbish parents torpedoed four sets of wedding plans."

Miranda, mouth hanging open, looked at Jane.

"Tell her about plan number five," Caroline said.

"That was a bummer. Having completely given up trying to find anything that could remotely appease his parents, we decided to elope. In our beloved France. But then, just a week before my flight to Europe I slipped on an invisible patch of black ice. Yup, blammo! I landed in a cast and a sling at the same time."

"Oh my God, what did you do?"

"Not elope. No, but we actually successfully tied the knot right out there in Caroline's back yard. Attempt number six. Gorgeous place for a wedding."

"That is an incredible story." Miranda stared at Jane.

"Oh honey, she's only getting started." Caroline smirked and shook her head as she sipped her tea.

"Should've taken that epic wipe out as some sort of sign. Nick turned out to be *not* British. And *not* poor. And *not* in architecture. And *not* with me."

Miranda just stared at Jane. "How did… how did all that unravel so fast?"

"How did he turn out to be a Canadian heir to thirty million who was actually running a liquor business and sleeping with one of our friends? Oh, let me tell you." When she'd finished speaking, Jane smiled at Miranda. "So, you can write my story if you want. I mean, don't make it about me, but you can use the events if you like."

"Wow. Only if I can also include how you saved the day after that lout, Nick, buried the jeep up to its axels in the sand down in rural Mexico. What a jerk. You were so lucky you happened upon a pepper farm and not a coca farm! Oh my, you so could have ended up dead."

"You know, I don't know what they were growing. I didn't ask. I just described it as peppers so my mother didn't have a heart attack."

Miranda looked wide-eyed at Caroline, who sipped her iced tea and nodded.

They all agreed that truth was stranger than fiction.

"Or there's my baby sister. Her love life took some bizarre twists and turns too, but they were all of her own making."

Miranda smiled, thinking back on her own experience. "It seems to me that most of our roads are ones we've driven down willingly—we just didn't know quite how to read the directional signs, so we took some really weird off ramps."

Jane gave her a knowing nod. "Those are pretty sage words to come from a comedic author. So, your next book... it's a drama?"

"Oh God, I hope not!"

* * *

"I think this is pretty good. I really love the part about the coca farm. That's crazy," Burke said as he was marking typos on the manuscript.

"Tell me about it. I'm glad it didn't happen to me."

"I'll have to think about the younger sister's story." He put the papers down and looked at her. "Being in love with one brother and then suddenly falling for the other, who had secretly always been in love with her? I don't know, that sounds like some bad Hallmark Channel movie. It's hard to understand how someone could get themselves into that position. It shouldn't happen. People should know better."

"But it did happen. That's the point."

"I suppose so," he said, but he sounded unsure. He sounded uncomfortable. "I think you should go with the fake British guy and the mousy girl who was just happy to have anyone love her."

Miranda looked at him. "Is that how she comes across? If I write her like that Caroline will never talk to me again."

He looked at her, raising an eyebrow.

"She is Caroline's sister-in-law after all." She moaned and laid her head back against the couch. "Writing is so hard. And while this is a fun story, I feel like I'll never rise beyond the level of fluff."

"Oh no, I disagree. Your characters have real motivation. They have struggles, particularly identity struggles they endure and develop though. Just because your challenges are humorous ones, doesn't make it just fluff. I would say you've progressed to the level of… fluff-plus."

She chortled at him and shook her head. "Well, I guess that's progress," she said, a rather wry tone in her voice. "At least Mad-Kat loves it. Mad-Kat is my greatest fan."

"Oh no, Miranda Wright. I'm your greatest fan."

She could feel her smile growing as though it started deep in her chest and then overtook her, bursting over her face. She felt like she was glowing. "You're too kind. You have the patience of a saint to work with me like this."

He set the manuscript down. "C'mon! You pay me in great breakfasts!" He winked at her. "That dish today is one I will never forget. What did you call it? Poached eggs in morel mushroom sauce? I've never had anything like it."

"It's my friend Claudine's specialty. She gave me the recipe. She calls it magic food."

"And she would be right. But I'm not just here for your amazing food. Don't forget, I'm a geek in disguise. Love books. This is serious fun to me. I'm going to get another coffee. Want a refill?"

"Yeah, if it's still set to decaf, then sure. Anything with caffeine will make me shaky. Shakier than I am already. I think a macchiato. No, a latte. Hmmm, maybe a…"

"How about I surprise you? I think I might know a trick or two. After all, I've seen this coffee maker before once or twice."

"That's right—you have one in the shop. That's so funny, the little things we have in common."

Burke had turned out to be more helpful to Miranda than she would have anticipated. He was a very good critic, but more importantly, he was a good person to talk with about character motivation. They would sit and discuss these imaginary people and it felt as though they were gossiping about neighbors and relatives. She was beginning to understand what it meant to have intellectual companionship in a relationship. She'd never known that before and had to admit that it was a powerful draw. Maybe that was where she and Gregg had gone wrong? They had a family together but no real intellectual give-and-take. No shared headspace. But he had found that with Chenguang, hadn't he? And she was finding it with Burke. She had thought love was taking care of someone. It was about being needed. But Burke didn't need her and she didn't need him. They just… enjoyed one another. She found it immensely satisfying.

Their kiss at the art gallery had changed everything about their relationship. Now they would snuggle on the couch, she would work on her laptop and lean into him, Burke's arms around her. She would work for a while and then read him what she was working on. Through his questions and suggestions, she would re-work the passage, making it infinitely better, or get whole new threads to weave into the story. He was like a walking thesaurus. When she marveled at his ability to pull words out of the air, he would remind her, "Well, I do own a bookstore. It's rather indicative of a person who likes to read."

Miranda found she could relax around Burke in a way she had never relaxed around anyone. Only with Caroline had she ever been able to be this real about herself, this transparent. Little by little, she let him in to how she really saw the world, into her insecure self as well as her professional one. She marveled that it was like having a best friend. A best friend you could kiss.

She rested her hand on her belly and she noticed that her body was changing. Softer. Now she had a little muffin top again. More like her old self. She simply didn't have that pounding drive to work out for hours every day. Maybe it was because that obsession had been a way to force her tears, not to mention her fears, out through her pores, to wash it away with sweat. Maybe she didn't seek the gym quite so much because she didn't have the same demons to exorcise. Yes, she was starting to be happy. With Burke she felt this sense of peace. A relaxed happiness like all those knots in her psyche finally untying and letting go.

She focused on her computer. She could hear him bumping around in the kitchen and the sounds of the coffee maker very distantly, as it ground the beans, whirred and steamed up some milk. He came back in a few minutes holding two coffee cups. He stopped right in front of her. She stared out over her computer, totally lost in thought, and then realized she was staring right at his crotch. He was standing, motionless, just waiting for her. She sat up and slid the computer off her lap, next to her on the couch. Tentatively, she reached out her hand and touched his stomach. He flinched ever so slightly. She could tell from dancing with him that he had a nice physique. She reached under his shirt and touched the skin on his stomach, playing a bit with the hair on his belly. She had never touched his skin like this before. He was a real man and he had a real man's body. He felt like a man and not a boy. Still staring at his mid-section, she reached up with her other hand and undid the button of his jeans. She heard his sharp intake of breath, but he didn't move. She smiled and unzipped his zipper. He was getting ready for her fast. She started slowly, almost teasing him before she made him breathe and moan. He remained frozen the whole time, as if afraid to move, as if afraid to break the spell. And still, he didn't spill that coffee. She made him tremble and cry out. There was no hope for it, those coffee cups were hitting the floor. They fell with a crash.

Miranda's eyes flew open and she sat bolt upright in bed. She looked around the room. She was alone. Burke had come over early yesterday and spent a good part of the day with her, working on the manuscript in the morning. He had made those lovely coffees. They had brunch at her place, Claudine's special dish to conjure up some magic, then drove to his. Then in the afternoon they took her car and went to the NC Aquarium and saved a few mannequin turtles, pretending to be turtle vets in an interactive exhibit designed for children. They went out to dinner at their new favorite Mexican restaurant where they always danced and drank margaritas on Saturday but never seemed to have time to eat dinner. She had dropped him off at his place with a kiss in the car and a promise to see one another again soon. She had come home alone.

She had not touched him yesterday morning. Her gaze had indeed lingered on his crotch for a few moments, before she had come to her senses and looked up into his face, smiled and accepted the coffee. But he'd noticed. She was sure he'd noticed.

She looked at the empty space in bed next to her. "Oh my God. I've got it bad for him," she moaned, as she fell back into her pillows.

Chapter 30

Would you be willing to get together? Maybe we can meet halfway, in Raleigh, for the day? I would really like to see you. Girl time would be good. Would you like that?

That was unlike Emma. There was no demand. There was 'meeting halfway', although Raleigh was not near halfway between them.

You want to get together? Miranda had texted back.

Yeah. I promise that I won't ask you do to my laundry. Or cook. Or pay for my dinner. Or listen to me whine endlessly.

Lol. Sure. How? Where?

I'll fly in. Raleigh's the nearest big airport to you, right? We can meet anywhere. Just let me know.

So, they made plans to meet the next weekend. Miranda made the three-and-a-half-hour trip to the state capital, and they met at the Marriott downtown on Saturday afternoon. Emma was flying out on Sunday morning. She didn't even ask her mother to pay for her flight or her hotel. They met up at two in the afternoon and went shopping. Emma wouldn't let her mother pay for anything. In fact, E didn't buy anything they looked at, although her mother could see the desire in her eyes as she tried on a few outfits. Despite her invitation, their time together was light, their conversation insubstantial. When it came time for dinner, Emma paid for both. They hit Soho, a sushi restaurant just a block up from the hotel, which wasn't too pricy. Finally, she started to open up.

"Mom, thanks for meeting me."

"It's been fun, E. It's been great to get together. I was worried that something was going on when I got your text."

"Well, I have a few things I need to say. And I just couldn't fathom saying them over the phone. And certainly not in a text."

"Oh." Miranda took a sip of her hot tea.

"Yeah. I do. I've been really crappy to you, Mom. I just wanted to say… I'm sorry. Um… I've been thinking a lot about our last conversation. About being honest. If I'm being honest, really telling the truth, to myself, and to you, I don't think I've been a stellar daughter. No, let me say this before I forget how to say it. Dad always pushed me. He always wanted me to climb my personal Mount Everest. To rise above every challenge."

"That sounds like your father."

"Yeah. And that did push me. Dad would point to the task and say, 'That's Mount Everest! Take the hill.' And that might be making honor society. Or winning the league championship in soccer. Or getting into medical school. And he would love me when I won. But you just… loved me. No matter what. And you're the one who showed me the way over that Mount Everest, whatever it was. Helping me with my homework. Making it so that I had the time to study. Coming to every soccer game I ever had. And I… I don't think I really understood that. Or appreciated that. And I wanted to say thanks. And I wanted to say it when we were together."

Miranda could feel her heart pounding in her chest. She pinched herself to make sure she wasn't dreaming. She smiled at her daughter and took another sip of her tea. "You know, when you were little, we used to go to the Outer Banks every summer for vacation. I remember that you were fearless about the ocean. You always went in further than you should, daring yourself. And oh, how your father encouraged you."

"You were always so nervous." There was still that hint of derision in Emma's voice. Miranda thought that was just going to take a while to wear off. But she liked this new Emma. This new Emma was at least flirting with self-awareness.

"Yeah. Beach days weren't so fun for me. I had to watch you like a hawk. Since you had no fear of the ocean, you also had no judgment of when the swells were too big for you. You didn't know how to respect the ocean's power. I had to carry the fear for both of us, so I could never relax."

Emma was quiet for a few moments. "Since were truth telling here, actually, I was scared out of my mind."

"You were?"

"Oh yeah. But Dad was always saying 'don't be a weenie'. I really didn't want him to see me as a weenie." They were quiet again for a bit. "I don't want him to see me as a weenie now, either."

"Honey! Why would he see you as a, a… weenie? He loves you."

"He loves me when I'm perfect."

"He loves you all the time!"

"He says I embarrass him."

"What?"

"I know." Emma's voice was barely a whisper. "That's what he always said about you."

That stung. Not that it was a surprise to Miranda. Gregg had told her a thousand times to change what she was wearing, to not say what she said, to not laugh when she did, to not show her dumb paintings to anyone, to get in better shape. He had a quality of tone that made fun of her, probably of anyone. But to think that he had subjected Emma to it? That's what stung. Then she realized that Gregg was indiscriminate in his criticism. He was a two-dimensional character living in a two-dimensional world. It was black and white, wrong and right and he was always right. He would never recover from that particular affliction. He was incredibly smart and super successful, so he usually was right. Unbearably so. "I'm so sorry, Emma. It's not a club I was eager for you to join."

"I get it why you divorced him. He didn't divorce you, did he? You divorced him."

"Let's say it was a mutual decision. But I can't understand why in the

275

world he would say that to you."

"Because I'm in academic trouble."

"You are?" Miranda could feel the shock reverberating through her.

"And he teaches at the medical school. He found out from a colleague that I'm struggling. He yelled at me, asked how I could do that to him? Embarrass him like that? Actually, I'm more than struggling. Mom, I hate it. I hate anatomy. It's horrible. It gives me nightmares. And patients—they bring in patients to give us case-experience. Ugh, it's like listening to them whining and whining and then it hit me—if I go into medicine it will be a whole lifetime of listening to people complaining."

A small smile crossed Miranda's face. "You know, that part was never your father's favorite either. That's why he became a surgeon, so he didn't have to deal with the patients. He loved medicine. He never loved patients."

"Oh. So at least we have that in common. I've always felt like I was so much like him. I always wanted to be so much like him. But now we won't have anything in common and he won't love me. He'll love the new baby best."

Miranda was taken aback. Babies took all your time and energy. It was normal for the older child to feel dethroned. But perhaps not normal when that child was twenty-three. She decided she'd address that one later. "Emma, you need to have a career that you will love and that you will want to spend years doing. This isn't your father's life. It's not my life. It's your life. If you don't want to be a doctor, which I can understand—it never appealed to me either —what do you want to do? What do you love?"

Emma looked stumped. Miranda worried for a moment that the only thing her daughter loved was earning her father's praise. Then, with a horribly guilty look, Emma said, "I like clothes."

"You like clothes? I mean, I know you love shopping, but you like clothes? Like as a profession?"

"I like color. Texture. Design. Those things fascinate me."

"Oh, my goodness. Emma, why didn't you ever say anything?"

"How could I choose something like that? Dad would hate me." Then

Emma gave a little laugh, more like a snort. "I can only admit it now because he hates me already."

"He doesn't hate you. No, Emma, don't look at me like that, he doesn't hate you. Gregg is a man who has many talents and skills, but expressing love, well, that's not one of them. Separating out who he is from what everyone thinks of him is a challenge I doubt he can comprehend. If he didn't have his job, he wouldn't know who he was. You know what? I think this is a good thing for you! I think this is a really positive development."

"Flunking out of medical school and making my dad hate me is a positive development?"

"It's a dramatic exit from the path, to be sure, but you're going to start down a new road of discovering who you really are. Not who Daddy wants you to be. Or me. Or Emile." Emma immediately teared up and Miranda was sorry she'd brought up his name. "Honey, you need to find yourself. Finding out who you aren't is a good start."

They spoke for hours. It was a real heart-to-heart. Tears first, but laughter eventually, and, at the end, hope. Being your daughter's best friend meant listening. It meant gentle correcting. It meant loving her even when you didn't quite approve of the choices she made. It meant letting her be her own person, with bumps in the road and lessons learned, a bruised heart, and a hug to come home to. Emma still had a long ways to go to shake off some of the obnoxious habits she'd picked up from her father, but as Miranda made the drive back to the Outer Banks, she exhaled a deep sigh of satisfaction. No relationship as fractured as theirs was going to heal overnight. Or in a few months. Maybe not even for a few years. But it was a start.

Chapter 31

Burke and Miranda were enjoying a glass of wine while they watched the sunset from the gazebo over the water at the end of the long boardwalk. They had wandered out hand in hand, Burke carrying a wine bottle, Miranda two plastic wine glasses, Who'sMyGoodBoy dogging her heels. It had been a long day. Burke had worked at one of the businesses he had a stake in, doing some advance preparation for the season. Miranda had enjoyed a decent day of writing, drafting ten pages of her developing story and doing quite a bit of research for the book. They were both a bit tired. Their feet made soft padding sounds on the wooden walkway as they traversed the fifty yards to get to the lovely little gazebo. It was so private, so quiet this far out into the water. Herons were flying in and landing in the tall grasses that lined the long canal that led to a big, empty boat slip. The only watercraft that slip had seen had been brought there by Burke. Or before him, Austin.

    She could look back on that relationship with some peace of mind now. She thought the shock of finding out just how young Austin actually was probably equated to his shock at finding out just how old she was in return. They both had seen the world the way they had wanted it to be, cheerfully ignoring the abundant clues that had been before them all the time. It had been sweet with Austin. He was older than his years, more insightful, more principled than anyone could reasonably expect from a twenty-year-old. *Now twenty-one,* she reminded herself. What a man he would make some day. Not the man for her, but for some very lucky woman. She wanted the best for him.

She wanted him to be happy. She thought the world of him, but she didn't want him. The gulf in their experience, now that she understood what it was, loomed so large she could hardly comprehend how she had traversed it in the first place. *Rebound relationship,* Caroline had diagnosed for her. *It was a mad thing. A mad fling. Of course, you did it. You had to.*

But now she didn't want a mad fling—she wanted the real thing. Somehow, if she imagined what Austin would be like all grown up, she pictured a man like Burke. He had a depth of experience, had been married, had a grown son, was insightful and kind, with a generous nature. He didn't pull punches. While he always spoke with kindness and respect, he was also direct and pointed in his comments. Sometimes his insights were almost too revealing.

Burke was leaning against the gazebo railing and looking back at her house. "It's hard to not love Hayward House. You've done some nice things with it. This was always one of my favorites, with that cool, funky 'somebody lives here' vibe. And Salvo is kind of like the mythical lost city—still mostly undiscovered by the mega-mansion beach house builders." Burke turned and looked at the sunset again. "God, Miranda, you've bought a piece of paradise. I wish it would last. I hate to see what's happening to the island."

"What do you mean?"

"All the build-up. Every inch of island being taken for mega-beach homes. Ghost villages in the winter. Not for residents. Not for people who care about the island. We're losing the open space. They'll be no place left for the herons and all the rest of the wildlife."

Miranda looked at him as Burke watched a heron pick its way through the tall grass, hunting a last little snack before it bedded down for the night. The yellow sun cast golden and pink jets of light through the clouds behind him, framing him in light. "But you make your living on those people."

"I know." He sounded so glum. "A necessary evil." He was quiet for a long time and occasionally sipped from his glass or petted the dog. "It makes me sad to think of Hayward House being swallowed up by the mega-monstrosities. It's so peaceful here, but soon you'll have the sounds of late-night drunken parties and people throwing beer bottles around that the locals come and clean up in the winter. Vacationers' radios playing obnoxiously loud. Eventually you'll lose this amazing view. That little slice of green in-between your house and the sound, it looks too small to build on, but it's a lot, believe it or not. Some rich dentist is going to come along and buy it and put up a huge mansion there that he only stays in a week a year, and you won't be able to see the sunset from the house any longer. Hayward House has this awesome vibe to it and I hate to see that diminished by overcrowding."

"That won't happen," she said simply.

"Of course it will happen. It always happens. It's a miracle it hasn't happened here yet."

"It won't happen."

"Miranda, you can't hold back progress."

"In this case, I can. I bought the lot."

"The sound side lot?"

"Yes, that little slice of land between me and the water. I bought it."

"Wow." He sounded astonished. "Good for you. You'll always have a sunset." He took a while to finish his sentence. "That's nice. For now."

"No one is going to build up beach houses here. It won't change."

"Miranda, I hate to dispel your illusions, but it happens everyplace."

"It won't happen here. I bought the lots."

"You what?" He turned to her.

"I bought the lots. A local guy suggested it."

He stared at her. "You bought them? All nine of them?"

"Yep! All nine of them. No one will build here unless it's me."

"But, that must be," he calculated quickly, "a little over a million dollars."

"It was one-point-four million, to be exact."

"Where did you get money like that?"

"Well, partly it's the divorce from Gregg. I told you he was super pissed at what the judge gave me. Half of everything we had. Gregg's a very successful surgeon. He made a lot. Then my book has done really well. And I have that movie option from it."

"You have that much money?"

"Correction. I *had* that much money. Now I have that much land. My treasure trove has taken a significant hit, but despite breaking the piggy bank, I don't expect to starve any time soon."

Burke sat down on the bench and didn't say anything. He set his wine glass down next to him. The dog stuck his nose in it.

"So, Burke, tell me why you're not happy? I just told you that the island you love will be preserved, at least this tiny little corner of it. I would have expected you to say, 'Way to go, Miranda! Thanks! You're one of us now,' but you look further away from me than I think I've ever seen you."

The sun disappeared over the horizon.

"You're rich."

"I guess." She shrugged, but she felt a little flush of pleasure that she'd had some measure of success. After being told for so many years that she was a drain and not 'an asset', it felt really good to have achieved success all on her own.

"I'm not rich," Burke said.

"I know that."

Burke stood up and ran his fingers through his hair, turning away from her to look over the water again.

"Don't tell me you think I'm so shallow that I care about something like that?"

"I don't think you're shallow at all, Miranda. But this is about who's got the upper hand."

"The upper hand? You've lost me."

"Yes. It's about power. It's what ruined your relationship with your ex. He held all the cards. He always had the upper hand. You told me how he wouldn't let you make decisions and over-rode the ones you did make. You described how he controlled all the money and belittled you for not contributing financially in meaningful ways."

"He was the king of the snide remark." She stood up and walked over to stand beside Burke, looking out over the darkening water. He didn't say anything for a long time. The sky was quite dim when she ventured, "Okay, you need to tell me what's going on. You're going to have to explain this to me because I'm not following you."

He let out a deep breath and turned to her. "Your ex held all the cards in your relationship. Whether he took them or you willingly handed over yours, he held everything. His currency, what he cared about, wasn't you. It wasn't the love between you or your family. It was wealth and education."

"I embarrassed him." She nodded as she looked back at him.

"Yes, since he had all the education and all the money-making power, that imbalance led him to not respect you."

"Okay, Dr. Phil, I get that. Lived it. Been there. Done that. I've gotten that for a while now, even. Exorcised some of those demons in my book, actually. I don't see what that has to do with you and me."

"Miranda, you hold all the cards. You have the wealth and power. I have nothing compared to you."

"But if you don't value those things, how can that create an imbalance between us? I mean, you really don't care about money."

"Sure, I care about money. I'm very careful with mine. But you don't ever have to be careful. If you want to go out to dinner, you'll just go. Want to go on a trip, you'll just go. Want to put a flume in your house, you just do that, so you can swim. Want to buy up all the available land around you to ensure your privacy, then you do that."

"You resent it. You resent people with money."

"I suppose I do. I've watched them nearly destroy this island with their greed. Then the people who don't have enough money to buy a million-dollar beach house but have ten grand to piss away to rent one for a week, while they come here and get smashed and drive drunk and kill our people…our mothers and wives and daughters…" his voice trailed off.

"Burke, you know I love it here. I don't look down on you because you work hard to earn everything you have. Quite the contrary, I respect that. I really respect that." She put her hand on his shoulder. She could feel the tension in his muscles.

Burke put his hand over hers. "But, Miranda, that's where you've lived for more than twenty years. You've learned at the feet of a master. What else do you know but how you've been treated? How will you stop yourself from repeating what you've seen over and over again?"

"I would never…"

"Be careful. It's easier said than done. Think about it. What happens when you want to go skiing again, up to Aspen or Vail or wherever it is you rich people go? I can't go there and I'm sure as hell not going to let you take me places and pay for me. I have different priorities. I have a boy in college, but to be honest, I'm not going to even want to go to those places anyway."

She sat down on the bench. This was a big deal to him. She could hear it in his voice. Already he was putting her into a 'them' category, and he was an 'us'.

"You're right, Burke. I can't promise you that I won't make a mistake or say a dumb thing that might sound like I'm not respecting you. All I *can* promise you is that I do respect you. I don't want you to be 'us' and me to be 'them', but I need you to help me see and understand your world so that I can love you on your terms." She froze. She couldn't believe she had just said that. She hadn't meant to say 'love'. She was trying to work her way through a mass of complex emotions and stay calm at the same time, and through stumbling with her words she had just revealed to both of them how she felt.

She could just see his face in the dimming light. "I can't be bought. I can't be kept. I can't respect myself if that's what we become."

"Wait a minute. Are you telling me that I just accidentally confessed that I love you and you're still hung up on the fact that I have money?" She looked at him, totally incredulous. "Here I am freaking out at the words that just came out of my mouth, and you're standing there, totally calmly, worried that I'm going to like, I don't know, take you on vacation?"

A slow smile spread across his face. "I know you love me, Miranda."

"How?"

"You talk in your sleep."

Chapter 32

Burke felt a skip in his step as he walked to his car. *She loves me. I knew it!* Even the news and the weather report couldn't dampen his mood. The dog danced around his feet as he approached the car. Burke opened the door to let him in. "Who's my good boy? Huh? Who's my good boy?" he said as he scratched the dog's ears. As he turned the key and the engine started to hum, the radio came on with yet another update about the tropical depression in the Atlantic. The island was in the projected cone of possibility, but there was a lot of time still for it to turn out to sea. He changed the station and started to hum along with some song on the oldies station.

While he'd suspected it since November he knew now that he loved her. It had come upon him like a storm, overtaking his reason and preoccupying his thoughts. It had been like losing his rationality to an edgy happiness. But tourist season was approaching. It was time to make sure all the equipment was working at the rental place and to get the bookstore in order. It was late April. Soon Junior would be home.

He was looking forward to that more than he had in previous years. He had called his boy to again thank him for his earlier advice and to let him know that good old dad officially had a 'lady-friend'. He was sure his son would like her. Junior had said, "Spare me the details!" more than once, but had advised his dad to take it slow, let the relationship develop. "Make sure you really get to know one another. You know, you don't want to fall for her and then, you know, be surprised."

"Oh no, I feel like I really know her. My God, we've been friends for eight months."

"Dad… no details. I'll meet her when I come home."

"And it was good advice—I'm taking it slow, just like you said."

"No details!"

"She loves me," he said again as he drove to Watercraft Rentals.

When Burke pulled in, Ben was already there and working on tuning up the engine of a jet ski. "Mornin'," he called out. "We've got a whole mess of carburetors to clean out today and all the engines need tuning. You look awfully happy."

"Who me?" Burke said, a wide grin splitting his face. "I'm always happy."

"Well, I'm glad you can spend a few hours away from Miranda."

"Just a few hours. She's bringing lunch up for us."

"Good stuff? Not more of that girly cooking? And nothin' that looks like dog food?"

"Ha! She said she was bringing up meatball subs."

"Well, that'll be all right, I guess."

They worked for a while in silence, then Ben asked, "So, you tracking that storm?"

"Won't come ashore. It'll blow back out to sea and head up north east."

"I hope so. It just sucks to have one so early in the season. Damn global warming. The storms are earlier and more frequent every year. If this one does hit us, I'll need you to help me board up the place."

"Of course. Why would you even need to bring that up?"

"Well, you'll have your house to board up. And The Book Shelf."

"The Book Shelf Café."

"Yeah, whatever. And you'll have to board up Miranda's place too, and that's not small."

It hadn't struck Burke until that moment that his family had already accepted Miranda as one of the group. Almost as one of the family. And that he would have a whole nother house to board up.

"Plus Doughnuts of Rodanthe. Oh, wait, she's calling it Ro-Dough now. Dumb name." Ben was muttering. "No one will know what the heck that is. You'll have to help Mad with her shop."

"Yup, we all will. With those big glass front windows. I told her to get the metal shutters."

"Since when have you known Mad to listen to you? Or anyone for that matter." Ben chuckled. "She'll take your money, but not your advice."

"Isn't that the truth," Burke said under his breath.

Miranda brought the subs up shortly before noon. As she was unpacking, Mike and Kat pulled up.

Burke was surprised to see his sister. "Hey, Kat, I thought you were going to man the bookstore today?"

"I'm taking a long lunch break. Besides, when I heard that Miranda was cooking, I didn't want to miss out."

Miranda handed Burke a fruit iced tea. "I brought lots," she whispered and gave him a wink. "We're expecting Maggie and Jim, too. Oh, and here they are!" Another truck pulled up into the driveway and parked in the small lot.

"What have I done to you?" He looked at her, feeling a little guilty.

"Nothing I haven't asked for."

They sat at the little picnic table to eat.

"So, why the impromptu party?" Burke asked the group.

"We ladies are headed up to help Mad with getting Ro-Dough ready," said Maggie. "The walls still need some paint and there's a ton of cleaning to do. The equipment's being installed in two weeks and everything has to be perfect before that can happen."

Mike took a big sip of tea. "Do you guys want help with the engines or would you rather I help out Mad?"

"Burke and I've got a handle on things here. We can work on the engines. Miranda, are you still willing to repaint our signs?"

"Oh sure. I thought I could work on that day after tomorrow if the weather holds."

"You're painting the signs for the shop?" Burke asked her.

"Yeah, Mad said they needed to be refreshed; they're looking kind of dull. Well, that's something I can do."

Maggie filled her glass with tea and sat down. "They just upgraded the storm to tropical. You won't believe what they named it: Austin. I think we need to have a plan for if it comes this way."

"We've got a plan," Ben said, his mouth full of food. "We'll caravan from house to house and board everything up. Burke's got metal shutters on the Buxton shop, so that's easy."

"Hey, it doesn't do itself," Burke said.

Miranda looked confused. "But it won't become a hurricane. It won't come on shore. I mean, it's not hurricane season, right?"

"Ah, you mainlander you," Ben replied. "Sometimes hurricanes, like tourists, come out of season."

Miranda turned to Burke. "I'll help you with the shop. Can I help you? Or is it something that takes burly guys?"

"Tell you what, you help me, and I'll help you board up your place. But the storm won't turn into a hurricane. They aren't going to evacuate the island. It'll blow out to sea. Ninety-five percent of the time they don't come and hit us. Particularly not this early. Ocean's not warm enough to really stir anything big up yet."

* * *

The storm didn't blow out to sea. It made a bee line for the Outer Banks, as if it couldn't wait to pound the island with havoc and devastation. It grew quickly, from a tropical depression to a named tropical storm to a Category 1 and then a Category 3 hurricane. Suddenly everyone was rushing around trying to prepare, secure supplies for the generators, and get the boards they needed before the evacuation orders came down. Burke was able to buy enough plywood for Haywood House, but he had to go to Manteo to get it. He showed Miranda how to put the boards up over her windows, and then ended up hammering in all the nails himself.

He had kept his plywood from the last storm, and Mike helped him to put it back up over the windows at Burke's own house. Then they did the house at Watercraft Rentals. Then they trucked over to Mike and Kat's. Miranda brought food and stayed out of the way.

Miranda insisted on helping Burke ready the bookstore for the storm. He showed her how to unlock the metal blinds from the top, lower them, and secure them shut, but first they moved the stock to the middle of the second floor of the house.

"We'll stack everything up here in this room. In this old house, this room and that back one are the least likely to get wind or water damage."

"I saw something on TV about wind blowing the roofs off the houses, and that was just a one-hundred mile per hour wind. A Category 3 storm sounds really scary. They aren't nearly this daunting from Charlotte. Or Lexington. It's just a major rain event by the time it gets there."

"That's part of the reason why they're calling for evacuating the island."

"Is the roof of the bookstore safe?"

"From blowing off? Oh yeah, sure it is. Building codes require roof straps on the buildings at the coast. If the roof is going to come off, then the whole structure is going to be flattened anyway, and there's not much we can do to prevent that. We're going to bring as much of the inventory as we can fit into the two rooms upstairs. And we'll cover them with the tarps and tie them down. That way if the roof leaks, nothing that's in the attic now will get ruined. And if the storm surge gets really high and there's serious flooding, there won't be books downstairs to get wet." He looked around at his beloved bookshop. "I'll have to replace all the drywall though. And the wiring. That'll be a bitch of a job. Yeah, we'll sandbag the front, just in case."

Miranda stroked one of the beautifully crafted bookshelves as she walked by it. "What about these? Won't they get ruined?"

"They'll be all right. That's hardwood finished with marine varnish. They'll dry out. And it probably won't be that bad."

Miranda worked on boxing up books and carrying them upstairs for a while. The dog followed her closely, every step of the way. "Hey, you never told me you have an apartment here."

"Um, you never asked?"

"I found a studio apartment when I went looking for the bathroom. Who stays here?"

"Me. Sometimes. And him." He pointed to the dog.

She bent down to pet the pooch. "Who'sMyGoodBoy certainly loves it here. He showed me where the dog treats are hidden." The dog wagged his tail and tried to lick her face. "But, why? You have a house up island." She looked around. "Are you worried, or something, about someone breaking in?"

"Oh no, nothing like that. Not here, no, not here. No, it's just that sometimes it was nice to have another place to be."

"Burke, that sounds really kinda strange, I have to say. You have a perfectly nice house."

"Well, when my boy went to college, I put in the studio. I would come up here with the dog because the house seemed so empty. I just knocked around there and, with my boy gone, it was too much like, like…"

"Like what, Burke?"

"It was so much like coming home from the hospital after Joette died. I just never thought that would happen. And I remember coming home and being alone. Everyone was at the grandparents, and I'd never felt that alone and she was gone, forever gone." Burke moved another box and tried to pull himself together. His daughter Juliet, his little pumpkin as he always called her, had been pronounced dead at the scene. But Joette had survived a few days. He'd really thought she was going to make it. And then she didn't. "And it felt like that, back at that bad time, so I thought it would be good to have another place to be, to sort of shake things up. To keep me from getting, you know, depressed. It's kinda weird, I know…"

"I totally understand. I moved into the condo in Charlotte, which is beautiful, but it was just another city. And it was so big and empty, and I just knocked around in it. And I realized I needed something totally different. Someplace else to be once in a while. And I ended up here."

"Yeah. You ended up here."

She gave him the warmest smile. "When everyone evacuates, I'd like for you to come with me. To Charlotte. We can stay at my condo. I'd like to introduce you to some of my good friends who live there. Take you to some of my favorite places. I mean, if you haven't made any other plans. It might be nice for us to get away together. And for me to share some of my world with you."

He looked at her. "I'd love to come to Charlotte with you for a few days, to ride out the storm." The smile that burst across her face made him feel warm.

"Okay. Okay then."

He thought she nearly skipped out of the room as she carried her box of books upstairs, the dog trotting along at her heels. After they boxed up and moved books from the downstairs, and after he'd packed up his precious Jura and moved it to the 'safe room', they started on the attic.

As he was rearranging the boxes in what had become their storage room, she came in with a box of books. "Mr. Mitchell. I have a bone to pick with you."

"What?" From the look on her face he thought he might be in trouble.

"Why are all these signed books of mine in the attic?"

"Um, well, um, I think they'll be big hits this summer!" He thought fast. "Signed and all—I thought we could do some special nights with the author. Doesn't that sound good?"

"You never sold any of my books after that October book club, did you?"

"I sold two."

"Uh huh. And you had me come back in January and sign thirty more, so you'd have a lot of unsold inventory?" She put the box down with a thump, then put her hands on her hips and raised her eyebrows at him.

Oh shit, is she going to be mad or flattered? "Look, Miranda, I uh, well. Look, okay, I did lie to you. I wanted to spend time with you and to get to know you better because I, well, I, um, I really, really liked you."

"And so you pretended to need me to sign all those damn books. And the whole thing was a set up? You didn't just have on hand all those snacks and the wine?"

He knew he must look like a kid caught with his hand in the cookie jar. He shook his head.

"And did you conjure up that rainstorm too?"

He walked over and put his arms around her. "Look. I have to tell you the whole truth."

"Uh huh."

"I love you. I've loved you since I first saw you. And I would have done anything, even buy a whole mess your books, if that meant I could spend five more minutes with you. I hope you're not mad. I didn't mean to manipulate you. I was just hoping for a chance."

"Wow. That's sweet. I mean, in a stalkerish kind of way."

"Can you forgive me?"

He was happy that she laughed at him. "Yes, I think I can manage that. It's not like I couldn't tell that you were fighting yourself to remain disciplined for all those weeks."

"And nothing's changed. I still am." He kissed her. "We're taking it slow. I'll wait as long as you want."

Chapter 33

"Dude, are you ready to drive?" Taisei asked. "Time's a wastin'. Hurricane's a comin'. Pretty nice that they named it after you this year."

Austin threw a couple more shirts into his bag and zipped it up. "I'm ready, man. And we have plenty of time to get Austin out of town before Austin hits town. It won't move this far west for days, *if* it hits. It'll probably move out to sea. They mostly curve back east and head out to the Atlantic."

"Well, don't tell that to the people in charge! If we do get a direct hit, they might cancel exams!"

"They're not going to cancel exams."

"They might. They did in *Harry Potter* one year."

"Fiction. That's fiction."

"And don't you feel like you're living a fictional life?"

"Hah," Austin said, but he was struck by Taisei's comment. When he looked back over the last year he had to admit that it did feel quite unreal.

"The roads outta here will be a nightmare if we delay," said Taisei. "I've gotten stuck in that traffic with Mom before. Now, while I think you'd be more fun, I still don't relish a three-and-a-half-hour trip turning into a five, six, or seven-hour one. I want to get home - the crib of Mama Ah-Bey is plush. It is the Ah-Bey-Say-Day place to be."

"So, what? You've got waiters and a pool and a restaurant onsite?"

"Almost, man. When the extended family's in town, which I hear they are, the service really ratchets up. It's not to be missed."

"Nag, nag, nag. I'm ready to go. We need to gas up before we head out of town."

"Thanks for driving, dude. Since Mama Ah-Bey confiscated my wheels, you've been super cool about letting me use yours and chauffeuring me around."

"No worries. Trust me, Taisei, you've not been a pain at all. And I appreciate your offer to let me shelter from the storm with you at the superlative crib. And Taisei?"

"Yeah, man?"

"Take your shit to study. Hurricane Austin is not going to flatten UNCW. This isn't Hogwarts. You will still have exams."

They made the drive in heavy, but not excruciating traffic. As Austin drove, his mind kept returning to the conversation with his father. He reached to the radio and turned down the volume.

"Hey, can I ask you a question about your mom?"

"Sure," Taisei said, obviously still listening more to the music than to Austin.

"How old were you when your folks divorced?"

"Six, maybe seven years old. It was a long road. For everybody."

"You haven't mentioned your dad much."

"Nah, dude's not much interested in his American family. He's on his third family. I've never met those kids. I do know my little brother from his second wife. He's actually cool and I like him a lot. We skype in Japanese. We mostly both bitch about dad, but at least we have each other. What does this have to do with my mom?"

"So, Mama Ah-Bey never remarried?"

Taisei shook his head.

"Did she date much?"

"Oh sure. No one Nana ever approved of, but I never knew if that was because Nana didn't trust Mom's judgement, or if she didn't like the actual guys, or if she was afraid Mom would fall in love and move away again, leaving her alone in that big old house. You know, people do weird things for love, even to those they love. People can be really fucked up."

"You think your mom is, uh, still not dealing with stuff?" Austin didn't want to phrase it the same way his friend had. "It's been a long time."

"You know, my friend, I've decided that there are some things you aren't gonna get over. Like my dad. He sucks as a dad. I'm not ever going to get over that. And it finally dawned on me that when I would wreck the car, or that semester I got those Fs, or that time I got busted for under-age drinking, that neither got my dad's attention nor did it seem to hurt him in any way. It just hurt me. It just fucked me. Shinzo, my Japanese half-brother, he pointed out to me that maybe I didn't want to fuck myself. Maybe the best way to get even with Dad was to be successful."

Austin marveled at Taisei's confessions. He'd heard him skyping late into the night in Japanese. He knew Shinzo was out there, someplace, a half-brother who was about fifteen now. But his roommate didn't usually spill his innermost secrets to Austin. They ate pizza together, they went out to listen to live music together, they went to parties to meet girls together, but they really lived their lives in parallel play. They were friends. Good friends. They weren't some type of bro-soulmates.

"Taisei Ah-Bey-Say-Day, these are deep thoughts. You are turning into some kind of Master Sensei."

"Ah, Austin Powers, Master and Sensei mean the same thing. Talking to Shinzo has been… enlightening, this past year. It helps that we have a common enemy. Why do you ask about my mom?"

"Oh, because my dad is dating this woman. He seems to really like her."

"That's a good thing. No? Is that not a good thing?"

"Oh yeah, it's a good thing. He should date. He's dated since I was in high school. It took him a long time. He's never really gotten over… losing his wife. He's never fully dealt with it, I think."

"You can never fully deal with shit like that. I mean, have you? Have you, really?"

"I don't know. You have a mom. You know what that's like. I don't remember much about my parents. So, my dad was both dad and mom, father and mother, sort of. You have the mom experience. I can't tell you what it means to be loved by a mom."

"It's awesome. You never feel so loved, but it's like being loved by a tiger. She's always there waiting to pounce. Maybe eat you alive. And I don't know what it's like to be loved by a dad."

"It's awesome. You feel loved, absolutely, but it's like being loved from a distance. You have space and time to do your own stuff. No one nags you for anything. No one pries into your business. Dad is always there for me, and definitely my best friend. I want to be just like him when I grow up."

"I thought you were grown up?"

"You know what I mean."

"Yeah. And I want to be anyone *but* my dad when I grow up."

"So, your mom never fell in love again?"

"Don't know. She doesn't tell me about her love life, thank God, but if I had to put money on it, I would think not. You think your dad has?"

"Yeah. I think he has. He hasn't told me any specifics about her. Says I'll meet her when I come home over the summer, and that's fine. I'm too busy now and I'll be home shortly after our rescheduled exams. But he's never asked me for permission before."

"So, how are you with, maybe, having a new mother?"

Austin braked to give the car in front of him a bit more space. The sky was gray and cloudy already. This was a fast-moving storm with absolutely huge outer bands. He thought about this woman of his dad's as a new mother. He couldn't tell how he was feeling. "She's more than just a lady friend, that's true. And he needs to move on. But that means she'll be there, won't she? Like for holiday dinners. And summers when I come home. Family dinners. Spaghetti and taco nights. I might end up working with her at the shop or the rental place, I mean everyone gets involved in the family businesses. I can't imagine my dad ever choosing someone who wasn't a part of the island community."

"If he marries her, this will be the woman that your children call grandma, you know."

"Damn. I never thought of that." That felt heavy. That felt real. "What if I don't like her? What if I think she's no good for my father? What if she doesn't like me?"

"What woman wouldn't fall in love with Austin Powers? You've got the mojo, man!"

"You know what I mean."

"Raising parents is very hard," Taisei said as though he were a therapist. He stroked his scraggly beard and tapped the tips of his fingers together. "You have to remember, everything they run into, it's basically their first time. They look like they're so in control, but in reality, they're making everything up as they go along."

Austin burst out laughing.

"No, I'm serious, Austin. They screw things up. They make mistakes. They don't want to admit it. They think they need to be perfect, particularly in front of their offspring. They have these bizarre internal pressures. Even my Psych 432 professor agreed with me. I wrote my term paper on that. When they handle something badly, they can become like children again. My dad is a total case study of that. They nag us to take responsibility but that's no guarantee that they know how to do that themselves. Parents aren't perfect. They can have bad mojo. I've even seen my mom have some major bad mojo. Never Nana, though. She's pretty superhuman."

"I have a superhuman grandparent, too. So cool. But my dad? I have to disagree with you, Master Sensei. My dad is very cool. He's got things under control."

"Not if he's fallen in love. Dude, everyone loses control when they fall in love. That's part of the definition of the experience."

Austin mulled that over while they drove. Just what would that mean for his father? Probably that he would want everyone together and happy all the

297

time, just like he probably thought it would have been had that damn alcoholic not been driving at exactly that time, at exactly that place, on exactly that day and wiped out the other half of their family. That had forever altered his dad's life. All those family members—they simply weren't here. And Austin realized that, if he were being truly honest with himself, the cavernous maw left in their wake had nearly swallowed his dad at one point in time. Sure, he was a cool guy, but there was that shadow that lurked behind the facade.

Chapter 34

"Are you ready to go?" Miranda asked Burke from around the corner. He walked out of the bathroom with a towel wrapped around his waist. "Oh my, I think that's a no." She laughed at him. "I'm going to take Who'sMyGoodBoy out for a quick pee, while you get dressed."

"Or we could be really late to go to your friend's house?" He gave her a mischievous smile.

She looked at her watch. "I suppose the dog can wait. And it's not like we'd want to be early. That would be totally rude, no matter how good Claudine's cooking is."

He put his arms around her. "I will be amazed if she can light a candle to you, babe. But no, we wouldn't want to be rude." He kissed her. She playfully wriggled out of his arms and pulled off his towel in the process, swinging it around her head and laughing.

He stood there and shook his head while she danced her way through the door to the bedroom. They had just made love before their shower. It had been sweet and slow, almost a shy way of having sex. They were both new to this with one another, a little unsure of themselves, exploring this new facet of their relationship and each other. It had been nice. Yeah. Really nice.

He relished the time they spent together, cooking meals, napping on the couch, sharing their love of books, good stories, and an excellent turn of phrase. She felt like such a perfect match in so many ways. And if she wanted to fool around again, hell, all the better. He smiled and followed her into the bedroom. She was lying on the bed with her head towards him and her feet pointing away. While the majority of her clothes lay abandoned on the floor, she was still wearing lacy black panties and an almost nothing bra, also black and lacy.

"Come here," she said and reached for him, laying on her back and reaching her arms over her head towards him.

"You are the most beautiful thing I think I've ever seen."

She responded with a huge smile, all confidence.

He walked closer to the huge four poster bed, rather conscious of her staring at him.

"That's right, come closer. I won't bite you… much."

He laughed at her and took two more steps up to the edge of the bed. Whatever he thought about his tentative, let's-go-slow-Miranda up to now, she seemed to have a different plan in mind at this moment. He was happy to let her be in the driver's seat but was caught by surprise when she lay her hands on his hips, hung her head over the side of the bed, and completely took control over him. He hadn't been ready for that. He reached out to the post of the bed. Grasping it for support he closed his eyes and breathed in deeply. This wasn't the shy, sweet sex they'd had earlier. It was slow, however. Like the best kind of torture he could imagine. He couldn't have moved.

"Ohhhh, you're a good girl," he heard himself say softly. "You are so sexy." She was amazing. And she was his. The thought of this being their love life, this being the sex he would have when they climbed in bed at night, this being how she was willing to touch him, to arouse so many of his senses… and she was all his. "Oh fuck…" he gasped. Burke could feel himself drowning in Miranda, willingly melting into her sensuality, her delight in her sexiness and her obvious thrill in being so totally in control of his body and his mind and wrapping him around her little finger. He climbed into bed with her and all too soon, he felt his muscles tightening up, his heart beating wildly and the blood rushing in his ears, then he collapsed on top of her. Their interlude was both fuzzy and clearly etched into his mind. He could kind of remember when they were loud, saying the kind of things lovers exclaim in the throes of passion when the excitement takes them away from their ordinary selves and he could clearly call to mind the amazing look on her face as he took her. Just calling up the image could take his breath away. He lay there for a while wondering how he could be so lucky as to have a woman like this in his life. He loved her *and* she was a hellcat in bed? Usually, it was one or the other. He could feel himself starting to shake slightly. He wasn't sure why. Maybe in excitement. Maybe it was all just so much pleasure. He just wanted to bury himself in her for days. He could feel himself slipping, as if into quicksand, drowning in the lovely sexiness that was Miranda. His Miranda. His forever Miranda. She was in his mind and his heart and soul and he didn't want to miss out on any of this. Missing out on this? Suddenly he felt almost a sense of fear at the very idea of losing her. Of sharing her. Of not being with her.

"You're squishing me."

"What? Oh, sorry." He rolled over on to his side and she took in a huge breath.

"Thanks." She smiled at him. She was sweaty. Maybe that was his sweat on her, now that he thought about it.

"Sure, I think you deserve to breathe."

"I meant for that totally amazing, awesome sex."

"I have to say, you are the best fuck ever. I mean, you are fucking awesome." He kissed her. "Let's do it again."

She laughed. "Certainly. But not now. Now we have to shower again and head over to the dinner party."

He watched her slink her way into the bathroom, loving how her hips swayed. Who'smygoodboy jumped up on the bed. Burke gave him a scratch behind the ear as he heard the shower turn on. "You know, Junior, I'm a lucky man. A very lucky man." He would join her in the shower in a moment, but for now he was caught by a dawning awareness of just how deeply he was sinking into this relationship. This was a forever kind of thing. He didn't want to be away from her. He'd heard before of men who were pussy-whipped, lost in the throes of a woman's pleasure and the particular kinds of points she could drive a man to, but he'd always disregarded that as some kind of movie mythology. "I'm living it. Damn, I'm a lucky man."

Chapter 35

"Oh my God, now we're officially late," Miranda said as she made a rolling stop at a four-way intersection and eased into the right-hand turn.

"She's French, right? They invented fashionably late. She'll understand."

"Or she'll call us out on her suspicions, which wouldn't surprise me. Claudine can be very direct, totally sweet but she pulls no punches and suffers no fools. I hope you're ready for her."

"Hey, I'm with you." He picked up her hand and kissed it. "I'm ready for anything."

Miranda laughed. "Luckily, we don't have to be ready for more than excellent wine, a fabulous meal, and the company of truly wonderful people. We're well away from the hurricane, as worried as we might be for our homes back there."

"We did a good job boarding up. I'm not that worried. I don't think it will turn into a category four, but you never know. We're out. Family's out. My dad actually left the island, amazingly—usually he rides these things out. We have the dog." He turned around, saying, "Who'sMyGoodBoy?" The dog stood up on the back seat and wagged his tail excitedly.

"I swear, he really thinks that's his name."

"Yes, He'sagoodboy, yes he is, yes he is." Burke scratched the pooch's ears. Turning back to Miranda he said, "Thanks again for letting him come along. I know you're not really a dog person."

"No worries. I realize that you two come as a pair. There's no separating you from the hound. I get that. I accept your hound."

"He accepts you in his pack, too."

"Yes, I can tell he does. Between the fact that he has to be constantly touching me and the loving stares as I cook, I can tell I'm in his pack."

"Don't be offended by his humping. He's only trying to be like daddy." Burke snickered. "Aren't you, boy? Aren't you, boy? Who's my good dog? Huh? Who'sMyGoodBoy?"

Miranda sighed. "Like father like son."

Burke laughed. "Well, he is Junior."

"And we're here. Let's park over there. Plenty of room. We'll just pull in next to this one."

"And they have five cars… who can park five cars comfortably? This place is huge." Burke was a little wide-eyed. "Wow, look at the barns. They have barns. Like more than one of them."

Miranda turned off the engine. "Yeah, and you should see Mimi's painting studio out back! This big old house has been in her family for generations. Caroline is the fourth generation to live here and her son, Ty, makes the fifth. It's amazing that a family can hang on like this. Caroline's brother, Chase, has been super-successful and he actually pays for it all. He only lives here when he's in the US."

Burke sounded uncomfortable. "So where does he live outside of the US?"

"Oh, mostly France. His wife, Claudine, has family there. He has a lot of business ties there." Miranda gave him a level look. "You aren't going to freak out because they have money, are you?"

"Um, no."

"Look, in case this helps, Caroline grew up here while her mother and father had to rebuild the place. It was falling apart. I think the stress of it caused them to divorce, but by scraping by, Mimi managed to keep hold of it, keep it together and make a home here. Caroline never went hungry, but she never had excess either. They're really normal people, just like you and me. Mimi's sons, Caroline's brothers, have worked their asses off to make good in their careers, and they've been successful, particularly Chase. He's currently here in the states, so he's living here and will join us for dinner. So these people are just like you. They've worked hard to keep their family home. They've worked hard to make their businesses survive and feed their families, raise their kids. They're normal people."

"Okay, so no false superiority? No weird surprises? All right. I'm good. I'm good."

"Oh, hell no! This isn't Gregg's family. This is Caroline's family. You couldn't get more laid back and relaxed. Absolutely normal. You're going to have a great time. I promise."

Burke leaned over and gave Miranda a kiss, a nice long kiss. "As long as I'm with you, I'll be fine. I love you."

"I know. You talk in your sleep." She winked at him. Hand in hand they walked into the house with the dog walking so close to Miranda that she almost tripped over him. They rang the doorbell. Caroline came to the door.

"Miranda!" Caroline gave her a big hug and the dog stopped short, sniffed, barked twice, and shot past them, disappearing into the house. Caroline didn't miss a beat. "And I am guessing that you must be Burke? It's so nice to meet you after hearing about you for so long. C'mon in, c'mon in. We're just about to start our hurricane escape party." She pulled him inside and gave him a hug.

Burke laughed, "Not much risk of it still being a hurricane by the time it gets here, if it gets here."

"True, but you're not the only ones here escaping the hurricane! We've taken in a couple of other refugees."

As they walked into the living room Chase entered the room from the other side, carrying two children who were about six years old, one dark-haired and the other fair, one in each arm. "Okay, now you two, it's bedtime in forty-five minutes. How do you want to spend your time? Mommy and Daddy are going to eat dinner."

"Can Marcel read to us?" the child with long blonde hair asked.

"Well, let's ask him." Chase stopped by Miranda and Burke while Caroline made introductions. "I'm sorry I can't shake hands, since mine are kind of full. I'm looking forward to spending the evening together. Let me get these little tykes upstairs with their mannie and I'll join you directly." He gave them a fabulous smile and then he went up the stairs, children in arms, and called out to Marcel in French, asking if he would read to the children. The little ones immediately started talking quickly in French as well.

Miranda looked at Caroline. "You know, I am always caught by surprise at how very handsome he is. So, Caroline, would it be totally inappropriate for me to ask for his autograph? Or would it be like, um, being a fan girl."

Caroline laughed at her. "Of course, you can ask. I'm sure he'll be happy to. I mean, it happens all the time. They only ever get any peace here in Charlotte. They can hardly walk down the streets of Paris and not be mobbed by the paparazzi."

Miranda looked up the stairs. "You know, I've always secretly been a fan girl. I'll never forget The Golden Man ads."

"What are you talking about?" Burke asked, also looking upstairs.

"Oh, didn't Miranda tell you? My brother was, I guess he still is, a high fashion model, so he's pretty well known. He's into multiple businesses now. Colognes, clothing, watches. He really loves his line of watches in particular, so he's done well. C'mon, this way. Everyone's in the back room, at least they were when I left. People seem to keep migrating all over the house. Let's head to the family room."

As Caroline led them on Burke whispered to Miranda, "Just like us, huh?"

"Oh sure. You've got your hand into lots of businesses. So does Chase. No difference."

"I do doughnuts, coffee, and books. He does high fashion, cologne, and watches. I think it's different." He turned to Caroline and asked more loudly, "What's a mannie?"

"Oh, their nanny is a man. They wanted to avoid gender stereotypes with their kids, so they're allowed to wear whatever they want. You saw the twins.

Jacques often likes to wear skirts and he was the one with the long hair. Chloe, who is ten now, is around here someplace. She's currently sporting a boy's cut dyed a hot pink color, but she looked like Rapunzel until February. She donated her hair to Locks of Love. They do a lot with children's hospitals all around the world."

Burke leaned into Miranda again, "Oh yes, just like us. No difference." He continued to look around the beautifully decorated house and stare at the artwork.

"Remember, Mimi is my painting mentor. You'll see a lot of artwork here, both hers and her friends'. Artists trade with one another a lot, so this place has, over the years, become kind of like a gallery. I love it here."

As they walked by the kitchen, a woman who was just a few years younger than Caroline and Miranda was clearly in control of production. She had two assistants and was giving directions in rapid fire succession. In French. Then she saw Caroline and hurried over. "Mon Dieu! You are here. How wonderful that is. Miranda, it is so nice to see you again." She kissed Miranda on both cheeks. "Tell me, did you ever use the morel mushrooms I sent you?"

"Oh yes. I had to wait for the dried ones to come in handy. But yes, this is Burke and he has tasted your wonderful recipe for the poached eggs in morel mushroom sauce, although I know it wasn't as good as yours."

"Oh, you are sweet. I'm sure it was completely acceptable. Burke! How nice to meet you. And what did you think of the dish? You must be very special indeed, for Miranda to serve such a magic dish to you."

Burke was a little overwhelmed . "It was… amazing."

"Of course it was. Love is like that, no? Magic is a very good thing. Well, I must get back to work if I'm going to have the dinner ready for us all. We got a little behind because the children did not want to be bored and eat with the stuffy grown-ups tonight. So, it is good that you are late." She began to go back to the kitchen and then turned back around, and with a wink said, "I hope you had fun!"

As they walked down the hallway Miranda whispered to Burke, "I told

307

you so. Luckily, that was only in front of Caroline."

"I'm not sure I'm ready for this. She's the wife and she has kitchen staff? French kitchen staff?"

"Oh, my brother often drags this entourage in tow," said Caroline. "The mannie, a personal chef and an assistant, a business manager, his communications person, a tutor. It's crazy. That's why he built the guest house out back when he put in the pool, so they can all be here but not be in Mom's house. I mean she likes them and all, but maybe not that much."

"Oh, just like us. No difference there. None at all. I have a little house out back, too. It's called a shed. I keep my wetsuit and an old jet ski in it, along with the sheets of plywood for hurricanes," he whispered to Miranda.

"Everything will be fine. Hey, where did the dog go? Usually he's trying to trip me."

Caroline led them into the family room. The couch was L-shaped and was covered in a creamy leather, while other contemporary chairs dotted the room. An older woman was straightening up some toys. "Hey Mom, Miranda and Burke are here."

"Oh, it's so nice to meet you." Mimi greeted Burke with warmth and elegance. "No wonder Miranda looks so radiant these days."

They chatted easily and Burke visibly relaxed.

A young man with dark hair and Asian features walked into the room with Chase, catching Miranda's attention.

"Hi Ty, I see your hair is growing back. It's looking nice." She gave Ty a hug.

"Yes, it was awful of Mom to shave it on New Year's Day," Ty said sullenly and ran his fingers through his black hair. "I didn't bang the car up that badly."

"She told you, no drinking. Not 'til your twenty-five," Chase said as he walked up behind the young man.

"Uh, Uncle Chase, in the U.S. it's twenty-one."

"Not for you, buddy. I saw the shape that car was in. You need some time to mature. I think twenty-five. Maybe even thirty."

Miranda laughed and said, "I think that sounds like a good rule, Ty. Hey Chase, would you mind terribly if I asked you something really tacky?"

"Hey, is that Burke? I didn't know Burke was here!" Ty said more to himself than anyone. He left Miranda to talk to Chase by herself.

"It was so nice of you all to let us bring Burke's dog. I think he would have been nervous left back in my condo without either one of us there. Particularly as the outer bands stir up some thunderstorms. He absolutely hates thunder," Miranda said to Chase.

"Oh, we love dogs. We always had dogs. I really miss them," Chase said as he bent down to pet the pooch. "We can't have one and drag the poor thing back and forth across the ocean. What's his name?"

Miranda laughed. "He thinks it's 'Who'sMyGoodBoy'." On cue the dog ran in fast circles chasing its tail and then tried to hump Miranda's leg. She pushed him off. "I'm not quite as enamored as Burke is, I have to say. He usually follows me everyplace."

"What is that dog doing here?"

Miranda turned slowly, then froze. "Austin! What are you doing here?"

Austin turned his attention from the dog to Miranda. He came over and hugged her. "Oh my God, Andy?" Who'sMyGoodBoy excitedly jumped up and down, bouncing off the both of them.

Before she could say anything else, Burke looked over and, with clear excitement on his face, said, "Austin! What are you doing here?"

"Dad? You're here? How come you're here?" He gave his dad a hug. Both were all smiles .

"Miranda, how do you know Austin?" Burke asked.

Miranda was still so shocked at seeing Austin that she didn't catch Burke's question. "Austin, I can't believe I'm seeing you. Why are you here?"

"Taisei is my room-mate. This is his house."

Miranda laughed, but clearly was still a bit confused, "This is Caroline's house." She pointed to Caroline.

Austin pointed to Caroline as well. "It's Mrs. Ah-Bey's house. She's Mrs. Abe, Taisei's mom." Caroline was looking a bit shell-shocked. At that moment Claudine came into the room.

Burke turned to Austin, asking again in a slightly faltering voice, "Austin, how do you know Miranda?"

Miranda asked, "Austin… Taisei? You mean Ty is your roommate?"

"I've never heard him go by Ty. Taisei. Taisei Ah-Bay-Say-Day, I told you about him. Taisei Abe. Yeah. He invited me to come home with him when the evacuation orders were given. This is a great place. I've never been here before." He looked happily around the room.

"Yes, the Watkins' place is spectacular. Caroline was my roommate in college."

"Who are the Watkins?" Austin asked.

Chase volunteered, "We're the Watkins. Caroline is a Watkins. Like me. And Mom."

"Miranda, how do you know Austin?" Burke asked again, clearly becoming more confused at this happy reunion that he couldn't quite figure out. The dog barked excitedly.

Austin looked at Caroline, clearly confused. "You aren't Mrs. Abe?"

Caroline smiled generously. "I'm Caroline Watkins Abe. This is my brother, Chase. And this is really our mother's house. We all grew up here, but I guess we're all the owners now."

Miranda said, her voice evincing some shock, "I can't believe you live with my college roomie's son! It's such a… small world."

Austin smiled back at her. "Yeah, it is. Hey, Andy, why is my dad here? Dad, why are you here?"

Burke asked yet again, "How do you know each other?" The dog was jumping up first against Burke's side, then Austin's, then Andy's.

"Down, Junior, down boy. Dad, how do you know Andy? Are you here with her? Why are you with her?"

"Miranda's my girlfriend," Burke said and took Miranda's hand.

Austin looked from his dad to Andy, and back again with a growing look of shock. "Andy… Andy—you're dating my dad?"

"Who's your dad? No." She gave a nervous chuckle. "Burke's son is named Burke Junior. Not Austin. What? Darnell Mitchell is your dad…?"

"Darnell Mitchell? Not hardly!" Austin turned to Burke. "Dad, what's going on?"

"Wait, Burke is your dad? This is *your dad*?" Miranda looked between the two of them. "I think I need to sit down." The room fell silent as everyone stared at the three of them and then looked at one another.

Caroline broke the silence first. "Oh my God. This can't be happening."

"This can't be happening," Miranda echoed, her voice barely a whisper. She let go of Burke's hand and then took a seat. She was shaking slightly.

Austin turned to his dad. "So, the woman you've been telling me about all spring, this woman you've fallen in love with, is Andy?"

Burke looked at Austin. "How do you know Miranda? Why do you call her Andy? Wait a minute. Andy? Andy? Your girlfriend of last summer? Andy?" Burke looked quickly back and forth between the two of them. "You dated… my girlfriend?"

Austin looked incredulously at his dad. "You're in love with my ex-girlfriend?"

Ty's voice rang out into the silence that filled the room, "Wow, Austin Powers. This is really weird. This is the woman you talked about most of last year? My mom's best friend? That is some major mojo, dude!"

Caroline grabbed Ty by the shoulders and started marching him towards the door. "Ty! Get out of here now. This is none of your business."

He did a quick spin and was free of her grasp. "Oh, I think it is. Austin's my best friend. I had to listen to him moan all winter long."

At that moment Claudine swept back into the room, having snuck out at some point during the unfolding conversation. She was bearing a tray on which was a large bottle of vodka and some small glasses. "Oh, honey," Chase said, "I'm not sure now is a good time."

311

She shook her head and he immediately took two steps back. In her heavy accent she announced, "Oui! It is the best time for vodka. You Americans are thrown by the smallest little things. I'm sure you will all need a stiff drink before you can figure this out." She commenced with pouring out a half a dozen little glasses of vodka and she put a bit of lemon zest, a spring of something green, and two ice cubes in each glass.

Caroline reached for a glass, saying, "I'm not even a part of this, but I could sure use one of these. Thanks, Claudine." She slapped her son's hand, which was reaching for a glass. "Ty, don't you even think about this. You touch one of those glasses and I'm shaving your head again." Ty quickly took three steps back away from the tray.

Burke turned to Miranda. "How can Austin be your... your... you told me you had a man-friend?"

Claudine shook her head sadly and picked up one of the glasses. She went over to Miranda and picked up her hand and put the glass in it. "Trust me, you need this!"

Miranda looked up into Claudine's eyes. The woman was smiling at her encouragingly. "Thanks." She turned to Burke and tried to find her voice. "I did have a man-friend. Austin took me sailing last summer. Then, then...." She found herself at a loss for words.

Austin sat down next to her, seeing her distress. "Then we dated all summer. And up to Christmas."

"*That's* who you went skiing with? Austin, you went skiing with her? Miranda, you went to Aspen or Vail or something. Austin, you were up in the northeast?"

"No," said Miranda. "I changed plans after you and I had coffee. Because of what you said."

"We went on our Christmas vacation because my dad suggested it?" Austin asked.

"Now that's some major weird mojo!" Ty said as he reached for a glass again. Caroline was too quick for him and slapped his hand again. Ty withdrew to hide behind Chase.

Burke took two steps closer to Miranda. "How can Austin be your man friend? He's… so young."

"I did tell you that my man-friend and I had an age difference. I mean, I had no idea it was quite such an age difference. We discovered that on our ski trip. It was quite a surprise. And made me decide that I truly hate skiing. All kinds of skiing."

"Yeah," Austin sighed. "It ended our relationship. It was just something we couldn't get over. I mean, that's a big difference."

"No, no, your man-friend was an older guy. Some old geezer. A man. Austin's not a man, He's just a boy. He's my boy."

"How can you say that?" said Miranda. "He's a wonderful man. He may be your boy, Burke, but he's all grown up."

"Oh right. I suppose you can attest to that?"

Everyone in the room flinched. Miranda was visibly taken aback. Mimi was looking at Miranda right in the eyes and nodding slightly. Miranda could feel herself filling with confidence. She took a deep breath. "Yes, Burke, I can. Austin is one of the most wonderful men I have ever met. Up until this moment, I would have said he was just like his father."

Burke flinched. Claudine handed him a glass of vodka. "Burke, you in particular need this badly at this moment. I suggest you take a sip and collect your thoughts. You might want to be very careful about what you say next."

Burke sat down. He sipped the vodka. He looked at Austin, the pain clear across his face. Then he looked at Miranda.

"Burke, why do you say my man-friend was an older guy?"

He tried to speak a couple of times and had to sip his drink again. Finally, he said, "You told me you had an age difference with this friend of yours. Of course, I assumed it was an older man. It's outrageous to think that you'd be going out with a younger man! Twenty years younger! With my boy!"

"The fact that Austin turned out to be your son, yes, I'm also reeling from that. But why is it that outrageous that a younger man would want to date

313

me?"

"Well, younger's fine, maybe five years younger, but twenty? Twenty? That's beyond crazy. How could you not have known?"

Claudine made little *tsk tsk* sounds. "Burke, drink your vodka. Good boy. You know, you might need a second glass. Chase, would you? In France, we call it a May-December romance. I cannot believe it does not happen in the U.S." She took the glass from Chase and handed it back to Burke.

He looked up into her eyes with almost a pleading look. "Not with the woman being older. Not that much older." He was stammering, almost spluttering.

Now it was Mimi's turn to break the silence. "Of course, that happens, Burke. Even my boyfriend is younger. In fact, he's in his early fifties. That's nearly twenty years younger than I am."

"Mom, you have a boyfriend?" Caroline and Chase's voices rang out in unified surprise.

Claudine raised her glass. "Good for you, Mimi!" She handed Mimi a tumbler and they clinked their glasses and drank.

Caroline stared at her mother. "How could you have never told me about your boyfriend? Who is he? Oh my God, I know who he is. He's that artist from the studio you joined. Wow, Mom, he's hot. Oh my God, my mom is dating hotter men than I am."

Claudine turned back to Burke, "You see, Burke. It happens all the time. Even here. You don't need to be an ageist."

Burke looked at Claudine, obviously speechless.

"A president of France, Emmanuel Macron, loved his Bridgette, who was twenty-five years his senior. Oui! May to December relationships can be very nice and the calendar, it can work both ways. Burke, tell me, why are you so shocked that the woman you love is loved by another? And you clearly love and respect your son, Austin. So, the woman you care for is also cared for by another whom you love and respect?"

Burke was still unable to speak.

"Hmmm. Maybe you need to drink that? This has been a big shock for you, no? Oui! Of course, it has. It will take some time for you to sort this out, to get used to the idea."

"Get used to the idea?" He looked up at her. "I don't know about that. That's just... just... not right. It's like she's some type of sick cougar... predator... woman."

"Burke, I think Claudine's right," said Mimi. "Your problem is that you haven't had a chance to get used to this whole idea yet. Remember, Miranda and Austin have had months to work through the shock of discovering that not all was as it appeared. But this is all new for you. I would have to say that back at Christmas time, this was overwhelming to Miranda, too. Quite overwhelming. She was going to give up the beach house over it."

Austin put his hand on Miranda's arm. "No, you weren't! I would never want you to do that. That place is so you. You're so happy there."

Burke shuddered and turned away from them, downing his second glass of vodka.

Claudine's assistant walked into the room. With an excited flourish he announced in his heavy French accent, "Mesdames et messieurs, dinner is served!"

Chapter 36

Étienne, Claudine's chef, was most disappointed to learn that the true storm was an emotional one and it left no one in the mood to eat. He brought out small plates and set dishes around so people could snack as needed. They certainly seemed interested in drinking, so he rolled in a little glass cart loaded with liquor bottles of all kinds.

The evening had been the most brutal on Burke, who was furious with Austin and he couldn't even look at Miranda. Austin wished he was shocked that his dad was being such a jerk. He hadn't seen this side of Burke for a long, long time, but when his dad decided to fall apart, well, he could do it in style. He wanted to seem perfect, but he wasn't. Nobody was. But nobody should have said the things Burke said to Miranda. Poor Andy left in tears to go back to her condo and Caroline packed a quick bag and accompanied her. The dog howled as she left and the front door closed behind her. Austin felt helpless and hated seeing her so distraught.

When they were alone, Burke turned to Austin. "I just can't believe you, that you… would do that."

"Would do what?"

"Would use such bad judgement."

"What?"

"Well, for starters, she's a client. A customer. Tell me you don't hit on the customers at the shop? Oh my God, what do I not know about? Is this a regular thing with you?"

"What? No, I don't hit on the customers. I can't believe you would accuse me of…" Austin could hear himself spluttering and was unable to finish his sentence.

Burke was pacing. "I thought I could trust you. I obviously can't trust her, going after a mere boy like that. And she's old enough to be your mother."

"But she's not." Austin could feel his temperature rising.

"She's twenty years older than you! I can't believe you didn't know that. I can't believe she didn't know that."

"Dad, you might be interested to know that we never talked about our ages. Honestly, I pegged her for thirty-three. Thought her daughter was in middle school."

"She's in medical school."

"Yeah, believe me, I got that totally clarified by the daughter herself when she accused me of being some kind of pool-boy gold digger after Andy's money." Austin felt his face get hot at the memory.

"People with money." Burke muttered as he paced. "They think they can have anything. Do anything they want. The rules just don't apply to them." He shuddered again. "It's like she's some kind of child molester. She lied to me. She lied to you."

"Are you crazy?" Austin saw that his dad wasn't calming down with time, he was ratcheting up. Well, he'd seen this from Burke before. He was so together when things were going his way but after something triggered him, well, that was a different story.

"I think I've been crazy. Out of my mind for these past months, but now that I see what she's dragged you and me into, I'm sickened. She's a monster."

"Bad judgement? You called Andy bad judgement? Dad, she's amazing. She's wonderful. Clearly, she loves you. And you love her."

"No, I don't. How could 1 love someone like that? A predator? A manipulator? A liar?"

"You know, you're coming across as pretty eager to blame everyone but yourself. And you're probably more to blame than anyone."

"Nonsense. I'm the victim here."

"No, you're not. Jesus, Dad, take a look at yourself. After you first met her you practically stalked the poor woman. The monster here may be you. Given that you called me for advice about how to scoop up some other dude's girl, I think you're being pretty damn hypocritical. If I'd known, I'd probably have told you to go fuck yourself."

"There is no call for that language!" Burke raised his voice.

"So, Dad, why'd you do it? Why'd you go after her so hard?" Austin was surprised at just how sharp an edge his own voice held.

Burke collapsed into a chair. He put his hands over his face and gave a deep and painful sigh. He hung his head, his face still in his hands. Austin realized his dad was crying. He went over and sat down next to him and put his arm on his shoulder.

In a quiet voice, he asked again, "Why, Dad? Why did you pursue her so hard?"

Eventually Burke met Austin's eyes. Tears were falling from Burke's face. "I thought she was the one. It. It felt like *it*, from the first time I met her. Every time I saw her or was with her, it was the same."

"The book signing? That's where you met?"

Burke nodded. "Your Aunt Kat arranged a book club, and she asked Miranda to come. We read her book. It was stupid but funny. And I couldn't take my eyes off of her. I couldn't imagine how Kat had found her."

Austin knew just what his dad meant. He'd had that experience too, seeing her zoom up on that windsurfer, but he didn't think that was the right thing to say. Then it dawned on him. "The book signing? With Aunt Kat?"

Burke nodded again.

Austin looked away, trying to sort out how complex and interwoven this situation was. "Dad, I set up the book club and the signing event. Andy was lonely, and I connected her and Kat."

Burke stared for a moment, his face full of disbelief. "Now that's some major weird mojo."

"Look, Dad, I know you're really struggling with this, but hear me out, please. Andy and I met as two adults. We did nothing wrong. We found out that we had no future and we parted close friends, loving each other and wishing one another the very best. Dad, I have nothing to apologize for. Andy has nothing to apologize for. You met her and you saw in her the same things I did. She's wonderful. I want you to think about the idea that maybe this isn't about Miranda."

"Then what is it about? The woman I loved is a lying, false…"

"Dad, I think this is about you. I think you should apologize to her. For all those things you said to her, the things you called her."

"What? I can't. I just can't. After finding out that you and she…" Burke shuddered. "I just… can't." Burke went and poured himself another glass of vodka. Austin had lost track now of how many Burke had downed.

Chase ventured in a short time after that. Burke obviously needed to stay the night. Chase gave Austin instructions on where to put him up in the guest house and directed Austin to where he could find some extra clothes.

The next morning, Austin woke up early. When he went downstairs, his dad was deeply asleep on the couch. *Well, he should sleep,* Austin told himself. *He's going to have an awful hangover.*

Very quietly, Austin crept outside, the dog padding along beside him. He felt embarrassed that everything had been so public in front of Taisei's family, that they got dragged into all of this. He thought he might sit by the pool for a while and absorb the quiet. As he walked over to a chair to sit down, he saw Chase crouching down by the water's edge, holding a square box of little test tubes in his hand. He was studying it.

"Oh, good morning, Austin. I hope you slept well?"

"The guest house is very comfortable."

"I'm glad you think so. I always like it, too. I appreciate it that you and Ty were willing to bunk out there so Marcel could be close to the little ones. Mom's house only has the five bedrooms, after all. It tends to fill up quick when so many of us come back to roost."

"Mr. Watkins,"

"Call me Chase."

"Chase. I want to apologize. I'm so sorry you had to witness that last night. My dad is usually a more, um, open kind of guy. More laid back. He's going through… uh… something. He kinda fell apart. That whole scene was really weird."

"Oh, I'm sure it was uncomfortable, but weird? Maybe a little bit, but on the scale of weird, I don't know. I'd not even give it a five on a ten-point scale."

"I mean, the whole dad-and-son in love with the same woman thing, even I think that's pretty weird."

"It's different. I'll give you that. But I know a little bit about weird. Once upon a time, there was this girl who chased me down for years. Everyone joked that we would end up together. She followed me to college even. It was like having a professional stalker since birth. Then we actually, finally got together. Twenty-four hours later my brother waltzes in and scoops her up, right out of my arms. In front of the whole family. Marries her. It's a little weird to have to spend nearly every Christmas holiday with my brother and his wife, my former stalker."

"Well, yeah, that sounds weird. But my dad used to date my Aunt Mad, high school sweethearts or something. I think that was kinda' their situation. She married his brother. And now he's an investor in more than one business of theirs. At least you have some, uh, distance between you. Besides, you ended up with Claudine."

Chase laughed. "Oh yes, I got the way better end of the deal. But then there was being shaved from head to toe, painted gold, and photographed replicating great pieces of art." Chase raised his eyebrows as he described the scene.

"Okay, that sounds really weird."

"Yeah, I thought it was pretty strange, too. But I have to say, the sex tape was the weirdest. Made my career though. I'm not sure my mother has forgiven me yet."

Austin wasn't quite sure how to respond to that. "Uh, mind if I ask why'd you do that?"

"Oh, I didn't," Chase explained "The lifestyle comes with… hmm, complications. You could think of it as predatory surveillance. I didn't know about the tape at the time, of course, until it was released in retaliation for a failed attempt at blackmail. Then the court case in Europe was all over the news, and the anti-terrorism trial that I had to testify in because of my fake identity."

"Okay, now that shit is weird."

"Everything is all in how you see it. It's all perspective."

"What are you doing?"

Chase held up the vials and put a couple of drops into one of the glass tubes. "Oh, checking the chemicals in the pool, testing the water."

"Don't you have people who do that for you? It just seems like the kind of place where you'd have a pool boy or somebody like that."

"Yes, but I like to do it myself. I don't often have the chance to enjoy the simple things, so I relish the opportunity when it presents itself. I also think it's funny, because I've been referred to as 'the pool boy' on more than one occasion."

"I was accused of being the pool boy. I found it really rankled. Still does, in fact."

"Who called you that? If I may ask."

"Uh, Andy's daughter. Accused me of having less than honorable intentions with her mother. Of not caring for her at all. Just after her money."

"You know, with those types of comments, I always found that the power with which it lands has a lot to do with the person from which it comes. Remember that."

Austin nodded. "I don't have a pool, I have the ocean. That's all I do all summer. Set up the rentals. Make sure people are wearing their life jackets. Send them off. Take in the rentals. Clean them."

"What are you studying in school?"

"Business. Management specifically. I've taken some courses in finance and accounting, supply chain management, personnel, anything that I could see helping me to run the rental shop someday. But now, I really don't want to go back there this summer. My dad is being such a jerk. I've always wanted to live my life on the island, but what if my dad is being so stubborn and narrow-minded because he's never really been off the island? Never finished college? Never really experienced the wider world? I guess I'm feeling like all of a sudden I don't know what I want for my future. And I've always known. And not knowing, it's just so… weird."

"I know just what you mean. Precisely. I was a little bit older than you, but there was a time when I knew exactly, precisely what I wanted to do."

"What was that?"

"Accounting. Yes, you laugh, but I loved it. Numbers have always been easy for me. I passed all four parts of the C.P.A. exam on the first try."

"Damn. You must be legend. That's rare. All my profs tell me that's nearly impossible."

"Yeah, and I made management in my first job. Absolutely loved it. Then I met Claudine just over a year later and suddenly nothing I wanted the day before seemed to matter. But she didn't live in my world, so I followed her to her world. She became my manager, my agent, my everything. If I were being honest about it, she re-made me into someone totally new."

"Oh, yeah, Taisei, uh, I mean Ty, said you had a stage name."

"Well, that's one way to put it. But yes, I had a professional identity. I did all right. I used my success to both land the woman of my dreams, who I married and started my family with, and to set up the business of my dreams, which I oversee the accounting arm for and direct a lot of the profits to a foundation that engages in the charity work I really care about."

Austin looked around the grounds. "And you've done well by your family, too. This is a great place for Ty to have grown up."

"Of course. I'm an accountant. I understand money. Austin, have you done any internships over the summers while you've been at school?"

"Nah." Austin shook his head. "Just the family business. They've needed me. But I do most of the customer service, ordering, and book-keeping."

"Hmm. You know, I think you need to do an off-island experience before you graduate next year. How would you like to come and work for me? I could provide you with a great internship, a broad view of a complex business. You could help me with a product launch. Maybe you can learn some things that will help you run businesses on the islands, if that's what you choose to do later on."

"Really? That sounds… yeah. Really? Don't you need to see my transcripts? Essays and applications?"

"All I need to see I saw last night. In a difficult situation you comported yourself well. Very well. You were caught off guard, and yet you held it together. You treated Andy with care and respect. You even did pretty well with your father for a while there, too. But I get that, those relationships are much more complicated."

Austin understood precisely what he meant.

"So, if you're game, then when you and Ty finish up exams, come back with him. You can come with us. Do you have a passport? No? I'll have Henri work on that. We'll be headed to France first. Then Italy. You wouldn't happen to like cycling, would you?"

"Passport? Okay. Plane tickets?" Austin was trying to keep up with the sudden turn of this conversation.

"Passport you need, and in your own name." Chase gave him a wink. "Absolutely. Plane tickets, not so much. We're such a huge group that we take our own plane. Really helps with the kids' jet lag. And, unfortunately, we can't trust airport personnel with our luggage. Too many of our personal possessions would disappear and then show up on eBay. So, there's plenty of space for you, no problem. I do have to warn you of one thing though."

"What's that?"

"It's Claudine. She's got her eye on you."

"Um, Mr. Watkins," Austin suddenly felt like this was going down a road

323

that was too foreign for him. "I'm really not into older women. Particularly married, older women."

"What? Oh, that? No, don't worry. Not that at all. She has her eye on you professionally. She will want to pull you away from the business end of things. She thinks you have in-front-of-the-camera potential."

"What? What does that mean?"

"She runs a very successful modeling agency. She thinks you have the potential I had, way back when. Being the talent is a good gig. From my personal experience, I'd recommend it. And I can still teach you how the business works. One thing I've learned about my wife: she's usually right. I try to do everything she says. I'd recommend you follow suit."

"Um, if I say yes, do I have to be shaved and painted gold too? Or, uh, make a tape. I don't want to do that."

Chase laughed. "No, neither did I. Cross that bridge when you get to it, son. Cross that bridge when you get to it."

Chapter 37

"How are you this morning, honey?" Caroline asked in her gentle way. She pushed a mug over to Andy.

Gratefully, Andy accepted it. "I'm absolutely awful. Did you hear the terrible things he called me? A monster? A predator? A liar. I'm not those things." She looked at her friend. "Am I? He wasn't even twenty-one."

"Last I knew, men over eighteen were adults. They're able to make their own decisions. From what you told me, you tried to let Austin go at the end of summer?"

Andy nodded.

"And he reached out to you after you parted. You didn't chase him down. You didn't buy him. He came back to you. You just loved him. You know, I think you're going to have to face some facts."

"Oh? Which facts?"

"You're a highly desirable woman. That Gregg was a total fool and you should forget him. And that Burke never realized before that he's a middle-aged man who could be so completely outshone by his son. You aren't all those things he said. He'll regret his words."

"The one thing, the one thing I didn't want to have happen was to get hurt. This is worse than my divorce. The whole time with Burke, it felt like *it*, you know? Like he was the one. I didn't think I'd ever feel that way again. Well, I guess I shouldn't say again, because I never felt that with Gregg."

"And not with Austin?"

"No. Not really. He was so sweet. He was so fun. And he helped me come back to life. Healed me. But no, there was no *it* thing. Deep in my heart I always knew it had no future. But with Burke, I felt like we could have had a future. And I'd just so totally opened up to him... to just be crushed." Miranda lay her head down on the table.

"Yeah, from everything you told me, he sounded like the perfect guy," Caroline said. She put her cup down. "But nobody's perfect, Andy. Anyone can be on their best behavior for a while, but eventually we all crack under the pressure."

"If that's true, then Burke certainly did. He's so creeped out by this whole situation that he can't look at me, much less speak to me about it."

Caroline refreshed her coffee. "Well, if he can't talk to you, you guys can't work through it."

"Oh, there's no working through it. After that three-way fight? There's no working through it. Caroline, how do I go on from here?"

"Hell, girl, you can't see that?"

Andy shook her head.

"You write your next best seller!"

Andy just stared at her.

"Well, you might need to do it under a *nom de plume*, 'cause unlike your last book this one would be really, really autobiographical. Of course, your last book has now become kind of autobiographical too, given the whole younger man thing."

The two women looked at one another for a few moments and then slowly they started giggling. Then laughing.

"You're gonna be all right, Andy. I can't tell you what's going to happen or whether Burke will ever get his head on straight, but if you can laugh about it, then you're going to be all right."

Andy gave her a rueful little smile and sighed, running her hands through her hair. "Boy, you know when word of this spreads, I bet Paul will leave a message on my phone in about five minutes."

The hurricane hit the Outer Banks as a category three storm. Luckily it was a fast-moving system and it raced across the state, bringing a tropical depression to Charlotte and quickly moving out to drench Eastern Tennessee. After a few days the all-clear was given and residents were allowed to return to their homes. Caroline offered to return with Andy, since she had to drive Ty back. They agreed that Mimi was right. The beach house was her home. She loved it there. She wasn't going to let either Burke or the memory of him scare her away.

"Are you sure you'll be okay?"

"Sure, I'll cry. But you're right. I'll laugh too. I'll make it through this."

"The writing will be very therapeutic." Caroline nodded at her knowingly.

"Yes, I can feel it. I need to get it out. I'm kind of itching to get back to the beach and get to work on it. It's like last time. I have my story."

Caroline smiled at her friend, "And this story you can choose whether you want to publish or not. Maybe you'll just write it for you."

"Yeah. That's a huge difference. You're right. I can't write for my agent no matter how hard she tries to whip me. I write for me. Funny how I never put that together before."

"I can come for a few days and help you get everything back to rights. I'll take Ty back and then I'll come over to the beach house."

"That'll be nice."

"You know, he headed back already."

Miranda gave her friend a small smile. "It's okay to say his name. Burke. Burke headed back already." She had a brave look on her face but her voice cracked with emotion.

Caroline nodded. "He and Austin left before the all-clear was given. They went to join his brother and his wife, where they were waiting it out."

Miranda nodded. "It's gonna be so awkward, you know. So awkward."

* * *

Miranda arrived back at the beach house, relieved to find no real damage amidst the plethora of downed branches and general mess left by the fast-moving storm. The empty lots around her were also masses of debris left by the over-wash. She had been worried that Hayward House wasn't up high enough. It wasn't on ten-foot pylons; it was only about three feet off the ground, but it had survived the high water just fine. The highest watermarks were only half-way up the stilts. She was relieved that she didn't have water damage to repair. The flume would have to be drained and cleaned, but that was small stuff. Still, she needed to de-board all the windows and put the plywood in storage. That would be a job for any person alone to do, much less someone who had no experience doing it. She decided to wait until Caroline arrived the next day to worry about it. Until then, she would pick up the outside, hit the grocery store, and do what she could.

Chapter 38

Burke put the Caribbean-blue Microbus into park, got out and slammed the door shut rather harder than he intended. Little things could really annoy him these days. Almost two weeks ago now, he and Austin had left that palace, *the Watkins manor*, as he referred to it, just as the heavy rains were ending. They'd checked into a motel near where Ben and Mad were sheltering with friends. He and Austin argued constantly. Burke couldn't believe his boy was being so disrespectful. He couldn't believe that Austin would defend her like that. As though she were blameless. As though it was Burke who needed to adjust. And yet, this behavior was all too familiar at the same time.

Then Austin went and aired their dirty laundry in front of Ben and Mad. Burke was stunned. And they were speechless. Then Mad had the audacity to laugh. She *laughed* about it. Ben said that sure was weird but since he'd been down a weird road or two, he got it: real life was like that. It was messy. Burke had been furious, and they'd had the argument all over again, only this time with the four of them.

Then Austin shocked them all. He announced he was leaving. After heading back to campus and taking his exams, he told them he'd be taking the offer of an internship in Europe. He'd let his dad know where he was. He apologized for the inconvenience of leaving them without summer help on short notice, but he'd made up his mind. He'd see them all at Christmas. Maybe.

Things took a turn for the worse when Burke yelled at Austin that he wasn't trotting off to Europe with a complete stranger.

"Look, I'm making my own decisions here," Austin had replied. "I'm twenty-one years old. I'm not a child. Sorry, Dad, but you can't tell me what to do anymore."

"You have responsibilities. You have commitments."

"Honey," Mad said. "You work at your father's business. What will he do without you?"

A look crossed Austin's face that Burke had never seen before. "I don't work at my father's business. I work at my uncle's business. I love you, Dad, but you're not my father. I'm not yours. And I'm not living your life… or his… anymore."

Mad gasped. Ben took long toke of his beer. Burke was taken aback. He couldn't help himself when he mumbled, "You've never been more like him than right now. Running out on your responsibilities. Selfish. Stupid. Young. I don't want you to end up like him! I've never wanted you to end up like him."

"What? Dead? That's not quite his fault."

"What do you know?"

"What do you mean? What don't I know?" The question loomed heavy in the air. Austin stared at Burke expectantly.

Burke didn't want to say anything more. He'd said too much already.

"You have to tell me. My father was killed by a drunk driver. Some twenty-five-year-old tourist. A drunk mainlander who killed him along with my mother, your wife, and your daughter. What else is there to that story?"

"Burke! No! He can't know… no one should have to bear that." Madeline tried to pull Austin away, but he shrugged her off, grabbed Burke by the shoulder with one hand and spun him around.

"Tell me."

The tears were streaming down Burke's face and he could feel his body tremble. His hands balled into fists. The time had come all too soon, but clearly, it was time. "Bobby wasn't killed by a drunk driver." His voice had a tremble too. "He *was* the drunk driver. I didn't know that he'd been drinking.

330

He had a… problem." Burke could hear Madeline sobbing. "I didn't know he was driving. The girls were all getting in the car, to go together. He wasn't supposed to go along. I didn't know how much he'd had until I found the cans, but that was after they left. He'd hidden them. It was too late. They were gone. I didn't even know where he was—and he was behind the wheel. Then we got the call."

Burke looked into his son's eyes. The boy he had taken in, raised as his own, at the request of his wife as she, too, lay dying. "You'll need each other," she had whispered. It was the very last thing she'd said. Like a replacement family, but some things you could never replace. At first, he had been unable to cope with his own grief and his fury at his oldest brother for ruining and tainting everything he ever loved. Seeing even a glimmer in Austin's behavior of the restless bad boy that had been Bobby triggered Burke. Bobby was all over Austin's face. He looked just like his father. The spitting image. And now the taint had spread to Burke's new relationship. The woman he had lost himself in, drowned himself in, and now he was drowning in grief and anger and disgust and he couldn't quite sort it all out. He couldn't find himself. It was like his brother's ghost coming back to haunt him, reaching out from the great beyond to ruin his happiness yet again. But he could never explain that to Austin. He couldn't even explain it to himself.

"So, my father murdered… everyone. Why did you never tell me?"

"You didn't need to hate your father. You didn't need to resent him. I carry enough of that for the both of us."

The silence hung heavily.

"You may not be my father, Uncle Burke, but you are my daddy. I love you."

"Oh Austin…" Burke grabbed Austin in a bear hug.

"I'm still leaving."

"Austin, no…" Burke felt his world crumbling. Austin was his world. He was his everything. The only thing he'd really loved. The only thing he could count on. He was his family. "You can't…"

"Dad, I've never really lived my own life. I've lived out my family's dreams. I get it now. I've grown up just to take Bobby's place. But I can't do that. I can't right his wrongs. I gotta find my own place. I gotta go." Now Austin was crying too.

"It's that woman, she's changed you."

"Yes. I know you can't see that it's for the better. You might need to vilify her. You might need to vilify your brother. I understand it if you need to vilify me, too, for a while. But what if there are no villains or victims? Maybe it's not win or lose. Sometimes we make bad choices. My father, for whatever reason, made some really suck ass choices. I'm gonna try to make good ones. Andy was a good choice. She was a great friend to me. I care for her deeply. If she were twenty years younger, who knows? But she's not. She wasn't put on this earth for me, not for anything other than as a great friend. And someone I trust. Someone I love. Burke, I wish her all the best, even if that's her being with you. Especially if that's her being with you. I'm telling you, she never did anything wrong. If anyone is to blame, it's me. But this is your deal, Dad. This has to do with you."

"She's changed you."

"Yes, Burke. She sure has."

And he was gone.

Mad and Ben had the courtesy to say hardly anything to Burke while he wrapped himself in silence until the roads were cleared and the Outer Banks re-opened to homeowners. He was silent for the three-hour drive to Salvo, deep in a dark funk of resentment. When Ben dropped him off at his place, he said, "Burke, there is another way…"

"I don't want to talk about it."

"You should listen to Austin. Bobby didn't mean any of this… You should call Austin. He's still your boy."

"She's turned him against me."

"She hasn't. You've turned him against you. And if you keep this up, Austin won't be the last. You're being unreasonable, Burke."

"She's turning you against me now, too. Damn her."

Ben sighed deeply and shook his head. "I'll come by tomorrow to help you take the boards down."

"I don't need your help. I'll do it myself."

"Fine. Suit yourself. Call me when you're ready to be reasonable." Ben shrugged and headed back to his car. "But show up tomorrow afternoon to help get the rental place back in shape."

Burke got up early the next day and took the plywood off the windows by himself. He made a list and then started fixing what had been damaged and didn't go to the rental place at all. He drank about six beers as he picked up the considerable debris in the yard. He lined the cans up on the porch railing. "See, Bobby!" he shouted out across the sound. "I don't need to hide mine. Right here. Out in the open. See that! Damn you!" He picked up an empty can and crushed it in his hand, then threw it against the wall.

Eventually he went inside to relax and watch a game on cable, but cable hadn't been restored yet, so he fell asleep on the couch. He woke up crying. He spent the next day fixing the damage to the shed, drinking no beer at all. Late afternoon on the third day he wandered over to the rental shop to find Ben and Mike finishing some of the last repairs.

"Well, look who decided to show up?" Mike muttered.

"Looks like you've got it under control," Burke muttered back at him.

"Damage at your place?" Ben asked.

"Fair bit. Attended to. Damage here?"

"Fair bit. Attended to. No thanks to you."

Mike turned to Burke. "Investors are supposed to show up. Not sulk."

Before Burke could make a retort, Ben said, "Did you check in with Grandpa?" Then he added, "And Mike, give it a rest. You're not helping."

"Funny, neither is he. He needs to show up and grow up."

Burke felt instantly guilty. He had been stewing so much in his own sauce that he hadn't called his own father to see how his place had weathered the storm or what help he might need.

Ben broke into his thoughts, laying a hand on his shoulder. "Bro, this has you by the throat. You've got to get a hold of yourself. You're like, going crazy over this. I mean, the shit with Bobby, that's old news. It's yesterday's nightmare. But you turned that around. You did right. And this new shit, yeah it's weird but that's all. You're acting like it's the end of the world."

"Fuck you," Burke said and turned around to head to his car.

He heard Mike say, "Or don't grow up," as he walked away.

"Mike. Not helping." Ben sighed.

It took him three more days before he drove over to Grandpa's. Now here he was, having just slammed the car door shut, walking up to his father's house. He walked in without knocking and found his dad making coffee in the kitchen. As he came in, his dad poured two cups, added milk and sugar to one and handed it to Burke.

"Sounds like you need this," the old man said. "The way you're slammin' your car door you sound pretty pissy." He picked up the other cup of black coffee and took a sip. "Ah, that's a good cup o' joe. Nice to have the power back on."

Burke sat down at the table and took a sip of the coffee. He didn't say anything or even look up at his dad.

Grandpa shook his head and sat down at the table with his son. "Took you long enough. I've got some things I need you to fix around here. Storm damage. Your brother left it for you. Been a week since the all-clear."

"Sure, Grandpa."

After several minutes of silence Grandpa said, "Since you haven't asked me what needs to be fixed, I suppose I should tell you the most pressin' thing on my list?"

"Yeah, sure, Grandpa. What's top of the list?"

"I got a problem with somethin' got damaged. It's real special to me. A real treasure. I'll be honest, I'm mighty worried. I hope it can be fixed. I hope you're up to it."

"I'll fix it, Dad. I brought the tool kit. What is it?"

"Good, 'cause it's one of my most important things. Hey, you want some more coffee? Let me get you another cup." He got up and as he fussed with the coffee, said. "Yup, it got broken in a storm. I thought it was so strong, but I didn't realize that old damage had never really been attended to. I guess I didn't look at it hard enough to see. Just saw what was on the surface and took that as the truth. But this time, when the wind blew, it's, well, I'm worried. It hasn't blown over quite yet, but it's leanin' hard."

Burke realized that when he arrived he hadn't even looked around to assess the damage to the house or any of the outbuildings.

"Don't worry, Dad. There's nothing around here that I can't fix."

"I'm glad to hear that. I'd be mighty vexed if you couldn't fix it."

Burke looked up at his father. "Of course, I can fix it."

"Oh, well that's good to hear. You promise? You'll stick around 'til the job is done? Won't run out on me and leave me here?"

"When have I ever let you down?"

"Never! You have never let me down." He emphasized the words with several pokes of his finger to Burke's shoulder. The old man sat back in his chair. "So, you promise?"

Burke rolled his eyes, "Just tell me where it is, and yes, I promise. So, what is it?"

"It's you."

Burke was stunned. He shook his head slightly.

"Yes, you heard me. It's you. Dumpin' all the work on Mike and Ben. Bein' short with Ben and Mad. Drivin' Austin off, him not comin' home now 'til Christmas, if then. What are you thinkin', Burke? You're like a broken version of my son. You're more like Bobby now than I've ever seen you. And he was a broken man. He broke nigh' everything he touched. Himself. His family. Your family. But you fixed that, best as anyone ever coulda done. You are Austin's daddy. And, if we're gonna be serious about it, you are his father, too. The only father he can remember. You've got him in the here and now, but you can't grasp the present while you got this stranglehold on the past.

Son, you gotta let go."

"Dad, I'll think I have. I'll think I've moved on. Forgiven Bobby. Put it to rest. Years pass by and it's not eating at me, like it did there at first. It nearly destroyed me at first. To think I should have seen Bobby for what he was… that day of all days. Should have known. Should have done something. Now it's like he's reaching back from the grave and trying to wreck and burn it all up again."

"Yes. Grief is like that. Sometimes it comes back. Sometimes it brings its friends. I'm telling you, son, you are not responsible for his terrible choices. It's not your fault that you didn't prevent him from causin' the accident. Now you have a chance to be happy. Burke, let me tell you: this is not your brother, may he and those demons that tormented him rest in peace. This is you. And you're just putting a stranglehold on your own happiness. This, what's happening now, is no one's fault but your own."

"You know… everything?"

"I suppose I know what's fit to tell. What's fit to hear. What do I not know that I need to, to understand why this thing with this woman has you so twisted up? So twisted up that you're alienatin' everybody. Wait? Is this about Madeline? Just how much past are you holdin' onto?"

"What?"

"Well, you were pretty serious with her back in high school, then your older brother came home from the army and saw what a beauty she'd grown up to be and swooped right in. You were pretty pissy about that, too, as I remember."

"No. This is not about Madeline."

"You sure? 'Cause this time it looked to me like you won. No need to be pissy."

"No. I got over that years ago. We've been friends for nearly two decades. That's ancient history. Long forgotten."

"Oh, sands of time and all that, huh? Well, good. 'Cause I remember that you were pretty vexed yourself when you and your brother overlapped with

Madeline. She sure was a pretty thing back then. Now you and Austin fell for the same woman."

"I don't want to talk about it."

"Then you'll stay broken. And you'll break your promise to me."

Burke had been down this road of forced conversation with his father before. His father believed that you never went to bed angry and you didn't leave the table until you'd talked out the whole problem. It was bad medicine but better to get it over with.

"It's not about Madeline. It's about Miranda and Austin. It's… disgusting."

"Why is it disgusting?" Grandpa asked him. "Why are two people who meet each other and hit it off, two *adults* who are not attached to anyone else in any way, wrong?"

"Because she's old enough to be his mother."

"Did she know that?"

"She claims not to."

"Austin is mature for his years. Always has been. What's Austin's story?"

"He claims he pegged her for her early thirties."

"I can see that. She's a good lookin' woman. Got that baby face. That ageless look to her." They were both quiet for a while. "People do that. They see what they want to see. Don't want to see what doesn't fit in. Stupid, yes, but human nature, nonetheless. Son, say Austin had been thirty. Say she had been thirty-four. What would you say then? If you hadn't also met her, I mean."

"Well, age-wise, that would be fine."

"Why?"

"Well, they would be of age. But she's old enough to be…"

"Yes, yes, yes, you've said that. But I think what you mean to say is that now you believe she can't be his mother, because of what's passed between them."

Burke's hand shook on the coffee cup.

"Chalk one up for the old man. Guess Grandpa pegged that one. Well, son," he put his hand on Burke's shoulder, "I got news for you. She was never gonna be his mother. His mother was Lindsay and they'll never be another. Had Joette lived, then she would be his mama, like you are his daddy. And they'll never be another Joette either. Austin's a grown man. No woman you bring into this family will ever be a new mother to him. She'll just be your wife."

Burke could feel his heart slamming in his chest. He could hear it thumping in his ears. "I thought I loved her. I really thought I loved her." What he didn't want to admit to his father was the ache of missing Miranda. How it gnawed at him. It hurt, physically. In the heat of the moment, he couldn't shake it. He had believed all those nasty things he'd said to her, but then seeing how hurt, how very wounded she looked, tore him apart with guilt at his accusations. How could he be so cruel to someone he loved so much? And how could she have torn him apart like that? The feelings were overwhelming and too complicated to sort out, so they just stewed within him.

"And you'd seen her as maybe fittin' in? Becomin' part of the family?"

Burke nodded. "But she would betray all my respect for Joette."

"She's not Joette. She will never be Joette. You choosin' someone else does nothin' to change the memory of her. You fallin' in love again does not tarnish the love you hold for the mother of your child. This lady's not Joette: she's Miranda. And Andy. Your son met Andy and he still cares for and respects her. You met Miranda and you fell in love with her. But now that she can't become Joette you're feelin' your dreams are dashed. And somehow you're blamin' your dead brother for it."

Burke would have felt like his father had been reading his diary, had he ever kept one. How could he *know*?

"I saw you at the graveyard. I didn't want to bother you. But when I saw the roses, I figured I could put two and two together. I'm happy for you, Burke, if you haven't blown it yet, that is."

"How can you just ignore that the woman I love was also the woman your grandson loved?"

"Oh, I don't know. Maybe it was because I met her last summer. Oh yeah, you look so surprised. Austin brought her out for me to meet her. I knew what was going on when I saw her with you in March."

"And you can live with that?"

"The way I figure it, Austin met her and fell for her. Believed she was so wonderful that he never even thought to find out how old she was."

"Yes, sir, that's how I understand it."

"And then you met her, not knowing that her man-friend was actually Austin?"

"Right." Burke nodded reluctantly.

"And you never thought to find out? Never thought to actually size up your competition?"

Burke felt pretty defensive at this statement from his father. "Well, I found out about her marriage and her ex-husband and her daughter. I thought her man-friend was some old geezer."

"Watch it!"

"Sorry sir. Some mainlander."

"Well, he is now! So, you didn't know that you were trying to move in on your son's girlfriend?"

"Nope." Burke felt very uncomfortable.

"But you liked her so much that you moved in on her anyway?"

"Yes, sir. I don't feel too proud of that."

"Tell me, son, why'd you do it then?"

Burke knew there was nothing for it with Grandpa but the truth. "Because I wanted her. Because I thought she was incredible. Because I thought she was someone I could fall in love with."

"And you did fall in love with her?"

"Yes. Yes, I did."

Grandpa looked his son square in the eye. "And should I be yelling at you? Cursin' you out for your behavior? For stealin' your son's very girlfriend from him? How could you do that, Burke? I didn't raise you that way. Austin's girlfriend?"

"But Dad! I didn't know. Of course, I wouldn't have done it if I'd known! I wouldn't have come within ten feet of her if I'd known. But I didn't know."

"Precisely! Exactly Burke! You didn't know. Neither did Austin. Neither did she. You are all innocent. Furthermore, you are not related to her. Austin is not related to her. It's not what you're afraid it is. It's weird, and messy, but you're all innocent." He let that soak in for a while. "And so is Bobby. He's dead. He had no part in this."

"Innocent." Burke sounded like he was puzzling it out. "And it's so… weird." He shook his head.

"Well, if she's so wonderful that both you and Austin could love her like that, and you can't handle it, then I have one thing to say to you, one piece of advice."

"Yes, sir?"

"Move over and let me line up! A woman like that is a fine and rare thing. Let me have a shot at her 'cause you're just a jackass, Burke! You're holding her responsible for something she didn't know and for the same mistake you made. You saw what you wanted to see. You didn't ask what you didn't know about, because you really didn't want to know, now did you? You're faultin' her for being human and Austin, too. And you're bein' such a jackass that you're drivin' everyone away from you. It's not little miss Miranda who's breakin' up this family. It's you. It's not your long dead brother whose wreaking havoc. It's you. If you're so much better than the rest of us, move on over and get out of the way. I only got a short time left on the planet and before I die, I'd like to be as happy as you've been all spring."

Burke felt as though he could hear ringing in his ears, or maybe he just couldn't believe his father was saying this. She would never be Joette. She didn't have to try. She would never be Austin's mama. No one would. He might not be Austin's father, but he was the boy's daddy. Now Austin was a grown man. Burke didn't shoulder that responsibility anymore. He had fulfilled Joette's final request. And he had done it well. Austin was a fine man. There were some things a man couldn't live with. But could he live with weird? He'd lived through weird before. Serving as Ben's best man was weird. This would be weirder. He looked around the room. For the first time in weeks he felt like Bobby's ghost was gone. Then he looked up at the wall of the kitchen.

"Grandpa? That's new. Where'd you get that painting?"

"Oh, new little artist moved onto the island. Felt like my family might have been less than gracious to a new neighbor and I dropped by to pay my respects. She was very kind. She seemed so touched she gave me a painting I admired. She seems like a nice lady. Very talented. Were I a younger man, I would have asked her to dinner. But I'm just an old geezer. Now I just think she'd make a nice daughter-in-law. Did you hear? She bought Hayward House."

Chapter 39

The doorbell rang. Miranda wondered who it could be now. She'd had an endless parade of people come by the house since her return. "Hang on! I'm coming," she called out from upstairs as she pulled off her painting smock and hung it on a peg. She hoped it wasn't Burke. She really wasn't ready to see him. After all the horrible things he'd said to her, had accused her of, she wasn't sure she ever wanted to see him again. The doorbell rang again. "I said I'm coming!" she called as she started down the stairs. When she got to the front door, she found Kat and Mad waiting for her, their arms full.

"Hi, honey!" Mad gushed and came in through the door, planting a kiss on Miranda's cheek. "Glad to see you're home." Mad went in through the house to the kitchen.

Kat gave her a smile, but no kiss, and said, "We brought lunch!" She, too, walked in the house past Miranda and followed Madeline.

"Well, hi guys. Uh, is everything back to rights at your place?"

"Oh sure. What's left Ben and Mike will take care of," Madeline chirped, unconcerned. "We wanted to make sure you got everything straightened out here, so we brought lunch and we're here to help."

"Yes, and it's time for things to get back to normal. I brought your latest chapters with me. I took them with us when Mike and I went inland for the storm. I have to say, I absolutely love that your character falls for the young British aristocrat. Oh my God, but I hate his parents already. I can't imagine where you come up with these story ideas, Miranda."

Kat didn't seem to notice the shock Miranda thought must be evident on her face at seeing her new friends show up so unexpectedly. It seemed that to them nothing more had happened than a hurricane washing over the Outer Banks. Of course, they couldn't see it had washed away her hopes and drowned her happiness. To her, this wasn't some passing storm. She wasn't going to get over that argument and just move on to blue skies. Maybe islanders could just pick up and move on. She couldn't. Maybe she was a mainlander after all.

The girls started unpacking the bags of food and making lunch for the three of them.

"This isn't quite a Miranda special, but I think you'll find our subs are both tasty and still fall into the classification of girl-food." Kat winked at her.

Madeline shot a look at Kat, who gave her a slight nod.

"Well now, has Burke been around at all? Come by to see you?"

Miranda shook her head.

"I didn't think so," Kat said. "He hasn't been by the bookstore either. I've had to run the whole thing by myself."

"Same at Watercraft Rentals. Not hide nor hair of him. And forget about Ro-Dough. Poor Ben and Mike are run ragged trying to cover for him."

"Is he… okay?" Miranda wondered if something had happened to him, or if he had packed up and left.

"Of course, he's not all right! He's devastated." Mad shook her head sadly.

"He hates me." Somehow, she managed to get the words out, although her voice was barely audible.

"Hates you? Hardly," Kat answered sagely. "My little brother loves you."

Miranda coughed and blinked a few times. "No. If he did love me, he doesn't anymore. If you knew, you might hate me too."

"Nah. Burke hates that he's an asshole. He hates that he can't handle that real life gets really messy sometimes. But he doesn't hate you," Kat assured her. "He couldn't hate you."

"Honey, we know all about Austin." Mad patted her hand. "And we know all about Burke's meltdown and what he said to you."

Miranda looked from one face to the other. "How? Did Burke tell you?"

"No," Mad replied, "it was Austin who spilled the beans, not Burke, believe you me, it wasn't Burke. He's not the type to want to talk about deep stuff, or anything embarrassin'. At least not about *him*. You know, that's partly why I left him."

Miranda could feel the room spin for just a moment. She had to admit it to herself, that was one surprising twist wrapped up in another. "Austin… told… you? And you what?"

"Didn't you know? We were sweet on each other in high school. Dated from seventh grade through our senior year. But he was a tough nut to crack. He always seemed to feel that he had to project this perfect, totally put together image. Well, honey, none of us is quite perfect or put together that well. When Ben came home from service, it shook me up. You always knew what he was thinkin'."

"Well, yeah, because it was always spilling out of his mouth, usually at inappropriate times!" Kat laughed. "My brothers are night and day. You know everything, and I mean everything about Ben. That man doesn't have a filter."

"And Burke has enough filter for the whole family. He got all the filter genes, that one did." Mad laughed. "So, I broke up with Burke and married Ben."

"That kinda' shocked Burke." Kat nodded knowingly.

"Yeah, it sure did. Poor thing. But he stood up with us at the weddin', nonetheless! Nah, he was good with it. Truth be told, I was a bit much for him. That man was just so overwhelmed in our relationship, but once he's committed to a path he finds it hard to change, even when it's good for him. We had a kiddie love affair. We were teenagers. And at some point I wanted the whole gamut of emotions and a person who let me see their flaws. Well, Ben does that. But then again, he lets everyone see his flaws." She burst out laughing. "I found that I just loved that. He's so close to life, you know? Life is right there on the edge of everything Ben does."

"And Burke?" Miranda asked.

It was Kat who answered. "Oh, he's come a long way. He's not, uh, terribly flexible, but he always does the right thing. He's pretty hard on himself when he puts a toe out of line. Or Austin. Probably why that boy turned out so well. Miranda, my brother is a good man. A really good man. He's not as perfect as he would like everyone to believe, but he's no slouch either. I hope you can find it in your heart to forgive what he said in anger. He shouldn't have said those terrible things to you. I know he didn't mean it. Not really. He's torturing himself over what he said, he feels guilty about how he handled everything with you and his boy, and he doesn't know how to handle the whole thing about you and Austin."

"I think it's bringing up unfinished business from when we were kids, when I left him for Ben." Mad nodded sagely.

Kat didn't look so sure, but she turned to Miranda and said, "He'll come back round. He just needs time to process it all. It's weird for him, you know? He struggles with weird. He struggles with the past. He's really struggling with Austin leaving him."

Miranda nodded. "Austin emailed me that he's taking an internship this summer. He got an offer from Chase, the uncle of his roommate. He's off to Europe."

"Yeah. Austin dumped his daddy on me and Ben when he said he wasn't gonna' take it anymore. Said in no uncertain terms that Burke needed to get his ever-loving shit together because Austin wasn't going down that bullshit path with him again."

"Austin said that?" Miranda was stunned.

"Well, it was colorful, but I can't remember quite who said which colorful words. Those could have been mine, actually, now that I think about it. But they hold true nonetheless!"

"What path with him again? I think I need to catch up here. Austin told you that we, um, we, dated, last summer? That we had no idea..."

"Of your age difference?" Kat smiled. "Miranda honey, you look at least ten years younger than you are, probably more, bless you. I think I can understand how it happened."

"But when we realized, I mean, we just couldn't go on. We ended it as soon as we found out."

"And then you met Burke!" Mad said around a bite of sandwich. "And you had no idea of who he was. That he was Austin's uncle. The man who raised him."

"His daddy. And doesn't that bother you?" asked Miranda.

"Hey, life's weird. It's like that. You have to keep goin' on, even though it gets messy sometimes."

"Just keep going on? Mad, I wish I could, but I feel so humiliated. All the things he said."

"My brother is a wonderful guy." Kat smiled. "And a jackass. He doesn't deal with, uh, surprises very well. Or the past. He likes to have everything planned out and predictable. He likes to come off like he's perfect. I know he loves you by the degree of his total meltdown. The last time he melted down, well, it wasn't very pretty." Kat set down her sandwich. "I think there is something that you need to know about Burke."

Miranda nodded. She didn't think she wanted to hear this. She steeled herself.

"He was married, way back when. Joette was lovely. Really special. But she was killed in a car accident, along with their daughter, Juliet, who was seven. A drunk driver killed them."

"Oh my God, that's awful. Austin said a drunk driver killed his parents too. That's why he lives with Burke."

"Yes. It was the same accident. The drunk driver was Bobby, my oldest brother. Austin's biological father."

Miranda gasped and stared at Kat. She didn't know what to say.

Kat nodded. "Bobby was an alcoholic. Not that we understood back then just how bad he was. He was driving the car. All four of them died. Juliet, Burke's daughter, died at the scene. Lindsay, Austin's mother, made it to the hospital but they couldn't save her."

"And what happed to Bobby?"

"Bobby hung on until Burke made it to the hospital, but he was beyond speaking. I think he knew what he'd done though. I don't know if my brother died of his injuries or his guilt. Burke rarely ever mentioned Bobby again. Didn't go to his funeral. He wasn't in any shape to, actually."

"And Burke's wife?"

"Joette lingered a few days. Burke was sure she was going to make it. He just couldn't accept what the doctors were telling him. It was a miracle she hung on as long as she did. I'm sure she did it for him. She asked Burke to take Austin, to be a father to him. It was her dying request to him. Personally, I think she was worried about how he'd make it without her."

"Worried about him? But he's, he's so, I mean he's got it so together."

"He does now." Madeline nodded. "But back then he was a mess. He spent a few months drunk as a skunk himself, he just couldn't face it. He couldn't live in a world without Joette and Juliet."

"But Austin!"

"Yup. Five years old. He stayed with us for a while," Kat said. "Grandpa and Mama led an intervention with Burke. We were all there. Grandpa asked him why he was doing the very thing that allowed Bobby to take his girls away from him? What was he gonna' do? Go out and kill some other family? Hadn't enough people died? And what about Austin?"

Mad shook her head. "That was a rough, rough day. But he got on the path to getting everything back on track. It took him a while."

"It was hell on poor little Austin. Things like that, losing your parents, then seeing all you got left fall apart, made little Austin grow up fast. He knew he was supposed to go and live with Uncle Burke. He was named for Uncle Burke. Burke Austin Mitchell. But he was afraid to live with him for a while. That's when he started to go by Austin." Kat looked so sad.

Madeline leaned back in her chair. "Ben told me once that Burke blamed himself for the accident. He'd been nagging his oldest brother about being so damn irresponsible. Burke pissed Bobby off, which was why he split and took the car. I'm not sure he gave anyone any choice. He just got in the car and they took off, tires spittin' gravel. He didn't want to be around his nagging little baby brother. After they'd left, Burke found a stash of empty cans, hidden. Not long after that, we got the call."

"I think it's survivor's guilt," Kat said, nodding.

"Burke felt guilty for boozing it up for the first few months after they died. It was a couple of years before he was himself again." Mad shook her head.

"No, he's never really been himself again." Kat stared into her iced tea glass.

"Well, maybe lately he has been." Mad looked at Miranda.

"Yeah, maybe." Kat nodded. "My little brother is wound pretty tight."

Miranda took a deep breath and looked down at the table. "When my husband left me and took up with a much younger, much more successful replacement, I was so shocked. So surprised. Unprepared. I felt devastated. Nothing of my life was recognizable. I didn't know who I was or how I felt or where I was. It was like being thrown away with the trash."

"And how did you cope?" Kat asked her. "What did you do?"

"Honestly? Actually, you know, I employed a bottle of scotch as my therapist initially." Miranda took a deep breath. "It didn't work for me either. Then my best friend's brother confronted me, did his own little intervention. Talked some sense into me. And I found writing. And a personal trainer… but writing and books."

"Books. That's what brought Burke around. He opened his little bookstore and he lost himself in books. Books saved him. And Austin. And probably all of us." Kat looked out the window at the sun glinting off the water in the sound.

"Is Burke an alcoholic?" Miranda asked Kat.

"Not that I can tell," said Kat. "But while he's got lots of wisdom to share for everyone else's bumps along the way, he's shitty at coping when it comes to his own tragedies. At least that's my opinion. But then again, he's only had two real tragedies."

"What was the other tragedy? What else happened?"

"He thinks he's lost you."

"But he drove me away. He said horrible things."

"In shock and anger. If he doesn't regret them yet, he will soon. He's a jackass. And he's a really nice guy."

"And you all aren't, well, upset by what happened last year? And last month?"

"You know, I'd be more upset if there wasn't a *next* month and a *next* year for you two." Kat reached out and squeezed Miranda's hand.

Miranda reached out her hands, one to Kat and the other to Mad and gave them a squeeze. "You are such dear friends. Thank you for coming over today. I hope that no matter what happens—or doesn't happen—between me and Burke, that we will always be friends."

"Oh darlin', it was a great day when the wind blew you to our island." Madeline smiled back at her.

When they left, Miranda could feel a knot deep within her starting to unwind itself. Only this morning she had been feeling an overwhelming mix of hurt and fury and humiliation and fear. Hurt from what he thought of her. Fury at what he had said to her. Humiliation at how the situation had so publicly revealed itself. And fear that everyone else on the island would find out and they would treat her like some scarlet woman. But they did know, and they didn't care. They didn't see it as wrong. Weird, maybe that, but not wrong. She started to think that maybe it wasn't wrong, it was just… odd.

And Burke would have to find his way through. For the first time, she wondered if he might find his way back to her? Then she wondered what she would do if he did. Could she forgive him? He wasn't perfect. He was pretty flawed, in fact. But then, so was she.

Chapter 40

Miranda was up in the studio painting. She'd been back for almost two months now and after cleaning up from the hurricane, had started to write. And paint. She studied her canvas. She could hear a car turning onto her little road. With the string of visitors coming by since she'd returned to the beach, it was amazing she'd been able to accomplish anything at all. She'd always been a planner, a checklist kind of person. Productive even in that Zen art of keeping a house where all your hours of diligent toil were washed away like a sand mandala as soon as the family arrived with their chaos of books and briefcases. Now, she was learning to go with the flow. She walked over to the screened window and looked down. It was a cute little Caribbean-blue Microbus.

"Moment of reckoning." She set down her palette and brush and started to head downstairs. "You just never know when's the last time you're going to see someone. Wow." She paused on the steps to catch her breath and try to slow her heart rate. She went down a few more steps. "I thought you really meant it when you said you'd never see me again. Maybe fate had other plans." She shook her head and wondered what was going to happen next. She thought he would be at the door by the time she got there, but he wasn't. She walked out and down the wrap-around porch, stopping at the bottom step. He was sitting in his car, windows down, car off. After standing in silence for a few moments she called out, "Are you coming in? Or are you just gonna' sit there?"

He looked up, as if surprised to see her there. "Oh, yeah." He got out of the car and rather awkwardly moved in her general direction. He looked her up and down. "What are you wearing?"

She gave a quick glance down at herself. "Painting smock. I've been painting."

He opened his mouth as if to say something. Then he shut it. He looked around.

"Oh, for God's sake, Burke. Why don't you come in and have a glass of iced tea?" She turned around and walked inside. Either he would come, or he wouldn't.

By the time she had gone into the house, taken her painting smock upstairs to hang in the studio, returned downstairs, and started towards the kitchen, he was just coming in the front door. *So, he wasn't going to come in then,* she thought. She went to the fridge and pulled out a pitcher of mango mint iced tea and filled two glasses. By this time, he was standing in the kitchen on the other side of the counter. *Not too close. Not close at all.* She slid the glass over to him. Looking as though he felt reluctant, he took it.

"I promise you, it's not poisoned. See?" She took a sip of hers.

"I don't think it's poisoned."

"Good. Drink up then."

They both sipped their tea, not speaking for a while.

"I see you got all the boards down. Much damage?" He didn't make eye contact.

"Hardly any, actually. And the boards, yeah. Caroline and I were working on them, but then a couple of really nice neighbors came by to help us. Islanders are great, aren't they? Taking care of their own."

"Yeah, islanders are great people." Burke looked so awkward. "Who came by?"

"A guy named Mike. Another guy named Ben. Just checking in to make sure the new islander was okay. Pitched in to help."

"So, they've been by."

"Yeah. They were terrific. I'd still be taking that plywood down if I were by myself."

"Oh." The painful silence stretched on again. Finally, Burke said, "So Ben and Mike came by."

"Yeah. And Kat. And Mad. They say you've been really busy, um, for the last six weeks or so."

"They did?"

"Yeah," she said. "Haven't you been? Kat said you disappeared for a couple of weeks after the storm but lately you've been working long hours at The Book Shelf Café and Mad says you've been in to help her a lot at Ro-Dough."

"Oh, yeah. Well, that's true." Burke nodded. He still was looking around and not looking at her. Certainly not meeting her gaze.

"And Ben said you've been working at Watercraft Rentals too, to pitch in for some of, um, the uncovered shifts."

Burke surprised her when he answered, "Yeah. Austin left."

"Uh huh. Sounds like a good opportunity for him, though. A really good opportunity."

"Oh, you know?"

"Uh, yeah. He wrote me before he left to tell me he wasn't coming home. Tell me about the internship."

Suddenly a look of consternation crossed Burke's face. "Wait a minute. Let me get this straight. You said Ben's been by. Kat's come around. You mentioned Mad. And Mike? Yeah, you said he helped take down the boards. Anyone else I should know about? Anyone *not* come by?"

"Grandpa swings by. He is one sweet old man. He comes by each week to check in on me. Make sure I'm not leaving the island."

"Grandpa? Each week? For how long?"

"Since the storm. I mean, they all come for Friday night dinners. Didn't you know? I thought you didn't want to come. We went out to shag at Miguel's last weekend but it's so popular now we couldn't even get on the floor. He's really indebted to you for getting that started, you know."

Burke glanced at her.

"Um, yeah, Kat told me how it was actually you who got all that started. So, did you know he's planning on expanding his restaurant?" She tried to say it as brightly as she could.

Burke looked incredulous.

"Did you not know?" She said the words very slowly; it was dawning on her that his family had basically adopted her, included her in everything they used to include him in. Which meant they might be excluding him. "They just always told me you were too busy."

"So, everyone's taken your side, huh?"

"What? Burke, I don't have a side. There are no sides in this. They keep telling me to be patient with you. To give you some space. Say you'll come around eventually. They've never left your side, Burke. This is all you. I feel terribly embarrassed, of course, but as awkward as this is…"

"Weird," he interrupted her. "It's weird."

"Okay, weird. As weird as this is, I never meant to hurt you. Or Austin. Or me. Had I ever known that I would meet you, I never would have… I mean had I met you first… oh, dammit." She could feel herself tearing up.

He looked down into his tea. "Ben thinks I'm an ass."

"Yeah, if you think that's bad, you should hear what Grandpa says."

"Every week, huh?"

"Yeah. He keeps coming by to check on me, but I think he's really trying to check on you. I have to keep telling him that you're not here. Either that or he just really likes my iced tea."

"I like your iced tea."

"Oh my God, Burke, that's the nicest thing you've said to me since we left the beach to get away from the hurricane."

"No. The nicest thing I said to you was that I loved you more than life itself." Burke wandered around the kitchen, looking lost, Miranda watching him. "You were in the shower. You couldn't hear me say it. Miranda, I…" he started but he couldn't seem to get any other words out.

He'd said that? She felt shaken. She was so afraid he was going to say he

353

hated her now. Still. "Burke, you came all the way over here…"

"What did my dad say?" It was an abrupt change of topic.

"Well, he, uh, said you were being a jackass."

Burke nodded like this wasn't a surprise to him.

"He said that you needed time."

Burke nodded again.

"He asked me to not give up on you, but said he respected my right to throw in the towel. Said everyone has their limits of tolerance for weird."

"So that's it?"

"No."

He looked at her.

She took a deep breath before she said, "Grandpa said you're unable to forgive your brother, Bobby. You're still mourning Joette. And Juliet. You're caught, believing that you can only replace Joette with someone who is so perfect that she couldn't actually ever exist. Burke, I would never have wanted to replace Joette. There's no way I could ever fill her shoes. She was the love of your life. The mother of your child. I'm a mother. I understand that. Gregg remarried, but Chen is Emma's friend. And Emma will be more like an aunt to that baby when it's born, not like a sister. No one will ever replace me in Emma's life. No one will ever replace Joette in your life. Austin's mother can't be replaced either."

"I'm a jackass." He looked down into his tea.

"Yup. You're right." She took a sip of her tea and then walked around the kitchen counter and stood in front of him. "But you don't have to keep being one."

Burke looked Miranda in the eye for the first time. "I've been doing a lot of thinking. My father's right. While this is totally weird, I think I had more going on, correction, *have* more going on, with Austin growing up and leaving, with me having to face some unfinished issues with Joette's death. With the loss of Juliet, my precious little girl. With my brother, Bobby. I've had a lot of time to just… sit with it."

"I'm so sorry, Burke. There's nothing I can do to change the past. Not yours. Not theirs. Not ours."

"I've thought it over. There's what a man can't live with and there's what a man can't live without. I know I can't live trapped in the past. I think I can't live without you. I'm willing to try to live with weird."

Miranda could feel her heart pounding in her chest. "You think you could live with weird?"

"Maybe? Yes?" He sounded unsure. "I'm willing to try."

She didn't say anything for a long time.

"Are you able to maybe try living with weird, too?" His voice was very quiet.

She looked at him and found she was unable to speak.

He stepped over to her and touched her arms, gently holding her. "Miranda, can you forgive me? I'm a jackass. I've been a total jackass. I'm sorry. I'm not through this yet but I have at least come to the realization that no one is at fault here. Except maybe me. Can you forgive me? Do you think you could ever forgive me?"

She took a deep breath. "Let me show you something." She took his hand and led him out of the kitchen, through the living room to the stairs. "C'mon." She led him down the upstairs hallway into a little library with her desk for writing and out onto the sunporch. There were multiple canvasses on a couple of easels and quite a few leaning up against the walls.

"Wow, you've been busy."

"I've never shown you my paintings."

"These are good. Why didn't you show me? You could be in that gallery, Miranda."

"It's not these I want to show you. It's this one." She walked around an easel that stood with its back to the door. He joined her, walking around it. "It's almost done. I love it. It's so perfect. Look here. See that? It's a black-bellied plover in the tall grass, just peeking out. They're very shy, you know. And over here, that's a Eurasian Wigeon. You have to be very, very lucky to

355

see one of those."

"But, but in the center…" Burke was clearly struggling for words.

"I know. It's you. On the kayak. It's how I've thought of you. That look on your face. You look content. You look happy."

"It's amazing. It's… me."

"Can I forgive you? I've spent the last six weeks trying to understand this whole crazy thing. And understand you. And me. And Austin. And all that thinking led me to this." She pointed to the painting. "So, yeah, I think I can maybe try to live with weird."

Epilogue

They walked out of the theater, hand in hand. She looked down at her new tattoo. She couldn't believe she'd let him talk her into it. *Well, I guess I've got it pretty bad for this guy,* she thought, and it brought a smile to her face. The tiny tattoo encircled her finger, a match to his.

"I could use a drink after that," he said.

"Yeah. Me too."

They walked to their car and drove a short distance to one of their favorite haunts: Tony's Pizza and Empanadas. Tony greeted them warmly and showed them to a table.

"What can I get you, my friends?"

"I think I'll take a beer. And a scotch," Burke answered.

"I'll just take the beer.

"And bring us a few empanadas. Whatever you think is good," Burke said.

"I know just what you like!" Tony replied.

Miranda looked around at Tony's place. Caroline had turned her onto it, and it was undeniably offbeat and cool. Now that she and Burke spent a few months each winter in Charlotte, they had favorite places like this. It was nice to have both the beach and the city in their lives. But today had been weird. Of all the strange things that had happened to her, she had to admit that what she had just experienced was one of the weirdest.

"I'm so glad we didn't go to the premiere," he said, rather heavily. He hadn't said much since they came out of the theater.

She hadn't meant to write it. It had just burst out of her as she tried to make sense of the crazy twists and turns of her life, as she tried to understand her feelings and figure out how she had ended up in that spot. But she had written it. She had let him read it. They spent the summer and fall talking about it, about what had happened between them, trying to make peace, and using a work of fiction as their virtual therapist. And he thought it was good. Her best yet. Reluctantly, he urged her to let her editor at least see it. And then it was a crazy train that left the station and *boom!* It was a best seller and *flash!* It was going to be a movie. And they had just walked out of the theater having witnessed the adaptation of her work to film. They had called it *Chicapocalypse.*

"All the way out to California? For a movie? No way." She tried to keep it light. "Maybe we should have just caught this one when it hit streaming."

"Yeah. I mean, it would have been nice to see him at a premiere. I enjoyed the last one we went to. It was really nice of him to fly us out there for that."

"Yeah. But not this one. You know, I bet he didn't really want us to come either. Even though he invited us," she added. "I can't imagine he would want to stand there, with us, and all those flashing cameras. You know, I have to admit, it was a little weird. Even for me. And I wrote the damn thing."

"Well, you are a very successful author."

"Of fluff-plus books. That get made into horribly embarrassing movies. Where's that beer?" she said as she looked around.

Tony showed up and brought Burke his two drinks and a Negro Modelo for Miranda. "Folks, your empanadas will be out in a few minutes." Burke downed his scotch right away.

"That feels better. That was so weird." He sipped his beer.

"He did a great job though," Miranda added. "I mean, in the role."

"Yeah. Who knew this would ever happen to him? When he went off to that internship, I really thought he would come back. Be the first one in the family to finish college. Come back to the island."

Miranda took a sip of her beer. "And he still might. He might come home."

"You remember he called it *subsistence living*. As though owning my own business, hell, more than one business, my own home, the bookstore, a vintage car in mint condition—as if *that's* subsistence living!" Burke growled a little, deep in his throat. "I had no idea that's what he thought of our life."

"I'm sorry I ever told you that." She arched her eyebrows.

"I hope he's happy. He's certainly not subsistence living now."

She reached out to touch his hand and started tracing the wedding band tattooed on his finger. "I guess when you are mentored by Chase Watkins anything can happen. Remember when we thought a semester leave of absence to tackle a product launch would be a such good experience for him?"

"And then he would come back." Burke took a large sip of his beer. "It wasn't supposed to be forever. He wasn't supposed to become a mainlander."

"Well, after that one modeling job it was like everything took off. I mean, this is his third movie. If he's not a household name yet, he will be soon."

"I'm glad he told us when he signed on for this one. I needed a lot of time to get used to the idea."

"Yeah, me too." Miranda sipped her Modelo.

"Do you think anyone will ever figure it out?" Burke looked at her intently.

"That he was basically playing himself in yet another semi-autobiographical novel of mine?"

"Yeah. That you and me and… and… do you think they'll ever know?"

"Hard to say. He lives in a fishbowl. So many crazy things come out about him, I think the bigger question is would anyone believe it? Or would they care? I mean, everyone in the theater was laughing their heads off. Maybe no one would give a shit if they found out just how close to home that story struck."

"That was weird," he said again.

"Well, we've lived with weird for five years now." She smiled at him and traced the tattoo on his finger again.

"Yeah." He smiled back as he traced his finger along the wedding band inked into her skin. "And I guess we'll do it for another fifty."

The End

Acknowledgements

I absolutely adore the process of writing—from the flash of the initial concept, to waking up and capturing ideas before they slip away, to the endless editing and polishing of a story. At each point along this process there are people for whom I'm incredibly grateful—for their ideas, suggestions, corrections, encouragement, and connections. To me, the process of story creation is a rich tapestry to which many hands contribute inspiration, color, texture, and depth. This book would never have come into being without their energy embedded in the process. My family and my Readers Circle are so dear to me. Thank you for all you have shared as this work developed and matured.

In particular, Alexander spent many hours and long walks listening to the story—page by page—and gave feedback and ideas, many of which have been woven into the storyline. Ruben, Alexander and Ethan—the lovely men in my life—are the very embodiment of patience and encouragement! There is no way I could have written this, my fifth completed novel, without their love and support. My Reader's Circle consists of dear friends who graciously read the stories in various stages, giving valuable critical feedback every step of the way. Special thanks goes to Michelle Abel-Shoup, who not only gave page-by-page feedback on TBTW, but who has been reading and giving feedback for the series of five books that encompass this family's story. Appreciation goes to Bharathi Zvara for her endless encouragement and critical thinking. Many thanks go to Erika Lusk and Angela Rosenberg for reading, re-reading and then reading the manuscript yet again. Katie Rosanbalm has a sharp eye for typos and consistency, which is greatly welcome. Linda Peterson's feedback and consultation was always valued, as were Melissa Green's creative suggestions. David Drake, who is mentioned in this work, is most appreciated for being my book mentor and giving me such generous advice about the publishing process. Appreciation goes to Priya Doraswamy for her sage advice and suggestions. Barbara Marcum, Gary Glover, Amy Langerfender, Kathy Donnald, Katie Brandert, and Bekki Buenviaje are all most appreciated for their encouragement, ideas, and feedback on the story. And a special thanks goes to Alison Williams, all the way over in Wales, editor on so many of my books, for teaching me how to write in the first place. Many, many kudos goes to my publisher, Beach Reads Books, endlessly patient and supportive, for making it possible for me (and you) to hold this work in our hands.

About the Author

Born an urban Northerner, Ci Ci Soleil has now planted her roots in the New American South. While squeezing chickens, a goat, and too many fruit trees onto tiny acreage not-quite-suited-to-the-task keeps her and her family busy, everyone realizes it's really the dogs who are in charge. Ci Ci loves spending her time writing, with the occasional painting thrown in for fun, although honestly, between her two boys, incredibly supportive husband, all those animals, and oh yes, that pesky day job, there is never enough time.